On Sundays We Go Long

A Novel

Ty Strange

Beach Life Books Santa Rosa, CA

Published by Beach Life Books Santa Rosa, CA. www.tystrange.com

This is a work of fiction. Names, characters, places, and incidents either are the product of the author's imagination or are used fictitiously. Any resemblance to actual persons, living or dead, events, or locales, is entirely coincidental.

Cover design by Peter O'Conner & Ty Strange
Formatting and layout provided by Polgarus Studio

ISBN: 978-0-9905392-4-7 (Hardback)
ISBN: 978-0-9905392-3-0 (Paperback)
ISBN: 978-0-9905392-5-4 (eBook)
Library of Congress Control Number: 2017939486

For my college roommate, best man, and inspiring friend, Rick Kunkle, aka Roomie. Your time with us may have been short lived, but it was instrumental, immeasurable, and never to be forgotten.

Week 1
August 31

LIFE WITHOUT ENDORPHINS IS AT BEST SEDENTARY AND UNIMAGINATIVE, reads the roughhewn redwood sign perched above a pair of Dutch front doors, one of which has its top half swung open. Slowing to a trot, thirty-three-year-old Dillon Percy blows one final snot rocket to his right, climbs the stairs onto the large wraparound porch, kicks off his stinky running shoes, and gives the redwood sign his usual post-run deferential nod, passing underneath and into the two-story, five-room Bed, Run & Breakfast Inn. At one time the place had been a farmhouse, back before asphalt paved over the horse-and-buggy dirt roads in California's rural west Sonoma County; but after many decades of permitless additions—front, back, and side porches privately enclosed; questionable roofing jobs that elevated and added new roof lines, which cover a hallway maze connecting irregular-shaped bedrooms—the modern-day clapboard structure resembles a charming patchwork quilt in need of fresh paint.

"Morning, Terri," Dillon says, entering the kitchen where his employee stands dicing onions on the kitchen island. "Our guests up yet?"

"Humping like bunnies," she replies with a wicked, potentially envious, grin. "How was your run?"

"I see," he says, reflexively glancing at her exposed long, lean legs jutting out from black skintight running shorts. "Good shakeout run, about eleven miles. Yours?"

"Magical! On the way over, I spotted three deer out in Beardsworth's pasture. Their cute little heads jerk from one side to the other, tracking me as I go by. So sublime . . ."

Dillon can appreciate Terri's endorphin-inspired enthusiasm, though her "sublime" interpretation differs from his, and often makes him roll his eyes. "Okay . . . I know breakfast should wrap up by eleven, but if they're slow in getting around, we'll extend it . . . no problem."

"Righty-o. From what I could tell when I walked by their room they're burning calories galore. They'll be *hungry.*"

Again with the grin. Dillon has only two formal rules at his Bed, Run & Breakfast establishment beyond treating every guest like an endurance athlete: he doesn't sleep with the help, and the help doesn't sleep with the guests. Twenty-six-year-old Terri makes rule number one difficult at times with that grin; those toned legs; that small, firm ass proudly—and constantly—displayed in short or long tights; bobbed raven-black hair that has come-hither sex appeal whenever she quickly turns her head in your direction; and constant sexual innuendos. *Oversexed grad student?* Dillon ponders the probable answer.

"Where's Miles?" Terri says, now dicing tomatoes.

"Miles?!"

Only Terri's *chop, chop, chop* and a faint *thump, thump, thump* from the headboard bumping the wall in the Helsinki-themed room upstairs answer.

"Must've gotten distracted along the creek," Dillon says.

"*Wooooowooowooo Woooowoooo,*" Miles vocalizes, padding through the open back door and into the kitchen.

"There you are, girl. What'd you find out there?" Dillon says to his three-year-old Siberian husky as she describes in great detail her morning adventure.

"*Owwwww Wooooowooowooo Woooowoooo . . .*"

"You don't say, sweetie," Terri says, as if she understands husky.

For all Dillon knows, Terri might know husky. He washes his hands in the deep, double-sided sink, flicks water at Miles, who continues talking, unfazed, and begins cracking eggs into a large mixing bowl. He briefly whisks them, adding in whole milk, salt, nutmeg, vanilla extract, and cinnamon, then continues whisking.

"Your ex called," Terri says.

Chop, chop, chop.

Thump-thump, thump-thump, thump-thump.

Dillon's whisking turns vigorous, bordering on pulverization; dark flecked egg yolk splatters across the counter.

"I told her I'd pass along the message, which I paid no attention to. Per your wishes."

A moment later, Dillon unclenches, allowing the French-toast mixture to settle. He pulls out a loaf of day-old Texas sourdough bread, slices off several thick slices, and lets them soak in the mixture, flipping each after a few seconds. "Dale should be by around noon to assess the toilet in the Athens Room. If I'm out running errands, tell him I think the seal underneath needs replacing."

"I thought you fixed—"

"That was the Munich Room," Dillon says, grimacing not only over the laundry list of repair jobs he and the local handyman, Dale, have tackled over the summer months leading up to the official opening, but also the remainder of the to-do list that scrolls endlessly on, including painting over the exterior's faded shade of brown. "I don't have time to do this one before the weekend."

"Speaking of the weekend," Terri says, finishing up with the mushrooms and moving on to the various-colored bell peppers that have been soaking in sweet-and-spicy oil and vinegar overnight. "I have a paper due on Tuesday, so . . . could I cut out early on Saturday and Sunday . . . after breakfast?"

"Sure. Miles and I can clean up. Right, girl?"

"*Woooooowoooowooo Woooooowoooo Woooooowoooowooo.*"

"Thanks," Terri says, jutting her hip to bump his as he passes by. "I'll make it up to you next weekend. I'm all yours."

That wicked grin yet again.

Thump-thump-thump-thump-thump—

Wrapped in luxurious cotton robes, the lovers from the Helsinki Room have taken a break and are now seated at the kitchen island, where Dillon serves them omelets and French toast smothered with handpicked blackberries from the property. Fresh-squeezed orange juice and aromatic coffee complement the spread.

"You owned this place long?" Nolan says between bites, working his way through breakfast with obvious gusto.

"Six months. Just opened it for guests last week." Dillon takes stock of the late-twenties, Canadian newlyweds and ultra endurance junkies: both fit, runner-lean, and average height. Their hair color and style, as well as complexion, even match, like designer luggage. Dillon learns that Nolan had proposed to Mya when they crossed the finish line at the previous 100K Lost Soul Ultramarathon up in Lethbridge, Alberta, Canada, saying, "If we can survive this together, we can survive anything." Mya thought him dehydrated and delusional at the time, kneeling such as he was, laughing it off, but a few bagel chips, a cup of chicken broth, and an IV drip later the proposal still lingered in his eyes and she promptly said yes.

"We're looking for aboot fifty kilometers today," Mya says, daintily picking at the omelet, pulling out the bell peppers. "Trails, preferably."

"That's thirty-one miles, eh?" Nolan says.

Dillon grins. "Runners in the US know meters and kilometers. It's the only part of the metric system anybody learns."

Nolan nods.

Dillon continues to size up the couple, impressed that they can "hump like bunnies" *and* still be up for several hours of running. *Marriage is like that . . . at first. Then a division of duties ensues, followed by excuses, until one Thanksgiving morning you come back early from a run, sore Achilles' heel and all, to find your wife enjoying her own version of an endorphin high . . . on top of a galoshes-wearing stranger, her ass bouncing up and down.* They were dark blue, the galoshes; red handprints framed by white, her fleshy paddled ass.

"With some strategic traversing," Dillon says, "you can get close to thirty miles in with minimal trail repeat over in Annadel. Long climbs and varied trail types—single track, technical, fire road. It's a twenty-five-minute drive from here." Dillon reaches over to the rustic sideboard and grabs a foldable waterproof map of the state park. Using a grease pen, he outlines a route that fits the couple's mileage requirement.

"That sounds lovely," Mya says, leaning back in her chair, sipping coffee as she peers around the large open room that serves both as kitchen and dining area. Dillon has preserved the old farmhouse charm: open cabinetry in the kitchen with beveled-glass windows that expose drinking glasses, serving plates and dishes, and pantry items; wooden tongue-in-groove slats arranged horizontally and repainted in a cheery yellow; and the oversized kitchen island extending sixteen feet in length that can seat ten, five tall stools facing the other five from across the thick wooden block that acts both as dining surface and prep area at the end closest to the sink and stove. It provides Dillon with a bird's-eye view of those seated around the island, encouraging lively conversation, and allows him to keep the breakfast festivities going until everybody is satiated from food and conversation about local running venues and personal race stories. For those less gregarious guests, a nook off the kitchen offers two small tables for privacy with a wonderful window view of majestic Mount Saint Helena across a bed of vineyards to the northeast.

Dillon slides the map in between Nolan's and Mya's place settings. "Park here at the Cobblestone Trailhead on Channel Drive. Make sure you lock up any valuables; break-ins have been known to occur. Start running up the road to the end, and hang a right onto the fire road." He circles the western access point to Richardson's Trail. "It starts climbing right away."

Both Canadians scour the map with eyes of delight as Dillon gives an overview of the route, where water sources can be found, places of scenic note, and what to watch out for this time of year—poison oak, ticks, rattle snakes—adding in what extra running gear and nutritional products are available in the guest supply room off the kitchen should they need anything.

"The masseuse, Nicola, said she'd be here around eight tonight if you'd like a massage," Dillon says, reminding them of the perk from the honeymoon package they had reserved.

"Oh, that'll be wonderful!" Mya says.

"Nicola's hands are magic," Terri says, passing by the group, heading toward the laundry room, a basket of linens in hand. "She'll find muscles you never knew you had," she continues, complete with *that* grin and her gaze directed at Dillon.

Definitely oversexed . . . bordering on nympho.

Nolan, Mya, and Dillon watch Terri stride from the room, each glute proudly honoring *Homo erectus* for evolving to upright mobility, Miles at her heels, talking.

"Runner?" Nolan says.

"Competitive one in high school and college," Dillon says. "Now she runs for recreation while working on her master's down at Frisco State."

"Dare I ask in what?" Mya says.

"Human sexuality."

A blushing Mya whispers to a grinning Nolan, "I told you she was outside our door this morning."

Dillon hangs and shakes his head, contemplating *another* shakeout run.

Tuesday Midday
Power Lunch

In fluid motion, passing over the start/finish line painted across the Tartan Track of lane one, thirty-two-year-old Chase Brandon glances at the latest Garmin GPS–enabled sports watch wrapped around his wrist: 1:06. Halfway through the last of six 800-meter repeats, sweat drips down his forehead, mixes with sunblock and salt, and stings his eyes. He summarily dismisses the teary discomfort with a swipe of a finger under his Oakley sport sunglasses as he enters the first turn, hugging the inside portion of the lane like a sweat-soaked shirt clinging to perspired skin—an annoyance that Chase, shirtless since arriving to the junior college track, avoids throughout the favorably warm, protracted Sonoma County summers. It's purportedly compensation for the long, frigid winters he spent bundled up in Wisconsin throughout his youth, or so he tells people.

Emerging out of the turn and entering the back stretch along the east grandstand, Chase opens up his stride, lifts his knees higher, thrusts his hips forward with added force, and drives each foot of his trailing leg into the surface, leaving it all behind until his quads balk, sending signals of distress to his brain. His breathing whistles and gusts, rough and hollow, lungs begging for six liters of oxygen but receiving half that, the resultant lactic acid build up sounding synaptic alarms.

Off to the side two groundskeepers sit in a small utility vehicle waiting for football practice to conclude. One hunches over the steering wheel, his paunch deployed like an airbag, a finger drilling through layers of earwax; the other, pencil thin, sits upright with an appreciative once-a-runner glint in his eyes.

Turn two, headed for the apex, shaded by a giant sprawling oak tree on the inside portion of the track, Chase pumps his arms harder, propelling each in turn, back and forth, like connecting rods on a steam engine under a heavy load. That carries him into the home stretch, past another oak tree, less than 80 meters of worn-down track left to go. Rising lactic-acid levels work against him now, additional effort thwarted by muscles that can no longer respond in a timely manner. He zeroes in on the looming point of the finish line, growing by the meter, channeling all his mental energy into relaxing any body part willing to listen, his flaring nostrils and agape mouth inhaling the surrounding oxygen and velvety waft of dusty oak tannins like a vacuum. Ten yards out, his upper body stiffens, forcing him upright and rigid. The bear has jumped him, runner's rigor mortis in full bloom, but its damaging impact is too late, his velocity carrying him over the line, his finger jabbing the LAP button on the watch to capture the final split. *Beep*—"2:10" briefly stares back at him . . . *Hell yeah!*—then the watch resets for the next split and continues on, 10, 11, 12 . . .

No longer running from time's perpetual movement, Chase drifts to a trot, legs wobbly, lungs gasping. His brain endeavors to orchestrate an intervention of mass proportions: Lie down and curl up in the fetal position until the perceived danger passes. Chase pushes all the corporeal and mental noise aside, committed to finishing the one-lap recovery prescribed after each interval, despite the fact that he has completed the final one. This is what the schedule calls for, what facilitates the flushing of lactic acid from the body, or at least a portion of it, so he plods along until body and mind simmer down on the fly 300 meters later. From there the recovery is tolerable, better mechanically, and less likely to draw attention from the nursing students exiting their classroom across the way, though that wouldn't necessarily be a bad thing, his delirious mind muses.

The recovery lap complete, Chase commemorates the event by pressing Stop on the watch: *beep.* Off the clock and walking, his body loses its former structure, now rubbery, head drooping, the sweat sheeting down his chest. He basks under the noon sun, awash in blissful fatigue, the thumps in his chest slowing—though still pumping well above resting levels—going over the splits for the day in his mind: 2:16, 2:19—*had to wade through clueless joggers hogging lanes one through four*—2:14, 2:13, 2:15—*damn football team crossing the track as they please*—2:10. The planned, negative-spilt progression—each interval faster than the one prior—doesn't quite pan out, but the effort is there, which Chase takes solace in, though once uploaded online to his Garmin training journal it'll be forever scribed as such, excuses or no excuses in the notes column. No sense in crying over what can't be undone. Besides, he needs to keep moving for his 1:30 meeting back at the office.

Chase stops beside the west grandstand, where he'd tossed his tech shirt earlier and removes his sunglasses, clearing the smeared sunblock and sweat coating them. Eyes exposed to brilliant sunlight, he blinks repeatedly until the UV-protected lenses are cleansed and replaced. Vision improved he scans the stadium. Both oak trees on the north end of the football field stand stoic in solitude, leaves motionless. A crow struts nearby, its black plumage casting a stubby shadow against the ruddy track surface; it shoots furtive glances Chase's way, hops onto the football field, and heads toward a crumpled energy-bar wrapper sitting next to a scuffed leather football left behind. He raises a hand to his sunglasses and squints at the glare thrown from the long strands of bare aluminum benches scaling the east grandstand. His heart pulses in his ears, the moment's only soundtrack. He crosses his arms, rests each hand on the opposing shoulder, arches back his neck, and hugs himself, stretching out his upper torso.

Loosened yet steeled for the hardest part of any of his track workouts, Chase kneels, wipes down his face and arms with his shirt, then closes his eyes, bows his head, and gropes at the laces of each spiked racing flat, unlooping, unswooping, and unpulling the memory of his parents' shoe-tying lessons. Behind closed lids, dark shadows manifest from the year 2001, cast by the floodlights encircling the University of Wisconsin–La Crosse track and field stadium. His coach approaches him outside the chain-link fence past the finish line as he unloops, unswoops, and unpulls his 1,600-meter event winning track spikes at the 3-A High School State Championships. Coach's somber demeanor belies his congratulatory words. Frozen in place, knelt down, hands holding damp shoelaces, Chase knew. He wondered why he hadn't heard his name shouted out by his parents during the bell lap as he streaked down the homestretch. In the heat of the race he just assumed the din of the packed stadium drowned them out, when in fact they'd met the same fate as the SS *Edmund Fitzgerald* earlier that afternoon.

Spikes off, eyes open, shadows chased away by sunlight, he dons and laces up thicker-soled training shoes. Gathering his shirt and rising, he wraps it around his waist, tucks a portion of it into his shorts, and quenches his thirst from the water fountain. Walking with a racing shoe in each hand like relay batons toward the stadium exit he no longer finds himself alone, taking note of a woman with short jet-black hair in *very* tight running shorts and a sports bra heading out onto the track for laps of her own. *Nice!* He breaks into a warm-down trot, wishing he had time to stick around to chat her up, tapping the Start button of his watch—*beep*—his oft-traveled sidewalk route back to the office precisely 2.17 miles.

The air movement around him revives his senses, the evaporation of sweat on his skin cooling the body efficiently per nature's objective, a welcome change from the oval furnace he's spent his lunch hour baking in. Passing by the adjacent high school, Chase glances up to the second story of the Ivy League–inspired brick building, waving a baton toward the window where friend and fellow runner Spencer will most likely be standing, settling down his class for their post-lunch history lesson, perhaps setting the record straight about Paul Revere's *supposed* midnight ride or, more important, who John Galt was.

Traffic swirls around Chase, working his way downtown, pausing at intersections as needed before crossing, his mind on work. *Let's see, back to the Grogger Winery ad campaign . . . wine in a box . . . hmmmm . . . okay, how 'bout "Juice box for adults. Silly straws sold separately."* Chase bursts out laughing at what amounts to a futile print-ad campaign he has reluctantly agreed to take on. *Wine in a box . . . a box! . . . this is wine country; who do you think you're going to sell?—Honk!* Chase reflexively waves a spiked shoe without looking, not that he knows who has honked, or cares to know. *I know: "When you're at the end of your rope . . . Grogger's Box Wine . . . Box cutter included!" Shit, this campaign sucks.*

Beep. Warm-down complete, Chase slips his shirt on and braces for the air-conditioned shiver that awaits him at Chase Creative Ads.

"Nice nips," Chase's lead adman, John, says as Chase passes by his elder colleague.

Chase tucks his chin to his chest as he heads for his office to grab his gym bag, observing two sizable protrusions underneath the short-sleeve tech shirt from the New York Road Runner's 10K event three years ago. "AC is really cranked down today."

"Or running *really* turns you on."

"Not as much as the woman I saw across the track."

The older colleague chuckles. "With you they always look great from a distance. Any brainstorms on Grogger's?"

"Grogger's Box Wine . . . pairs well with sippy cups."

"Might test well with support groups for recently divorced women."

Chase nods. "We'll figure something out," he says on his way to the changing room, or what suffices as the changing room: the two-stall men's bathroom. The handicap stall provides adequate space to change, and after slathering his pits with a scentless deodorant—complex varieties react harshly with his body chemistry's post-run metabolic output—he rinses his face with several cold splashes from the sink. Once back in suitable office attire that shows no residue of athletic influence, he's ready for an afternoon of creativity.

Perched atop a large blue Swiss exercise ball in lieu of the traditional office chair, Chase listens intently to his two junior ad lackeys spin various ideas for the Grogger's campaign: fashion the wine box into a faux picnic table with folding legs for an outdoor wine-and-cheese picnic. Between ideas he chugs from a large plastic bottle filled with a "chemical shake" as his training partners often call it and tease him about, which actually contains Hammer's Recoverite, a popular sport recovery drink.

"The problem is," Chase says, "box wine is perceived as cheap. It's not a new concept. It was around and dismissed years ago as a fad. So we're up against negative perception on this one no matter how *good* it might be today, especially here in wine country. We need to pair it with something positive— yes, pun intended—like another product or . . . better yet, an initiative like, say . . . going green! Yeah, it's the green thing to do. The research shows"— Chase scrolls through a series of documents on his iPad while sipping from another plastic bottle with UCAN Hydrate, a hydration drink—"that it has a smaller carbon footprint by . . . here it is . . . nearly sixty-seven percent. Let's generate some ideas around that. It's already perceived as inexpensive, the bulk nature of that is built in, so we don't want to reinforce that aspect."

The lackeys sit motionless, complete with reverent expressions as if taken in by an evangelist.

"It can't be aged in a box so there's no angle there either. It's portable but that's only relevant for destinations or venues that don't allow glass. And if you're going to lug large quantities of alcohol around, it's going to be beer kegs; again, not a good association. Green is the theme. Excellent!" Chase slaps his hands together. "Show me some concept boards by the end of the week."

Chase bounces up from the Swiss ball and struts out from the conference room, "Banana Nut Bread" Clif Bar in hand poised for consumption, his audience left enraptured in the wake of his creative storm, their collective whisper of "Man, you were really on a roll today, Chase! That must've been some run," proof of his power, or his imagination.

Wednesday Afternoon
Period Six: US History

Peering out the second-story window awaiting a mix of tenth through twelfth graders to filter into his classroom, thirty-two-year-old Spencer Lingard cracks a slim smile as his friend Chase runs along the sidewalk below and waves a shoe toward the window. *Probably circled their track ten thousand times . . . at least . . . they should dedicate lane one to him.* Spencer watches Chase shrink from view. *Seems boring to run in circles on a recovery day . . . at least run the grassy loop in front of the JC—*

A distressed-sounding *buzz* sends students scurrying through the door to their desks.

"All right, wild ones, settle down." Spencer moves over behind his desk. "We're going to start off today with a pop quiz."

Trepidation spills across the tile floor and washes up to Spencer's running shoes.

"Can anyone tell me in what country the industrial revolution started?"

More than half the eighteen students raise their hands.

"Conrad. Glad to see you're participating today."

From the back row, Conrad's partially raised hand above broad shoulders remains at half mast, his expression stunned. "You never call on me, Mr. Lingard."

"You never raise your hand. I'm confident that you didn't do so today simply to *look* like you read the assignment. This is your moment to shine *off* the football field."

"Well, sir . . ."—he clears his throat, his quarterback eyes scanning the classroom as if under heavy pressure by a blitzing defense—"since this is US history . . . the United States?"

"Is your answer a statement or a question?"

Nervous laughter laps the room, sacking the quarterback.

"The United States."

"Better, but wrong. Spend a little more time on your studies and a little less time on the playbook. Only six percent of those playing football at the high school level make a college team, and less than two percent of college players make it to the pros, and those that *do* are lucky to play three years for all those years of sacrifice. Steve Young managed to earn a law degree *while* playing professional ball. Intelligence is the new sport." Spencer scans the room as arms and hands reassert themselves, saluting knowledge. "Crystal?"

From the back row the recently transferred Oakland student's bespectacled eyes flash freeze like a deer in headlights when her head snaps upright.

"Lose the cell phone . . . Zac?"

"Great Britain, Coach."

"Yes, as *most* of you read, around 1760 the jolly good Brits, Conrad's esteemed eighteenth-century heritage, improved the process of spinning and weaving wool, moving it from household piecemeal production to full-scale mills, offsetting the growing cotton trade from India. Next question: how is this relevant to today's information revolution?"

Fewer arms rise, most provisional at best.

"Katharine."

Katharine contemplates the question further, as a game-show contestant does, one who rushes to hit the buzzer first but without an answer at the ready.

"It wasn't in your textbook; it's okay to conjecture," Spencer says. "Historians do it all the time."

Katharine nods politely, smile reserved. "So, understanding the underpinnings of the industrial revolution can provide insight into what will transpire throughout the information revolution."

"Underpinnings?" Oz says. "My car has those; *squeak, squeak, squeak . . .*"

Chuckles bubble up.

"Oz, we talked about this . . ." Spencer says, undermining Oz's continuing attempt at gaining Crystal's attention.

"Thank you, Katharine. Another one, more specific?"

More hands rise, confident in speculation.

"Josh."

"It impacts how we live socially? I mean, it impacts how we live socially, like where we live, our standard of living."

"Better. Another? . . . Nate."

"Comparatively, tech startups began in garages as a way to have fun and experiment, then visionaries like Jobs and Gates took the ideas mainstream."

"Excellent. That's the importance to understanding the fundamentals of a historical event or time period: it allows us to derive and extrapolate just about anything to anywhere by placing our lives into a broader context. It inspires us to improve upon or alter what's gone on before us." Spencer faces the chalkboard—one of only two left on campus, the other in a honors math class—picks up a piece of chalk, and scratches out the day's assignment. "And to that end we're going on a"—*tsk, tsk, squeal, tsk, tsk*—"scavenger hunt."

Shoe soles scuff freshly waxed floor tiles. A pen drops, lands, and rolls, evading its owner's reach.

"Hand down, Crystal," Spencer says, etching out SCAVENGER HUNT across the charcoal-colored surface. "Your all-encompassing doctor's note won't be necessary."

Thud! Crystal's rejected arm against her desktop resonates throughout the room of world and US relief maps hanging in the disquieted space.

When Spencer turns toward the students, their palpable thoughts confront him: *Run around the hallways gathering crap? Barging into classrooms? What if Jones sees me or Ninh or Brian? What are we, freshmen? This constitutes hazing. Lame!*

"Did I forget to mention it's an *Internet* scavenger hunt?"

"Yes!" Conrad roars as if he's thrown a touchdown pass.

Crystal rolls her eyes.

With the aid of a front-row student in a pleated dress eager to please, Spencer passes out Chromebooks, going over the assignment: break into four teams and research one aspect of the industrial revolution and its importance to understanding today's information revolution—economically, socially, politically, or culturally.

"Here is a list of research sites," Spencer says, returning to the chalkboard to list them out, ones more valuable than generic search engines like Google, which he likens to a worldwide popularity contest in the sense that results are skewed by paid advertisements as well as complex algorithms based on visitation frequency and content quality; it ranks up there in mystery with the collegiate Bowl Championship Series (BCS) computer-generated rankings.

- Internet Public Library
- Smithsonian National Museum of American History
- The History Engine
- Library of Congress
- United States Historical Census Browser

"Dogpile is my go-to search engine," Zac says. "It combines—"

"Dog *Pile* . . ." Oz says, laughing so hard he nearly falls off his chair.

"Oz, get it together or extra hill repeats are in your future," Spencer says, though the threat doesn't completely quell Oz's amusement. "Dogpile *is* good"—Oz bursts into another fitful bender to which Spencer muses, *and he's on our varsity squad* —"in that it culls from other search engines like Google, Yahoo!, Bing, Ask, and LookSmart, to name a few. However, to use *any* of these sites effectively without getting irrelevant results you'll need some research skills." Passing by each row of desks, Spencer puts into motion a stack of papers with Internet search tips and tricks:

- Place quotes ("") around a phrase to return results that contain that exact phrase.
- Add the minus sign (-) in front of a keyword to eliminate it from the search.
- Add the tilde operator (~) in front of a keyword to return synonyms for it.
- The wildcard operator (*) placed after the keyword returns derivatives of it.

"But the best way to use a site like Google or Bing is as an intermediary to a source site. For example, it's quicker to search our local newspaper the *Press Democrat* with Google than it is on the paper's site itself."

Spencer writes out on the chalkboard the Google search format: *site:www.pressdemocrat.com sonoma county history.*

"To narrow your search to a time period add a year to the end: 1980s."

"Coach, at your age you really should work smarter, not harder," Oz says. "Type in a word or two and let Google fill in the blanks."

Spencer tilts his head, closes one eye, and raises the eyebrow of the other.

"So how many extra hill reps are we talking?"

Crystal scoffs.

While the four teams group themselves accordingly, based on counting off 1, 2, 3, 4 seat by seat, and begin their deep dive into history, Spencer settles in behind his desk and pulls out his personal iPad and catches up on his daily tasks. First he launches an app that tracks his training, logging the six and a half miles he ran from home to school that morning. He reviews his August total: 398 miles. *So close.* He sends a text with his summer's total to Chase, adding "Summer miles king again!" Based on Chase's Strava postings he'll be well under Spencer's 1,124 miles. Both men have kept track of every mile they've ever run—from paper-based *Runners World* training logs, through the spreadsheet era, Lotus 1 2 3 stored on floppy disks and Excel saved on rewritable DVDs, to today's web- and mobile-enabled apps. They each have different rules under which they track their miles, however. Chase doesn't count anything under three miles, while Spencer logs everything, including an ill-advised half mile New Year's Eve his junior year in high school when he had the flu, all in the name of preserving 2000's streak of having never missed a day of running. By the time "Auld Lang Syne" had been slurred throughout the Pacific Standard time zone and the *proper* Y2K celebrated later that evening, he'd thrown up enough times to earn a trip to the ER, but the streak was intact.

Next, he checks his personal email, finding a long-winded plea backed by numerous embedded web links from Walter, the local running club's president—Redwood Empire Runners Club—to his vice president, Spencer.

After two paragraphs, Spencer scratches his forehead, closes one eye, and scrunches up his lips as if reacting to an unexpected tart taste, then files the email away for another time when he can reflect on how best to talk Walter down from *another* wild idea—always an exhausting balancing act between prudent opposition and genuine support.

Next item: as RERC's de facto coach, Spencer reviews September's training schedule, makes minor adjustments to accommodate the upcoming cross-country season, and emails it off to the editor of the club's monthly newsletter. Before Spencer can move to the next item, Crystal's black-rimmed glasses frames bear down on him

"Yes, Crystal?"

"My Chromebook isn't connecting to the Wi-Fi."

Spencer takes it, examines the settings, twice attempts to connect, and determines she's not faking it to get out of the assignment. He surveys the technology cart off to the side: empty. "Team up with—"

"I want my own. How can *I* learn and contribute to the group if I'm looking through someone else's lenses?"

Spencer smiles, and not because her glasses contain no lenses; Crystal pays attention when motivated despite her ironically inspired disheveled attire: a zipped-up baggy Salvation Army jacket, and jeans with indie rock band patches sewn over spots of shredded denim. "Use mine, but *only* for today's assignment. I see one excursion to Facebook and you're voted off Technology Island. Got it?"

Crystal nods, snatches Spencer's iPad like a Capuchin monkey at a petting zoo, and returns to the "Economics" group, sitting across from Oz.

"You can see where we search?" Katharine says.

"Of course."

"What about privacy laws?"

"School property. When you join the workforce, your employer will have the same right to know where you go on the Internet. Their computers, their privilege. Do you think about who monitors your social-media posts?"

Katharine nods and returns her attention back to the assignment.

Spencer reaches for his smart phone from his day pack to resume his task list when he notices Zac and Donna, both runners on his cross-country squads, interacting with each other rather than their group.

"Zac, Donna, let's focus on the social aspects of the industrial revolution and not modern ones."

"Got it, Coach," Zac says, handing Donna the Chromebook. "She was having trouble connecting to the Wi-Fi."

Donna smiles, reacquires the device, and fixes her gaze on it. "But what if we can learn from past mistakes, Coach?"

"*You* can't," Katharine says from the "Politics" group.

Spencer accepts the Zac/Donna interaction externally, but internally . . . *Are they dating again?* He breathes deep, then exhales slowly. *On again, off again . . . relationship commitments at their age are fruitless. They're consumed with trying to figure out who they are and what they want—*

"Who's Maggie?" Crystal says.

Spencer reacts the same way Conrad had earlier, sans raised hand. "Excuse me?"

"His *girlfriend*," Donna says.

"Her text message says her parents are coming to town in two weeks. She added two smiley emojis. How cute . . ."

The class reacts with all the diplomacy of teenagers: hoots, hollers, and a whistle or two.

Spencer gives off a distinctive clearing of the throat, from which the class scurries back behind the Internet's curtain; except for Crystal.

"Should I reply?"

Spencer sighs and shakes his head. "Back to the economic aspects of the industrial revolution."

Maggie's parents are delightful enough during their one or sometimes two visits a year, though each trip brings along two topics that always put him on the defensive . . . both of which he immediately banishes when a new email catches his attention, this one from Rocco, the high school football coach, declaring which dates Conrad should be excused from class for away games. There's an added comment *not* to be a "Sir pain-in-the-ass" about it as Spencer had last year. Spencer smirks while typing his reply: "Sir Rocco, as long as you submit the proper release forms to the front office in a timely manner there will be no issues with excusing Conrad on game days. Historically, Spencer."

"Who's Chase?" Crystal says. "Is he being ironic with his name: noun *and* verb?"

Spencer closes his eyes for a moment. *Perhaps I should invoke her doctor's note.*

"We call him Hunt for short," Oz says, taking another enamored shot, though Crystal's return glare doesn't inspire hope.

"Just—"

"What does he mean by 'Quantity is for the jogger; quality is for the runner?'"

Spencer chuckles. He and Chase are always debating their mileage tallies, the underlying basis. It has all the flare of "uphill both ways, in the snow, the sand, against the wind—"

"He wants to know when and where Sunday's run is. Wait, he added, 'it better not be at Cobblestone again or I'm gonna—'"

"Economics group, what do you have so far?" Spencer says.

Suddenly speechless, Oz scratches his neck and glances at Crystal, then Conrad, then Kalyan, none of whom seem willing to present the group's findings.

Crystal groans. "There have been three major revolutions in human history as a result of innovation," she says. "Agricultural, industrial, and information. Their economic impact can be evaluated within the Kondratiev wave model and its four milestones: prosperity, recession, depression, and improvement. Logically, the next one will be the space revolution. Can I check my phone? My grandmother is in the hospital."

"Cool army boots," Oz says.

"A reminder that history shouldn't be judged by one account only," Spencer says, nodding toward Crystal, allowing her cell-phone access. "Social group, what do you have?"

Thursday After Work
Black Swans and Taxes

Thirty-five-year-old Jim Greyson stands patiently beside his two-tone black-and-silver Subaru at the Cobblestone Trailhead, awaiting his friend Jake, for their longstanding Thursday-evening Annadel run. He methodically sweeps his right foot back and forth in the dirt, a remnant of his Little League days at shortstop, mulling over the unsettling conversation he'd endured with another runner, a familiar stranger, who'd regaled Jim with the concept of "humans transcending biology." "Isn't that *so* cool?" the future transhumanist hopeful said before continuing on with his transcendental run. *Great. Another black swan on the horizon. I'm still waiting for the aftershock to the last global financial collapse. Now there's "technological singularity"?* Jim pauses a moment, peering down Channel Drive for Jake; unmaintained asphalt worn down by city life, blackberry bushes torched by the sun, and a mountain biker riding in circles examining his chain that's skipping gears fill Jim's vision. *I can't decide which threat is worse, artificial intelligence or idiocracy. Perhaps they're one in the same.* Jim pats the key pocket on his running shorts for the second time since locking the car. Key still there. *Technology already changes too fast to fully enjoy as it is. And it's increasing exponentially?* Jim shakes his head. *I miss the days when the only concerns were coming up with a catchy email address, running into a mountain lion in the park, having to pee during a race, choosing between regular or organic produce–organic pesticides are equally dangerous, people!–going bald, job security, retirement savings, health insurance covering all the new diseases discovered every year, running out of. . .*

"Your life has been filled with terrible misfortune," Jake says, approaching Jim. "Most of which never happened."

Jim cracks a slim smile, shaking Jake's extended hand. "Today's philosopher of choice is?"

"Michel de Montaigne."

"Probably didn't have to deal with black swans back in his day."

"True. The Black Plague pre-dated him by two hundred years. Ready to roll?"

"Easy nineish?"

"Cobblestone-Richardson loop?"

"Perfect."

The two friends since grade school exit the parking lot, jutting up the meandering single-track, tree-enclosed Cobblestone Trail that tests one's lungs quickly. Jim scoots ahead of Jake where the bone-dry trail narrows, using short, choppy strides to facilitate the maneuver; faint puffs of dust rise with each foot strike.

"What's your latest black swan?" Jake says.

"Technological singularity. Heard of it?"

"Artificial intelligence, 'our greatest existential threat,' as Elon Musk once put it."

"The Tesla guy? The guy who wants to build self-driving smart cars *and* send people to Mars?" Jim says rhetorically. "I think the fumes from his billions are clouding his judgment."

"Or bringing his visions to life. Even Bill Gates and Stephen Hawking have expressed concerns over AI."

"We're perpetually like cavemen fumbling with fire . . . artificial insemination was bound to breed artificial intelligence."

"Generally I encourage people to *not* sweat the small stuff," Jake says. "For you it'd be therapeutic."

"Doom is my mojo."

"Yes, it is." Their shoes skim over alternating shafts of sunlight and dark shadows. "If memory serves me correctly there are *good* black swans. Not all are doom and gloom."

"Such as . . . ?"

"Your poster, for instance."

Jim glances back to Jake. "Billy Mills?"

"Fits the criteria: nobody saw it coming, *yet* afterward everyone said, yeah, that makes sense."

Jim considers it; Billy's Olympic victory stunned everyone, and was influential from an inspirational perspective.

"Nice article in the *Press* yesterday," Jake says, snaking his way over a rocky section that requires well-honed agility.

Jim groans. "Doris insisted on it."

"You did win all three county half-marathons this summer. It's a great profile piece. Gives attention to local age-group runners and the club."

"I look constipated in the picture."

"Race photos are like that."

"I posed for it after the interview."

Jake bursts out laughing as they pass by a wooden bench, then promptly says, "Many apologies" to the bench's occupants when they implore, "Gentlemen, please keep your voices down" while the couple regard their view.

"That seemed unnecessary," Jim says, glancing to his left through an opening between a cluster of oak trees toward the steep hillside across the valley where a "cross" faces them. Constructed out of whitewashed stones, each piece laid out in a clearing of golden wild grass as if painted, the iconic cross has polarized many locals for thirty-five years, reactions ranging from adulation to condemnation. Its presence for Jim is simply another quirky local charm.

"What's the latest on the merger?" Jake asks.

Jim shakes his head, a mixture of worry and disgust. If he could wring his hands *and* run efficiently, he'd do so. "Nobody's talking, so we don't know if we'll have jobs next month or not. Just what I need right now . . ." *Get a little ahead and the other shoe invariably drops—*

"You never know. From the article in the *Press* it sounds like they're interested in expanding operations."

"They're only interested in the client list."

Jim and Jake crest the first climb, released from the treed confines and out into a small meadow, giving their legs brief respite before the next sustained climb. Jake pulls up alongside Jim where the trail widens and drifts back where it narrows.

"You ever sort that guy's taxes out?" Jake says, ducking back under the leafy canopy. "The celiac guy who wanted to write off his gluten-free groceries?"

Jim's head shake now conveys irritation; the variations are subtle, but they are there if you look close enough. "Well, as it turns out he can deduct up to fifty percent with a doctor's note."

"You're kidding."

"You know I don't kid. The guy's still bonkers. He doesn't understand cash flow to save his life. He comes in and only wants to hear how much money he can spend. I tell him he's bleeding his business dry, and he looks at me with a straight face and says, 'So how much? We can massage the numbers, right? Bottom line it for me.'"

"I couldn't run my business that way and survive."

"I know."

"Yes, you do."

They hit the end of Cobblestone and join up with Rough-go, whose aptly named trail requires full attention, the path winding its way through a minefield of various-sized rocks and boulders fully exposed to a blue sky that offsets the surrounding olive-green foliage. And though their pace slows it appears swift by comparison to the two guys cautiously negotiating the same route up ahead.

"Hey, hey, J and J," one of the cautious runners says, voice raspy, and wearing surgical compression socks to cover up his varicose veins. He steps off to the side of the trail, allowing "J&J" easy passage. "What are you guys doing on *my* trail?" He chuckles.

"Humbly honoring your history, Dale," Jake says with a sly grin.

"Wise guys," Dale replies. "They're wise guys, them two."

"Speaking of history," Jake says, several strides and leaps upon terraced terrain later, "what time are we meeting on Sunday?"

"Spence hasn't sent out the email yet."

"That's not like him to leave it so late in the week."

"First week back to school. Probably pretty busy," Jim says. "Plus I'm sure he's preoccupied with his team's prospects this year."

"Zac certainly has the potential to take them all the way. Last year was tough for him."

"We've all been there."

Jake nods as Jim leads them downhill toward Annadel's watery hub, Lake Illsanjo, at a fast clip for an easy run, though both runners' form show no strain from it.

"How's Doris—" Jake says. "Oh man, I almost forgot, how'd the thing go last night with the girl at that place?"

Jim cracks a smile. "*Ocean's Eleven*, and she said yes."

"Congrats, Jimbo!" Jake says, patting Jim on the shoulder. They turn onto and cross the Lake Illsanjo Dam, the surface of the lake sparkling with sunlight while dark- and white-feathered ducks glide serenely along, their webbed feet churning like egg beaters under the surface. "Did you set a date?"

"In a couple months. November seventh."

"That soon?"

"Her mother isn't doing well, so . . ."

"Makes sense. You're crazy about Doris. No need for a long engagement. Linda and I only had a two-month . . . wait a minute, Doris isn't pregnant is she?"

Jim lets out a rare burst of laughter that startles a group of hikers up ahead. "We're not in the pickle you two were in. *Man*, your parents are hardcore Catholics."

"Ohhhhhh yeah," Jake says, chuckling afterward.

"I still remember finding the unopened condom wrapper in your driveway back in grade school, and I asked your mom what it was. I thought she was going to cross herself to death."

Jake is laughing too hard to respond right away. "And you were like, 'But Mrs. Dearborn, what's it for?'" he spits out, unable to control his laughter.

"I still can't look at a condom wrapper without seeing the ghastly face she made."

"She talked about it for months; told me to steer clear of you."

"I wondered why I was never invited over after that."

"Yes, the great Condom Condemnation Act of '89."

They crest the final hill of the run and begin a long fire road–style descent that both runners and mountain bikers alike love. Jake pulls up alongside Jim, whose shorter stride requires quicker turnover in order to maintain his pace and position with Jake.

"Did you see Chase's latest billboard campaign along the freeway?" Jim says, watching a turkey up ahead split from its group, scatter up the path, and head off to the side, disappearing from view.

"The one about the Go Energy Bar?"

"That's the one. Did he tell you what the early pitches for it were?"

"Similar to the GU sport gel campaign he worked on back in New York . . . GU early, GU often?"

"Yep, except with a twist: 'Go early, Go often.'"

"Oh, lord love a duck!" Jake says, sling-shotting around a hairpin turn and continuing their spirited descent down Richardson, passing by three runners who had stopped and were taking a group selfie that included deer grazing in the background.

"He ate a bar and said he was in and out of the can the rest of the day."

"That could work for a Depends ad too."

The two reach the bottom of the trail, hang a left onto the asphalt of Channel Drive, one and a half miles from where they'd started. Their pace coming off the downhill doesn't ease, a gravitational tendency when finishing up a run on Channel Drive: the call of the finish beckons, the grade an ever-so-gentle net drop allowing legs, tired or not, to turn over with a modicum of extra effort. Side by side, the former junior high cross-country co-champions stride in silence, with nothing further to discuss, Jim stowing his day's toils behind him while Jake places his into perspective.

"I'm parked over at Spring Lake," Jake says, approaching Jim's car, both slowing to a stop. He reaches his hand out to shake Jim's. "Thanks for the run, and congrats on the engagement. And yes, I'd be honored to be your best man." Jake bows.

"That's why I didn't have to ask."

"Give Doris my best."

"See ya Sunday."

Thursday Evening
A Life Examined

Pace subdued, thirty-six-year-old Jake Dearborn works his way down Channel Drive after parting company with Jim, taking an unnamed trail into

25

Spring Lake that hugs the lake's northwesterly shore instead of the paved bike/pedestrian path. He takes comfort in the day's subtle exhale, the sun somewhere behind the hills toward the coast, its lingering rays painting the tips of the overhead Douglas firs a golden yellow. Entranced by the dusk light, his long legs glide over tree roots and unfortunately placed rocks much like a deer would scamper over them. And with no official name to the trail, Jake moves along in harmony with nature without labels, without even a timepiece on his wrist to measure it. His effort will be stored inside him, and any written record of it in his journal will be a mere, but mostly accurate, estimation.

Jake turns onto what many refer to as the Fisherman's Trail, quiet and vacant, whose many outcroppings expose the lake and provide easy shoreline access to patient anglers. The half-mile segment also plays host to numerous cross-country meets throughout the fall, a stretch he's raced along many, many times. Unfortunately, his moment of solitude and reverence ends abruptly when another runner from a side trail nearly bowls Jake over, bumping his shoulder and moving him off course.

"Whoa, sorry!" the reckless runner hollers, skittering to a stop while grabbing Jake's arm. "You okay?"

"We're good," Jake says, unfazed by the intrusion and thankful the stranger has grabbed him, which in all likelihood keeps Jake from getting up close and personal with the trail.

"I hit that turn pretty hot," the reckless runner says, glancing behind him.

"It's certainly hard to judge off the descent." He regards the guy as they resume running. "Jake's the name."

"Dillon. Where's this trail dump out?"

"Boat-ramp parking lot. New to the area?"

"Moved here eight months ago. I was exploring some of side trails today."

"Nice. It's easy to head right up into Annadel and forget about all the trails around Spring Lake. Don't let me hold you up if you're on a roll. I'm coasting the last of my run."

"Coasting you say . . . feels about right. It's nice to meet someone who's from here. I'm usually the one giving directions and course maps. I own a bed-run-and-breakfast inn just outside of—"

"So you're the one," Jake says, putting a face to the place. "Rumors have swirled all summer about a running-themed B&B in the area. Small running community; word travels fast. You . . . didn't by chance win the 10K downtown last weekend?"

"I did. I jumped into it that morning on a whim."

"Some in the club were asking who you were. Nobody knew."

"I felt bad not sticking around for the awards, but I had guests coming in early."

"I ran into a Canadian couple last Monday running out here. Said they were staying at a BR&B. Unique twist. Business good?"

"Really just opened it. They were my first guests. I missed the summer season, unfortunately. More repairs than I anticipated."

"Where'd you move from?"

"Newport Beach."

"Beautiful."

"Once upon a time . . ."

Jake lets Dillon work out the details to his last statement without interruption, enjoying the casual pace with the fellow runner whose lean physique and form has a refined flow to it, second-nature in style, suggesting a competitor lurking underneath. "Any more races on the horizon?"

"The fall always reminds me of cross-country. Might jump into some races down in Frisco."

"Colorado?"

"What? No, San Francisco."

Jake leaves his grin unexplained, having a little fun with the Southern Californian transplant. "We have a local running club that competes in a series of cross-country meets around Northern California starting in a few weeks if you're interested," he says, slowing his pace. "This is me." He stops next to a long-bed truck whose front and back door panels advertise his trade, DEARBORN LANDSCAPING. "Nice running into you." Jake smiles and Dillon chuckles. "We do our long runs on Sundays if you'd care to join us. We usually start at seven a.m. on Channel and go twenty or so."

"Tempting," Dillon says, shaking Jake's hand and turning to continue on. "Thanks for the run."

Jake wipes the sweat off his forehead with an old towel once he opens the truck, watching Dillon stride out across the parking area until he reaches the Spring Lake Dam, where he chews up the packed gravel in short order, hangs a right, and disappears into the wooded campgrounds. Jake grins. *We may well have found our fifth man.* The fortuitous encounter with Dillon will no doubt delight Spencer.

Jake steers his truck westbound from the park, through town, heading home, outside city limits where property lines expand and the density of life recedes. Turning off the poorly maintained, potholed county road, Jake pulls into the spacious gravel driveway. With a turn of the key, the aging engine gives way to peace, save for sporadic hisses, pops, and clicks.

Through the truck's windshield, where wiper blades have etched out an unclouded view amongst the plastered grime, he can see his eight-year-old daughter sitting at the dining-room table next to the large picture window eagerly doing her homework. "Robyn is an inquisitive one," her third-grade teacher had told him and his wife, Linda, last week after Robyn's first day back to school. Robyn's thirst for knowledge knew no bounds, certainly far beyond her years and it often brought a joyful tear to his face on occasion as well as shades of embarrassment on others. And not just the proverbial "Why, Daddy?" but insightful questions, like the time she asked him, as he laid down weed fabric at a job site, how weeds grew if no one planted them, a question he himself had never considered. The answer involved a discussion on how seeds travel with the winds and settle in the soil and eventually grow. After that conversation she carefully studied the air every time the wind picked up, searching for "weed seeds," hoping to pluck them from the sky before they landed and sprouted in their yard.

He can see his wife of Robyn's age plus eight months moving through the air conditioning–less homestead, still dressed in hospital scrubs, opening windows to maximize the air flow of the cool evening breeze.

Jake opens up the glove box and pulls out a rumpled, earth-stained journal. He flips to where he had left off the previous Sunday, reviewing the beginnings of a new prose poem, "Footfalls in Annadel." He reviews and polishes each sentence, reducing them to their pure essence, pleased with the opening stanza:

The dry twig snaps, breaking the predawn slumber, awakening ancient Pomo footfalls that came before him. Old-growth redwoods stretch high, basking in autumn's first sun rays, outlining the meandering trail below. The ground shifts subtly under the weight of his shoes, set to a rhythmic cadence, dispersing pillowy clouds out from underneath, forever scribing the journey both in soil and socks.

He returns his attention to the homestead, admiring a scene that never tires him: Robyn has retreated to the bathroom off the kitchen to wash her hands; Linda has set the table and is carrying large serving bowls with steam trailing each; Juggles, their fifteen-year-old mutt of a dog, slowly circles the table, nose pointing straight up; Robyn returns to the dining room, fills up all three water glasses from the pitcher on the table, marches over to the big picture window, presses her forehead against the thick glass, smiles, and waves to him.

Friday Night
Spencer's Weekly Email

> From: Spencer Lingard <MarathonMan@gomail.com>
> To: Team Thirsty Boys <SundayRunDL>
> Subject: Sunday's Run . . .
>
> Dear Sirs,
> Congrats, Jim, on your engagement! I can't wait for another Tahoe
> bachelor weekend getaway like the one we had for Jake, assuming
> Doris will allow it after the great Chase debacle of '08. In hindsight,
> hanging out with miss Ph-Double-Ds wasn't a bright idea.
> Any thoughts for a start time this week? Chase, can you do 7
> a.m.? I can hear the groan already . . . my apologies. Maggie
> and I are attending the Save the Wine Country Creek Cohos
> committee meeting at 11 a.m. I need 20 this weekend and Jake
> is doing the same. Channel Drive again? And we might have a
> potential recruit for our club join us so let's not scare him off

with any blistering pace changes; I'm glaring at you, Jimbo.
Don't act surprised. Let's avoid philosophical debates (Jakey),
commercials (Chasester), and excessive coaching analysis
(yours truly).
Signing off,
Spencer

. . . I will reply to your email after I've had sufficient time to reflect on its
content.

From: Chase Brandon <ChaseMeIfYouCan@gomail.com>
To: Team Thirsty Boys <SundayRunDL>
Subject: RE: Sunday's Run . . .

"The un-American in Annadel." Why the eggshell tap-dance
with the new guy. I'm sure he ties his shoes one at a time like
everyone else.
You're killing me with your 7 a.m.s! When the forecast calls for
triple digits then it makes sense. Those days are behind us.
I propose starting at Howarth for a change of routes, and toilet
paper option. Just saying.
And in my defense, Tiffany *did* have two PhDs. In what I don't
recall.
Chasester

From: Jim Greyson <JimG@gomail.com>
To: Team Thirsty Boys <SundayRunDL>
Subject: RE: Sunday's Run . . .

Gentlemen,
Chase is the one that pushes the pace. I just latch on. Doris is
fine with a weekend getaway so long as you, Jakey and Chase,
aren't there. Tiffany? I thought her name was Amber. The next

time Chase says we're going to a "Tapas" bar, we should clarify what he means.

I second Chasester's Howarth start proposal. Until Sunday.

Jim

From: Linda Dearborn <LDRN@gomail.com>
To: Team Thirsty Boys <SundayRunDL>
Subject: RE: Sunday's Run . . .

I saw the new guy run. He can handle us.
Andrea. Chemistry and Psychology.

Happy Trails,
Jakey

From: Spencer Lingard <MarathonMan@gomail.com>
To: Team Thirsty Boys <SundayRunDL>
Subject: RE: Sunday's Run . . .

Dear Sirs,

Channel Drive at 7 it is (I'll have TP on hand if needed.) The new guy's name is Dillon and he's expecting to see us on Channel. Plus we can take him on our favorite loop: Shultz-Lawndale.

Signing off,

Spencer

Sunday Morning
Cobblestone Trailhead

One by one, a handful of cars trickle past Dillon as he runs effortlessly along the unkempt paved side road that butts up against the five-thousand-acre, heavily wooded state park of Annadel, tranquil under the early-morning September sky. The cars jostle over potholes defined by layers of futile repairs, the passengers absorbing each bump without thought. Dillon has parked at Howarth Park and run the two miles through Spring Lake over to the Channel Drive parking area, giving him an excuse to peel off from the group should the pace, or group, not suit him, though he has an inkling that Jake's invite suggested they'd be a good fit.

Jake's landscaping truck rumbles by as Dillon approaches the dirt parking lot, where a handful from the endurance community have already assembled, some making mechanical adjustments to mountain bikes while others stretch and make small talk, deciding on what layering options they should start their run or ride with. Their voices percolate in the stillness.

"Dillon," Jake says upon opening his truck door that creaks. He tosses onto the ground worn trail shoes, whose brand and logo are unrecognizable under layers of many muddy and dusty miles.

"Jake," Dillon says, happy to discover that his aren't the only socks marinated in Annadel's powdery soil, permanently infused into the fabric, their original color forever tarnished.

"Where'd you run in from?"

"Howarth."

Jake chuckles. "Chase and Jimbo will get a kick out of that."

"Oh?"

"You'll see."

Another car silently pulls in alongside Jake's truck. "Jakey," says the voice that exits the metallic green Prius. "Your truck getting bigger? Now it's blocking the sun."

"Every week I get this," Jake says, grinning. "Last week it was 'It could swallow my Prius whole.' You and your *petite* hybrid . . . I'm the first person you call when you need to make a trip to the grocery store. Dillon, this is Spencer; Spence, Dillon."

"Hi," Spencer says, extending his hand to shake Dillon's. "Just that one time, Jakey, for the plants."

"You're forgetting the move last month—eight trips across town," Jake says, whacking his shoes together, knocking off the last run's miles; a small brownish cloud floats outward. "The used washer and dryer set you and Maggie bought down in San Rafael, and the—"

"Time you, Maggie, and I took *my* SUV to Tahoe because yours didn't handle the snow well," says the shirtless guy who walks up to the group. "You must be Dillon. I'm Chase. Glad you could join us."

"Likewise." Dillon shakes Chase's hand, drawn in by the good-natured ribbing the trio have going.

"How's it going, Jakey?" Chase says. He places a hand on Jake's solar blockade and leans against it, stretching his right calf. "Robyn's doing?" he adds, pointing to a newly affixed Curious George sticker on the truck's back window.

Jake nods.

"Robyn like her new school?" Spencer says.

"She does," Jake says, standing up and shaking out his legs. "She's already reading ahead of her class, and was designated class librarian and recess monitor." He glances over to Dillon. "Robyn's my daughter; just started third grade."

Dillon nods. *Precocious and involved.*

"Where's Jimbo?" Spencer says, checking his watch. "He's cutting it close."

"That's him there," Jake replies as Jim's Subaru approaches, passes, and parks a few spots down from the guys.

"We're doing a seventeen-mile route from here—" Spencer starts to explain to Dillon.

"We used to call it eighteen until Garmin came along," Chase says. "Data to the rescue."

"You say rescue, I say splitting hairs," Jake says.

"And Jake and I are going to add three on at the end."

"That works. I parked over at Howarth so—"

Chase and Jim, who walks up, groan and feign annoyance.

"TP?" Spencer says, producing a roll.

"Jimbo, this is Dillon; Dillon, Jim," Jake says.

"Hey," they say in unison as Jim lifts a foot onto Jake's truck's bumper, tying the shoe.

"You like those?" Dillon asks, pointing to Jim's shoes, Hoka One Ones whose soles exceed Dillon's preference for padding, removing him from the sensation the surface provides to the soles of his feet, like the cushy ride a Cadillac provides compared to a Jeep's rugged one.

"They're okay. I only do my long runs in them. For anything fast they're too bulky. I'm really not sure what all the hype is about."

"It's all in the branding," Chase says.

"It used to be the runner made the shoe, now the shoe makes the runner," Jake says in theatrical fashion.

"*Quiz Show*," Jim answers.

Dillon's eyes shift between Jim and Jake, waiting for an explanation, but none is provided.

"Let's roll," Jim says. He turns and starts trotting, prompting the others to toss unwanted clothing into cars, close and lock doors, and tuck keys into small waistline pockets. All but Jake presses the Start button on their respective watches as their legs swing into motion. *Beep . . . beep-beep—*

"Shit," Chase says, stopping. "Mine hasn't linked up with the satellites yet."

"Movie quote game," Spencer says, sidling up alongside Dillon. "J and J are huge cinema buffs, so they try to incorporate a quote or theme into conversation and someone tries to identify it."

"Got it," Dillon says.

"Come on, Chasester, it'll link up soon enough," Jake says. "You guys and your precision. The body records and stores your effort. You don't need technology to tell you you ran X number of miles."

"When they figure out how to attach a USB to my chest so it uploads my run to Garmin, Strava, and Running2Win, I'll relax," Chase hollers, and once properly linked to the heavens, he rejoins the group.

"Your nipples are too big for a standard USB," Jim says.

"Running2Win?" Dillon says.

"Another training-log website," Jim says.

"It's more socially interactive than that," Spencer says.

"It's 'where runners live,'" Chase quotes proudly.

"I don't understand Strava," Dillon says. "It's like piecemeal training: 'Look at me, I sprinted two-hundred yards during my twenty miler today faster than everyone else' . . . nice job, kudos, big whoop."

All except Chase nod.

"It's good motivation for those who need it," Jake says.

"Sparks competition," Spencer says. "The high schoolers love it."

"What about those running-magazine articles," Chase says, "where so and so is designated the fastest third-grade teacher who lives in a town with a population over one hundred thousand and eats ice cream every day for lunch?"

"I think the *Guinness Book of World Records* inspires such esoteric pursuits," Jim says.

"Man distinguishing himself from the herd," Jake says.

"Look at me, I'm the king of the world!" Spencer says.

"*Titanic*," Jake says, a beat quicker than Jim.

Stretched five wide they embark up Channel Drive under a canopy of mature evergreens and oaks toward the one official road entrance into Annadel State Park, where a handful of driveways lead to humble homes tucked away behind hedges and undergrowth. Dillon listens to the original four's morning chatter halfheartedly while he observes their sinewy and varied running forms—runners can be just as easily identified by their form as much as by their fingerprints—quickly learning more about them from it than discussing running or politics. Chase runs like precision-engineered German machinery, his build stocky, and everything from head to toe working in harmony to contribute to forward progress. Dillon guesses him a former miler based on knee lift and higher than normal back kick. This is in sharp contrast to Jake, poetry in motion running alongside Chase, showcasing their divergent styles. Jake has at least six inches on Chase and lacks the same precision. Jake's stride, considerably longer, has a lower cadence, and his arms swing freely with less arc; an expressive gait carried out by sturdy tree trunk legs in keeping with the surrounding redwoods.

Spencer's head bobs quite a bit, though his talking and constant head turning while talking probably contributes to it. His stride resembles Olympian Mark Conover's: a shuffle of sorts, almost like he's dragging his feet along, though his busy turnover rate makes up for the low knee lift; an efficient form for marathoning. *Probably not much speed, but could hold a strong pace for a very long time . . . much like Conover, ol' "Shuffles" himself.*

Jim's form has a serious tone to it, like a prizefighter might exhibit during cardiovascular training: quick, light, choppy steps, well suited for trail running, having the requisite attributes for a fearsome downhiller, hammering down sketchy descents with reckless but assured haste. His upper body has an odd quirk to it, where his right elbow flares out on the forward swing as if he's throwing an elbow to protect himself at the start of a race, but with every stride.

"I hear you own the BR&B out off Hall Road," Spencer says, breaking into Dillon's inclination for sizing up the competition. "How's business?"

"Okay so far. Really just getting—"

Honnnnnnnk!

Each runner shoots startled looks over his shoulder; a black model-X Tesla advances on them with the precision of a stealth bomber. Like California quail, the five guys scatter, each darting off in slightly but distinctly different directions from the middle of the narrow road.

"Slow down!" Spencer yells as the car passes by faster than the posted fifteen-mile-per-hour speed limit and disappears up the road and down a long driveway. "Idiot."

"Electrics certainly have a way of sneaking up on you," Dillon says.

"I'm warmed up," Jim says.

"We were taking up the whole road," Jake says.

"Those things are so cool," Chase says. "The dashboard is a seventeen-inch touchscreen monitor. It's like driving a computer."

"Great. Run over by technology," Jake laments.

Dillon catches a glimpse of the car's personalized license plate: MOVE AWN. He thinks it ironic, all things considered.

The guys regroup back in the middle of the road, working their way around the locked gate that keeps autos out of the park proper until eight a.m. The original four pepper Dillon with basic questions, such as where he moved from, attended college, what type of running or racing he does most— road, track, trail, cross-country, ultra . . . Dillon keeps his answers short and to the point, avoiding embellishment, though he does let slip a snarky comment about his divorce as the reason for moving north, which he immediately regrets.

"Divorce is tricky," Jake says. "Do you stay in touch?"

After contemplating the matter, Dillon replies, "She's dead."

The rest of the group falls into a shocked kind of silence; of the *What do you say to that?* variety, exchanging glances among one another. Uncomfortable and furtive stares descend upon Dillon.

"Metaphorically speaking, that is," Dillon says.

The subtle shock dissolves into a couple of reserved smiles and one chuckle, but there still lingers a sense of confusion and uncertainty about the new guy's emotional state, an unintended consequence of dealing with issues on the run.

"Metaphorical death is the best kind of death," Chase says. "You can feel good about hating her without the nagging remorse."

And with that subtle stroke of humor, redemption swathes Dillon in layers of escape, avoidance, and relief. *Fun group.*

"Chase, you could sell the Hoka One Ones to Barefoot Ted," Jake says, shaking his head.

"That guy's *quite* the character," Dillon says, looking at Jim's footwear and imagining Barefoot Ted, running's quirky, self-experimenting evangelist, standing in them as if he were teetering on stilts.

"I know, right?" Chase replies in a girlish voice.

Groans emanate from the rest of the original four. "Not her still?" Spencer says.

"I broke it off. Her squeaky voice annoyed me. And she had *major* abandonment issues."

"At least we all agree on her," Jim says, "but what happened to the one with all the cats? She seemed *normal.*"

"Shawna?" Chase says. "Naw, I had to bail on her. We were doing it one night at her place and her cats were staring at me the whole time. All three of them, judging me. One even looked bored. Trust me, Dillon, stay clear of women with cats, and women who live in Sebastopol, for that matter."

"Not a problem," Dillon replies.

The guys work their way up Richardson's, jutting off at the hairpin turn onto Two Quarry, a mostly uphill single-track grind that parallels a small seasonal stream when winter brings enough rainfall. The trail meanders along ridges, briefly dips into narrow, tree-covered meadows, and undulates over shale that shifts under their feet. Chase opens a gap on the guys and Jim immediately responds to bridge it while Dillon instinctively follows until Spencer lets out a distinctive clearing of his throat that causes Chase to scale the pace back.

As Dillon shortens his stride to avoid tripping up Jim, he and Chase quietly inform Dillon that they have dubbed that sound "Spence-speak"—a guttural "ahem" that subtly influences, alters, and nonverbally conveys displeasure over whatever is going on at that moment around him—though it usually means only one thing during their Sunday runs—an idiosyncrasy Jim and Chase figure Spencer developed after nine years of teaching high school.

Once they reach the first summit of two climbs for the day, they stop to regroup, as Jake has fallen behind, slowing to join another runner he knows. While the guys stretch out calf and quad muscles, and shed outer layers of clothing, Chase takes advantage of the wooden outhouse, his vocal complaint of the stench and lack of toilet paper amusing the others.

Back on the run, circling around Buick Meadow and headed for Shultz for a winding technical, single-file descent, Spencer asks Dillon, "When'd you graduate from U-dub?"

"Oh-four."

"I think I remember you at the Pac-10 Cross-Country Championships my junior year. Your hair was longer then."

Dillon smiles. "Yeah, it was. Where'd you attend?"

"Oregon."

"A Duck man. When'd you graduate?"

"Two thousand and five."

"Tough course. That backside is a killer. Never did race well there."

"Tell me about it," Spencer says. "But you placed second if I recall, behind—"

"Chase, where'd you run in college?" Dillon says, uncomfortable under the spotlight.

"Ithaca."

"Cal Poly," both Jake and Jim say simultaneously.

"Jake was a year ahead of me."

"So now we have a duck, a husky, two mustangs, and a bomber," Chase says, summarizing the mascot consortium.

"We'll need to update our roshambo equation," Spencer says. "J and J . . . any creative thoughts?"

"Let's see," Jim says, facing east toward the town of Kenwood, their view rich rolling swaths of uninhabited valleys, some lush with vineyards, others with golden-brown fields of wild grass. "Duck chases husky away and bomber steps in duck crap. Husky startles young and old mustangs by barking. Bomber corrals old mustang and . . ."

"And collars husky," Jake says. "Young mustang chases duck and bucks bomber."

"And as always," Jim says, "old mustang craps on duck and eats young mustang's oats."

"Impressive," Dillon says. "But huskies don't bark as a rule."

"Really?" Jim says.

"They can, they just don't. They talk more than anything."

"Okay, then, how about," Jim says, "husky insults young and old mustangs with trash talk about . . . them prancing around groomed tracks, while huskies run cross-country. Hello, Iditarod."

"What about the Western States Trail Ride?" Jake says.

"Is that event still around?" Jim says.

"Speaking of cross-country," Spencer says, the group working their way from the bottom of Shultz over to the base of Lawndale for the long climb back to the stinky outhouse. He will go on to discuss—subtly recruit—the local club's cross-country team and the *opportunity* to race on the series, inviting Dillon to the club's cross-country BBQ the next weekend to learn more, if interested. Dillon is interested, and it has nothing to do with running with five equally fit guys, climbing the two-mile-long, tortuous Lawndale trail; it provides another distraction to further buffer him from his past life down south.

Week 36 Training Summary			
	Long Run	Mileage Total	Comments
Dillon	21	71	Found local running club. Fast group.
Chase	16.8	63	Love the new Garmin watch! New guy looks fit.
Spencer	20.50	84	First week back to school.
Jim	17	48	Merger rumors are hell.
Jake	20	70	Robyn's back in school.

Week 2
September 7

Monday Afternoon
Merger Uncertainty

"Jim, was that you running on the Prince Greenway this morning?" Tina says, walking up behind Jim seated within his narrow cubicle. "By the Hyatt?" Her girth blocks most of the entryway.

"Probably. Sixish?"

"Yes! That was you! You run so fast. I was, like, walking my Dinky on the bridge and I said to her, 'Is that Jim running so fast?' You run faster than I drive my car." Fork in hand she carves a thick slice of cake from her plate, perches it on her lower lip and engulfs it. "How often do you run? Once or twice a week?" Tina brushes a crumb off her upper lip. "Do you want some cake? There's cake for Barry's birthday. It's good!"

"I run every day," Jim says, contemplating the new accounting software that the company is transitioning to in anticipation of the looming merger with Pinnacle Tax Consultants. *This system is so clunky. Who designed it?* "No thanks on the cake."

"Every day! Is that good for you? That sounds like an awful lot. Did your doctor say it's okay to run every day?" She pauses to celebrate Barry's birthday again. "I don't even walk every day . . . well, except around here and at home . . . and Dinky's stroll, I suppose. So that's some exercise." She scrapes her plastic fork across the paper plate several times.

Jim clicks task buttons that result in pop-up warning messages. He shakes his head. *I only need to correct one entry from yesterday. Is that too much to ask for? Do I really need to reinvent the wheel?*

"Do you think the new company will keep us around?" she says, depositing her cake-consuming paraphernalia into Jim's wastebasket. "I mean will they shut this office down? We've been here for fifty years. Well, *we* haven't, but Darryl and Brendan have. They can't shut us down. The taxpaying community needs us."

Jim leans back, clasps his hands together, each thumb massaging the other in turn. "I don't know, Tina." He stares down at the wastebasket. Between the new accounting software forcing him to navigate two additional screens more than the legacy system did in order to make a simple debit adjustment, and Dinky's—Tina's secret nickname bestowed upon her by the other accountants in the office for many reasons beyond the fact that she *walks* her cat on a leash—incessant questions, Jim's eyes begin to glaze over when his desk phone rings.

"Jim?" the voice says before he can recite the proper office greeting, "Bennett Valley Accounting Services."

"Yes, it's me, Doris," he says. "And before you say anything, I was in a meeting when you called my cell earlier."

"I wasn't going to say anything," she says. "How was the meeting?"

"Entertaining. Carlos tried to connect his laptop to the overhead projector but first it required a software upgrade, and before he could initiate it he had to update his password, and he kept creating simple ones that'd get rejected. Once he satisfied that requirement he went to upgrade the software, but the IT department sent him a pop-up survey asking him how well he thought they had done in resetting his password, to which he started shouting at the laptop, which responded with a Low Battery warning message. I tell you, technology is quite needy."

"And that was more entertaining than talking to me?"

Jim chuckles.

"Gotcha! Could you stop by the store on your way home and pick up milk? I forgot it on my trip there this morning. Oh, and some eggs, bananas, pasta, and . . . olive oil . . . that's it."

"Sure," he says, jotting down the items on a notepad, the firm's name emblazoned across the top of it. He double underlines the logo and pens in a question mark next to it.

"Oatmeal! I forgot my list."

"I gathered."

"You sure you don't want some cake?" Dinky continues to hover around Jim's cubicle. "We could split a slice."

"Who's that?" Doris says. "Why's she offering you cake?"

"It's Barry's birthday today and Tina is going around announcing last call," Jim says, motioning Dinky to move on.

"I can't believe he runs *every day* . . ." Dinky's voice trails off as she waddles away.

"Did you take any cake?" Doris says.

"I ate the blackberry cobbler you packed in my lunch. It was very good."

"Good answer."

"Speaking of which, the club BBQ is on Saturday. You can bring some of it along."

"Is Chase going to be there?"

"Don't start. He's not that bad."

"Ha! He gets under my skin."

"Don't engage him—"

"He's always cracking jokes that aren't funny."

"Some are funny."

"He's never serious."

"He's single. I was that way once," Jim says.

"Very funny. Your idea of not being serious is letting the grass out front grow an extra day. Remember when he had everybody over for breakfast last summer? Before we went kayaking? After he pulled the last pancake off the griddle, he put the spatula *back* in the utensil bowl!"

"It's his house."

"How many times had he used it before that morning?"

"Maybe he washes it before using it. I used to drink from the same water glass all week before washing it."

"I cured you of that."

"And I'm not single anymore."

"It's because he's from New York."

Jim stands up and leans against his desk to stretch each calf muscle in turn, glancing around the office area, a bland catacomb environment that has all the energy of an Egyptian tomb. "He just attended school there."

"But he stayed after he graduated. He must've liked it."

"For a while. He says nice things about you. He likes your homemade pies. And he bought one of your homemade necklaces for his girlfriend last year. He's not a bad guy."

"I suppose . . . see you at home. Don't forget the groceries."

"I won't."

"Flour!"

"Got it."

Tuesday Afternoon
Kitty Hawk, We Have a Problem

"Orville and Wilbur Wright *were* the first to fly!" an animated Katharine says from the third row, her petite shoulders squared off as if ready for a fight.

"But—" Zac says, standing with arms akimbo like a condor at the front of the class after presenting research that challenges the "First in Flight" motto attributed to the Wright brothers.

"They *were*!" Katharine reasserts. "Set aside for the moment the fact that it's documented in like a gazillion textbooks, the 'First in Flight' motto is on every North Carolinian license plate. *And* the Smithsonian has *the* Wright Flyer on display. I've been there! I've seen it! First in flight!"

Dazed, Spencer fiddles with a piece of chalk that coats his hand and fingers white, taken aback by the Zac-Kat war of words, the subtext of which makes it appear that at one time they have dated and—

"Kat wants to fight, Zac wants to run," Oz says. When no one laughs he adds, "The fight-or-flight response, get it?" Only Spencer does.

While Oz lobbies for comedic recognition, Zac stands motionless, eyes shifting between Donna, Kat, Spencer, and his notes until he folds and then stuffs the notes into his back pocket. "The assignment was to research a historical milestone during the industrial revolution, and in exploring the importance of the flight at Kitty Hawk, I found archival evidence that suggests Gustave Whitehead of Bridgeport, Connecticut, flew two years *before* the Wright brothers. And the reason the Smithsonian doesn't recognize Gustave's flight is that they signed an agreement with the Wright estate in 1948 to officially recognize the Wright Flyer as the first manned and powered plane. It wouldn't be the first time an inventor or pioneer was cut out of the picture at the hands of a businessman. I'm just reporting the facts I found. Got it?" Zac flees to his desk and flops down on the seat, creasing his research.

"See, *flight*," Oz says, arms raised as if parting the sea. "Nothing?"

Crystal moans for a social-media fix.

Conrad yawns at a sport that doesn't make use of balls, protective gear, keep score, have timeouts, or use instant replay.

Donna winks at Zac and rolls her eyes toward Kat.

"There are times," Spencer says, brushing his chalky hands off on his jeans, "when new information comes to light that challenges what we have been fed as the *truth*. In reality, *truth* is often skewed by misinterpretation or ulterior motives. For example, it's been pointed out that Paul Revere was captured and jailed before he completed his famous midnight ride through the countryside. *And* he wasn't the one who responded to the signal lanterns that hung in the Christ Church tower, but rather the one who devised them. Henry Longfellow wrote the poem we're all familiar with, but it distorted the facts, a creative license if you will."

Katharine snaps her textbook shut, reverberations bouncing off the walls. If she isn't in a total nosedive over the attack on her native state, a jailed Paul Revere questions her former East Coast existence entirely. "Historical revisionism!"

Spencer glances to the wall clock, refuge a minute away. "Historical events are like cold cases, and from time to time new info comes to light that demands we look at the past in a different way, or refute the new notion with data. It's not a matter of *changing* history, but rather gaining a better perspective on it. A relationship with history *can* be fickle at times."

"You also have to consider," Donna says, her gaze shifting from Kat to Spencer, "that throughout history humanity is confronted by the same challenges, you know, like improvements in transportation, or ways to produce goods and services, or disease control . . . those universal influences inspire not just one person or group, but many around the world. Who gets credit becomes the real battle. Look at today's tech sector and the all the patent lawsuits"—Donna's gaze shifts back to Kat —"know what I mean?"

Kat's fierce eyes discharge competitive daggers in Donna's direction.

"*Katharine*," Spencer says with a peek at the clock. "I'm going to assign you an extra-credit project: put together an informed rebuttal beyond 'that's the way it's always been.' For the rest of you, pick either Orwell's *1984* or Huxley's *Brave New World* to read. In five weeks submit an essay on how your selection's visionary themes manifest themselves in today's—

Like a choreographed escape plan, the class lurches to its collective feet at the sound of the day's final bell, stuffs items from their desks into backpacks, back pockets, and book bags, and files out the door into the hallway that resembles the local Russian River during flood years, rising quickly from the many tributaries flowing into it.

Spencer nods at students who make eye contact with him, those with high GPAs like valedictorian candidates Katharine and Donna, as well as runners who refer to him as Coach regardless of GPA; calls out Conrad and two other students by name, giving them scholarly reminders about missed assignments so early in the school year; and concedes to Oz that his fight-or-flight comment was clever, but best left for Twitter, outside of class.

Once the class has emptied, he tidies his desk, gathers up his belongings, and places them into a small day pack after pulling out his running shorts and shirt. He ducks into the small classroom storage closet to change. Transformed to the role of coach, Spencer works his way through the emptied but littered corridors, through the back parking lot, and out to where the cross-country team has congregated. "Okay, wild ones, settle down," he says, approaching the noisy athletic charges languorously sprawled across the grass behind one of the soccer nets as if it's the latest teen hangout. "We have a *fun*"—Spencer lets the last word linger a moment—"workout today."

Moans emanate from the group. With the exception of a couple freshmen, the rest know what Coach means by *fun*: labored breathing, oxygen debt, and ultimately tired legs; for some, side stitches and nausea bordering on retching. For a select few, though, fun means a challenge, testing oneself, learning to live with suffering, distancing themselves from the pack who balk at the first barrier of fatigue.

"The roots of cross-country," Spencer says, "date back to the nineteenth century in Great Britain, where it started as a school game for children to model the traditional fox hunts—"

"Sounds like another history lesson, Coach," Oz says, picking at the grass and blowing the blades skyward. "I protest on the grounds that school is out for the day."

"Wise moron," Zac says, kicking Oz's foot with his own.

Oz mimics a mindless bobble-head, chuckles spurring him on.

Spence-speak.

Grass blades flutter to the ground.

"In honor of our sport's heritage," Spencer says, "we're going to run a modern version of 'hare and hounds.'"

"I love this workout," Zac says, double-checking his shoelaces. "How long, Coach?"

"You love *every* workout," Donna says.

"We call it the 'zombie run,'"Oz says, intensely scanning the group. "'Cause when we catch you, you become one of *us*!"

"Twenty-minute cap," Spencer says.

"That's it?" Zac says.

"Dude!" Oz says.

"There'll be a bonus afterward," Spencer says, which slumps a few shoulders. "Zac, lead the group through the drills."

"Let's go, rubes!" the senior and boys' squad captain commands, leading the rubes out onto the soccer field proper.

The group ambles to the farthest reaches of the goalie's box, and once assembled, Zac hollers the first drill, knee lifts, and launches out in front to demonstrate. Though everybody knows the routine by now, Zac's enthusiasm rouses them from their midafternoon lethargy and soon they flow into the rhythm of the drills, thirty yards out and back, launching into the next one of the series: butt kicks, which always brings on a chuckle or two during the first week into the season; high leg back kick, quick feet, running backward, which roots out those whose coordination skills have not yet fully developed; knee sweeps; and lastly skipping. To newcomers who don't understand the purpose of the drills, and to Oz who complains daily about doing them—"I don't want *running* homework too!"—Spencer explains that they prepare the body to run efficiently, reducing the risk of injury. "Think of them as dynamic stretching," Spencer would say, though it doesn't mollify Oz's discontent.

Bodies primed for running, Spencer and Zac lead both squads out along a mile-long route that works its way through and around the adjacent junior college to the front of the campus's original building, Pioneer Hall. They gather on a grass-and-dirt expanse with an approximately 500-meter, irregularly shaped circuit that weaves its way through a maze of majestic oak, sequoia redwood, and western sycamore trees; squirrel-filled pecan and European chestnut trees; and an "urban jungle" of bunya bunya, monkey puzzle, ginkgo, and liquid amber trees on the northern end, the latter of which drops sizable "seed balls" during the fall that challenge ankle stability. Colorful perennials and an immense rose garden cap off the sprawling refuge from the four-lane avenue of commerce a sidewalk's width away.

Spencer dishes out the details of the workout. "The purpose of today's workout is to simulate fast race starts as well as pace changes throughout. You'll also have the added challenge of incorporating real-time strategy in chasing down others. Today's hounds"—Oz has started walking stiff-legged with outstretched arms—"or zombies, will be the varsity boys' top five." Spencer retrieves his smart phone and locates the mobile app he and Zac have assembled to track each of the returning runners' past workouts, bringing up the last time they had performed this one. "The rest of you are the hares, running for survival after a thirty-second head start. Remember, zombies, you must run as a *pack* to tag hares, and as you tag them they join in with the hunt . . . at *their* pace, so pick your hares wisely. If the hares come up from behind you can't turn around to tag them, but they can tag you and bring you back to life. Remember, don't sacrifice good form for speed. This is a *fun* way to prepare the body for harder training down the road. Got it?"

Nods follow, some more enthusiastic than others, as the five "hounds" gather to discuss strategy and the "hares" head for the ancient oak tree that acts as the beginning of the loop they will circle for twenty minutes, or until all the hares have been converted into zombies, whichever comes first. To the handful of JC students walking between classes, taking curious glances at the group, the runners' less-than-enthusiastic reception may signify a lack of interest in what they're doing. Spencer, on the other hand, knows as their coach it has nothing to do with not wanting to be out there at that moment, but more to do with one simple fact: cross-country training is hard. It doesn't matter that it's on grass without hills or that he calls it "fun" or that Oz calls it a "zombie run" or that the whole team shares the experience, an ode to "misery loves company" and building camaraderie; running fast for short periods of time early in the season, faster than race pace, after a long summer of less specific and structured training, is always a shock to the system.

But perhaps the thing that concerns the group the most is the bonus part of the workout that Spencer doesn't disclose until *after* they've completed the prescribed workout. This is Spencer's magic touch, his signature mental training tool, the part he reveals when they are tired and ready to call it a day, a psychological supplement that steels the mind for the tougher aspects of competitive racing, managing whatever race day throws at them.

Owing to Oz's impatience, the zombie apocalypse doesn't materialize; the wise moron tagged one of the slower runners sooner rather than later, which slowed the zombie pack down considerably in assimilating eleven of the faster hares. But Oz's ability to channel failure and fatigue into caffeine ups the ante throughout the bonus part of the workout, carrying the dispirited on his shoulders—"Don't count the miles, make the miles count!" he tells them. Spencer has them do "Group Ladders," where groups of seven are formed based on team ranking, then set into motion twice around the grassy circuit in the opposite direction, running single-file, the last member sprinting to the front of the group, allowing them to simulate racing together and mid-race surges.

Afterward, Spencer herds the spent crew back to campus, reversing the route they warmed up on, the pace noticeably slower and the conversations less animated—except for Oz. Spencer starts with the slower boys and girls in back and works his way up to Zac and Donna, though he hangs back several yards, picking up bits and pieces from their conversation about the earlier Zac-Kat classroom tiff. Spencer half wants to eavesdrop and half doesn't, still trying to figure out if they are dating or not. And now if Kat is in the mix. *Never a dull moment with teenagers and their social woes! I never had time for a relationship . . . my worst problem was which belt buckle to wear to school, not who was dating whom.* Despite Zac and Donna's switch to a neutral topic about their first race in two weeks, Spencer continues to mull over the unknown: Will this affect their racing abilities? Winning demands focus and sacrifice. Should he step in and nip whatever this is in the bud? That thought doesn't sit well with him: too intrusive . . . unless it hurts the team's dynamics . . . alliances might form, dividing the group up . . . .

Spence-speak.

When Zac and Donna glance over their shoulders and acknowledge their coach's presence, he realizes his Spence-speak hasn't been uttered internally. *Oops.*

Back at the soccer field, Spencer addresses the tired lot as they perform post-run stretches. "Another solid job today. These early weeks of hard running always feel tough." His gaze drifts from one set of tired eyes looking for solace to another. "Within a few weeks you'll notice a marked improvement in your ability to run hard over longer stretches with less fatigue. Believe in the system. Okay, so no wild dance parties tonight"— smirks and mild laughter break out—"and be sure to get a good night's sleep. Remember, it's not the workout that makes you strong—"

"It's the recovery!" sings the chorus of returning athletes, which spawns laughter, and puzzled stares from the uninitiated.

"Exactly!" Spencer says. "The workout itself merely breaks the body down."

"Coach, my mom says I come home too tired," Oz says, his splayed body evidence of his state. "It's not good for my homework."

"You never do homework, Oz," Zac says.

"That's because I'm *sooooooooo* torched."

"Use your brain and not your legs and you'll be fine, Oz," Spencer says. Laughter and more joking follow. "All right, off you go."

After addressing questions from the newer runners about practice times and weekend commitments, Spencer retreats to his classroom, calls Maggie to let her know he's on his way home, and straps on his small day pack, cinching the straps snugly across his chest. Barely out the emergency exit doors, he breaks into a run, blindly waving to a teen couple by the back wall who have come up for air from their make-out session and holler, "Nice short-shorts, Mr. Lingard!" His pace quickens every fifty yards until he hits the five-and-half-minute-per-mile tempo he wants to hold the six miles home. He readjusts the straps of his day pack, shakes his arms and hands out, locks onto the steady pace, a staple of his marathon training program, and leaves the school day behind, transitioning him between his coaching duties and settling into life at home . . . in roughly thirty-three minutes.

Wednesday Afternoon
The Athens Room

"*Woooooowoooowooo Woooooowoooo*," Miles says when Dillon backs into the paint bucket, olive green sloshing over its lip and onto the canvas drop cloth.

"I know, I know, girl . . . I need to be more careful." Dillon drops a rag onto the spill and steps back to view his handiwork on the accent wall, nodding, pleased and relieved that the color's boldness hasn't overpowered the rest of the room as he feared it might. He peers around to the other walls, whose Greek sky blue, along with the light-gray trim, complete the official Olympic colors of the '04 Athens Summer Games. It's one of the last two rooms that requires refurbishing, and now only needs running memorabilia, Athens-inspired olive wreaths, and Grecian trinkets before making it available for bookings.

The other unfinished room will depict the '96 Atlanta Games or the '84 Los Angeles Games. He's leaning toward L.A. in honor of Portugal's Carlos Lopes's age-defying marathon gold medal, and America's Joan Benoit's gutsy inaugural women's marathon gold medal, though Ethiopia's Haile Gebrselassie, one of the world's greatest distance runners and admired humanitarian, made his Olympic debut in Atlanta. Both give him pause, however. Neither L.A. nor Atlanta's color schemes will be all that appealing or exotic compared to the international venues. In the end the decision, as with most he makes, will likely come down to a procrastination-forced coin toss.

"Athens . . . the birthplace of philosophy," says a familiar voice.

Dillon turns toward the doorway. "And democracy," Dillon says, wiping a hand on his jeans and extending it toward Jake. "Not to mention Meb and Deena: first US medals in the marathon in over thirty years."

"'Time is the wisest counselor of all,'" Jake returns, shaking Dillon's hand. "Athens's very own Pericles, nicknamed 'The Olympian.'"

"I'll have to add a bust of him to the room. What brings you out this way?"

"*Wooooowooowooo Wooooowoooo.*" Miles walks up to Jake and sits.

"Who do we have here?" Jake says, kneeling down, letting Miles sniff his hand and petting her behind the ears.

"Miles is her name." Dillon covers up the open paint bucket and dunks the roller and trim brushes into a bucket filled with water.

"*Wooooowooowooo Wooooowoooo.*"

"Like I said before, huskies talk, and she's quite the talker."

"I'll say. If you make it to the BBQ this weekend, bring her along. Robyn would love her. Our dog, Juggles, is getting up there in years and sleeps most of his days away."

"I'd loved to come," a woman's voice announces from behind the guys.

Both men turn their attention toward the doorway.

"You must be Jake. I'm Terri," she says, giving him a little wave.

"Hello," Jake says with a nod and curious grin. "You're more than welcome to attend."

"Dillon, the Tokyo and Munich rooms are ready to go, so I'm out of here. Doesn't look like you have any guests until Thursday night, so I'll see you Friday morning . . . for breakfast," she says, kneeling down to Miles, who has wandered over. "And you too, sweetie." She kisses Miles on the snout, rubs her ears a couple of times, stands, and exits the room, but not before giving a quick over-the-shoulder peek back, her hair twirling about. "Call me if something comes up."

"Lord love a duck," Jake says, watching Miles trot after Terri, talking up a storm. "She seems . . ."

"Like trouble," Dillon says. "The word you're looking for is 'trouble.'"

Jake grins. "Gotta get back on the horse sometime."

"Too wild for me. Let me walk you around the place. You working in the area?"

"A property down the road. You know, you're only a mile from the creek path. You can run it all the way to downtown."

"Really." Dillon shows him the room across the hall, its deep-red accent wall surrounded by gold-tone ones adorned with lush tapestries depicting Sensō-ji—an ancient Buddhist temple—and picturesque Tsutenkyo Bridge. "Tokyo '64, obviously. Billy Mills won gold in the ten thousand, and Abebe Bikila won his second Olympic marathon."

"Jim has a poster of Billy crossing the finish with his hands raised high."

Dillon grins. "He certainly stunned the world. Took down Gammoudi and Clarke."

"Where'd you pick up interior decorating?" Jake says as Dillon closes the door behind them and walks down the hallway toward the Helsinki Room.

"My ex. That's what she did, among other things." His tone turns somber. "I'm sure she'd take credit for it too. I *hate* that she has a hand in this in some small way. But it is what it—"

"Dillon?" a voice drifts up from the front of the inn.

Dillon leans out the second-story hall window. "Dale. I didn't know you were still here."

"The sauna was acting up so I replaced the thermostat. It's good now. I'm heading out to meet the wiff for dinner. I'll stop by tomorrow to see if you need anything," he says, waving as he turns to leave. "Hey, Jakey."

"Hey, Dale," Jake says, peering out the window alongside Dillon as Dale shuffles off and disappears behind the back of his old beat-up van. The panel doors squeak when he flings them open.

Dillon glances at his watch—*Dinner at 3? "Wiff"?*—then leans back and closes the window. "You know him?"

"Pretty much a legend around here. We think he runs in his sleep." Jake grins. "Certainly has more miles on his body than his van. And he's had that tin can forever."

"Sure explains his keen interest in helping out around here."

"Sub-2:30 marathoner back in the '60s. Runs every race in the county each year too. In fact, some say it's not an official race unless Rob Shore starts it and Dale finishes it," Jake says with an appreciative grin. "Rob's another local guy who fires the gun for hundreds of races a year."

Dillon proceeds to show Jake the other restored rooms: Helsinki, 1952, with its azure walls and pure-white trim commemorating the country's thousands of lakes and snowy winters; Munich, 1972, with its Bavarian blue walls, a gold accent wall, black trim, and wallpaper on one wall with a flock of doves floating above the city. He also shows off the other building detached from the inn, a 1,600-square-foot cedar yurt with a rolling hillside vineyard view to be enjoyed from the ensconced sauna, hot tub, or massage rooms.

Tour concluded, standing out by Jake's truck, Dillon describes the property, gesturing around the twenty-five acres, partially wooded underneath oaks and Douglas firs, with a small pond off on the backside and a shallow creek that feeds it. "I have a trail that works its way around the perimeter. It's a shade over a mile long with minor rollers, some good twists and turns, wetland patches in the winter, crosses a creek on the backside. Pretty sweet."

Jake gazes out, following Dillon's finger as it etches out the course he spent the summer mapping out and, with Miles's help, running along to carve it permanently into the earth.

"Percy's Loop," Jake says.

Dillon smiles. "I like it."

"Feel like a run?"

"Always."

After Dillon swaps out his paint duds for running shorts, shirt, and paint-free shoes, and Jake has done the same, they start out around the 1.1-mile loop in counterclockwise fashion, an ingrained habit from Dillon's former track days.

One trip around complete, gliding by Jake's truck again, Miles comes running out of the inn and makes a beeline toward them, rushing by and taking up the front position.

"*Wooooowooowooo Wooooowooooo.*"

"Mystery fartlek, girl," Dillon says. "You game, Jake?"

"This should be fun."

Immediately Miles gaps the men, signifying the first salvo in the running game that Dillon taught her when she was a pup, running around with her on the sand down in Newport Beach. Dillon shortens and quickens his stride to bridge the gap while Jake responds more slowly, his longer legs less adept at adjusting to the pace change. Once they rejoin Miles, the mystery begins: how long will she hold the current pace, hence the essence of the mystery fartlek, never knowing when one will start or for how long they will go, extending the basic use of "fartlek," a Swedish word for "speed play," which are generally run solo.

Based on the current pace and past experience, Dillon guesses Miles will take them about two hundred yards or so. It turns out to be nearly three hundred. "You showing off . . . for our guest today, girl?" Dillon says, breathing moderately hard.

"Nice," Jake says, slowing alongside Dillon. "You teach her that?"

"Yep. Didn't take much—" Miles gaps the guys again. "Miles! It's not your turn."

"Apparently she's thinks *we* talk too much," Jake says, responding quicker than before, jetting in front of Dillon and jumping onto Miles's back paws.

Dillon shakes his head, smiles, and accelerates, bringing up the rear, legs rebelling, stiff from an afternoon of manual labor.

Another three circuits breeze by, the guys and husky taking turns, trying to one-up the other, like playing a game of HORSE in the backyard around a basketball hoop, and then Dillon calls it a day. Panting, Miles trots into the house while the guys linger and sweat under the waning sun's rays filtering through the trees on the far side of the property that sets it apart from the neighboring vineyard.

"Don't let Spencer badger you into joining the club or run the cross-country series," Jake says, sipping water from a large thermos he pulled from the back of his truck. "He means well, but he can be pushy at times on recruiting. We've actually lost a few talented local runners to neighboring county clubs, so he gets territorial."

"No worries. He was pretty funny about it. I plan on joining."

"He's basically the organizer of the group, and his weekly emails are pretty entertaining. They used to go on for paragraphs until Chase once replied with '*War and Peace*.' I usually just scan them, hit Reply, type 'great,' and ask Jimbo when and where on our Thursday-night run."

Dillon nods, scratching off dried paint from his arms.

"Thanks for the tour and run. If you have any landscaping needs, let me know," Jake says, gesturing toward the front of the inn, where the center of the circular driveway lacks a visually appealing presence: an gnarled old oak tree surrounded by overgrown "weeds," plants in the wrong place as Jake jokes.

Dillon stares at the oak tree and the "plants in the wrong place." Beyond his general reluctance to accepting help, his financial situation is a factor, cash-strapped after a summer of renovation cost overruns. "I'll let you know."

Thursday Night
Spencer's Weekly Email

From: Spencer Lingard <MarathonMan@gomail.com>
To: Team Thirsty Boys <SundayRunDL>
Subject: Saturday's XC BBQ & Sunday's Run . . .

Dear Sirs,

Okay, I'm slowly catching up with back-to-school items. By next week I should have these emails out on Wednesday nights as usual.

First of all, welcome, Dillon, to the Open Team, and your first weekly email. I'm sure by now you've been forewarned about my tendency to wax on in these emails, but I assure you everything is vital and succinctly put, though today's email is the exception rather than the rule due to this weekend's XC BBQ, but I digress.

First item: be sure to attend the XC BBQ on Saturday at Jake's place (thanks again, Jake, for hosting!) Anytime after 2 p.m. Bring something to toss on the grill, a side dish to share, and your preferred choice of beverage.

Start thinking about what races you want to commit to this season. As with past seasons, we need a minimum of 5, plus the championship race in Golden Gate Park. I've listed the PA schedule below. A couple of the Saturday races I can't make, as they conflict with high school meets. We should be able to recruit a couple master guys to drop down and give us a 7-man roster for some of our races. If not, we'll simply make do as in the past.

See, that wasn't so bad now, was it. Wait! Sunday's run. I need to be home early since Maggie's parents are coming into town next week. *Apparently* we need to "renovate" our new place. 7 a.m. again on Channel? I'm going to run 20. How about we run up North Burma, South Burma, down Canyon, into and around Spring Lake and back to Channel?

And lastly, Leo sent me an email this morning. That "foot ache" he's been complaining about for several weeks, turns out it's a stress fracture. He's out for the upcoming cross-country season.

PA Cross-country Schedule				
Day	Date	Race	Venue	Available
Sat	Sep 26	Redwood Empire Runners Club XC Open	Santa Rosa	Y
Sun	Oct 4	Garin Park XC Challenge	Hayward	
Sat	Oct 10	Renegades XC Challenge - Ancil Hoffman	Sacramento	Y
Sat	Oct 17	Agras XC Open	Crystal Springs	Y
Sat	Oct 24	Willow Hills XC Open	Folsom	
Sat	Oct 31	Dipsean XC Challenge - China Camp	San Rafael	Y
Sun	Nov 8	Santa Cruz Slug XC Invite	Santa Cruz	
Sat	Nov 14	Presidio XC Challenge	San Francisco	Y
Sun	Nov 22	PA XC Championships	Golden Gate Park	Y
Sat	Dec 5	USATF Club XC Championships	Bend, OR	Y

Signing off,
Spencer

. . . I will reply to your email after I've had sufficient time to reflect on its content.

From: Chase Brandon <ChaseMeIfYouCan@gomail.com>
To: Team Thirsty Boys <SundayRunDL>
Subject: RE: Sunday's Run . . .
You lost me after "okay." Looks like the 5 races are already decided upon. Glad there are choices.
I propose we take turns on who decides the Sunday start time and location. Dillon, thoughts? I told Leo not to wear those damn minimalist shoes on every run.

Chasester

From: Linda Dearborn <LDRN@gomail.com>
To: Team Thirsty Boys <SundayRunDL>
Subject: RE: Sunday's Run . . .

7 is fine at Channel. Linda wants me to remind you, Spence, to ask Maggie to bring over more chapters of her newest manuscript. I don't think Leo's shoe choice is the culprit. He had other issues going on and didn't address them.
Happy Trails,
Jakey

From: Jim Greyson <JimG@gomail.com>
To: Team Thirsty Boys <SundayRunDL>
Subject: RE: Sunday's Run . . .

Gentlemen,
Channel is getting old, fast. I might not be able to make the Renegades Challenge. Heads up, Chase, I'm bringing Doris to the BBQ. I saw Leo running laps on the grass this morning at Juilliard Park.
Jim

From: Dillon Percy <BRB@gomail.com>
To: Team Thirsty Boys <SundayRunDL>
Subject: RE: Sunday's Run . . .

Thank you, Spencer, for the warm welcome and the eloquently stated, well worded, informative opus. It wasn't long . . .
For the Sunday runs, the earlier the better. I like to be around when the guests are eating breakfast if possible to talk shop.
I'm open to any starting venue at this point, though Howarth is closer for me.
Race schedule should be manageable on either day unless I have a full house.
Anybody enjoy a good Belgian-inspired beer? I have a case of Allagash White I can bring to the BBQ.
Cheers,
Dillon

From: Spencer Lingard <MarathonMan@gomail.com>
To: Team Thirsty Boys <SundayRunDL>
Subject: RE: Sunday's Run . . .

Dear Sirs,
Opus? Nice one. Allagash White? I believe Dillon just became our new best friend.
Channel Drive at 7 a.m. it is. We'll consider a different start venue next week.
Signing off,
Spencer

Friday Evening
The Dearborn Homestead

Tap, tap, tap. Jake looks up from his journal to find Robyn standing on her tiptoes, staring at him with wide eyes through the driver-side window of his truck. He rolls down the window. "Hi, sweetie, I'm almost done."

"Mom says you're like Play-doh."

"The clay?"

"No, silly . . . the Greek flossifer."

"Sometimes it's good to take a moment and put life into perspective."

"She also said you're stinky."

"*You're* stinky."

"No, I'm not. I smell good, like cinnamon." She places her wrist under his nose and he takes a whiff. "She also thinks your face is too scruffy." She rubs his facial scruff.

"I doubt that."

"Okay, it was me. But it tickles my face when you kiss me."

Jake grabs her and kisses both cheeks. Her delightful squeals fill the evening sky, inciting the neighboring donkeys to bray. "Tell Mom I'll be right in."

"Okay." Robyn skips back toward the side door to the kitchen, stopping halfway there and squatting to examine a yellow dandelion. She peers at it intently for several seconds, carefully uproots it, and continues on skipping with it into the house.

Jake returns his attention to the journal, rereading the last stanza he's been working on since arriving home:

The season's warm days and quick-cooling evenings infuse the air with the aroma of anise that permeates his nostrils, harking back to adolescence and his first days of trail running. Ahead, wild turkeys rustle in dry leaves a safe distance off the trail. He never pays them much attention, though once a rafter of turkeys hindering his progress scattered as he approached, except for one loner, who frantically trotted ahead some fifty yards before stepping to the side, lost its footing, and tumbled several feet down the embankment.

Content with the connotations that morning's run in Annadel had inspired, Jake flips to another page of the journal, scribbles in the current date, and pauses to recall the route he had run, adjusting for the extra loop around Lake Illsanjo that he added. His head shifts side to side ever so gently, a mental abacus whose beads are sliding to total the final count: twelve miles at hard effort up the hills, steady effort on the flats, let loose on the downhills. He closes the journal and tucks it back into the glove box. Exiting the truck, he catches sight of Robyn standing with arms akimbo in the picture window facing his direction. He smiles and waves. *Yes, she smells good, like cinnamon.*

Friday Night
Check, Please!

"Your pizza will be here momentarily," the waitress says, pausing at Chase and his date's table before moving on.

"Hmmm," his date, Sandra, mutters. "Does she mean our pizza will be here for *just a moment*? Or does she mean it will be here soon?"

"What?" Chase says after sipping his wine. "Our meal will be here soon is what she meant."

"But she said 'momentarily.' The proper usage for the adverb 'momentarily' is 'for a moment.'"

Chase shrugs, unconcerned over the nuance. "Hopefully it'll be here soon. I'm starving."

"Hmmm . . . you shouldn't begin a sentence with 'hopefully.'"

"You're kidding?" Sandra's exposed cleavage in the little black dress, breasts wobbling with every hand gesture, is losing its appeal.

"Placing it at the beginning modifies the entire sentence. . . . 'It is to be *hoped* that the meal arrives soon.'" She poises her index finger in the air like a symphony conductor would on a high note, raising it higher on the word "hoped."

"That's the dream." Chase's eyes wander around the small upstairs seating area of La Vera Pizza, praying for help in one form or another, appetizers, meal, more wine, the check, the sound of a fire alarm.

"But by saying, 'It'll be here soon, *hopefully*,' it means you are hopeful it will arrive quickly."

"Irregardless . . . I'm hungry. My run this evening was tough and I'm ready to—" He catches sight of Sandra's pinched facial expression with another "hmmm" ready to tumble forth. "Oh, right, *regardless*. Did you say you were from Sebastopol?" Chase considers quaffing his wine, but settles for a chug. *Last time I let Jakey's wife set me up.*

"No, I live in Petaluma, remember? But I'm not from here. I grew up in Wisconsin."

"Really? I grew up in Green Bay." *At last, a diversion.*

"Madison!"

"I'm sure there's a story there," he says, *hopeful* that he has derailed her grammar rant. While she launches into her Madison, Wisconsin, to Petaluma, California, pilgrimage, he mentally checks out, scanning the restaurant for their server, hopefully bearing plates of much needed-calories, or is it bearing plates of much-needed calories, hopefully? No such luck, grammatically speaking, either way. He switches to going over his evening workout, still fresh in his mind as well as his calf muscles, fatigued and periodically twitching from exertion and dehydration: 12.3 miles total, broken up into four 2-mile cruise intervals with two minutes of recovery between them, and each successive interval faster than the previous one—*10:16, 10:05 . . . 9:45?* He wants to review the Garmin data to double-check the third segment's split, but that would be rude, ruder than *momentarily* tuning her out. *Felt too fast, which explains why my last spilt was 9:59.* Without thinking, he glances at his watch.

"I'm sorry. I'm boring you, rambling on like I am," Sandra says, her wineglass in need of a refill.

Chase looks up, attention divided, then regroups. "No, no . . . I'm just hungry . . . low blood sugar and all. I should've had a protein shake before meeting you here."

"Linda said you run with Jake. I watched you win the mile at the last summer series track meet. What was your time, four-twenty-something?" Her hand moves over to cover his hand that is fiddling with the stem of his wineglass.

"Twenty-one," he replies, forgetting about his waning blood sugar and hunger pangs. "I had hoped to break twenty, but was forced to go wide on the last turn to get around a group that had bunched up; cost me a couple seconds."

"Are you training for anything?" Her hand caresses the back of his hand.

Chase refills her wineglass with a free hand. "Cross-country is coming up. We run a handful of meets around Northern California that's part of a grand prix series. And in December there's the USATF National Club Cross Country Championships. They're in Bend, Oregon, this year. We have a new guy that recently joined our club. He's pretty fit so we should do well this year."

Dinner arrives and before long Chase's blood sugar levels stabilize, his enthusiasm back on track, dazzling Sandra with past ad campaigns he's worked on, making her laugh with cheesy jokes, and enjoying casual glances at the cleavage she offers when she leans forward.

Chase remains seated, checking his Facebook feed, emails, text messages, and run data after Sandra has excused herself to *powder her nose*, as she put it. He felt certain a grammatical joke could've been made from it, but refrained. He's taken care of the check and is ready to walk her to her car and end their "interesting" evening. But has it really been that bad? He can see why Jake's wife set them up: she's smart, witty, works in the wine industry—a sommelier, passionately promoting Sonoma County–produced wines—a runner who's completed three marathons, all under four hours. Her figure grabs his attention, much bustier than the average petite blond runner. He guesses a C-cup on her five-foot-one frame. She's just a bundle of energy to take on an empty stomach, and the incessant grammar corrections skewed his perspective to some degree. Either way, he's leaning toward cutting his losses, heading home to relax and rest up after a long day and week at the office, and hard workout that evening.

"Ready?" Sandra says, approaching the table, freshly powdered, smile as big and white as when she arrived to the restaurant ninety minutes earlier.

"Yeah." Chase rises, takes the shoulder wrap from her chair and places it over her bare shoulders from behind. She purrs at the touch of his hands on her skin; he feels a spark.

Uh-oh.

Outside they stroll along downtown Santa Rosa sidewalks in front of brick-exposed buildings whose windows tout American and international cuisines, wine bars, local brews, used books, antiques, fair-trade handcrafts— all modestly decorated in their cavernous cement-floor dwellings, historical in nature, from a time when architecture revolved around railroad passage, its entirety rebuilt in the wake of the 1906 San Francisco earthquake that leveled downtown Santa Rosa. Interspersed amongst the commerce a series of whimsical, five-foot-tall statues depicting Peanuts characters pay tribute to Charles M. Schulz's forty-year presence in the county. Charlie Brown dons winter gear, holding skates, a hockey stick, and a helmet atop his head; Snoopy characterizes Joe Cool, complete with sunglasses and Keds shoes, a basketball cradled in one hand and a skateboard dangling in the other; and Lucy strides animatedly along holding a cell phone.

The usual Friday-night energy, muted as it is for a "cow town," as Chase often refers to it, saddles the evening with an un-rushed eclectic medley of flannel, plaid, and belted jeans . . . hoodies, T-shirts, and low-hanging beltless jeans . . . San Francisco Giants baseball caps crown bearded faces . . . casual Friday attire entertains out-of-state colleagues in business attire . . . chic button-down shirts, slacks, and sport coats interlock with chiffon dresses in high heels . . . dressed-up young women date dressed-down young men . . . Chase once joked that it would take a half-day tour in San Francisco to witness what a short stroll around downtown Santa Rosa would net in ten minutes.

Negotiating a series of left and rights on their way to her car parked several blocks away, Chase faces a crossroads on whether to extend the evening or call it a night. The conversation has stalled since leaving the restaurant. Is this a sign she's bored? He glances down at her. She smiles back. Not bored; he knows that smile. He ponders his current physical state and Saturday schedule: *I am tired, but I don't have to run in the morning. I could sleep in and make her breakfast instead . . . and do my easy seven at noon, before the BBQ.* That sounds good, and it becomes clear to him: he's horny, and the view from his height down her deep cleavage further fuels his lust. The grammar girl is a pretty cool catch after all, and *hopefully* there won't be much opportunity to talk . . . hopefully.

"Well, this is me," Sandra says upon arriving at her car.

Chase admires the late-model BMW. "Nice wheels."

"I think it's sexy, don't you?"

"It certainly has some nice lines. They did a great job on the bumper treatment."

"You should see how it handles the curves."

"I'll bet the suspension is top notch."

"The real excitement is under the hood."

"I can imagine it out on the open—" Before Chase can finish his sentence, she lunges at him, her bumpers mashing into his chest, her lips meeting his like a head-on collision on the Autobahn.

Chase wraps his arms around her, tightening his core muscles to keep himself from falling backward, her shoulder wrap sliding to the sidewalk. He lifts her petite frame up onto the fender of her BMW, where her legs instantly wrap around his waist, her tongue shifting gears in his mouth.

A minute later, Sandra breaks off the kiss. "I don't need to be anywhere. Let's head to your place. My stupid brother is in town and crashed on my couch." She resumes kissing him.

"Okay," is all he can muster until they pause again. "Drive me over to my car and you can follow me home.

Things unfold quickly at Chase's condo. The entry-hall light strobes to the beat of errant shoulders, elbows, and hips bumping the light switch; the front door may or may not have been locked behind them; the stainless-steel kitchen shimmers when another bumped light switch lights up the recessed panels underneath the cabinetry; the day's mail scatters across the floor upon colliding with the Scandinavian nesting table; Chase's shirt, socks, and shoes, and Sandra's high heels and little black dress are strewn in their wake.

He breaks off their impassioned kiss long enough to push her back into the leather club chair, where she flops back and reclines, her attire at this point a black thong and matching bra, hair tousled, grin delirious, breasts straining the satin material with every deep breath. Dilated pupils gaze up at him. At the press of a dimmer switch diffuse track lighting casts an uninhibited tint over their silhouettes. To complement the aura, Chase pushes buttons, adjusts knobs, and increases the volume on his Onkyo home theater receiver; "Free Bird" floods the living room from eight Bose speakers.

"Really? . . . Lynyrd Skynyrd?" Sandra says. "That's not really a turn-on for me." She raises and stretches out a leg toward him, her pointed toes teasing a butt cheek.

"It will be in nine minutes and four seconds," Chase says with confidence, facing her. He kneels and with both hands wraps them around her legs at the knees, yanking her toward him in one clean jerk. She chirps at the sudden movement that forces her legs apart and sinks her petite frame deeper into the seat cushion, her back flush on the leather.

He leans in seductively, lips grazing an exposed thigh, kissing each one in turn, the power ballad beginning its slow, meandering journey, from soothing lullaby that lingers teasingly long like his tongue toward her thong, until the guitars kick up a notch several minutes in, holding steady for what seems like an eternity, squirming as she is to the vibrating strings, until the melody crescendos, and crescendos, and crescendos evermore, the thong no longer properly arranged, and before long the guitars reach titillating speed, the velocity faster and faster, the guitar licks harder and harder, the drums pounding and pounding in her ears until her hands are stretched out behind her, palms bent back and pressed against the leather for support, both feet planted firmly on the carpet, toes curled, her body arched as if suspended in a backward flip, her gymnastics-sized body poised for the highly anticipated dismount. . . .

Wearing black designer boxers and standing shirtless, Chase flips the last pancake over on the griddle as Sandra walks into the kitchen draped in one of his many cotton T-shirts from a road race. This one, from Rochester, New York, has a Saint Paddy's Day 10K logo splashed across a white background from 2005, where he set his still-standing 10K road PR of 29:12. On her it reaches the same part of her thighs that her little black dress had. She squeezes his butt and reaches for a coffee mug, her C's wandering freely under a pair of four-leaf clovers.

"Morning, you gorgeous stack of pancakes, you," he says, pulling the mug down from the top shelf, handing it to her. He grins to himself, answering in Jim and Jake's absence: *A League of Their Own.*

"Morning." She takes the cup, bites his shoulder, leaving a small imprint, and heads to the Cuisinart coffee maker, filling the cup. She hops up onto the counter. "I think I'm coming around to Lynyrd Skynyrd. May have to add it to my collection."

"It grows on you." He lifts the last pancake off the griddle and places it atop the others stacked on a platter. He turns the gas burner off, slides the griddle to the back of the stove, and returns the spatula to where it normally resides, inside a ceramic jar full of wooden spoons, a whisk—

Sandra giggles.

"What?"

"Nothing." She holds a plate out to him, upon which he places a couple pancakes and ladles fresh blueberries over them.

"My thighs are sore," she says, using her fork to carve out a double-layered chunk of pancake. "I need to get in better shape. Not that I'm complaining."

Chase chuckles, though it isn't the first time he's heard what he deems the ultimate compliment.

"How'd you get into running?" she asks him, examining the shirt she has on after he hops up on the counter next to her, digging into his stack.

"Well"—he finishes chewing—"I actually played soccer growing up. Pretty good at it too. Played the central midfielder position all the way into high school . . . then"—he takes another bite, chews it thoroughly, and washes it down with fat-free milk—"then sophomore year my grandfather, ol' coach 'Brando,' the toughest guy I knew, dropped dead of a heart attack during practice . . . right there on the sidelines." He hops down for more blueberries. "He'd coached me on just about every team I'd played on, so I had no desire to go back out on the field after that. I kind of checked out for a while from everything until one day I'm out behind the bleachers smoking a joint and poking fun at the track nerds running around in circles in their little split shorts when a shadow falls over me from behind and clears its throat. *Busted.* I sat there staring at the ground then started to turn when the shadow says, 'I don't want to see what I smell, son.' So I just sit there not sure what to do when the shadow continues. 'Look, we all admired Coach Brando. I know it hurts, but you know he'd be all over your ass for sitting on the sidelines right now.' In my haze I almost thought the shadow *was* my grandfather, but it was the track coach."

Chase works his way through another pancake chunk. For the first time in retelling this story, he makes the connection between his track coach's throat clearing and Spencer's Spence-speak quirk.

"He told me, 'If you're not going to play soccer let's put those feet to better use. With your soccer background and speed you'd make a damn fine miler. Might be a good way to run off your grief, one lap at a time, until you figure things out.' So the next day, I showed up, dressed in my soccer shorts, everybody snickering at my getup. He told me they were doing a mile time trial, so I jumped in and finished second in 4:41. I was wheezing so hard I thought my lungs were going to burst, but damn if the shadow wasn't right . . . it felt good."

"That must've been tough." She rubs his back. "I can't imagine . . ."

He inhales deeply, holds it, then lets it seep out. "I can handle tough, but a senseless world . . . that's a tougher matter: my grandmother died of a broken heart a month later."

Sandra leans her head against Chase's shoulder.

Chase pokes here and there around his plate, taking occasional bites, wanting to ask what inspired *her* to start running, to learn more about her life, but instead vulnerability besieges him. It never fails. Extended pillow talk is his doom, reliving his grandparents' early departure followed by his parents'; off to college with no one to go home to for the holidays.

Sandra runs her hand through his hair, which reels him back from the past. She leans in to kiss him but he keeps it short, hops off the counter, and scrapes the leftovers from his plate into the sink, turning the water and garbage disposal on for several seconds.

Sandra hands him her empty plate, squeezes his butt again, and heads out from the kitchen. Minutes later, the kitchen cleaned, she returns, ready for her trip home. She kisses him on the cheek and says, "Call me if you want, or don't . . . it's up to you." She smiles and lets herself out the front door.

Except for the distant meow of a cat, Windsor's farming town turned bedroom community silence engulfs Chase. He gazes out the window that overlooks the Windsor Town Green, its wide grassy greenbelt empty, and the eclectic storefronts below the condo—restaurants, cycle shop, candy shop, knickknack shops—not yet open. As peaceful and serene as it appears, Chase has to summon the strength to push aside the gloom inside, eventually gearing up for a weekend of marketing creativity, running, analyzing workout data, and connecting with friends.

Saturday Afternoon
Annual XC BBQ

"Robyn, sweetie, this is Dillon and his dog, Miles," Jake says when man and his husky enter the homestead's backyard, his arms full of banana bread, a serving dish filled with roasted potatoes, and a case of Allagash White.

"Very nice to meet you," she says. "I'm Robyn, spelled with a *y* because *y* is the best letter in the whole alphabet." She takes out her *Agent Carter* notebook and jots in it. "I shall call you Dilly and Miley."

"*Wooooowooowooo Wooooowoooo.*"

"Oh, that's a funny noise," Robyn says, scribing another entry.

Miles tilts her head up toward Dillon.

"If I can live with Dilly, you can live with Miley," Dillon whispers.

"And this is my lovely wife, Linda," Jake says as she walks up to them. "This is Dillon."

"Hello, Dillon. Let me take some of that off your hands." She offloads the food items. "I'm sure the guys can help you with the beer."

"Mom, it's *Dilly*."

"Yes, sweetie, I forgot the *y*."

"*Wooooowooowooo Wooooowooooo.*"

Linda laughs. "You're right, Jakey."

"Mom, Dilly's dog barks funny," Robyn says, wrapping her arms around Linda's legs.

"You know it's not nice to make fun of others," Linda replies.

"I mean it's different," she says, now playing around Jake's legs as if they were a jungle gym.

"That's not a bad thing," Jake says.

"I know."

"She's talking, not barking," Dillon says.

"Really?!"

"Really."

"Oh, then we have things to discuss, Miley. We must go!"

Miles eyes Dillon, who nods, and trots alongside Robyn, moving away from the trio, talking a mile a minute.

"Here, let's find a home for that beer, and I'll introduce you around," Jake says, giving Linda a kiss afterward.

"Nice meeting you, Dillon," Linda says.

"And you."

Jake walks Dillon around the spacious backyard, a patchwork of green and brown grass owing to the drought engulfing the region, that plays host to a dozen wooden picnic tables loosely clustered around a large BBQ pit. Around the perimeter of the property tall eucalyptus trees sway to a gentle breeze. Through the trees Dillon watches two horses saunter around a dusty corral, grinning when he spots a pair of donkeys in the same corral, one nudging and chasing a large plastic ball while the other chases the first, nipping at its hindquarters.

"It's amazing," Dillon says.

"What's that?" Jake says.

"How much your place, and mine, makes you feel so out in the country and away from everything, yet we're only ten minutes outside town."

"That's what makes this area special: a little heaven on Earth . . . and a trail always within reach," Jake says, approaching a lively group sitting around a pair of picnic tables pushed together. "And this motley crew collectively represents the founding mothers and fathers of the club." He gestures to the consortium of senior-division-and-up female and male runners sitting in various modes of running shirts from years gone by. "Founding mothers and fathers, Dillon; Dillon, founding mothers and fathers."

A chorus of *hey* greets Dillon. "Founding mothers and fathers," Dillon says. "Hey, Dale."

"The shower working in the Toyota Room?" Dale says.

"Like a waterfall." He hands Dale a beer.

"Ooookay, we'd better keep moving," Jake says, turning and moving on, "or you'll be employing the entire table for beer."

Various forms of "But Jakey" fade behind them as Jake walks Dillon over to where the Sunday crew has staked out a table and several lawn chairs. "This is more our demographic."

"Dillon," Chase says from his seated position, shirtless.

"Chase. Guys," Dillon says, setting the case of beer down. It is instantly emptied and placed into the oversized cooler.

"Maggie couldn't make it?" Jake asks Spencer.

"She's on a writing tear."

"What's she working on now?" Chase says.

"She doesn't let me read anything until the second draft."

"Why not?"

"She says I'm too literal."

"Nooooo," Jim says.

Spence-speak.

"Who's the hottie," Chase says, gesturing across the way.

Dillon turns toward the hottie, a woman with short black hair and shorter running tights conversing with Robyn and Doris on the other side of the fire pit.

Jake chuckles.

"Terri," Dillon says. "She works for me, helps with breakfast and housekeeping."

"Hmmm," Chase says, sipping his beer. "I think I saw her out at the JC track last week."

"She teaches a class there a couple days a week," Dillon says.

"You two . . ." Chase gives Dillon the inquisitive eyebrow treatment, shifting his eyes back and forth between employer and employee.

"Nope. I don't mix business with pleasure."

"Or trouble," Jake says, popping the cap off an Allagash White. Doris's cackle catches his attention and he watches his daughter take notes like a journalist as she and Doris converse with Terri.

Dillon scratches his chin.

"What's her story?" Chase says.

"She's working on her master's in human sexuality—"

The beer that reaches Jake's lips sprays outward in all directions. The guys standing directly in front of him take quick cover.

"Smooth, Jakey," Chase says, chuckling along with the others afterward.

The commotion catches the attention of Terri, Doris, and Robyn, as well as others in the vicinity, and all are staring in the guys' direction, scrambling to cover up their shared embarrassment. Robyn marches over to her dad.

"Dad, I have questions for you and Mom."

"Lord love a duck," Jim says.

"That's my dad's words, Jimmy."

"I'm sure you do, sweetie," Jake says. He composes himself and successfully takes a sip of his beverage. "But not now, okay?"

"Chasey, why are you 'fraid of commitment?" Robyn asks.

More beer spews out from its intended palate, this time from Chase, spawning raucous laughter. "Whaaaaaat?"

"My new best friend, Terri—spelled with an *i*, though I wanted to change it to a *y*, but she said she preferred *i* and I agreed because she's pretty smart— said you were checking her short shorts out, but if she went out with you— and she said she thought you were cute with your little dimple and blue eyes so it could be a possibility—you'd only sleep with her, then find something wrong with her and tell her goodbye."

Chase sits stunned. Dillon hangs his head. Jim is about ready to say Jake's patented catchphrase again, but stops short. Spencer tries to suppress laughter but fails.

"It's not funny, Spencey." Robyn glares up at him. "You're not married, and you're living in *sin*."

Spencer clams up, smirk wiped clean.

"And you thought Doris was going to be your worst problem today," Jimmy whispers to Chase.

Chase gives Jim the stink eye and turns toward Robyn. "It's complicated, Robyn with a *y*."

Robyn fixes her tiny hands on her hips and juts her head forward. Chase flinches, bracing for the unbridled scorn of a young girl. "No, it's not, Chasey," she says. "Grown-ups always say things are complicated. That way they don't deal with them. '*It's complicated. . . .* ' If it's complicated, then you talk about it more!"

Jake adjusts the 2008 Pikes Peak Ascent cap on his head. "Sweetie, let's discuss this another time, okay? Why don't you go ask Mom what she wants for her birthday?"

"You already know what she wants, and this is *wayyy* more important."

"I'm sure it is but—"

"Okay, moving on to my next topic," Robyn announces, setting down her notebook.

Everybody within earshot holds their breath, drinks far from their mouths.

"These are my new shoes." Robyn bends over as if stretching her short hamstrings, pointing to her new red Crocs that have sunflower stickers across the tops.

Relief, smiles, and nervous chuckles spread over the group.

"Yes, sweetie, the guys think your new shoes are very nice," Jake says. "Now, go find Daddy a napkin to clean up with."

"Yes, you are very messy . . . and scruffy!" she says as she turns away, jotting again in her notebook. "We must work on that!"

Jake lets out a sheepish chuckle. "Trouble. Lord love a duck, trouble."

"Hmmm," Chase mutters. "I don't find things wrong with women."

Dillon grins as groans, guffaws, and a Spence-speak besiege Chase.

"How about the one who insisted on wearing socks during sex?" Spencer says.

"Who wears socks during—"

"Or the one that ate like a wood chipper?" Jim says.

"Chomp, chomp, chomp . . . sharks eat slow—"

"Or the one with the intense eyebrows?" Jake chimes in.

"Hey! She looked serious *all* the time, especially when she smiled. In fact, when she smiled, she looked fanatical, and when she laughed . . . holy shit!"

Belly laughter brings more attention their way.

"Pfft . . . *Spencey's* the one living in *sin*," Chase says, sucking down beer.

"Lord love a duck," Jake concludes, raising his bottle and toasting the group. "To another fun cross-country season ahead."

"Hear, hear," cheers the chorus.

Five bottles clink.

Sunday Morning
Keeping Pace

"Not peiveit . . . peever," Chase says thirty minutes into their run, exiting the paperless outhouse at the top of Two Quarry—much to his "Charmin chagrin" as he had lamented upon entering. He's correcting Jake's misunderstanding of the word Chase used to describe his date from Friday night to the guys. "Like a grammar Nazi. Apparently there's this whole subculture who go around *peeving* over the incorrect use of grammar."

"Peeving? Who came up with that name?" Jim says.

"Are the peevers peeved that their obsessively obnoxious linguistic tirades are referred to as peeving?" Spencer says.

"She corrected our server when the dinner arrived that her use of 'momentarily' was inappropriate, and it should instead be reserved for occasions that refer to 'a moment in time.' I was just glad she waited until *after* the food had been served."

"Airlines announce that they'll be landing *momentarily*," Dillon says. "I guess what they really mean is that the pilot is getting ready to perform a touch-and-go like in flight training?"

"Tower, this is Ghost Rider—" Jake says.

"*Top Gun*," Jim answers.

"She spent the entire time during dessert bemoaning the recent *travesty* over dictionaries including the word 'literally' to informally mean 'something that is not literally true but is used for emphasis.' She was so busy explaining it to me that I ate her dessert . . . and she didn't even notice . . . literally!"

"Robyn loves the desserts at La Vera's," Jake says. "It's our once-a-month dinner out."

"I ended up eating two orders of their molten chocolate tower."

"Not the tiramisu?" Jim says.

"*Sleepless in Seattle*," Jake says.

"I didn't—" Jim says.

"You were thinking it."

Jim turns toward Dillon. "It's true."

"There's no doubt that the English language is being watered down," Spencer says. "I see it in class. Everything is done in shorthand. It doesn't help that they're being raised in a sound-bite world."

"Makes for lazy writing and poor communication," Jim says. "Emails from coworkers are horrible."

"Is it 'raised' or 'reared'?" Chase says.

"Is that 'bite' with an *i* or a *y*?" Dillon piles on at his first attempt to join their lively banter.

"Lord love a duck."

"Let's get going," Jim says, turning toward the Marsh. *Beep.* "'Cause this conversation is going nowhere."

Beep, beep. Beep.

The witty repartee comes fast and furious, so much so that Dillon is hard pressed to find a way to crack into it consistently, let alone know who has uttered what at times. The previous Sunday run had been more or less an introduction of sorts, the sniffing out of who had done what and when and where, and even whom. The years and miles this group has behind and underneath them shows in their camaraderie. Dillon's ease at physically keeping up with them on the trails had done little for him in keeping up with their pithy banter. They have a beat all their own, a rhythm born from shared adventures, conversations, sweaty miles, social gatherings, road trips . . .

"How's it different from passing notes in class like in *them olden days?*" Jake says on their way around the Marsh, a wide expanse filled with an abundance of cattails, tules, and native grasses. The jeep-wide trail allows them to run three abreast up front and two abreast in back. "Those weren't composed in Shakespearian prose."

"I can't defend most forms of electronic communication, but at least Twitter forces you to say what you mean and get to the point without rambling on," Chase says. "If you ask me, there's too much verbal diarrhea out there."

"Like talk radio . . . woof!" Jim says.

"Who listens to talk radio anymore?" Dillon says. "It's all streaming music, podcasts, and online message threads."

"People without jobs, complaining they don't have jobs," Chase says. "That's who."

"It's a cesspool of political, sports, and religious ignorance," Jim says. "And that's a Monday."

"Harsh," Dillon says.

"At least they have an outlet to vent and express themselves," Jake says. "Discourse is important."

"I guess as *we* evolve so too does our language," Spencer says.

"Unfortunately, with technology *real* conversation suffers," Jake says. "Texting and talking are not the same; just as reading and listening differ qualitatively."

"That's been my experience," Jim says, shaking his head. "Coworkers and clients pick and choose what they respond to in texts and emails, skipping what they don't want to address or deal with. It's *very* frustrating. I end up walking over to their cubicle or calling them."

"If we're not careful, we'll devolve to grunt, grunt, grunt, or simply wink, wink, wink," Dillon says.

"Tell Linda thanks, Jake," Chase says.

"Was it that bad?"

"It wasn't awful—shit! Don't get me started on how 'awful' is used incorrectly."

Their conversation leans out once they hang a right onto the Ridge trail, a spectacular, three-and-a-half-mile, undulating single-track thrill run under a dense canopy of northern oak trees, manzanita trees, and Douglas fir. Stretches of it are technical, testing their agility, limiting extended or easy discussion, especially when Jim, leading the group, surges ahead and strings them out, dipping into their racing reserves until an emphatic Spence-speak reins them in. Other sections stretch out along a smoother surface, gently downhill, which allows them to roll *very* fast, and again, with Chase taking up the charge this time, towing Jim and Dillon, they open up their strides, a trio in sync with one another, floating along to the beat of the trail's contours. Spence-speaks fade behind them, no longer effective in governing that blissful state of perpetual-motion nirvana, flexing their fitness outside racing's confines, whose only limitation is the length of the trail.

Once they reach the end, which drops them out onto the upper portion of the Marsh trail, the trio eases off the pace, turns left, and coasts along, waiting up for the stragglers.

"*Wow* . . . that was sweet," Dillon says.

Chase and Jim grin as a pack of runners approaches.

"Here they come," Jim says, giving Dillon an elbow.

Dillon notes nothing out of the ordinary. "What?"

"Fit Kits," Jim whispers, at which Chase sports a prideful grin.

"Okay," Dillon says, skirting the trail's edge to allow five women and two men to pass, all talking and laughing and waving to the guys.

"Didn't you notice they all had pretty much the same gear and clothing options on?" Chase says.

"I suppose they did," Dillon says upon further reflection.

"I worked on an ad campaign for Sonoma Runner's Depot," Chase says.

"They wanted to know how to attract new runners to their store. So I suggested they incorporate the concept of 'cycling kits' from the cycling world—you know, coordinated outfits from head to toe. They target potential runners who need *accouterments* to inspire them."

"Dress for the job you want, not the one you have," Dillon says.

"Something like that. Not everybody is self-motivated like us, so getting out there requires dressing for the part, so to speak. Heck, research shows that some run *because* of the all cool outfits and gear."

"Sounds basically like an upsell technique," Dillon says.

"The print ads around town and in local magazines depict the average runner wearing all the latest gear and devices, and it lures them in, and, yes, salesmanship does the rest. Before they leave they've been upsold on every imaginable running-related item on the market: compression socks, water packs, cooling shirts, ice vests, cushy insoles—"

"As if the shoe manufacturer forgot to put them in," Jim says.

"Tech gear, laundry detergent, running safety bracelet, tech visor, sport sunglasses, store-brand shirts and shorts, sports bras, sports food, sports drinks, sport watch. You'd be amazed at what they end up buying."

"No nipple guards?" Jim says.

"Funny, you didn't mention shoes," Dillon says. "That's all you really need."

"You're a retailer's worst nightmare."

"I avoid anything called depot, mart, or warehouse."

"Fair enough."

Non–Fit Kits Jake and a perturbed Spencer catch up with the other guys, and the pace resumes business as usual until Jake works his way to the front and proceeds to become one with the contours of the narrow downhill ledge extending out from the northern flank of Bennett Mountain. And in doing so Jake strings the others out, speedsters included. With each sweeping left-hander, Jake holds his pace until the very last moment, braking briefly where the trail tucks into a crease of the mountain slope that allows streams to cross. He negotiates it with a deft left-foot plant along the bank, knee bending and leg absorbing his weight until, like a bungee cord stretched to its maximum, it springs back full-tilt, shooting him sharply to the right and several yards farther ahead of his followers.

Behind him the others handle the same effort with various degrees of skill or caution—some running through the minuscule stream, others jumping it—each time slipping farther and farther back from Jake. Dillon and Jim can make up most of the gap to Jake once the trail lengthens out, but as soon as it hooks left and tucks into another crease, Jake scatters their efforts to the wind, all but whistling through the tall redwoods towering above them. This yo-yoing lasts for a mile or so until the trail transitions to technical track, necessitating stutter-stepping and jitterbugging and extreme downward focus, preventing all from taking in the panoramic views of Lake Illsanjo in the distance. Here Jim shines the most, the only one agile enough to *mostly* match Jake's pace, drifting back only incrementally without losing sight of him; Dillon scales back his pursuit amidst painful visions of a twisted ankle; Chase drops back to Spencer and his shuffling stride as he usually does on such rocky terrain, his Tartan Track reflexes no match out here in the wild.

At the bottom of the Marsh Trail, where it intersects with Canyon, they regroup, Jake's expression of pure bliss more than enough to stifle a Spence-speak. Jake is rarely the instigator of such Sunday surges, but when he is, he puts everybody to shame, showcasing his trail-running prowess, and reminding them that out in the wild beyond the roads, the track, and the gentler short-and-sweet cross-country trails, Jake towers over them all.

Week 37 Training Summary			
	Long Run	Mileage Total	Comments
Dillon	21	65	Nice having a group to train with on Sundays again.
Chase	20.65	45	Great track workouts.
Spencer	20.50	76	Solid tempo run on Tues.
Jim	20	34	Not sure I'm fit enough for XC this year.
Jake	20	70	Love the new energy in the group.

Week 3
September 14

Monday Night
Prenuptial Balance Sheet

Seated at a small meticulously organized desk, in a chair from the kitchen that wobbles when he leans forward, Jim nervously logs into Pinnacle's Tax Consultants legacy system for the third time, keenly aware that, like in baseball, it's three strikes and you're out, or in this case locked out should he swing and miss again.

Several feet away from Jim, seated at a small round table in an office chair with a strip of duct tape down the center of the cushion, a caster wheel that squeaks, and whose lumbar support bothers Jim's back, Doris sifts through her clutter of Post-it notes, recipe cards, and a stack of pages ripped out from various magazines, looking for the note card with her computer's password on it. The busy couple are in the smaller of the two rooms of their cramped turn-of-the-century bungalow rental, situated in the Burbank Gardens Historic District. Its location affords Jim easy running access to his favorite route, the Prince Greenway; for Doris, easy walking distance to downtown Santa Rosa.

"Jim?"

"RememberYourPasswordThisTimesTheCharm7. No spaces, and cap each word."

"Something else."

"Okay."

"I took fifteen of my charm bracelets down to the lady who runs the local crafts consignment shop this morning. You know, there on Fifth Street?"

"Sure."

"So how do I book it?" she says, finding the note card. Once logged in she scans the spreadsheet Jim set up for her home business, Doris's Crafts & Things. "I didn't sell her the items, so it can't be booked as a sale, right?"

"Right."

"But without the sale, I can't take it out of inventory."

"Correct."

"But if I leave it in inventory, then I don't know how much I actually have to sell without doing a hard count."

"You'll need to set up another inventory bucket called Consignment." Jim pushes away from his desk and walks across the hardwood floor to Doris past a bookshelf that holds a plethora of accounting textbooks, signed books authored by Billy Mills, three historical tomes on the cinema, and a dozen baking and arts-and-crafts manuals. "Move those items from the main bucket to the consignment one; that way you can view what useable inventory you have on hand, what inventory is tied up in consignment, and an overall snapshot for your monthly P&L statement."

Doris's eyebrows rise and her lips scrunch up.

"Think of consignment inventory as items in limbo. And when they're sold or returned you can reverse the amounts as needed." Jim adds another column to her spreadsheet, tying the new column to the inventory one with a formula that will perform the math automatically.

"Limbo, *limbo*, limbo," Doris sings, wiggling in the chair.

"There," Jim says, leaning back. "Simply enter the amount you gave her, make a note to whom it went, and you're all set."

"Limbo, *limbo*, limbo."

"You goof." He walks back to his desk and sits. "Speaking of inventory, I noticed on our grocery inventory spreadsheet that you bought five extra boxes of cereal last week."

"They were on sale. You're going to eat them eventually."

"Right, but we need to keep our monthly cash flow up. We can't tie it up in inventory for the two or three months it'll sit on the shelf until I get to it."

"How can buying sale items *not* save us money?"

"It does in the long run, but it ties up our cash for things we need to spend it on in the short term. Make sense?"

"I suppose. Want me to return them?"

"It's under twenty dollars."

Doris tinkers with adding and removing values from the new column, watching the other column change automatically. "Still trying to figure out the new software?"

"I was," he says, staring at a popup message that reads, PINNACLE TAX CONSULTANTS: YOUR CREDENTIALS HAVE EXPIRED. PLEASE CONTACT THE ADMINISTRATOR. He shakes his head. *I don't feel expired.* "Now I'm just tying to log back in."

"Are you getting the hang of it at least?"

"Sort of. Everything is backward from the old system. I spend more time doing basic tasks than before." *Technology is great until they change everything. As if I have time to constantly learn new ways to do the same tasks as before.* He lets out a ruminative sigh.

"You'll figure it out. You always do."

"I'm afraid when the new management team comes out here in a couple weeks, they'll let go those who aren't up to speed on *their* system."

"You worry too much."

"You don't worry enough."

"You worry enough for the both of us."

"As long as we balance out," Jim says, and smirks.

"We do. Our relationship balance sheet as of last month says so," she mocks, closing out from the spreadsheet and begins viewing pictures posted online from the club BBQ. "Why does Chase always go around shirtless? I can understand it when he's out running on a hot day, but at the BBQ yesterday . . . is he *that* in love with his body?"

"I don't know. He's in marketing. Maybe he's advertising the goods."

"Please. He's just drawing attention to himself."

"Like I said . . ."

"I suppose. Terri seems nice, except for the overly tight butt huggers she wears. You can see her ass crack in this pic!"

"Who?"

"You know, Terri, Dillon's little *helper*. She's working on her master's—"

"Oh, her."

"'Oh, her.' I know you guys were talking about her at the BBQ."

"I hadn't noticed."

"Good answer. Jimbo, *limbo*, limbo," Doris sings, wiggling again. "I hear Chase has some oral anthem he dazzles the ladies with."

"What? Where'd you hear that?"

"I hear stuff. You almost done there?" she says, now spinning around in her chair, her feet lifted off the floor. "Jimbo, *Jimbo*, Jimbo."

"You goof."

"Hurry up. I want to try something new."

"Did you read another article?"

"Maybe. I'll bring a glass of water so you don't cramp up this time."

"Right. One less thing to worry about."

Tuesday Late Afternoon
Yard Walking

"Well . . ." Jake says, rubbing the scruff on his chin, politely conveying the absurdity of the new client's vision for their home's front-yard renovation. "Palm trees really aren't in keeping with the neighborhood, let alone the region." From the sidewalk where he stands, Jake surveys the surrounding Skyfarm homes, overlooking the elongated Santa Rosa plain, whose yards, like his clients, are large and irregularly shaped depending on their location. Some have terraced hills with manicured lawns, some have gentle slopes with shady oak trees, and others have both terracing and slopes, with large boulders and indigenous plants strategically placed. Jake had converted the front yard three houses down and across the street, which is how the man standing before Jake learned of him. "They really are more a Southern California look."

"Precisely!" the client says. "That's what we're going for, the San Diego vibe. That's where we're from."

Jake removes his 2010 Mt. Ashland Hill Climb Run hat, scratches his head a couple times, and studies the unreasonably tan, sixtysomething gentleman with white hair dressed as if ready to play a round of golf. "They won't provide any shade, and unless you fill the yard with beach sand and lay out towels and chairs, they really won't go with any indigenous vegetation."

"Beach sand . . . I hadn't thought of that," the client says. His eyes scan the yard. "Do you think—"

"County's largest cat box."

"I guess you're right about that."

"I can appreciate your attempt to create a unique environment, but I think there are some fresh ideas that are better suited for the area, and won't resemble every other yard in the neighborhood. For instance," Jake says, stepping onto the lawn and wandering around as if pulled by some invisible natural force, explaining his vision, "the landscape should reflect the relationship it has with the abundance of sun exposure the property receives as well as the late-afternoon summer breezes, the way it sits here with a southwesterly downward slope toward the city, and take advantage of our Mediterranean climate—wet winters and long, dry summers."

The Southern Californian tiptoes behind Jake while he performs his complimentary consult.

"My wife wants a hedge of bushes along the driveway, about yay high," the client says, using his hand to demonstrate, placed at thigh level.

"She probably meant shrubs," Jake says, continuing his trancelike walk.

"What?"

"A hedge along the driveway will give the property a boxy appearance," Jake says. "I think you'll find an open, airy presence will have better appeal from both house and street views."

The guy scratches his chin, either in deep consideration or wrestling with the conundrum placed upon him: what his wife wants and what Jake has proposed.

"Well, she found theses bushes, I mean shrubs, down at Home Depot that she fancied."

"The big-box outlets don't always sell what is ideal for the local area."

Now the guy scans the property, wringing his hands, either panic setting in or an approaching tee time. Relief replaces his dour expression when a late-model Mercedes S-Class Sedan enters the driveway. Upon parking, the engine goes silent, the driver door flies open, and out steps an animated and deeply tanned woman whose huge pearl-white smile matches her car's color.

"Harold!" the woman, who's wearing a tennis outfit, says. "Landry called and wants to know what's keeping you!" Several bracelets jangle from her forearm as her arm flaps about.

"Oh, right, yes, thank you, darling," Harold says, and turns to Jake. "I'm must rush off for a fund-raising event down at the Fountain Grove golf course. My wife can take over from here. Francine? This is Jake. Jake, Francine."

"Hurry along, Harold," she says, stepping up to and stopping at the edge of the lawn. "You know how they are."

Harold shakes hands with Jake and rushes off, climbing into his sterling-silver Mercedes SL Roadster parked on the other side of Francine's car.

Jake smiles despite the fact that he'll need to start over with the client's better half, but at least now he will be dealing directly with the person who appears to run the show.

Happy that he convinced the beach lovers that bringing the beach to them is as not as much fun as going to the beach, especially when he spoke of Santa Cruz and Capitola a couple hours down south, Jake steers his truck out toward west county, making a stop at another client's home to check on their new automated sprinkler system. System reset, he heads toward the Willowside Trailhead, an unofficial spot off the side of the country road by the same name, to take a run along the creekside path. Once outside town, however, he instead works his way over to Dillon's BR&B in hopes of finding a running partner.

"*Woooooowooowooo Wooooowoooo.*"

"You don't say, Miles," Jake says, petting the official greeter.

"Jake," Dillon says. "What brings you out here today?"

"Looking to get in a run along the creek. You run yet?"

"Not yet. I might be able to go now, though. Let me check to see when my guests are due in."

Jake's phone rings as Dillon steps away. "Hi, sweetie."

"Hi, Dad. Mom wants to know how far you're running tonight."

"That doesn't sound right."

"Okay, it was me. It's because I have a school project and I need your help. I want to make it about hort . . . horti . . . culture. So how far?"

"I'm going to do around . . ." Jake says, glancing at Dillon, who's returned, "twelve?"

Dillon nods.

"Okay, since you don't wear the watch Mommy bought you, I'll figure it out," she says. "Twelve times six is"—a long pause follows while she mumbles under her breath—"twenty-four. You'll be home in twenty-four minutes!"

"Are you sure?"

"No. We've only gone up to twelve times two on the number tables."

"It'll be more like seventy-five minutes. And you forgot the time it takes for me to drive home, sweetie."

"I always forget that part. I'll remember next time."

"I'm sure you will. I'll be home the usual time, right before dinner. We can work on your project after that, okay? I need to go run with Dillon right now."

"It's Dilly, Dad. Is Miley there too?"

"Yes, she is. Would you like to say hello?" Before Robyn can answer, Jake places the phone in the direction of Miley, who stands next to Dillon, staring up at Jake.

"Say hi, girl," Dillon says.

"*Woooooowooowooo Wooooowoooo.*"

"Miley says to say hi to you too," Jake says, putting the phone back to his ear.

"No she didn't, Daddy. She said that Terri with an *i* should talk to me about the birds and the bees because parents don't know how to talk to their kids about them."

"That's a lot of info for such a short conversation."

"Like you always say, Daddy, subbb . . . text."

"We can talk about this—"

"I like birds and bees, Daddy. They go tweet, tweet, tweet and buzz, buzz, buzz."

"Yes, they do, sweetie. I need to go now."

"Okay. Bye."

"Lord love a duck?" Dillon says.

Jake smiles.

"Terri?"

"It was bound to happen. I just assumed she'd be married by then."

Dillon and Miles pile into the front cab of Jake's truck, and he drives them over to the Willowside Trailhead. There they embark along the creekside path, heading east toward downtown, a dirt path most of the way—four and a half miles' worth— until it reaches the downtown area. Here it switches to concrete with decorative railings, a handful of rustic-styled wooden bridges that cross to the other side of the creek, painted benches, and colorful inlaid tile murals on the walls that flank the undulating route, ducking city streets and Highway 101.

"Business picking up?" Jake says once they settle into a conversational pace, Miles leading the way.

"Here and there. Pretty spotty for the most part. I need to advertise more. My aim is to bring in customers from other parts of the country, even attract the international crowd."

"Chase should be able to help you out with some copy. He's a jokester, but he is good at what he does."

"He is pretty funny. The whole 'metaphorical death is the best kind of death' bit was genius."

"He worked for a couple big ad agencies in New York after college, and did well. But his humor didn't always go over so well with the clients, or his bosses for that matter."

"Like what? Aren't commercials supposed to be entertaining?"

"For pharmaceutical products, not so much. He was working on the Xanax campaign and joked during a pitch session, in front of his boss and the clients, 'Xanax: Botox for the soul.'"

Dillon laughs. "That's brilliant."

"Before Chase returned to his office, he'd been fired."

"Perhaps a little too much 'truth in advertising' with that pitch. I might hit him up for some ideas. If nothing else it'd be entertaining."

"That it would. Getting the word out to the club would be wise too. We're hugely networked."

Still outside city limits, the guys and Miles glide and pad by a large vineyard of Sauvignon Blanc grapes a week away from harvest. Not more than a minute later they cruise by pastureland with a horse-training ring near the fence line, a young woman tirelessly trotting her steed around and around it. Miles glances at the horse twice, but otherwise dismisses the larger four-legged animal as unworthy of further attention. At the next adjoining parcel, another pasture, Miles has the same reaction to the dozen or more cows grazing, who regard the trio with sedate eyes and unhurried mastication.

"I'm obligated to ask you the following . . ." Jake begins.

Dillon glances over, expression quizzical. "Okay."

"Linda is the club's official matchmaker."

"I gathered that from Chase's conversation last Sunday."

"She's determined to settle him down one day, but it's been no easy task. She's asked about you after the BBQ—"

"Tell her thanks but my focus is elsewhere these days. I have no time for distractions."

Dillon's rebuff swirls like the eddy in the creek to their left, serenaded by rhythmic foot strikes against the dirt and gravel, and Miles's panting.

"Pretty bad breakup?"

Crunch-crunch-pant, crunch-crunch-pant.

Dillon cracks a wry smile. "To know me is to run with me."

Crunch-crunch-pant, crunch-crunch-pant.

"In other words it's a long story," Dillon says.

Crunch-crunch-pant, crunch-crunch-pant.

"Long runs and long stories go hand in hand," Jake says, offering a salve.

Crunch-crunch-pant, crunch-crunch-pant.

Whether it is the lent ear or the toxic silence of rancor, Dillon mentions that his ex simply didn't understand his daily training without Olympic aspirations attached to it—why do something that doesn't have a future?—then deftly moves on to another topic. Jake doesn't press. He empathizes with Dillon's reluctance, the desire to deal with the wound himself in his own way even though that *way* is simply to ignore it and let Miles, work, and the miles bandage it. As with all unattended wounds they eventually seep through the mind's protective gauze no matter how tightly wrapped.

All in good time.

Crunch-crunch-pant, crunch-crunch-pant.

Wednesday Night
The Cohabitation Principle

"How's the novel coming along, Maggie?" her dad, James, says as he passes her a serving bowl filled with mixed vegetables.

"Good, good, I think," Maggie says. "I don't know . . ."

"Honey, no, it's great," Spencer says, receiving the vegetables from Maggie and scooping out a sizable portion onto his plate. "It's brilliantly conceived: Huxley's *Brave New World* meets The Wachowskis' *The Matrix*." He passes the side dish to Maggie's mother, Joyce.

"Oh, that's interesting," Joyce says. "Is it like *Vanilla Sky* with Tom Cruise? I really enjoyed that movie."

"No, it's more like *Inception*," Maggie explains, "where people are under the influence of a special, but in this case legal, drug that makes them superconsumers."

"So commercialism rooted in science fiction," her dad says.

"Well, I suppose—" Maggie says.

"Actually the near future, given where science research is today," Spencer counters. "And the implications are frightening, a plausible alternate precursor to the Matrix trilogy: a consumer world blinds humanity to the harsh realities of life."

Spencer's summation drifts over the dinner table for several quiet moments, inviting further discourse.

"Your new home is lovely, dear," Joyce says.

"Thanks, Mum," Maggie says. "It needs some repairs, but we *love* the location."

"Difficult to find," James says, explaining that when Maggie told them they lived in Santa Rosa, he took that to mean they lived *in* Santa Rosa, not on the fringe.

"Your father kept turning back when it looked *too* country."

"All I ask for are sidewalks and streetlamps," James says. "Not a herd of deer running across the roadway."

"We eventually stopped and asked for directions."

"From a man who had a gauche scrap-metal sculpture in his front yard made from an old rusted water heater. It bore a striking resemblance to the Tin Man from *The Wizard of Oz*."

Spencer politely smiles. Their three-bedroom, two-bath home rests on Rincon Valley's eastern border off Los Alamos Road, tucked away in a mature neighborhood of Santa Rosa. For Spencer it's conveniently located near the Cobblestone Trailhead, and the distance from school to home allows him anywhere from six to twelve miles of running. Maggie loves the solitude, and her office has a picturesque window view up toward Hood Mountain, which inspires her daily writing routine. And true, the early '80s–built home requires some tender loving care, but that's the only way they could break into the real estate market *and* live on the fringe unencumbered by city life.

"Maggie mentioned school is back in session," James says to Spencer, passing him a piping-hot casserole dish from across the table. "What's it like teaching these days?"

"Dad, you just left four months ago," Maggie says.

"*Wikipedia* is often their one-and-done research source," Spencer says to James, who shakes his head; he's a tenured college English professor taking a yearlong sabbatical to write essays on the use of language in modern political rhetoric.

"*Wikipedia* is to knowledge what Cliff's Notes is to literature: a shortcut."

"Dad . . ."

"I encourage them to use it as primer," Spencer says, "but to delve deeper with critical thought to fully understand the basis for the results." As Spencer hears the words leave his mouth, a pet peeve his father quipped about many years ago dawns on him, how the introduction of the handheld calculator removed students from performing arithmetic by hand. "I suppose through progress we elevate to a higher level of—"

"'History is a nightmare from which I am trying to awake,'" James says.

"Now you're quoting—?" Maggie says.

"That's his favorite saying," Joyce says.

"And they're distracted with everything," James says. "I can see it in their faces, an email or text or Snapchat or *something* is waiting on their phones, and they're thinking more about that than my lecture. Frankly, lecturing their *smart* phones would be more—"

"Mum, how was the drive down?" Maggie interrupts, much to Spencer's dismay, though James can go on for hours on how he feels technology is ruining the classroom experience where *real* discourse takes place, getting students excited about what they're learning, developing conversational skills, traits not obtainable online or in chat rooms no matter how much funding is granted for technology.

"It started off nice in Portland, but by the time we arrived in Ashland, it rained like the dickens," Joyce says. "It was coming down so hard your father had to pull off the road twice."

"Where are you two heading from here?" Spencer says.

"Arizona," James says. "My niece is getting married in Flagstaff."

"She's marrying a professor too," Joyce says. "We viewed their engagement photos online. They look so happy."

Spencer shifts uncomfortably in his chair, regretting the question.

"Have you two, you know, considered making things official?" Joyce says, buttering a roll.

Spencer takes evasive action, quickly scoops a generous helping of avoidance from his plate, and shovels it into his mouth.

Maggie lands a swift kick to Spencer's shin, causing him to tighten his lips to muffle a yelp and expulsion of food. "No, Mum, we're really busy; Spence with school, running, and club matters, and me on my novel. Did I tell you an agent from New York showed some interest in my last project?"

Though Spencer has diverted his attention to Maggie, chewing and nodding along, he can feel James's eyes on him, measuring him, mentally chastising him. Spencer had at one time been a *good* catch in James's estimation, the one she should *marry*, but now, many years later . . .

"Still with the running?" James says.

"James, now don't start—"

"It's a frivolous activity, a complete waste of energy."

"Dad, there are worse vices. Spence hardly drinks, doesn't smoke or spend hours watching TV—"

"I think what your father is trying to say," Joyce interjects, "is that we don't understand it."

Spencer wants to defend himself, the lifestyle aspect, the cardiovascular benefits, the mental clarity it often provides, but doing so will only extend the debate. With the exception of Maggie, who runs two or three times a week for fitness and socialization, her entire family—two younger brothers and one older sister—have never participated in organized sports. No good will come from open dialogue on the matter, at least at the dinner table. They don't understand, and have no personal experience to draw from or appeal to.

"Eight years is a long time for cohabitation is what I'm saying," James says.

"James, it's been a long drive today, and we've only just arrived," Joyce says. "Let's enjoy dinner and take this up another time."

"Right, right. So, Spencer, what are they teaching for US history these days?"

"The world hasn't changed over the summer, Dad."

As Spencer immediately takes advantage of the topic transition and lays out for James the current discourse for his class, Spencer can't help but overhear the side conversation going on between Maggie and her mom about the wedding her parents will be attending.

"Your dad has put on some weight since last Christmas," Spencer says, slipping into a pair of running shorts and a racing shirt—from the '04 Portland Marathon—and crawling into bed.

"Mum says since he went on his sabbatical he has a shorter walking route than before." Maggie slides into bed wearing sweatpants and one of Spencer's old running T-shirts whose race name, year, and logo are too faded to read without proper light.

"I could write out an exercise—"

"Don't bother. He hates to sweat. Mum bought him an exercise bike and he hangs his coats and hats on it."

Spencer pulls his laptop off the nightstand, rests it in his lap, opens it, and navigates to the next school paper that requires his attention; Maggie mirrors his actions but instead locates the last paragraph she's written of her novel.

"Dinner was good," he says.

"Thanks."

Spencer turns his attention to the homework paper he has up on the laptop, reading the first paragraph. "Love you."

"Love you too."

Spencer watches Maggie, typing a new scene. "What's wrong?"

"Nothing," she replies with a brief glance his way, her fingers still in motion.

"It's the marriage thing again, isn't it?"

"No."

He leans over, reading the new story lines. "Did you figure out how to do that thing with the guy?"

Maggie doesn't reply, her focus intense.

Spencer turns his attention to his own work, but becomes distracted and instead opens up a new email to compose to the group, regarding the Sunday run. He begins typing.

"It has been a while since we talked about it," Maggie says as she snaps shut her laptop and sets it back on the nightstand.

"It has, but nothing has changed."

"Then let's change it." She slides further under the sheets and rolls over on her side toward him.

"Actually we have, come to think of it. We bought this house. We have joint checking and savings accounts. We both own and share the car. What's a marriage license going to do that tops those commitments? I love you. I tell you that every day. Is it the running thing?"

"You know it's not, so stop deflecting."

"You read the article I gave—"

Maggie rolls her eyes. "Yes, a ring doesn't define the marriage, and a piece of paper doesn't define a life. And, yes, Oprah Winfrey didn't get married and is in a great long-term relationship."

"This way we won't take each other for granted—"

Exasperated, she groans. "Not *Molly* again. That was at running camp years ago, and you never actually dated her, so you have no idea how she turned out. She could've been messing with you."

"I don't know, she seemed pretty serious and happy about the prospect."

"Listen, I'm not looking to get married so I can let myself go and sit around the house all day."

"True, you already sit around the house all day."

She reaches over and punches his shoulder. "I'm a writer, smartass."

"Better than a dumbass . . . and *owwww*. Add that to the bruise from your kick during dinner."

"Let's just agree you're being an ass."

"I'm jesting."

"No, you're avoiding the subject."

"This is true."

"I don't like being the *teacher* at home and you acting like your students." She rolls over and turns off her bedside lamp. "Don't avoid it forever. I may get bored. And, yes, I know standing by for eight years doesn't make my stance any stronger."

"Once things settle back into a regular routine, we can discuss it again. Right now I need to review these papers for tomorrow."

"Where are you meeting for your run?"

Spencer smiles. "Cobblestone."

"Again? I'm meeting the girls at Parktrail this weekend."

"Cobblestone is convenient for the guys," he says, leaning over to kiss her good night. "I love you."

She twists backward to receive his kiss. "You better, or my next novel is going to be about a guy who trips while running, suffers a concussion, and forgets the best thing that ever happened to him."

Spencer stares at Maggie as she curls up under layers of protection and finds a comfortable spot. "That's harsh. And Liane Moriarty covered that in her book, *What Alice Forgot* . . . and it had a—"

"Mine will be a tragicomedy with a *Titanic*-style ending. Love you."

Thursday Night
Domestic Irony

"Get down," Chase shouts, coming out from his office/weight room and into the living area a few minutes past nine p.m.

"Meow."

"Off!"

His predominately gray American wirehair cat jumps down off the kitchen counter and saunters over to the empty food bowl. "Meow."

"Hold on to your fur balls, will ya?" Chase says. He removes his GoFit weight-lifting gloves and tosses them back into the multipurpose room, where they land on the leather couch. Still shirtless from his session, he strides into the kitchen, gathers a can of cat food from the stack in the pantry, flicks the tab open, and jiggles it until the Spam-like mold plops into the bowl.

"Meow."

"Picky, picky, picky, aren't you? It's cat food, not tea and crumpets, Your Lordship." Chase fetches a fork and breaks up the round mold into manageable chunks. That proves good enough and his cat, Dogma, aka His Lordship, licks and nibbles away.

Chase tosses the can into the recycle bin, rinses the fork off, and places it in the dishwasher, then washes his hands.

Fresh from this upper-body session and craving protein, Chase hefts a three-and-half-pound tub of Muscle Milk over to the kitchen counter. Retrieving a specialized plastic bottle that has a stainless steel blending ball inside, he scoops in several ounces and fills the bottle up with fat-free milk. He caps it, shakes it vigorously for several seconds, and pops the cap, taking hearty chugs.

"Meow."

"Nope. Doesn't go well with cat slop. Besides, this is more expensive per ounce than your meal." Dogma resumes licking the bowl until it's spotless.

Chase polishes off the protein drink, and after rinsing the bottle out and placing it into the dishwasher, he stations himself in the living room and sprawls out on the plush carpet, settling into the first stretch of a thirty-minute routine. From a seated lotus position, he grabs the remote, turning the wall-mounted Samsung fifty-one-inch flat screen on and navigates to the recorded items from the night before and earlier that day. He scrolls through the list of shows—*Modern Family*, *Wheel of Fortune*, *Mike & Molly*, *Forever*, *Storage Wars*, *Dance Moms*, *SportsCenter*, the movies *Fever Pitch* and *Hitch*—and when he flashes by *Total Divas*, Dogma meows. "That sounds about right."

Shifting from the lotus position, he moves into a glute stretch on his right side, the remote still in hand, a finger pressed against the Fast Forward button. But instead of pushing Play at the show's beginning, he skips forward to the first series of commercials. He sets the remote down and sinks deeper into the stretch, making mental notes as the commercials play out. *Nice use of imagery, taking the viewer from their dreary day to a fantasy world . . . and it's simply bath soap.* The next commercial commences, promoting gourmet dog food—though the crossbreed Labradoodle that rushes into the kitchen appears confused between its desire to retrieve a ball first and its intellectual disdain over being the owner's living hypoallergenic pillow—followed by one that has many cats running around in a meadow, but ironically is not selling anything feline-related.

"Meow."

"That's a good one. People love cats in commercials; the aw-how-cute factor."

Dogma stretches out a leg of his own, adding licking his ass to the mix.

"Yeah, adorable."

Chase moves to the other glute and methodically on through his nightly routine, incorporating thick stretch bands of various colors and torturous sticks and dense foam rollers to aid in the process, all the while zipping through hours of television programming, uncaring about who says what to whom, when, or why. His conversations around the water cooler at work don't recount the plot of a Lifetime Network movie or the pseudodrama from a reality television show, but rather the commercials that aired during those shows, especially throughout prime time, noting the likely target demographic watching them.

Body decompressed and mind filled with fresh ideas, he gathers up the multitude of exercise aids, returns them to their proper storage locations, and heads for the shower. Once cleansed, he goes to the kitchen where he prepares another shake, this one a Whole Foods complete meal. Dogma stares at Chase as he begins imbibing. "'Better living through chemistry' as Dupont used to say." Product consumed and glassware rinsed and properly stowed, Chase plunks down on his large sectional couch, pulls his MacBook Air from the coffee table, and navigates to the folder and files for the Grogger's Box Wine campaign. He tunes the Sirius device to the alternative rock station and begins going over the notes from the last meeting with the client, addressing the snag that cropped up with the Go Green theme: the client kept insisting that the grapes used weren't green. The word "meathead" came to mind at the time, though all Chase said to the client was, "That's the beauty of boxed wine . . . no one can see what color they are!" This did not amuse Mr. Grogger.

Chase retrieves a box of Grogger's wine from the kitchen and sets it on the coffee table. He stares at it intently, rotates it, and views it from all sides, including lapping the table four times.

Dogma twice eludes Chase's careless passes, eventually settling in Chase's spot on the couch. "Meow."

"Yeah?" Chase says, the coffee table between him and the couch. "Hmmm . . . you might be right. I see a woman after a long day at work, tired, on her own, independent and on a budget, kicking back in a pair of her favorite sweats, a plate of cheese and crackers on the coffee table, a book open in one hand, a cat purring in her lap, and a glass of Grogger's Box Wine in the other hand."

"Meow."

"Or we could just have you using the box as a scratching post."

Chase's cell phone rings. "Hello."

"Chase. Dillon."

"Hey, Dillon. You're up late for a breakfast guy," Chase says, noting the time on his Seiko watch: 11:33 p.m.

"Yeah, sometimes the candle burns at both ends. Speaking of which, can we get together next week? I'd like to pick your brain on some marketing ideas."

"I'd love to. Let's meet for a run. What are your easy days next week?"

"Monday, Thursday, and Saturday. Pretty much the same each week."

"Perfect. I usually run during my lunch hour."

"No problem. Come out to my place on Monday and we can run out in the vineyards."

"Really? The vineyards? Is that allowed?"

"I'm friendly with the landowner so it's cool."

"It's not Grogger's Vineyards, is it?"

"No. Why?"

"No reason. You running on Sunday with us?"

"Planning on it."

"See you then," Chase says, ending the call.

"Meow."

Chase stares at Dogma, the phone conversation still fresh in Chase's mind. "That's it! Grogger's Box Wine, wine on the go, a picnic basket of sorts, with cheese, crackers, summer sausage, utensils, napkins. They could be sold at specialty stores for tourists to the area, even bed-'n'-breakfasts! Yes, a disposable, self-contained wine-country picnic, shaped like a picnic basket."

"Meow."

"Yes, it's time." Chase scoots the cat over and sits, turns on the TV, and cues up *Last Week Tonight* with John Oliver. "It's all the news I need." Chase goes to scratch the top of Dogma's head, but the cat turns, hisses, and lashes out a paw, drawing three fresh lines of blood on Chase's exposed arm. "Ouch! That hurt, you turd."

"Meow."

Early Friday Morning
Wake-up Call

Chilly warm-up complete, Dillon begins his third trip around Percy's Loop, cranks up the pace, and drops thirty seconds off his per-mile average over the next quarter mile. The cool dawn air hints at fall's imminent arrival, nostrils intoxicated by dewy sagebrush and ripened blackberries left unpicked on thorny vines. He waved Miles off at the end of the last lap, preferring to negotiate the workout solo, her waning objection peeling from his mind along with the predawn voicemail left on the inn's landline from his ex-wife. *Sorry, girl, this one I need to run on my own.* Not even a call afterward from his younger sister informing him that she'd be in town Halloween week fully counters his mood.

Despite Miles's vocal objections each time Dillon passes by her, the first of the three fifteen-minute progressively faster segments comes effortlessly, treading the trail that has more of his footprints on it than any settler before him. Two hundred yards into the third loop, Dillon's watch beeps, beckoning the second segment. He responds without hesitation, chopping another thirty seconds off expeditiously, down to six-minute miles. It's more feel than precision, the pace, despite the GPS watch strapped to his wrist. He doesn't rely entirely on Garmin's real-time data, as Chase does, resting his faith on Satellites 10,000 or more miles away to pinpoint his movement through Earth's din. It's a nice-to-have, a reference point to be taken with a grain of salt. Nothing more. Internal cues and ambient conditions tell Dillon all he needs to know.

"*Woooooowooowooo Wooooowooooo,*" Miles pleads as he flashes by the start/end point of the circuit roughly six and twelve minutes later, each time hushing her so as not to wake the guests, though one couple have appeared on the porch since his last pass-through, in bathrobes, holding mugs steaming with coffee and admiring his effort against the backdrop of the sunrise.

Dillon ratchets up the pace on the next beep's command, increasing his turnover rate, from eighty-eight steps per minute to ninety-two, working his way down to five-and-a-half-minute miles. He streaks by the same tall brown grass deadened by summer, the gnarled oak tree that branches out in various directions like an octopus, and the west-leaning wooden pump house, finessing the terrain as demanded, swiveling of hips through the S-curves, stutter-stepping to bridge the trench, tilting of the head away from low-hanging branches.

The sweat that beaded up on his forehead during the middle segment now forms rivulets, branching out in all directions. He licks his lips. The salty taste lingers on his tongue. Next loop, Dillon glances at his watch, the temptation too great to ignore: three minutes and change left. Now fifty-seven minutes and nine miles into his morning catharsis, working through the purifying stages—challenging to demanding to rigorous—he fiddles with the pace, nudging it faster. It isn't necessary or part of the plan or prudent, but he can't help himself, like a glutton for punishment, the slow burn of negative segment splits piling up and aching like an abscessed tooth that begs probing.

Another quick glance at his wrist: twenty-eight seconds to go. No body part screams, but tugging at the frayed mental thread does. This is why Miles has been left behind. He doesn't need company. He doesn't want company. He needs self reliance, to stretch himself mentally for the times every racer finds himself in: no-man's-land, the place where the gap between you and the next guy is too far to consider, or the gap behind is too great to threaten; or leading the race with the hounds chasing. Be you the hunter or the hunted, solitude requires mental resilience.

Beep, beep, beep, be— Dillon presses the Lap button on the watch, passively acknowledges the fastest single loop split to date on the display, and decelerates, his body and mind sighing, the promise of restoration on the horizon. He jogs until he reaches Miles and pats his right butt cheek.

"*Wooooowooowooo Woooooowoooo, Wooooowooowooo Woooooowoooo, Wooooo-wooowooo Woooooowoooo*," Miles says, running alongside him now.

"I know, I know." Dillon concedes that *he's* in the doghouse, and not for the first time.

"*Wooooowooowooo Woooooowoooo, Wooooowooowooo Woooooowoooo, Wooooo-wooowooo Woooooowoooo*," she continues on for the two warm-down loops and on into the BR&B.

Sunday Morning
Annadel Lore

"Gentlemen," Sir Jake says, commencing the official ceremony, "we have before us a new pair of footwear in need of proper initiation for their maiden run in Annadel."

Dillon's eyes shift from one guy to the next—Chase, Spencer, and Jim—waiting for the moment where someone bursts out laughing, no longer able to maintain the ruse. But no one strays from their stoic roles, Dillon's new Adidas road shoes sitting on top of a dented and scuffed-up silver platter he holds, standing in stocking feet behind Jake's truck at the Cobblestone Trailhead.

"Sir Jim, commence in preparing the Lake Illsanjo Basin elixir," Jake says.

Jim reaches inside an old gunnysack, extracting a dried mud cake the size of an irregular-shaped patio brick. He breaks off a piece and drops it into a bowl that, like the platter, has seen better days.

"Sir Chase," Jake says, "do us the honor of adding ancient drops of rainwater."

Chase produces an oversized beer jug many years removed from its bottling date, removes the stopper, and pours nonpotable water over the mud cake, sealing the bottle up afterward.

"Thank you, Sir Chase," Jake says. "Sir Spencer, will you do us the honor of mixing earth and water."

Spencer steps forward, pulls out a gardening trowel from the back of Jake's truck, pokes at the mud cake, breaking it up in the shallow water, and stirs it. The mud cake dissolves and turns a murky brown, chunks floating.

Dillon stands mesmerized, not entirely sure of the ritual unfolding before him. He's seen some funny initiation rites of passage in his day, like the time his freshman year at U-dub when the seniors from the cross-country team wedged pennies between the dorm-room door and the doorjamb from the outside while he and his roommate slept inside, rendering them jailed the next morning, causing them to miss the team van to the park for their Sunday-morning run and thereby incurring the wrath of the coach. But the current one takes the cake, well at least the mud cake.

"Gentlemen," Jake says, "the elixir before you brings to life the mud flats left wanting in the wake of 2008's Great Lake Illsanjo Spill Gate. Not since then has this once hidden chunk of earth been wetted. Today we reconstitute the history it once held, going back fifty years, and bestow it upon Dillon's virgin footwear, christening it with historical significance, an archaeological dig uncovering an ancient time and place, bearing witness to former Sonoma County running greats gone by, Aldridge, Jordan, Spina, Rodriquez, Trask, Laurie, Cox, Stamps, Bei, Sumpter, Conley, Luna, Byers . . . the list is as multifarious as it is illustrious."

Spencer has thoroughly mixed the muddy water and replaces the trowel in Jake's truck. Jim hands the bowl with the Lake Illsanjo Basin elixir to Jake, and takes a bow.

"Thank you, Sir Jim. Dillon, your task before you, should you choose to accept it"—Jake pauses a brief moment as perceptible smirks fill the other men's faces and, what Dillon perceives as thought bubbles, which he completes for them: *Mission Impossible*—"is to anoint your new shoes with the history and lore of Annadel Park. Do you accept Annadel's humble offering and accept 'Sir' appended to your given name?"

A handful of RERC club members, including Dale, run by the ceremony, commenting, "Looks like another J&J production." "Those two are classic." "Remember that time . . ."

"Less jabbering, more running," the group's caboose, Dale, adds.

Dillon decides he's too far down the proverbial trail to turn back now. He's never one to preserve new running shoes at all costs by foregoing trails, though sullying them before their first run is unprecedented—even breaking them in is often done around the house or at work, on carpet or tile, far removed from nature.

"I accept, Sir Jake," Dillon says, stepping forward with silver platter in hand. He gazes into the muddy water; a murky reflection ripples along the surface.

"Most excellent choice," Jake says, pulling from his own bag of tricks an old paintbrush.

Dillon wants to laugh, but doesn't. *How are these guys not busting up?*

Jake dips the brush into the Lake Illsanjo Basin elixir and swirls it around until it is thoroughly soaked and just as dark brown. Like a priest, he flicks the brush at each shoe in turn with the holy muddy water of Annadel, anointing Dillon's new $130 pair of shoes. Ordainment complete, Jake dries the brush with a towel and replaces it in his bag of tricks. "Sir Dillon, may your shoes never fail you . . . or your feet." Jake barely finishes before laughing, which opens the floodgates for Jim, Spencer, and Chase, and immediately Dillon.

"You guys are certifiable wackadoos," Dillon says, slipping his newly anointed shoes back on.

"Welcome to Club Wackadoos, Sir Dillon," Jim says. "Now, let's roll."

Beep. Beep. Beep.

"Shit! I lost the satellite again," Chase says as the others trot away.

A quarter mile up Channel Drive past the park entrance gate, the guys veer off to the right, up a steep, twisty single-track trail named North Burma, sorting themselves out single file where the trail narrows—Jim; Dillon; Chase and Spencer side by side until Spencer concedes his position; and Jake. Despite running easily, their heart rates skyrocket, limiting conversation to short bursts of words. Reduced to Twitter-length sentences, along a seasonal creek fed by a highland vernal pool, Jake and Jim explain to their newly initiated knight the inspiration for the shoe ritual: Back in 2008 park officials failed to completely close off the release valve, draining the lake down several feet and exposing a large portion of the bottom. During a Thursday-night run, Jake and Jim ran by the depleted lake, stopping to take it in, and ultimately came up with a zany idea—like many of their unusual activities and events—for how to make use of the dried-up mud cakes that were forming under the warm spring temperatures.

Once they scale the ascent, the short-burst conversation switches to Spencer's common law in-laws' visit, then returns to longer sentences along an undulating wetland segment that oscillates between complete coverage from overhanging trees and chaparral, to open meadows of wild grass, boulders, and tree stumps.

"He really said, 'running is waste of energy'?" Dillon asks.

"I felt like I'd stumbled into a catered intervention," Spencer says.

"We should start calling Maggie *Saint* Maggie," Jim says.

"Sir Spencer and Saint Maggie . . . it has a nice *ring* to it," Chase says. "Oh no, wait, there's no ring!"

Spence-speak.

"Life demands change, buddy," Chase says.

"There's a quote floating around the Internet that basically says change isn't necessary," Dillon says, stutter-stepping over two salamanders darting across the trail, "just as survival isn't mandatory."

"Don't tell Darwin," Jim says.

"Is this still about Molly?" Jake says.

"Who? Roller pig? Are you *nuts*?" Jim says manically fast.

"*There's Something About Mary*," Jake says. "And Molly."

"Molly?" Chase says.

"This one time, at running camp—" Jake says.

"*American Pie*," Chase says a beat before Jim. "Chase for the gold!"

"Spencer worked as a camp counselor one summer up in Humboldt," Jake says, "and he and this other counselor named Molly were out under the redwoods getting busy every night—"

"Quite the *woodsman*," Chase says.

"This conversation is making my head spin," Dillon says.

"Anyway, on the last night of camp all the counselors are seated together, talking about their respective dating situations, and Molly says she can't wait for marriage so she can let herself go. Spence freaked out."

"It's not that, Jakey."

"Are you still using Oprah as an example?" Jim says.

"Maybe."

"Did you ever watch her show?"

"Not really. I figured I'd appeal to the woman in Maggie. Everybody listens to Oprah."

"You know Oprah let herself go and struggled with her weight for a while."

"Perhaps not the best example."

"She did run a marathon," Dillon says.

"Chicago, right?" Chase says.

"Oprah once was quoted as saying," Jake says, "'Running is the greatest metaphor for life, because you get out of it what you put into it.'"

Oprah's daytime wisdom invites a Spence-speak, but none comes forth.

They reach the fire road, coast along it for a quarter mile, and veer left at the next trail juncture, continuing their Burma route though now on the south side—a steady, couple-mile climb along deliciously carved trails. Up ahead Dale comes into view and begins zigzagging, enduring comments about his stiff gait and slow pace, to which he counters, "You'd better keep running, wise guys," as they stride by him. On *his* trail, as he reminds them.

South Burma has recently been reshaped after a couple wet winters rendered many sections of it dicey at best, for hiker, biker, and runner alike. Horseshoes had created craters. Fat mountain-bike tires left wide muddy treads. Heavy rains exploited the ruts, creating streams, deepening and widening them. Now it's smooth and, if approached from the other direction, a downhiller's treat. Today the group settles into a long, sustained climb that's never too steep to disrupt their steady cadence, but steep enough to imperceptibly improve their running economy over time—making faster paces on the flats possible with less effort. It stokes the cardiovascular system, boosts their VO_2 capacity, and enhances the mitochondria factor—increasing quantity, advancing size—the desired effects for any endurance athlete and acquired entirely without thought during casual conversation.

"What's with the scratch marks, Chase . . . on your arm?" Jim says, attaching to Chase's heels. "Girl get rambunctious?"

"Dogma," Chase says.

Dillon glances over a shoulder. "You mean karma?"

"Dogma is his cat," Jim says.

"You have a cat? I thought—" Dillon says.

"Ironic, right?" Chase says.

"Why'd Dogma scratch you?" Jim says.

"He's not a fan of irony," Chase says.

"So . . ." Dillon says.

"A girl I dated this past summer left him behind when she—and I kid you not—ran away and joined the circus, so that I could, as she phrased it, 'reflect on our time together.'" Chase snorts. "She'd named him Eat Pray Love, but I rebranded him Eat Sleep Shit. After a while that was a mouthful, and I prefer dogs over fur balls . . . so, Dogma."

"She left you for a circus clown," Dillon says. "That had to hurt."

"Pfft."

They reach the highest point of the day, 1,400 feet, exiting diffuse forest sunlight, now exposed to forceful morning-sun rays, which brings a new challenge: negotiating a twisty downhill track that embraces the contours and natural obstacles of the land. Instead of relocating numerous hefty boulders, trail landscapers have worked the path around them, sometimes between them, letting man and animal negotiate them on their own terms.

Silently and deftly managing their way through the boulder-like alley, the guys descend into Buick Meadow, the first such human traffic of the morning, causing deer and fawn to glance up from their foraging. A few startled deer step away from the migrating quintet, while others track the direction of the threat and resume nibbling nature's offerings when the guys move farther away.

Chase has picked up the pace on the flatter terrain, charged to the front, and prepared for the Marsh Trail descent when a woman standing at the trail juncture asks, "Where does this trail go?" Her arm points in the direction the guys have come from. It may as well been a Spence-speak.

Chase groans, slowing to a stop beyond the woman and the group of Fit Kits clustered around her.

Beep.

"What's that?" he says, walking back to the woman.

The other guys have stopped as well, with Jim and Dillon wandering off to the side and out of view to "water the trees."

"We're trying to decide where to run next," she says.

"This is South Burma, takes you down to Richardson."

"How far is it?" a man from the group asks.

Chase presses a button on his watch. "One point nine seven miles."

"That's precise."

"What's the best way back to Spring Lake?" the other woman says.

"Depends on how much farther you need to run?"

Chase's answer spawns a spirited conversation among the five Fit Kits, during which Jake turns to view Buick Meadow, watching the sun slowly roll up the meadow's shadows for the day, revealing additional wildlife: turkeys, rabbits, and squirrels.

They all speak at once: "I only need another ninety-five minutes." "We've already run five point ten miles." "My watch says three and a half miles." "You forgot to restart it after our last stop." "Shoot. And now it's running while we're standing here." *Beep.* "I need ten more miles, guys." "How much time would it take to get back to where we parked?" One guy pulls out his smart phone and calculates what their current pace has been up till that point. "Our average pace so far is 11:26." "But that was mostly uphill." "We'll be faster on the way back . . ."

By this point Chase turns away from the discombobulated conversation, one that is irritating him to no end, to join Jake, but his movement, as well as Jim and Dillon's return, catches the Fit Kits' attention.

"What do you think, shirtless guy?" a man says, the tallest and most overdressed of the Fit Kits: thin jacket over a long-sleeved shirt and long running tights.

"His Native American name is Guy Who Runs Sans Shirt," Jim says.

"*Dances with Wolves,*" Jake says.

"Pfft." Chase faces the Fit Kits. "First, run based on miles, not minutes or hours—"

"My coach says to run by time." "I prefer distance." "*Time* goes by faster for me." "But having a mile goal makes you *run* faster." And so it goes.

"Mileage goals force you to focus and run a consistent pace throughout," Chase continues. "Adds accountability to the equation. Duration goals allow you to run all willy-nilly."

"Willy-nilly?" Dillon says.

Chase shrugs and rolls his eyes. "Like this conversation." He turns as if ready to resume running.

"Running by time does have its benefits," Jake says. "Instead of focusing on a set distance, it allows you to focus on your effort."

"If Jack goes for a five-mile run, and Jill goes for a forty-minute run, who gets to the pail of water first?" Jim says.

"Ten minutes left in a run is an absolute time parameter, whereas one more mile to run is an unknown quantity, time-wise," Spencer says.

"So, Jack fell down, and Jill tumbled after him . . ." Dillon says. "I always hated those math word problems in high school."

"Time for the body, mileage for the mind," Jake says.

Buick Meadow begins to empty, wildlife slowly wandering off into the dense foliage, moving on with their day while the guys stand over the carcass of the topic.

"Distance forces pace," Chase says.

"Why didn't Jill have a crown?" Jim says. "Did Steve Harvey announce the wrong winner and take it away from her?"

"The body doesn't recognize distance, only the time *and* effort it spends exercising," Spencer says. "It's six of one, half a dozen of the other."

"Hold on a minute," Dillon says. "Having a fixed distance provides visual feedback; you can *see* the finish. But feedback for time is discontinuous; you can't see the finish without constantly checking your watch. Your mind perceives each variable very differently."

Irritated, Chase says, "No matter how you slice it, the missing *variable* is 'pace.' Without it the argument is moot—"

"Where'd the Fit Kits go?" Spencer says.

The guys turn toward where they had come and spot the last of the Fit

Kits disappearing up the boulder-like alley and Dale coming into view.

"That's humbling," Jim says, scratching his head.

"Where do you think we lost them?" Chase says.

"Somewhere around Jack and Jill fetching the water pail," Spencer says.

Beep. Beep. Beeeep.

"Speaking of water, did you see the pack on the tall guy's back?" Chase says. "There must've been one hundred ounces in it!"

"It's called a *Camelbak* for a reason," Jim says.

"I know, but wow!" Chase says. "He's packing enough water to last the entire day. That's like twelve cups' worth."

"Slosh, slosh, slosh . . . that's what my stomach does when I drink too much," Dillon says.

"Perhaps he has a high sweat rate," Jake says.

"He didn't look all pitted out," Jim says, coasting back under a protective leafy canopy, the sun backlighting them.

"The sport-drink industry sure did a number on endurance athletes with *their* claims that the body's thirst mechanism is faulty," Dillon says. "You know, 'if you wait until you're thirsty it's too late. Drink, drink, drink.' What a crock."

"And it's that mantra that gave rise to a *very* modern-day problem of overhydrating," Chase says. "It was unheard-of back in the '70s."

"'Hyponatremia' is the medical term," Spencer says. "Scary stuff."

"Someone died in the Boston Marathon because of it. They were encouraged to drink at every mile," Jim says.

"Like all the other overindulgences in our society," Chase says.

"Tim Noakes wrote a book, *Waterlogged*, that showed hydration recommendations were based on outdated and flawed research," Spencer says.

"He authored *The Lore of Running*, right?" Chase says.

"The runner's Bible; one in the same."

"Who is he?" Dillon says.

"South African scientist, whose research basically throws corporations under the bus by debunking their self-serving, in-house research claims," Spencer rattles off.

"Tell us how you really feel," Jake says.

"He found that there is no correlation between fluid consumption and hydration, and the occurrence of heatstroke. It's the intensity of the effort that spikes the core temperature, not the duration of the activity. You're more likely to get heatstroke from a 5K than a marathon."

"I take it you read his book."

"Last year, Zac started bringing a water bottle to the track, drinking from it after every interval. I told him it was actually slowing him down. I eventually convinced him with Noakes's research."

"Eat when you're hungry. Drink when you're thirsty. Sleep when you're tired," Jake says. "Buddhist proverb"

"Come race day, run like hell. Chase Brandon, Buddhist proverb addendum."

"Now I'm thirsty," Dillon says.

"Anybody have an extra energy gel?" Jim says.

"I need to pee," Spencer says.

Chase groans and stops. *Beep.* "Are we stopping? Are we stopping?! Are we STOPPING?! There's no stopping! There's no stopping in running!"

"*A League of Their Own,*" Jim and Jake say together as Spencer ducks behind a tree.

Week 38 Training Summary			
	Long Run	Mileage Total	Comments
Dillon	21	74	Tired from workload and extra miles. Good week.
Chase	20.67	64	Feeling good about XC! Dillon could be tough
Spencer	21	68	Visit from James and Joyce curtailed more mileage
Jim	20	44	Doris's mom isn't doing well
Jake	20	70	Fall is upon us, my favorite time of the year

Week 4
September 21

Monday Early Afternoon
Runners' Porn

"Wow, this place rocks!" Chase says as Dillon shows him the media lounge at the BR&B. Chase stands with his hands on his hips and scans the walls, taking in posters of world-class runners Steve Prefontaine, Frank Shorter, Billy Mills, Lynn Jennings, Doris Brown, Deena Kastor, Emil Zátopek, Lasse Viren, Jim Ryun, Derek Clayton, Ron Clarke, Ryan Hall, Henry Rono, and many more. Between the gaps of the posters, bib numbers are tacked up from various races around the globe: the 100th running of the Dipsea (#359); the 100th running of the Boston Marathon (#1972); the Peachtree 10K (#421); the London Marathon (#918); the Lilac Bloomsday (#1441); Comrades marathon (#41719); the Western States 100-miler (#238); Cascade Runoff (#1); Rock-'n'-Roll San Diego Marathon (#236); Penofin 10K (#85); Sound-to-Narrows (#206); and New York Marathon (#2001), to name a few.

Commemorative long- and short-sleeve T-shirts, of the cotton variety, nearly a thing of the past, hang from a clothesline strung high along one wall. On them are long enduring, famed races, Penn Relays, Mt Sac XC Invitational, Hood-to-Coast Relay, Pre Classic, Kinney Cross-country Championships, Rainbo (bread) Breakfast Run Marathon, and the Terry Fox Run, among others.

On a towering bookcase that spreads six feet wide, two middle shelves showcase the evolution of finishing medals over the years, from small medallions with simple inscription to today's overly large bling—more the attraction than the event itself for many who enter. Two other shelves hold videos and DVDs of running-oriented movies and documentaries, from *Chariots of Fire* and *Running Is Life* with Lass Viren to *Prefontaine* and Jim Ryun's black-and-white video of the first state high school track meet to host a sub-4-minute mile. Bud Greenspan's prolific Olympic Games collection covers several slots. The rest of the shelves host numerous books on running, both fiction and nonfiction, from *The Loneliness of the Long-Distance Runner* to *Born to Run* and every title in between.

On another wall, celebrating the democratization of self-portraitures, hangs a large thirty-two-inch digital picture frame where previous guests have uploaded before-race, mid-race, and post-race selfies.

"This room is like porn for runners!" Chase walks over to the magazine table, picks up a *Track & Field* issue from the mid-'70s with Frank Shorter on the cover, and thumbs through it, soaking in the black-and-white photos from yesteryear. "You're not old enough to have run some of these races or have all this memorabilia. How'd you come by it all?"

"My college roommate's father was a runner and huge track-and-field fan. After he died, I was helping my friend clean out the garage and we found most of this. His father used to show me items from his collection every Christmas when I visited during college, but I had no idea he had all this. My friend didn't want it and gave it to me. My ex hated it . . . tons of boxes stacked in the garage. She wanted me to toss it or at least sell it on eBay. I couldn't bring myself to part with it."

Chase is deep into his kind of porn until a woman's voice competes for his attention. "Hi, Chasey."

He turns to see Terri standing in the archway to the media lounge. "Hi," Chase says, dropping the magazine. "How's it going?"

"Enjoying all the porn?" she says with a mischievous grin.

Rarely one to be thrown for a loop, Chase freezes momentarily, the recent RERC BBQ flashing before his eyes. "Oh, yeah . . . this room is awesome."

"Dillon, all the rooms are ready except Athens. I just put those sheets in the dryer."

"I'll finish it. It's unoccupied tonight anyway."

"I'm going to hit the sauna, then head out. I'll see you in the morning," she says, turning to leave. "Bye, Chasey." She glances back long enough for him to catch her sultry eyes.

Chase stands there unable to take his eyes off her ass as it disappears through the kitchen.

"Dogma got your tongue?" Dillon says.

"Yeah, that's it."

"*Woooooowooowooo Woooooowoooo*," Miles says, running up to Chase.

Staring at Miles, Chase imagines Terri in the sauna, wrapped in a fluffy white towel, skin warm to the touch, beads of sweat forming.

"Let's hit the vineyards," Dillon says, turning toward the front doors.

"Yeah, let's."

Dillon and Miles break into a trot while Chase sheds his shirt and configures his watch. "I'll catch up in a minute." Thirty seconds later he strides out and spots Miles up ahead impatiently waiting. As soon as he reaches her, she turns and ducks under the wooden fence. "*Woooooowooowooo Woooooowoooo.*"

"Okay, okay, Miles," he says, limboing his way through the slates. "You're more demanding than Dogma."

Chase catches the slower-moving Dillon and the trio hits the main tractor-wide dirt path that wraps entirely around the 1,300-acre vineyard, giving them a flat eight-mile run through the Russian River Appellation. Chase glances at his watch after they adjust the pace and settle into their easy recovery run.

"Fast enough?" Dillon says.

"Anything between seven and seven fifteen is good," he says. "You sure we're okay running out here?" Chase scans the area as if he fears local vineyard thugs will jump out and stomp them and bury their bodies between the rows and rows of neatly arranged Pinot Noir and Chardonnay vines.

"Rich Beardsworth owns the land. We met when I first bought the inn.

He'd stop by every day to see how things were going. I first thought he was just bored, but he really embraced the concept. He struck a deal with me: if I featured his label, he'd comp me some cases. I said throw in running access to his vineyards and we're golden."

Chase stops searching for the wine boogeyman and instead soaks in the vibe of running through the lush vineyards, listening to Dillon elaborate on how they till the path during the winter, which provides an unstable surface and helps a runner build strength, and when spring and summer arrive, the same path is packed down, allowing faster and faster paces for the summer racing season.

"How have you been promoting your place?" Chase asks after they've covered the beauty, tranquility, and functional quality of vineyard running.

"Mainly target marketing online with Google and Yahoo! ads. I did register the inn with a couple online bed-and-breakfast directories."

"That's a good start, but limited in what you can display in small JPEGs. This type of product/service is very visual. You need to convey it in a grander way, create escapism like no other." Chase sweeps an outstretched arm back and forth to punctuate the point. "Do you have a website?"

"Yeah, but it's not very professional, and to your point there aren't very many pictures on it. Mostly descriptions, rates, and so forth."

"Definitely need to polish that up. Brochures?"

"Just business cards."

"Okay, I know a guy . . . actually it's a high school kid, a runner that Spencer coaches: Zac. He maintains the club's website. He's good. Brochures I can help you out with too, and I know a guy from my days in New York who can assist with some international presence. Europeans will love this concept."

The trio slants left where the fence line did the same.

"That sounds good," Dillon says, "but I'll have to scale some of it down, you know, budget-wise."

"Nonsense. I'm sure we can work something out. You have a wine connection, and a place to house and entertain guests."

Dillon chuckles. "This area sure loves to barter. Jake offered landscaping with the same suggestion."

"That's one of the charms of this cow town. I'm sure Jim can assist you with your accounting needs."

"Cow town?"

"You really shouldn't call it that if you're not from the area, but coming from New York it really felt like a cow town to me. When I moved here I thought I was landing in wine country. You know, classy people sipping wine and all that shit. Only after a few months did I realize 'wine country' meant this is where they *grow* the grapes. It's very agricultural. It's all good now, though. Besides, the Clo the Cow billboards are brilliant. They're how I heard about this area, actually. 'Clo for the Gold' is my fave."

Dillon nods. "I hadn't given it much thought. I like the peace and solitude."

Based on previous interactions with Dillon, Chase adds "escape" to Dillon's pensive list. Chase can't help but size up the open team's newest arrival, his competitive nature. Would he challenge Chase's top spot in the club? Dillon certainly looked the part, and his prowess on their Sunday runs in Annadel demonstrated his fitness. But racing fit? Competitively fit? *Now, that's the question. His online Athlinks profile should give me a sense of his racing history.*

"How'd you land in Sonoma County?" Chase says, passing by a pair of red barns, tractors and neatly stacked grape bins resting inside each. "I'd thought Napa would've been your first stop, given your Newport Beach roots. Apples to apples as it were."

"I was tired of apples," Dillon says. "I read a lot of Jack London in high—"

"Me too!"

"Yeah? *Valley of the Moon* spoke to me."

"Rural self-reliance, I get it. *Call of the Wild* is my favorite. Read it every year."

"Tale of survival—"

"*Woooooowooowooo Wooooowooooo?*"

"No, Miles, he's not going to fight you," Dillon says.

Chase chuckles. "You're right about Napa. It presents an upscale theme park–esque wine event; their Wine Train is a good example. Sonoma offers the wine *experience* wrapped in rustic authenticity. There, it's a business; here, it's a lifestyle."

"Suits me just fine."

The trio ventures left again where sunlight flickers off colored foil ribbons hung along the vines, an attempt to dissuade birds from eating the grapes.

"So, your place is nicely ensconced in the vineyards with close proximity to downtown and Annadel, all great hooks for potential guests. The Sonoma wine-country aspect alone is gold, and toss in your running-themed accommodations and you can get a ton of mileage from it. Also, you might consider expanding your demographic to cyclists. They spend shitloads of money on travel, and we have a few high-profile cycling and triathlon events in the area that attract athletes from all over the world. Heck, I'm envisioning add-ons like sherpa packages for some of the bigger events in the county, like Vineman, the Santa Rosa Marathon, Kenwood 10K, Levi's GranFondo . . . throw in a shuttle service to and from the event, some on-course pics, treat them like elites, they'll go crazy for services like that."

"Those are some great ideas. Ambitious, but great."

"It's what I do."

"I also want to host guest lectures from time to time, like have a coach come in and discuss training, or a shoe guy come in and talk shoes, or a yoga or Pilates instructor come in and give a free session. I already have a masseuse that comes by."

"Yeah, yeah, those are all great ideas. Spence would love to talk coaching. He's basically a guru, versed in just about any training program ever devised, and as he would say, 'Coaching is the cornerstone to success.' Dey's Percy Cerutty, Lydiard, Vigil, Hudson, Canova, Daniels. And Bowerman, Elliot, McMillan, Larsen, Benson—"

"Okay, Bubba. *Forrest Gump*, got it," Dillon says, shaking his head. "You too?"

Chase chuckles. "Once you're networked into the club, I know they'll support this and can help out with special events. This is exciting! Sure beats pawning off box wine."

"Wine comes in a—"

"Don't get me started."

The trio work their way along the last of the five main sections that define the vineyard's irregularly shaped polygon perimeter, ducking back under the wooden fence and onto the BR&B property, where they come to a stop, walking the rest of the way in. *Beep.* Chase saves the data from the run and scrolls through the menu choices to view the stats.

Dillon chuckles.

Chase glances up and grins. "I know." He returns his attention back to the Garmin. "No different than people checking their Facebook status every five minutes, though. At least this has a *practical* application."

Wednesday Late Afternoon
High School Cross-Country Tri-Meet at Spring Lake

"Nice job, Zac," Spencer says, standing at the one-and-half-mile mark as Zac glides by slack-jawed and with minimal head bounce. "You have at least two hundred yards on the next guy. Don't press."

"Go, Zac!" Donna shouts as she jogs up to Spencer. "Nice legs, babe!"

"Still warming down?"

"All done now, Coach."

"Good," Spencer says, glancing at the XC scoring app on his smart phone. He taps the SRHS icon. He peers back toward the other runners now coming into focus along the Fisherman's Trail. He catches sight of the jersey colors and taps the corresponding team names in their ordered sequence, which stores each runner's current placement and calculates each team's projected finish. With three squads competing and three race iterations in play, the app tracks the two races that matter to him: SRHS versus Maria Carrilla, and SRHS versus Montgomery. "Mind if I ask what yours and Zac's . . . *relationship status* is? I don't need details, just a general idea of what's going on."

"'Relationship status,'" Donna says. "Is that what *you kids* are calling it these days?" Her toothy smile embarrasses Spencer. "We've kissed if that's—"

"Naw, naw, naw," Spencer sputters out, on the verge of covering his ears. "Spare me the details."

Donna laughs. "Such a prude."

"Nice job, Gavin. Stay with that group." Gavin is nestled in the second pack of five. Spot two. "Let's go, Galligan. Get your head up and focus on Gavin." Spot six.

"Come on, guys!" Donna shouts. "Looking sweet!"

"Lift your knees, Rodger," Spencer says. "Stride out on this flat stretch. Nice Job." Spot eight.

"Is that a new timing app, Coach?"

"It tabulates a running team score."

"How are they doing?"

"Not enough data yet. So are you two dating?"

"We did over the summer, but I wanted to keep things simple, so we talked it over. I like how things are when we're just friends. Way to go, guys! He understood, I hope, anyway. Besides, his parents are getting a divorce so he's got *that* to deal with, and it's going to be a mess . . . those two are always arguing. Woo-hoo, Dan!"

"Nice job, Dan. You have three guys on your shoulder. You know what to do across the dam if they're still with you." Spot twelve. "Let's go, Oz!" Spencer shouts as Oz comes into view fifty yards away. "Stay focused. You're our fifth man today." Spot seventeen.

"How's my mane, Coach?" Oz says as he passes by, running a hand through his shaggy mop atop his head.

"Run, Oz, run!" Donna shouts. Oz flips up a rear flap to his running shorts, flashing a glute. "Uh, baby!"

"Don't encourage him. He needs to start applying himself. Nice job, Jonathan. Don't look behind you. Work your way up to the next group. You're a miler . . . tear 'em apart next time through here."

"Give Oz a break; he's only a sophomore. What's with the 'mane' comment?"

"During warm-ups he asked which guys he should try to beat since there are three teams racing at once. I told him to 'run dumb like a horse.'"

"Horses are dumb?"

"'Don't think, just run' is the meaning of the phrase."

"I don't get it. Do you have enough data yet?"

"Should be an easy win today. During a horse race, horses don't think; they just race. Actually the original quote is 'Act like a horse. Be dumb. Just run' by Jumbo Elliott."

"Jumbo . . . Jumbo . . . that's an odd name. *Jumbo.*"

"Nickname for James. Now, go get some sweats on before you chill down. It cools down quick this time of the year. Good race today."

"Okay, Coach Prude. We did other stuff—"

"Naw, naw, naw . . ." This time Spencer covers his ears.

"Okay, settle down, wild ones," Spencer says, standing in front of the orange-and-black contingent gathered around the lakeside picnic tables that act as base camp for the squads. "Oz, stop clowning around and sit."

"Just *horsing* around, Coach," Oz says, his smile big.

Groans and chuckles rise from the group, along with, "You stud, Oz."

Spencer lets Oz strut back and forth like a Kentucky Derby winner a couple times. "Okay, Oz, that's enough. Don't make me call the vet to put you down." Oz flops down on the bench. "Nice job today to all of you. First race of the season is under our belts and we know where we stand fitness-wise. For those of you who struggled toward the end, take heart in the fact that I didn't rest you up for this meet. As I mentioned last week, we're going to train through some of the league meets. Next week we're racing at Foothill Park against Windsor and Rancho. Rancho will be our first challenge for the guys, so we'll lighten the load beforehand. Okay, be sure to stretch good this evening and ice anything that aches. Off you go."

While the teams gather up their belongings, Spencer pulls out his cell phone and calls Maggie.

"How'd the meet go?" she says upon answering.

"The boys won easily. The girls didn't fare as well. Sarah and Julie graduating last year effectively made this a rebuilding year for them. Donna is showing some potential."

"And Zac?"

"He cruised it. Donna told me that his parents are getting divorced."

"Like he needs more on his plate. He's too much in his head as it is. Did you ask Donna if they're dating?"

"Doesn't sound like it, but dating these days seems complicated."

Maggie snickers, eliciting a Spence-speak.

"I received another rejection email today," Maggie says.

"Which agency?"

"Beachcomber Reads. They're the small boutique in Santa Cruz."

"Did they say why?"

"Let's see . . . I still have it up on the screen . . . 'Dear Maggie, Please forgive this impersonal note regarding your query, which I have carefully considered but must decline. As our agency receives a tremendous number of queries, we are unable to respond to each submission individually, but we thank you for the opportunity to review your work. I hope you will not be discouraged by this reply; I am limited by my own preferences both in terms of content and style when reviewing a manuscript, but agents' tastes vary widely, as with all readers, and so I encourage you to continue querying your manuscript until you find the right person to be its champion. With best wishes, Thomas Harper.'"

"Sounds like the others. 'To be its champion'? That's not inspired writing."

"Nope."

"I know you don't want to hear this again, but maybe it's time to go the indie route."

"I don't know, self-publishing . . . my parents won't understand it if they can't find it in a bookstore."

"Something to consider. It's a great story. Linda raved about it, and she thought *The Time Traveler's Wife* was vapid. At least it gets out there. Let the public discover you if the agents won't."

"How far are you running tonight? I have dinner ready to go."

"Only an hour. I'm doing ladders."

"Have a good run. Love you."

"Love you too. Cheer up. You're a great writer. The world just doesn't know it yet."

"Okay, *Coach*."

Spencer replaces his phone in his small day pack, cinches it up, swings it over his shoulders, and adjusts the chest straps. He lifts each leg in turn onto the picnic bench, retying his shoes. Once set, he starts off across the parking lot, waving to a coach from a rival school, reversing the finishing stretch of the cross-country course, heading east at warm-up pace. Two miles in, he accelerates until he hits his perceived 3K race pace—9:01—holds it for sixty seconds, and backs off. He jogs at a shade under an eight-minute-mile pace for another sixty seconds, accelerates again toward his 3K pace, this time holding the effort for two minutes, and then shuts it down. Today's ladders will follow the 1, 2, 3, 4, 3, 2, 1, 2, 3, 4 format, each step of the ladder requiring an equal amount of recovery with a two-minute cap, and as the ascent reaches the upper rungs the pace slows, shifting toward his current 10K race pace of 30:48—though well off his college PR of 29:59.

While the workout is part of his current marathon training cycle, integrating a modest amount of speed training early in his ramp-up to CIM—California International Marathon—in December, it also reminds him physiologically and mentally of the intensity that cross-country racing demands. With the season kicking off soon, his plan is to "run through" all the meets as part of his training, a dilemma he has resolved in his desire for an Olympic Trials qualifying time over his overall contribution to the RERC's grand prix efforts. Of course, he decided this before Dillon's arrival. But for the time being the miles dissolve methodically and resolutely, much like the sun behind him.

Thursday After Work
Home Course Preview

"Sorry, I'm late," Jim says, slowing to a walk, approaching Dillon and Jake, who stand in the start/finish area of the cross-country venue where the RECR

Open will be held on Saturday to kick off their season. "Doris needed help setting up her booth at the street fair downtown."

"No problem, Jimbo," Jake says. "I won't tell Spence."

Jim's version of a Spence-speak raises more concerns than anything else.

"You should get that checked out," Jake says, grinning and patting Jim on the back until the hacking stops. "I was giving Dillon an overview of the course."

"Seems kind of silly, doesn't it, that we preview the course every year, considering we've raced it dozens of times?" Jim says. "It's been a tradition of ours since junior high. Spring Lake was Jake's first race." Jim strikes a theatrical gazing-into-the-distance pose. "The Great 'Cup' Escape."

Jim and Jake chuckle but offer no explanation.

"Ooooookay . . . It sounds like I've run most all the sections at some point, and Jake said it basically consists of three loops, a big loop, a small loop, then repeat the big loop."

"Yup. Let's roll," Jim says, walking over to the official start line that has yet to be chalked out. "We start back here and head that way." He points east, toward the boat ramp. *Beep, beep.* "It's a wide start, so crowding is not a problem off the line, but the footing is terrible."

Dillon casts his view downward the entire fifty yards of pockmarked grass, dirt, and weeds, until they reach the boat-launch parking lot. "You said it's a little longer than 5K?"

"Three point three six, to be exact," Jim says, "though Chase claims whoever wheeled it out must've been drunk because his Garmin never records more than three point three one."

"I can live with that margin of error."

"I'd say there are two areas that require some strategy," Jake says. "The first is where we met along the Fisherman's Trail. Screaming off the dam descent you make two tight turns and the trail narrows, so you'll need to be in front of anyone close by otherwise they'll bog you down. The trail does eventually open up, but it'll take extra effort to pass them, especially the last time through. It comes right before the one- and three-mile marks."

Dillon nods, running through the parking area that rises and extends long enough that he envisions the field stringing out. It's been a couple years since his last cross-country meet down in Orange County, competing for the Newport Track Club, but already the competitive urges percolate in him, his mind putting together a strategy that will be unique to this course and useless on another, a facet that makes the sport of cross-country more appealing to him than racing on the oval track, which he's never been as proficient on despite his talent. Road racing exacts some strategy based on course location, but because they race on streets, with their prescribed width and measured gradients, it makes it less critical. But cross-country, with the added benefit of team competition, raises the stakes considerably, making it beneficial to preview a course so that one can formulate a strategy. Even the official 3.36 miles is an approximation given the less precise nature of trails.

As the trio recons the course, Jim and Jake point out areas that require, at faster speeds, more caution, where the pack usually bunches up, and unusual aspects of the course, especially the dam on the northern portion of the course that they now cross, a route that Dillon has not previously encountered. Reaching the end of the dam, Dillon peers beyond it, searching for where the trail picks back up, but finds nothing. His confusion clears when Jim and Jake veer right and straight down the forty-five-degree slope. He follows suit, stutter-stepping, skidding, and braking as much as he can to prevent an end-over-end tumble and painfully embarrassing face plant. Jim runs in that just-controlled manner, while Jake glides down, disappearing at the base into a cluster of trees, like a deer in a hurry.

"You're kidding, right?" Dillon says to Jim at the base.

Jim grins. "And we get to do it *twice*. We call it Double Down Dam."

"Catchy," Dillon says, shaking his head. He's raced on some unique courses in his day but never has he seen a section like the Double Down Dam descent, especially the way it shoots them blindly onto the bike path, where they needed to make a hard right.

Dillon and Jim catch up to Jake twenty yards later, shunting to the left, along the first section where moving ahead of those close by pays dividends. As Dillon finds himself in last position, he realizes that timing the dam descent, negotiating the bike path, and hitting the pinched trail requires some thought. You can conceivably recover from poor positioning the first time through, but not the second, where less than a half mile remains to sort out the final finishing order.

"It's flat and hard packed along here so if you have anything left in the legs, you can really roll," Jim says. "The other clubs won't be as familiar with the finish, so it's good home-field advantage."

"What's the . . . is it PA, competition like?"

"Pacific Association . . . very strong," Jim replies. "Arguably one of the stronger associations in the country. The open division is pretty one-sided for the top team spot. The Agras squad out of Yolo County is a sponsored team and recruits some of the best talent throughout Northern California and Nevada.

"Spencer calls them 'hired guns,' but that's an exaggeration," Jake says. "Like I mentioned before, he can be territorial when it comes to club matters."

"How's our club faired?"

"In the Open? Not that well," Jim says. "We've certainly never won the entire series, that's for sure. We've pulled out a single race win here and there. I think the highest we've ever placed in the grand prix is third. It's tough to compete against a club that can put all their scorers in the top twenty, and three in the top five."

"We've won the master's division, both men and women, and we've won the senior and super-senior divisions a few times over the years," Jake says.

Once back to the boat-ramp parking lot and jumping onto the bike path that meanders around the start/finish area and toward the other dam, Jim points to where the finish chute will stand.

"What about the other clubs? How many show up?"

"Let's see," Jim says, "there's the River City Renegades out of Sacramento, East Bay Runners down in Oakland, Dipseans down in Marin, Strawberry Hill Harriers . . ."

"South Bay," Jake says.

"The Chico and Humboldt clubs from up north put teams together from time to time. There are more, but those are the more competitive ones. You may have noticed in Spencer's weekly email there are a number of meets to choose from, so not every team runs every race since only five are needed. But it does leave the opportunity for individuals and teams to maximize grand prix points if they race them all. It makes for a long season, but it certainly helps out. Of course, even if you're tied for the top spot after racing all the meets, things usually shake out at the PA Championships."

"I noticed the club national meet on the schedule too. Do you guys run that one often?"

"Spencer puts it on the schedule every year, and he usually goes, along with a couple master guys. But the rest of us don't. After a long fall of tying up Saturdays, and some Sundays, racing, it's hard to convince significant others for a multiday road trip. The years they're held in Golden Gate Park, we run."

"I ran the one in Frisco back in '06. The course was sloppy that year."

"Colorado?" Jake says with a smirk.

"Lovely place this time of year," Jim adds.

Dillon glances at Jim and Jake, smiles, and chuckles. "I take it people around here don't like the shortened version of San Francisco."

Jim and Jake serenade Dillon with a golf clap.

"*Men at Work* for those keeping score at home," Jim says.

"Duly noted . . . dudes."

Leaving the pavement behind they ascend the southern dam.

"What kind of times do the winners generally post?"

Jake and Jim's combined grin and exchanged glance, along with the hushed aura left in the wake of Dillon's hubris, chafes the underbelly of his self-consciousness, but that's simply his mind-set: just about any race he enters, he considers himself a contender until proven otherwise. "You know, for perspective."

"My PR on this course is 17:33, and I was tenth that year, if that helps," Jim says.

"The race director told me that Harris James pre-registered. He's won it a few times, all under seventeen minutes," Jake says. "Chris Schillings usually shows up. He holds the course record . . ."

"Sixteen forty-four," Jim says. "Chase has won it a time or two."

"So competitive, then," Dillon says.

Jake and Jim nod.

The dam fully negotiated they hang a sharp right and embark on a three-quarter-mile-long trek over rolling and, in spots, technical terrain, alternating between single and double tracks that eventually merge with the top of the boat-ramp parking lot. From there it's an encore of the Double Down Descent, and a final push along the Fisherman's Trail into the finish.

While Jim and Jake toss out bits and pieces of course insight, Dillon formulates his plan of attack. His finishing kick will not be reliable this early in the season, especially after coming off a summer where high mileage and fartlek predominated his training diet. So that means he'll need to work the middle miles, like the rolling segment they're on now, to separate from as many as possible to avoid getting out kicked at the end by the milers like Chase. The middle miles are often the toughest for those who aren't well conditioned or mentally tough. After a typical fast start and first mile and half, as this course provides, anaerobic systems will show early season strain, legs will balk, and abrupt uphills will push back inattentive competitors. Their lost momentum can be exploited by accelerating the last yards to the top, gapping them, leveraging gravity's pull where one hill folds over into the next one.

"The Agras will be here on Saturday, as well as Strawberry Hill, and the Chico Running Club, which has put together a strong team this year with a couple Chico State alumni," Jim says, slowing to a stop at the not-yet-set-up finish line. "They should be able to give the Agras a run for the money."

Dillon isn't familiar with the competition in Northern California like he had been in Southern California, and really has no idea how he will fare up here, but that doesn't diminish the excitement of getting back into racing again after six months of relatively unstructured training and toiling away on the BR&B, retooling his life. The fact that he can run with a club sweetened the deal, and the growing bond he's developing with Jake, Jim, Chase, and Spencer enhances it immensely. Racing with a new team on new courses with new competition suits him.

"I need to head back to the BR&B," Dillon says. "What time is the open race?"

"Women at nine a.m., the master men at nine forty-five, and the open men at ten thirty," Jim says.

"Terri can cover for me if I need to leave before breakfast is finished," Dillon says, turning to leave. "Thanks again for the course preview, guys. I can't wait to mix it up again."

Dillon strides off, though floating better describes the movement, the tingle of competitive anticipation—fear, excitement, panic, bliss—diving into the chaos of uncertainty, measuring himself against others, will against will . . . that's what he's been missing since moving north, an acceptable way to express an array of emotions that doesn't require long talks about why he's feeling this way or that way.

Friday Night
Reading, Resting, and Learning

Jake lies stretched out on the couch wearing running shorts and a RERC club sweatshirt in the quiet living room at the homestead, his head propped up by a faded decorative pillow, an open paperback in his left hand, the hour hand on the old grandfather clock in the corner nearing Roman numeral IX. He turns a page, and as he does, he catches sight of Robyn marching toward him wearing a pair of Linda's hospital scrubs and toting a small duffel bag. "What are you up to, sweetie?" He smiles at the many folded cuffs she's performed on the pants and top to accommodate her small frame. "Aren't you supposed to be getting ready for bed?"

"Mom wants me to make sure your vi-tals are okay before you race tomorrow," she says, setting the Kaiser Permanente bag on the coffee table. She unsnaps the flap and opens it, producing a toy stethoscope.

"Mom's not home from her shift yet." Putting Robyn to bed entails a three-act drama with an epilogue or three before the final curtain.

"Okay, it was me," she says as she hangs the stethoscope around her neck, "but I want to practice." She pulls out a tongue depressor. "Open wide and say ahhhhhhh."

Jake rests the book on his lap, bookmarking the spot with a finger. "Eeeeeeeeeeee."

"No, silly, ahhhhh. And stick out your tongue."

"That's not nice to do, stick out your tongue."

"It's okay. I'm a nurse, so it doesn't count as being bad."

Jake sticks his tongue out and makes the requested 'ahhhhh sound, after which Robyn places a plastic depressor on his tongue and peers down his throat, shining a tiny flashlight inside. Once satisfied, she removes the depressor and places it in a Ziploc bag. "This goes to the lab, stat."

"Do you know what 'stat' means?"

"Everybody does, Daddy. It means *now.*"

"So if I tell you it's time to go to bed, stat, you'd have to go to bed *now.*"

"No silly. It only works if you're wearing this uniform." She points to the top's floral print.

Act one.

"I see."

She grasps his hand, turns it palm side up, and wraps her delicate fingers around his wrist. She counts under her breath while staring at the grandfather clock. Ten seconds later she releases his hand and scribbles a note in her *Agent Carter* notebook.

"Okay, lift your shirt so I can read your heart." She places the ear buds into her ears, brings the stethoscope's diaphragm close to her mouth, blows across it, and applies it to his exposed chest.

"You *read* books, sweetie. You *listen* to hearts."

"Why can't you do both?"

Jake grins as she moves the diaphragm randomly around his chest. "How am I looking?"

"Your chest is scruffy. Now, cough."

Jake burps instead.

"Daddy, that's gross." She pinches her nose with her free hand. "It smells like pot roast and carrots." She scrunches her face like a prune.

Jake lets out a cough, and a second one upon request.

"It's past your bedtime, sweetie. Time to go brush your pot-roast-and-carrot teeth."

"I had chocolate ice cream with strawberries on top for dessert. See?"

Act two.

She leans toward him, opens her mouth, and breathes on him. Jake makes a prune face. "Daddy!"

She removes the stethoscope, places it in the bag and pulls out a toy plessor, testing it on her knee. Deemed safe, she taps his right knee, the rubber end nothing more than thick foam. As soon it meets his knee, he jerks the leg up high in the air, lets it hang there a second, shaking it for effect while Robyn squeals with delightful laughter, and lets it fall back to the couch.

"You should tell . . . Bu . . . kow . . . ski to change the *i* to a *y*," she says, pointing to the book in Jake's lap.

"He's like Terri; he prefers the *i* because he's pretty smart."

"When can we go over to Miley's, Terri's, and Dilly's for breakfast? I want to play house."

"I thought you were a nurse."

"I can do both. I have time."

"Only if you get ready for bed."

"Do you want to know your test results?"

Act three.

"Give it to me straight."

Robyn studies her notebook before giving it to him straight, beaming smile included. "You're fit to win tomorrow!"

"That's good news, but you know Daddy doesn't win races. He lets the other guys win."

"You should take turns."

"I'll suggest that. Now Daddy needs his sleep for the race, but you have to go to bed first."

"I need to feed Juggles."

Epilogue one.

Robyn kisses his scruffy cheek, giggles, and skips away with her duffel bag.

"I'll be there in ten minutes to tuck you in, okay?"

"Okay."

Jake glances at the grandfather clock, the minute hand twenty minutes further along into the night. He returns to Bukowski's *The Last Night of the Earth Poems,* reads for another ten minutes, takes in Robyn's second epilogue and drifts off to sleep himself.

Friday Night
Peace of Mind Lives in the Details

By six thirty p.m. Jim has consumed dinner, homemade stroganoff, yellow corn on the cob, and a garden salad with scant dressing. He drinks his last glass of water for the day by nine p.m. And now, post-shower, he's methodically setting out his club race uniform, a traditional singlet by any standard, though the club does have one style that covers the shoulders, more of a muscle-T look for those who have the kind of time to lift upper-body weights on a consistent basis. Jim does not possess that kind of time, desire, or vanity. The royal-blue singlet bears the club's full name in an oval: REDWOOD EMPIRE arches across the upper portion, and RUNNERS CLUB underneath. The foreground of the space inside the oval depicts two figures, a man running behind a woman amongst evergreens. The background has an approximation of Annadel State Park's peaks with rays of morning sunshine springing out from its ridges. The design is as old as the club itself, some forty-plus years and counting. Tradition goes a long way with the '70s grassroots club, back in the days before the running boom raced in.

After neatly placing the singlet on the bed, he gathers the appropriate, and mandatory, colored running shorts, black, from the variety he can choose from: black, dark gray, dark blue, and a hideous lime-green pair that Doris bought him as a joke, though he wears them anyway because shorts are shorts and they cost money. He lays the black pair next to the singlet.

Next he collects a pair of socks suitable for racing, the key criterion is that the cuff rises above the ankle. Doris often finds socks, on sale, that barely clear the tops of his shoes, and after a training run in the park he can count on finding debris inside his shoe that shifts around during the run, at times causing discomfort though not always enough to merit a debris-removal stop most of the time. He further inspects the chosen pair of socks to ensure they haven't seen better days, from downhills playing havoc on the big toe, often punching through the material, before setting them on the bed next to the other items. The ensemble is complete, minus racing shoes, which he's already tucked away in a side compartment of the gym bag. The training shoes he'll wear for the warm-up and -down are sitting on the hood of their car in the garage, a strange and humorous sight to Doris. Jim offers no explanation for it.

Uniform assembled as a dry run of sorts, he places the singlet into the gym bag, on top of the other clothing options he initially loaded: two long-sleeve tech shirts; a short-sleeve tech shirt; a pair of light running gloves, though unlikely to see the light of day at this meet; a regular cotton T-shirt to put on after the warm-down; another pair of running socks in case the first pair become soggy during the race, another unlikely event; and a sweatshirt. His running watch is in its proper side pocket, along with backup safety pins should the registration table run out, though in his twenty years of racing that has never occurred.

Once completely packed, he zips up the bag and lays out what he'll put on first thing in the morning. With the black running shorts still on the bed, he adds sweatpants, a short-sleeve tech shirt, a long-sleeve tech shirt—warmer than the others for morning's first nip—which he will wear over the other, and a jacket should the morning feeling extra chilly to him.

Jim regards the gym bag for several moments, mind going over the contents, and then scans the bedroom, the closet, the chest of drawers, the half-full laundry basket in the corner, the master bathroom, attention back on the zipped gym bag. Unzipping it, he flips through the stacked layers, counting off everything again. Satisfied, he re-zips. The items on the bed require a mental dress rehearsal, the order in which they'll be put on—shorts, both shirts, sweats, socks. Everything accounted for, he transfers them to the chair in the corner, heads out of the bedroom through the living room to the kitchen to prepare the items that he'll need for the morning, and those items he'll take along to the race.

"How's it going?" Doris says from the couch, watching a pharmaceutical commercial. Jim shakes his head. "Sorry . . . Forgot."

A distraction during his pre-race ritual often causes him a restless night's sleep, ruminating over whether he's forgotten an item or not. Thirty minutes of uninterrupted peace is all he asks for to ensure everything is ready to go when the alarm sounds in the morning, allowing him the peace of mind to prepare his game face. Doris suggested at one time years earlier that he make a list and go off that, but he thought that too silly. She'd replied, "And you call *me* goofy."

In the kitchen he tunes out the TV voices and fills two plastic bottles with water and sets them on the edge of the counter, closet to the back door. He takes two ripe bananas and places them in a Ziploc bag so the banana scent won't permeate his clothing; it also provides a convenient disposal pouch for the peels once consumed. The containment pouch ends up next to the water bottles. The travel portion of the packing complete, Jim preps the coffee maker, setting out a cup next to it. A flick of the switch will be all that his body's morning wake-up call requires, keeping him on schedule.

He breaks the silence after scooping himself a small bowl of ice cream and takes a seat next to Doris. "What are you watching?"

"*Monk* reruns."

"Really?"

"No," she says, laughing.

"At least I don't shave my legs before a race."

"Who shaves their—it's Chase, isn't it?"

"Just for cross-country and track."

"Maybe it's because he can't go shirtless."

Jim shrugs. "He might need all the help he can get; Dillon's going to give him a run for his money this season."

"Chase being chased. Chase on the run. Chase the hunted—" Doris sings.

"Doris . . ."

"What? You're thinking it too."

Though Jim shrugs, it still stings that Chase's arrival knocked Jim off his hard-earned perch. And there *is* a part of him that wants someone to challenge Chase, his measured approach to racing, sitting back and waiting until the end to out-kick the others—no guts, no glory. "Thanks for buying the spumoni."

"Anything to keep your superstitions intact."

Jim nurses a spoonful, recalling how nervous he was the night before his first race back in junior high school, and how his mom served up some "fancy" ice cream, as she referred to it, to calm his nerves. He won the race, indelibly etching the tradition into his pre-race evening ritual.

"Spencer called while you were packing. He wanted me to remind you that the race is at ten thirty, and to arrive no later than nine thirty."

Leave it to a history teacher to dwell on the past. "I was late to one race."

"Ready for tomorrow?"

"I don't know. My left calf felt a little tight on my run today," he says, reaching down to rub it. "I sneezed a couple times at work. Might be coming down with something. Plus, I didn't put in enough tempo runs this summer."

The newly engaged couple absorb the TV's images until a high-blood-pressure, medicine commercial airs, prompting Jim to stop massaging his calf and begin checking his heart rate, pressing two fingers to his neck, eyes fixed on the second hand incrementing on his watch.

"So you're ready," she says.

Jim grins. He pulse rate is a steady forty-six despite not enough tempo runs over the summer.

Saturday Morning
Redwood Empire Runners Club XC Open, Santa Rosa

The predawn nip that chased Dillon around the BR&B while he prepared breakfast for early-rising guests has warmed noticeably as he approaches the hub of the Spring Lake race venue. The marked temperature differential, a signature trait of California's fall months, coaxes the sweet odor of anise from the surrounding dewy brush, black licorice permeating Dillon's senses, reminding him that cross-country season has once again arrived. Between the olfactory infusion and witnessing the flurry of activity at the finish line, where women give last-second efforts before plunging across the chalked line and into an ever-narrowing chute made of colored triangular flags, Dillon feels the familiar tug of cross-country's visceral spell.

He spots and walks over to the RERC tarp, protected under a foldable tent, providing shade from the sun that drenches the exposed start/finish area. Soon the others from the open team—Chase, Jim, Spencer, and Jake—congregate under the tent and like a universally scripted ritual they begin their warm-up fifty minutes before the scheduled race start. With the women's race all but wrapped up and the master men's race about to begin, the guys follow the course's marked route in order to get out ahead of the next racers, allowing an opportunity to cheer on fellow forty-and-up club members at some point when they race by.

The chatter among the group lacks the Sunday conversational vibe, replaced with causal banter to avoid long stretches of silence, holding nerves at bay, the kind of information easily digested; in one such instance, Dillon asks Chase if he actually shaved his legs for the race, and Chase proudly says yes, citing that his first sub-4 mile was accomplished clean-shaven, which prompts Jake to say, "Jim puts on his game face while Chase puts on his game legs."

Between bursts of conversation and cheering on the race in progress, Dillon plays out the race in his mind and periodically performs a mental body scan, searching for anything that might pose an issue, but nothing sends signals of worry. Two miles complete they split off into their own pre-race worlds: Chase heads for the bathrooms; Spencer chats with another club member; Jim stretches and converses with Doris, his demeanor rugged under intense sunlight; and Jake explores and explains the wildflowers growing on the field's fringe to Robyn as she leads him around by the hand.

Dillon takes up residence on the RERC tarp, and after several minutes into his pre-race stretching ritual, established at the dawn of his running career, honed and practiced before every race since, he catches sight of Chase and Spencer performing running drills from the start line, the *new* way to prepare the body for hard running. The concept makes sense in theory, functional dynamic stretching, engaging key muscles to fire in their proper sequence for maximum performance; after all, you don't see a lion stretching before it streaks after a gazelle. But it lacks the one thing Dillon loves to do before a race: mentally prepare. The time spent stretching allows him to focus, or not focus in some cases. Drills are too physical, the mind concentrated on *them*—form, rhythm, avoiding others—rather than the competitive one looming large. His daily life is so entirely consumed that to carve out time to mentally gear up for races days, even hours, beforehand is a Herculean effort. Running a marathon without training is an easier undertaking.

So seated, statically stretching old-school-style, he lets his mind go blank, eliminating the analytical aspect, a near flat-line state, letting go of a restlessly anticipatory night's sleep: How will it feel after several years removed from cross-country? Is the desire to *hurt* still there? How will the team fare? Can he beat Chase? Instead he gazes passively out at the scene, an abundance of memories, like comfort food, stretching back to grade school: groups of three to seven runners pass by in warm-up or warm-down mode, chattering about their upcoming race or discussing their recently contested one; officials pore over race results for accuracy in the timing tent next to the finish line; volunteers, clad in orange vests, stand like traffic cones, fulfilling their assigned roles as course monitor. A small crowd huddles around a makeshift wall—event trailer, side of a tent, plywood board leaned against a tree, the park's brick-and-mortar bathrooms—scanning printouts of results from their race, some taking notes to determine quick team scoring, others making conversation with the person standing close by about nothing in particular other than their shared experience on the course. The conversations around Dillon are decipherable if he paid attention, but their words blend together like a melodic chorus that fills the provisional amphitheater.

Repositioned and into his last seated stretch, he catches sight of a vaguely familiar woman, running with her teammates. Her confident form says as much: torso very straight and tall with squared-off shoulders, and a foot cadence that blurs like a hummingbird. He squints, attempting to bring her into focus for confirmation, but it's too fleeting as she pushes beyond his vision. He's not curious enough to holler her name, to engage in chitchat while he prepares for his race, especially if she is who he thinks she is, a familiar stranger he has run into at various races down south in Orange County. No need to dredge up what she may or may not know about his recent past; not now. Like the conversations that swirl around him, he purges her from his mind.

One by one the other guys gather back at the tarp, swapping out warm-up clothing for race gear. Some have begun switching out their training shoes for cross-country shoes, as Dillon is now doing. He observes that no one has opted for spikes, which makes sense given the modest amount of time they'll be on asphalt, and the dry course whose hard-packed trails from the long, dry summer will feel like pavement. There will be a time and place for spikes later, when the season turns to rain and courses become soggy. But not today. So knobby-patterned, thin-soled shoes will toe the line.

Racing flats on, Dillon swaps out his long-sleeve shirt for his never-been-washed race singlet, crumples up and flattens out the bid number—114—and secures it with safety pins, the first such holes to pierce the new uniform. Once pinned, he strides off toward the bathrooms, spending the time he has to in line performing standing stretches he saved for the occasion—quads, hamstrings, calves, hip flexors—and after voiding his balder, he runs against the grain of the course, along Fisherman's Trail, accelerating for sixty, seventy yards, pumping the heart rate up to near racing levels. Strides, he had explained to his ex-wife, allow the body to offset the rapid start to the race. She didn't understand why, like so many other aspects of his training and running, citing the energy expense: "Why not just save it for the race?" Six strides with thirty seconds between them leaves him flushed, leg muscles primed for intense activity.

"Five minutes until the start of the open men's race," comes the megaphone announcement from somewhere in the start/finish area. "Please make your way to the starting line. *Five* minutes." Such announcements always ratchet up Dillon's nerves, forcing a singular focus: quick bladder check should a last-minute pee break be necessary, and if so, what hidden area or tree is best to approach; double-checking of shoelaces and their proper tension and lace security; bib number in place and properly aligned. A deep breath when all systems appear to be a go; the slow trot, sometimes walk, to the start; searching for teammates while secretly sizing up the competition; watching other racers dart out from the start line for their last-second strides. He slithers through the back-and-forth striders, as well as spectators crossing the course to get to the side they want to be on for picture taking or cheering friends and family on. He hears a young girl's voice shout, "Go, Dilly!" and though he can't see Robyn with a *y*, he waves in the general direction the cheer came from. A spirited roar springs up from behind him, and upon turning he sees Dale chugging into the finishing chute, the final competitor to the superseniors' race, which puts a smile on Dillon's face.

Rob Shore starts them and Dale finishes them. Must be an official race.

Dillon gathers with his new teammates, shaking their hands and exchanging "good lucks" with each. There will be more hand shaking with the others queued up at the start line in the future when their names and faces become familiar, but for now this is a bare stage on which to act out a new chapter in his life.

"One minute. You should be at the start line now," comes the deep, resonant voice of Rob Shore. "Onnnnnnnnnnne minute."

By force of habit Dillon tosses in one more stride, giving him the opportunity to walk up to the *front* of the start line and position himself there rather than be relegated a row or two behind. The RERC open team has picked a suitable starting spot that affords them a direct line to the boat ramp without the need to negotiate curbs or the semivisible drainage pipe up ahead. Their front-line presence, after last-second jockeying by the field, exposes three spots, Dillon, Chase, and Jim up front, with Spencer and Jake directly behind.

"Thirty seconds!" bellows Rob Shore off to the right, an older gentleman with a permanent tan and white hair, noise-canceling earphones on, his arm outstretched above his head, a starter's gun in his hand.

Sound vacates the area, the kind of stillness often found during reflection or prayer. Like a moment frozen in time the collective held breath on the line stretches across fifty yards with harriers hunched over, back feet planted firmly behind them, and, for some, a hand poised over their watch.

"On your marks . . ." *Crack!*

Beeeeeeeeeeeeeeeeeeeeeeeeeeeeeeeeeeeeeep.

Dillon lurches off the line, holding a slight forward lean to facilitate acceleration for several yards until he reaches a suitable speed, righting his torso for efficiency. The first hundred yards are critical, not just for establishing position but for avoiding getting clipped from behind, sending one down in a heap in front of the herd that'll trample the unfortunate soul. It happened once in Dillon's running career, a high school meet that started on asphalt, leaving him bruised and skinned and ultimately out of the race. But while a fall in the first hundred yards will trigger a restart, Dillon is determined to avoid it altogether.

A clean start, riding the cresting wave, Dillon settles into a comfortable rhythm across the pockmarked patch, reaching the parking lot safely, the leaders winding their way through a sparse section of cheering spectators consisting mainly of fellow club runners and racers' significant others. Amidst shouted names and club affiliations that resemble a flash mob, the fleshy spectrum from the start has slimmed to a svelte fifteen feet as the elongated pack charges by trailers hitched to idling cars waiting to launch small boats held at bay by human traffic cones.

Up the slope to the sound of a handful of spiked shoes grinding the asphalt like fingernails across a chalkboard, Dillon spots Jim off to the right, a stride-length ahead, then catches sight of Chase to the left, latching on. Together they comprise the last spots of the top ten.

Good positioning. You're where you need to be. Now, settle in and relax.

The first gradient complete, a right turn marking the occasion, Dillon fans out and, guided by eagerness, opens up his stride, going by a couple guys, including Jim, who can't match Dillon's cadence and stride length. The pack shoots off the pavement and onto a flat fire road, giving Dillon a wide perspective to size up who has taken up the early charge. Three of the top five are Agras. No surprise there. The others consist of the Chico Club, Strawberry Hill, and a couple rogue unattached runners, whose placing won't affect team scoring, according to Spencer.

The fire road ends, jettisoning them onto a rutted S-curved trail that dips, where those less familiar with it slow enough to allow Dillon to move up to the fifth spot without excessive expenditure of energy. *Relax, relax, don't blow your wad early. You're good, settle in.*

The course sweeps around a trio of large water tanks and up a short rise that pushes them over the bike path that Dillon normally takes back to Howarth Park; but today he skims over it at five-minute-mile pace. The ground blurs by faster than he's experienced in some time, his eyes and mind poised for the first Double Down Dam plummet, the crunch of gravel under rapid foot strikes ringing in his ears.

Like F1 pilots peeling off from formation, the first, second, third, and fourth runners veer to the right and down. It looks easy. It's anything but. In a heartbeat Dillon reaches the edge of the precipice; in the next thump vertigo rushes in; and in the next, plunging down the escarpment, his stomach drops as if enduring inflight turbulence. Many years removed from his last cross-country meet, cobwebs still intact, allows Jim and another guy to fly by while Dillon digs his heels into the ground and squints at the sun's cruel position.

Get it under control, dude. Relax, relax, relax . . .

Near the bottom, Dillon releases the brakes and glides under the canopy of oaks, straying to the left to minimize any further braking for the hard right onto the bike path. Beautifully executed, Dillon reclaims Jim and jumps on the heels of the other lost spot, following him closely onto the Fisherman's Trail. As Jim had warned, getting caught behind on this section cost Dillon precious yards as the four up front zip through unabated, opening up a small gap that, if left unchecked, will act like a fissure and spilt the race up for good, even this early. Dillon lets the misstep drift through his mind and out of existence, focusing on the moment they clear the tight confines and, once clear, jets around the blockade, but the blockade has regained his composure and previous speed and holds even with Dillon. Moments like this amount to a poker game, who will blink first, drift back, and take up residence behind the other. They've crossed the mile mark, not one-third into the race. It wouldn't be sensible to *race* him now, this early, expending valuable mental and physical energy on one man. The logical play would be to relax and observe the guy's reaction: if he maintains pace, slip back and sit on his shoulder, even nudge it to assert a lurking presence; let him do all the work by leading, a tactic that can wear the guy down in the long run.

That's prudent in theory, but a restless competitive mind yearns for more: the growing fissure needs to be addressed . . . now, not later when it'll be too great to overcome at their pace. Committed to this, Dillon maintains his position, mentally blocks out the shorter guy to his right, focuses on the quartet thirty yards up front, and makes sure the gap doesn't grow; and that's the way it stays, pouring out from the Fisherman's Trail, hanging a wide sweeping left past two kayaks ready for voyage and onto the bike path toward the southern dam. Cheers spring up, his name shouted mere feet away, though he sees no faces attached to the voices—with the exception of Robyn with a *y*, who shrieks and bounces up and down like a bunny alongside Doris, who screams so loud it all but goes sonic. Chase's name follows shortly afterward, and fifteen seconds later a scream that *does* go sonic.

Nice grouping, but note to self: Jim starts off aggressively.

Another cheer comes his way, a familiar voice, female, from the small pack of women approaching from the opposite direction. It's her, no doubt, the woman he noticed while stretching. The recognition, the past, the pain, flee quickly from his mind, her cheers fading behind him.

Past the crowd's energy and the rise to the southern dam in sight, the guy alongside Dillon falls off the pace, slipping back a couple strides. Dillon wastes no time, surging up the stubby climb to unhitch him. The gap doubles. At the top, veering right and going for the kill he dips into his anaerobic well, his first at the halfway point of the race, until silence nips at this heels.

Alone, Dillon straddles the unpaved division between bottled-up Spring Lake and its tree-adorned shores, and Bennett valley's protected prime real estate southward sprawl until he leaves the dam behind with a hard right and dip that propels him alongside pitched tents and the smell of bacon, the undulating segment where he predetermined the need to separate himself from speedier legs. The four in front have splintered, now strung out roughly ten yards apart, giving Dillon fragments to pick off one at a time. The closest fragment rounds the next bend and, caught off guard, approaches the abrupt hill poorly, lumbering like a truck until gearing down to match the incline. Momentum lost, Dillon catches him near the top and rolls over the peak with a favorable line that puts Dillon on a smoother path among the rockier choices, shunting him down a narrower path, effectively blocking the guy from being able to regain his spot for another half mile without some very aggressive passing maneuvers, a tactic Dillon is prepared for. It's not necessary, though, when he hears Chase's voice: "It's me."

The miler is hitched, a complicated blessing: great for team scoring, but . . . teammate or no teammate, Dillon *has* to make Chase earn a higher placing, despite the thought of futility that flits through Dillon's mind: that as a miler, Chase will likely wait until the final quarter mile and gut him like a fish along the (as if to add insult to injury) Fisherman's Trail. Chase is the type of runner Dillon needs to distance himself from, and yet there he is, hanging on.

Amidst Chase's shaved sub-4 legs, Dillon works the remainder of what is left to his pre-race strategy until they spill out onto the fire road toward the water towers one last time. Dillon hasn't closed the gap on third place, and the leader has furthered his advantage by another twenty yards. Too far to consider, Dillon pushes him out of his mind and focuses on the Agras man directly in front, keenly aware of the crunch of gravel looming close behind.

Passing by the water towers he inches his way closer to the Agras runner. Breaking up the one/three Agras finish will help greatly in RERC's quest to win. Dillon's legs feel decent enough, taxed but not balking, though his breathing begins to sound laborious, which means he's been drinking from the anaerobic well too much. The clock is now ticking on when the leg muscles will cease to keep him going at his desired pace. Like the other noise, he lets that thought drift through his mind, acknowledging the dilemma but not analyzing it.

Cross that bridge when we get there.

The Double Down Dam. The plunge imminent. Breathing hard *and* pounding downhill, staying in control, balancing on tired legs that plant hard and push off prove a tougher feat than expected, but Dillon lets gravity grab him, quads contracting fiercely and releasing in stutter-step secession. He floats at the base through the tree line, negotiates the hard right, catches and passes the Agras jersey, and hits the Fisherman's Trail with a clear view.

Second place exceeds Dillon's fitness, however: his legs lack another gear and he knows it. Preservation time, holding his current spot for the final half mile, less than two and a half minutes' time.

His breathing now drowns out every other noise in the vicinity. Despite a dry mouth he works up some moisture and spits it hard to the ground. Sunlight flutters through overhead branches, creates a sporadic light show that annoys his vision and speckles the ground with intense bright spots among shadowy patches. On top of that, Chase lurks in Dillon's mind, running down the center of the trail, sneaking side glances toward the ground, watchful for creeping shadows, the brief hint of someone attempting to overtake him. Timed right, a quick surge can stave them off, make them back off and reconsider. Too long in deliberation, however, spots are stolen; no one gives an inch in cross-country.

Rounding the final bend of the trail, the boat ramp comes into view, relief twenty seconds away. Hope dangles before him until an Agras runner rushes by Dillon in his distressed state.

He has no answer.

"Let's go, man," Chase says, gliding by Dillon. "We've got company."

Chase gaps him like only a miler can. Dillon focuses on Chase's heels, willing himself to lock on, but the heels flutter away.

Ugh.

Dillon hears deep inhalations first and feels the brush of air next, followed by the sight of an Agras guy going by. Dillon silently groans, a helpless groan, a futile, slow motion, running-dream-coming-to-fruition groan, one where he can't escape the inevitable. As if easily relinquishing spots isn't telltale sign enough of his finishing demise, he glances back, further telegraphing his helplessness.

Never, ever, look back! You know better than that, Dill Weed!

Hands no longer relaxed, fingers choking the life out of each thumb, he rounds the corner into pandemonium, the finish banner looming thirty yards ahead, but it might as well be a mile as a Chico runner blows by Dillon's form as if he were a statue. He locks onto a spot just beyond the finish line, dredging up whatever fight he has left in him, another presence alongside him, leaning forward with a quick lunge at the line and passing the presence in the chute, but the finish line official hollers to a volunteer farther down the line to swap Dillon and the guy behind him their current spots, negating Dillon's fleeting last-second consolation prize.

Dillon slows to a stagger then stops altogether, wheezing as the other guy moves forward, patting Dillon's sweaty singlet and skin. "Nice race . . . new guy," the other guy says.

"You . . . too." Spots flicker in Dillon's vision and arid air seesaws back and forth in his windpipe like a pair of lumberjacks felling a mighty redwood. He rights himself and takes baby steps to keep moving. Disappointment replaces the flickering spots. *What did you expect? Jump into the race and walk away from everyone? Some ego you have. So you got beat. You're rusty, unfit. It's one day, one race. Shake it off . . . "Son, your ego is writing checks your body can't cash." The guys would like that one.*

By the time Dillon reaches the end of the long tapered chute, rips the detachable portion of his bid number off, and hands it to another volunteer, who places it on the growing stack in her hand, he has stabilized enough to walk over to Chase and pat his shoulder. "Damn milers," he says with a strained grin.

Chase chuckles as he sheds his jersey. "Shit, I tried going by you a couple times early on, but you never backed down."

"Nice job, you two," Jim says twenty seconds later, slapping backs and turning toward the finish line. "Come on, Jakey! Dig, baby, dig!"

"Man, the first one always burns," Spencer says, exiting the chute eighteen seconds after Jim. He hunches over and spits into the grass. When he straightens, spittle hangs across his chin, which he wipes off with the base of his singlet. He lets out a hack of a cough. "Feels like I have a raisin stuck in my throat." He lets out another hack, but produces no raisin. "At least it was a PR."

Dillon joins Jim, watching Jake—whose broad smile defies the intense moment—sprinting stride for stride with an Agras and Chico runner until their spent forms deflate across the finish line. When the close finish is sorted out by the PA official, Jake is sandwiched between the two, the Agras runner in front. Dillon glances at the race clock, registering the fact that the club's one through five runners are separated by only sixty-five seconds. *Great grouping.* He has no idea how the team placed, but no doubt his fold at the end makes it easy for the Agras to sew it up, perhaps the Chico squad, too. But there's room for improvement, and the season has just begun. Despite fatigue, defeat, and disappointment he smiles. *Man, I've missed this sport.*

"Nice job, Dillon," says a familiar voice.

Dillon turns around. "Hey, Kate. I thought that was you warming down." He leans in to give her a sweaty hug. She reciprocates without hesitation. "What are you doing up here?"

"I moved to the Bay Area earlier this year for work. I meant to look you up this summer when I heard you'd bought a place up here."

"No worries. I was pretty busy with things."

Kate nods, the kind laced with sympathy. "Sorry to hear about . . . you know."

"It's all good. Running for the Gazelles? Any good?"

"Only the best."

"Nice job, Jake," Dillon says as Jake wanders by, heading for the club tent.

"Thanks. How'd it feel?"

"Hard, but good. Didn't have anything at the finish."

"It's early."

"I should let you go," Kate says. "I wanted to stop by and say hi. Great race today. You doing the series?"

"If work doesn't get too hectic."

"I'll have to check out your BR&B sometime," she says, turning to leave. "Breakfast is my favorite meal of the day."

"Now, that's one I haven't heard before: 'Breakfast is my favorite meal of the day,'" Chase says, handing Dillon a water bottle.

"Do you have an aversion to shirts?" Dillon twists the cap off the bottle and takes a swig that burns yet soothes his raw throat.

"I like to air-dry," Chase says, tossing an arm up theatrically.

"*Jerry Maguire,*" Jim and Jake say in unison, stepping up to the guys.

"Where's Spencer?" Jake says. "Let's get our warm-down going. I have a long day of work out at the coast."

"Me too," Dillon says. "The inn's exterior isn't going to paint itself."

"Ugh," Chase moans. "I see a nap in my future."

"Spence! Warm-down!" Jim shouts across the field to where Spence is conversing with another club runner.

"I need to change shoes," Chase says.

"Where are we meeting tomorrow?" Jake asks, strolling over to the club tent.

"I can't make it," Dillon says. "Have a full house tonight. First time."

"Let's meet at—" Spencer says upon arrival.

"Noooooooo," Chase and Jim chorus.

Spencer feigns surprise and hurt.

"You aren't doing the usual twenty, right?" Dillon says, removing his singlet. His pale skin waves like a white flag. "Why don't you come out to my place and run in the vineyards. I'll have breakfast ready afterward."

Jim's, Chase's, and Jake's eyes light up. Spencer looks intrigued, though he voices his reservations. "Maggie and I usually go out and have brunch on Sundays."

"Have her come out at, what, nine thirty or so. Heck, invite your wife and fiancée," Dillon says, gesturing to Jake and Jim in turn. "We'll make a thing of it. There's plenty of room and a fun group on hand. One couple is from New Zealand."

"You don't have to ask me twice," Jake says.

"Me either," Jim says.

"I'm in," Chase says.

"I'll let you know about the breakfast in the morning, but I think that can work," Spence says.

"Oh, Spencer, step off the train once in a while," Chase says, walking, trotting, running—*Beep*—back out onto the course, this time in reverse order—per Jake's request so as to *unwind* from their racing effort—while volunteers methodically break down the various event support systems, club runners mill around, and Dale scoops up what is left of the post-race muffins.

Beep, beep. Beep.

Sunday Morning
Run & Breakfast

"You sure you can't sneak away for an easy ten?" Chase asks Dillon, tossing his shirt onto the porch bench at the BR&B, readying his watch.

"Wish I could, but the house is full, and it's too much for Terri to handle on her own. I'll run this evening with Miles. Right, girl?"

"*Wooooowooowooo Wooooowoooo.*"

Chase steals a glance inside the inn toward the kitchen.

"She's not here yet, buddy," Dillon says, patting Chase on the shoulder. "Have a good run, guys. You remember where to go?" Dillon points toward a spot in the fence line.

"Yep," Chase says. "Ready, guys?"

Jake nods, Jim yawns, and Spencer, well, he's still inside gushing over the media lounge.

"Spence! Let's go!" Chase hollers. "Should've never shown him that room. Maggie will never see him now."

"It is pretty cool," Jim says, rubbing his hands together and blowing on them. "So much history."

"Aren't you the least bit cold, Chase?" Dillon says.

"It's my early-morning wake-up call."

"It's eight fifteen."

"And your point?"

"Hi," Jim says, answering his phone he's retrieved from the porch railing. "No, you don't need to bring anything for breakfast. Dillon said not to." Jim rubs his belly. "Really, it's already a bed and *breakfast*. Just come over at nine thirty." He leans against the railing, half stretching a calf muscle. "No, he's not wearing a shirt. You goof. I need to go . . . love you too."

"Spencer, we're going!" Chase hollers again. *Beep.* "You tired, Jim?"

Jim yawns again, his form a lazy shadow of its normal purposeful self. *Beep.* "And my calves are sore this morning. That's what a PR will do for you."

"Why's Doris always bashing on me?" Chase asks. "What'd I ever do to her?"

"It's your giant man nipples. They freak her out."

Chase regards them and shrugs. "They look normal to me."

"That makes three PRs yesterday: Jim, Spencer, and Chase," Jake says, coming up alongside them.

"And the way Dillon ran like an animal from the start . . . no wonder we beat Chico," Chase says.

"Wait up, guys," Spencer hollers as he descends the steps from the porch. *Beep.*

"And we were only nineteen points behind the Agras," Jim says. "This bodes very well, gentlemen. *Very* well."

Spencer catches the guys at the fence line, ducking through it. "If we can get our fourth and fifth man ahead of Agras's fifth man, and Dillon and Chase in front of their second man, I think we can take them."

"I'll bet you mastered the Rubik's Cube as a child, didn't you?" Jim says.

"There's no doubt Dillon will move up," Chase says. "And that certainly motivates me."

"I'll *bet*," Jim says, adding a sly grin to the equation.

"Pfft."

"You'll have to move up as well, Spence," Jim says. "Remember, they tend to trot out bigger guns at the PA Championships, especially if they sense a threat of another club winning the series."

Spence-speak.

"It's less about *trotting* out faster runners than them *only* racing the bigger events," Jake says.

"I don't know about that," Spencer says.

"We'll cross that bridge when we get there. For now, we beat Chico, and that is celebration enough," Chase says, nudging a stride ahead of Jim, who overadjusts his move to stay with Chase, who corrects the differential with Jim, the pace now noticeably faster.

Spencer tosses in another Spence-speak from alongside Jake ten yards back and the surging duo backs off, allowing the group to re-form for a leisurely post–race day recovery run through the vineyards, Chase passing along the knowledge of the wine industry he researched during the Grogger's ad campaign: about the type of grapevines that fill their view—just a fraction of the 70,000-plus acres of vineyards in the county spread across sixteen agricultural regions with a wide variety of soil and climates, producing nearly twice as much wine as neighboring Napa County—as well as the appellation it resides in and how said appellation differs from the others, until the guys are drunk with knowledge and hungry for breakfast.

Dillon notices Doris staring at him as he pulls a pancake from the griddle. "Another one?"

She shakes her head.

"Dilly, the people in the little room want more," Robyn says, holding their plates as high as she can.

"Okay, but let's give them clean ones." Dillon exchanges dishes with her and slides a couple hearty-sized buttermilk pancakes onto each. He tops the stacks with fresh strawberries and places a dollop of heavy cream on the side. "All set."

Robyn carefully lowers the plates to eye level, inspects the food, and turns for the nook off the kitchen. Dillon smiles, watching her carefully walk away. "Who wants more pancakes?"

The couple from Boulder, seated at the island, both nod, and Dillon hands them platefuls bearing more calories for the hungry runners, who are on their way to the coast before heading north. They'd heard about the BR&B during their weeklong fast-pack adventure around the Tahoe Rim Trail, a 160-mile run/hike excursion. The stories they tell of epic views around the pristine lake from above, and the plethora of trails, intrigue him, enticing him to add it to his list of places to visit and run someday.

"Come on in, Maggie," Dillon says when she pauses upon entering the kitchen, scanning the scene. "Spencer's in the media lounge."

"Dillon . . . you've given your castle in the air a foundation." Her eyes sparkle. At Dillon's perplexed expression she adds, "From Thoreau's book *Walden*."

"I'm more a Jack London fan."

"I can see that." Maggie moves toward the island, says hello to Linda and Doris, and hands Dillon a bowl brimming with a mixture of fresh fruits chunked up. "I brought a little something."

"You really didn't need to bring anything, but thank you all the same," Dillon says, taking the bowl and placing it on the counter next to the homemade blackberry cobbler Doris brought and Linda's coffee cake. "I told the guys to tell you not to."

"They told us," Linda says. "They don't always understand proper etiquette." Doris, who is seated next to Linda, and Maggie, who joins them, smile and nod in agreement.

"Andrew, you ready for breakfast?" Dillon says when the Munich Room's guest wanders into the lively kitchen, searching for a place to sit at the island. "Have a seat here." Dillon gestures to a tall stool, placing a cloth place mat in front of it, along with a glass of orange juice. Andrew settles in. "Three-cheese omelet and pancakes sound good?"

"Mighty good."

"Andrew, these are my friends I told you about from the club: Chase, Jake, and his wife, Linda"—Dillon directs his finger in all directions, connecting the relationship dots—"Jim and his fiancée, Doris, and Maggie, Spencer's girlfriend. He's still in the media lounge, Maggie. You might need to rescue him. Everybody, this is Andrew from Santa Fe."

Heys and hellos greet Andrew.

"Nice to meet you all."

"Good luck rescuing Spencer," Chase says, eating while eyeing Terri without much discretion as she comes and goes from the kitchen. "He found the video of Alan Webb breaking Ryun's national high school record at the Prefontaine Classics back in '01."

"Andrew, I didn't see your name in the results from yesterday's race," Dillon says, cracking open three eggs. "I thought you were going to jump into the open race."

"Well, after talking with you Friday night, I decided it wasn't for me."

"I'm sorry about that. I shouldn't have said anything."

"What'd he tell you?" Jim asks.

"Oh, nothing off-putting, just that if I was expecting a race like a 10K road race to not feel discouraged if I found myself at the back of the pack after a quarter mile."

"Yeah," Jim says, nodding, "cross-country isn't like other running events."

"That's what he said. I'm not fast like you guys, but my forty-one minute 10K doesn't put me in last place back home."

"I always feel in a bind when someone asks me about jumping into a cross-country race," Dillon says, explaining the quandary he often feels in talking about racing with less competitively talented souls. "I certainly don't want to discourage anyone, but at the same time, I don't want them overwhelmed when the field leaves them in the dust right from the get-go. It's a rude awakening."

"They offer prize money for the top three individuals and clubs, so it makes it very competitive. And there's the grand prix series," Chase says. "Cross-country tends to attract competitively deep talent."

"It's more of a team sport than it is for individuals," Dillon says.

"Not to mention the team scoring can be confusing," says the woman from Boulder. "Michael explained it to me once, but as soon as he spoke about 'displacers,' he lost me."

"Displacers?" Andrew says.

Jake and Jim look at each other and nod.

Jake cups his hand and places it to his mouth, mimicking a harmonica, humming a summoning note.

In turn, like a barbershop quartet climbing the harmonic scale they stand, Jim the bass singing, "*Displacers . . .*" Chase the baritone, "*Displacers . . .*" Jake the lead tenor, "*Displacers . . .*" and rushing into the kitchen, Spencer the harmonizing tenor, "*Displacers . . .*"

"What's happening?" Dillon says.

Doris cackles while the entire inn quiets and focuses their attention on the off-pitch entertainment.

"Cross-country teams consists of seven hearty souls," Jake recites.

"*Doo-wop. Doo-wop. Doo-wop,*" Jim chants.

"The first *five* score points based on their placing," Chase recites.

"*Doo-wop. Doo-wop. Doo-wop.*"

"One, two, three, four, and so on . . ." Spencer recites.

"*Doo-wop. Doo-wop. Doo-wop.*"

"Their scores are then summed up," Jake recites.

"*Doo-wop. Doo-wop. Doo-wop.*"

"And the lowest score wins, just like in golf minus the walking," Chase recites.

"*Wooooowoooo. Wooooowoooo. Wooooowoooo.*"

Robyn giggles as she skips around the kitchen with Miles.

"Though the sixth and seventh runners are optional," Spencer recites.

"*Doo-wop. Doo-wop. Doo-wop.*"

"They can *displace* other team's top five scorers," Jim recites.

"*Wooooowoooo. Wooooowoooo. Wooooowoooo.*"

"*Displacers. Displacers! Displacers!*" they all sing.

To rousing applause, the quartet takes a bow and resumes their seated positions.

"Wackadoos," Dillon says, tossing Miles a dog treat for her contribution.

"In practice, most clubs don't have that kind of depth beyond the fifth man, so displacers' practical value is for the mid-pack squads," Spencer says.

"If you think cross-country is quirky, indoor track is crazier," Chase says. "Eight or more laps per mile in some cases, and some are run on wooden boards."

"Name the 'Chairman of the Boards,'" Spencer says.

"Eamonn Coghlan," Chase says. "First over the age of forty to run a sub-four-minute mile, and he did it *indoors*. He's a senator in Ireland these days."

"No kidding," Spencer says.

"Schooled!" Chase shouts.

"How about those races where volunteers throw paint at you as you run by?" Maggie says.

"What?" Linda says.

"Don't forget those muddy buddy challenges," Jim says.

"I don't get those," Dillon says. "Too messy for me."

"What's next, virtual races?" Jim says.

"They already exist," Chase says.

"You're kidding."

"Simply time your run and submit it to the event website," Chase says.

"Talk about *webbing* it in," Dillon says.

"No shit."

"Chase!" Doris shouts.

"Sorry."

"I suppose if they use a Garmin to track the route and mileage it'd be verifiable," Dillon says.

"At least it encourages activity in a modern way," Jake says.

"Unless they ride their bike or have someone else run it for them," Jim says.

"Kind of ridonkulous if you ask me," Chase says. "I want to enter one of those Disney Princess races." He smirks.

"They're for women only," Maggie says.

"I know!"

"Did you see where some guy entered one and as he crossed the finish line in first place the race announcer told the crowd *not* to applaud him?" Jim says.

"How embarrassing," Linda says.

"For who, the guy or the event?" Dillon says.

"Did they at least give him a tiara for the effort?" Chase says.

"Call the *Press*, the Algonquin Round Table has reconvened," Jake says.

As the rapid-fire conversation swirls around, Dillon works the kitchen like a street performer on a busy shopping plaza. He discusses with Andrew about where to go for a run later that afternoon out at the coast, to park at Shell Beach and run the trail that skirts along the cliffs high above the pacific ocean, lapping at the rocks below. "There are bathrooms near the parking lot. Pack a windbreaker, it gets chilly out there." He gives the Colorado couple maps of where to go wine tasting, offering them alternatives along West Side Road for smaller but respected wineries that don't charge for tastings like the well-known wineries out along Highway 12 do. He wanders over to the nook off the kitchen, topping off orange-juice glasses and coffee mugs, talking with three middle aged women who came into town from Santa Barbara to run the Clo-Cow Half Marathon down in Petaluma, telling him how they did and showing off their commemorative cowbell-styled medals that hang and clank proudly around their necks.

Dillon wanders by the media lounge, where he overhears Spencer's conversation with the New Zealand couple, though more him—a national athletics coach—than her, about the differing coaching philosophies between the two countries, and the impact the late, great Arthur Lydiard, a Kiwi, had on running worldwide. He walks by the large couch in the living area, topping off the coffee mugs of three aging ultramarathoners, men who are working their way south from Seattle on an early retirement celebratory road trip, running as many trails as possible during their journey. They are seated in front of Robyn, who explains to them why y is the best letter in the whole alphabet. Dillon pauses, curious himself, and learns that y opens doors while other letters like i and u close them. No doubt she has inherited Jake's philosophical gene. He continues on back to the kitchen, where he notices Terri has her lips near Chase's ear, whispering, before moving over to the sink to rinse off dishes. By the time Dillon enters the kitchen, Chase's cheeks have flushed.

With one final call for pancakes and nothing but head shakes in return, Dillon turns the burners under the griddle off, sets the batter bowl under running water in the sink, and tosses the spatula into the dishwasher.

"Aha!" Doris shouts.

The various conversations around the breakfast island stop midsentence, their attention directed first at Doris, following her eyes to where she is staring.

Dillon turns toward her. "What?"

"See, Chase, he washes *his* spatula."

Confused, Dillon glances over to Chase.

"He has a health code to adhere to," Chase says to Doris with a smile and addresses Dillon with, "I'll explain later."

"Time to go, Doris," Jim says.

PA/USATF TOP 5 TEAM STANDINGS AS OF 9/27/2015		
	Club	Total
1	Agras	10
2	RERC	9
3	Chico Running Club	8
4	Strawberry Hill Harriers	7
5	South Bay Striders	6

Week 39 Training Summary			
	Long Run	Mileage Total	Comments
Dillon	12	65	First XC in 2 years! Too aggressive for current shape, but it sure feels good to be back racing with a team.
Chase	12.23	58	Opener PR. Solid splits. Dillon is going to be tough
Spencer	12.50	76	Legs felt good despite high mileage. RERC PR!
Jim	12	59	Sore calves.
Jake	12	64	New experience: run through the vineyards.

Week 5
September 28

Tuesday Evening
The Sands of Time

Jake wraps up the last of the lawn-removal effort with his crew at a windswept home out near Bodega Bay, a quaint seaside town along the Sonoma coast known affectionately for Patrick's Saltwater Taffy, sold from a symbolically pink-and-white striped building, and abalone diving. Its historical claims to fame, though, are for hosting the first Russian structures built in California back in 1809, as well as for PG&E's thwarted effort to build a nuclear power plant at Bodega Head in the '60s, when, during the first reactor dig, a fault line was discovered, leaving behind a huge hole that eventually filled with water. The site was locally known thereafter as the Hole in the Head.

His crew gone, Jake changes out his work duds for running gear and steers his truck farther north along the twisty coastline of Highway 1, where the golden-brown hills to the east cascade with the joy of children at the start of summer break, skipping over the roadway and past neglected barns filled with stories and plunging over the cliffs and into the surf. He reaches the Salmon Creek parking lot, overlooking from its perch the Pacific lapping at the sandy beach below. He slides his truck in between two older, early model vehicles with signs of coastal cancer whose occupants rest serenely on the hoods, commenting on the breaking of the surf as the glass-off hour, as surfers call it, approaches—that magical time of day when the onshore wind calms and the water surface becomes smooth and glassy. Jake reclines, gazing at the immense blue life form breathing supinely in meditative repose, the distant swells rising and falling, the sun forty minutes away from kissing the horizon.

Jake exits the truck, removes his shoes and socks and heads down the path to the beach. Stepping onto the beach proper, the cool sand sifting between his toes, he walks a few steps before launching into a casual pace, adjusting to the shifting topography untouched by summer tides. He breathes in the salty air, noting which direction the generally constant wind is blowing from. Beaches north of Santa Cruz are very different from their southern brethren. It's not unusual to see throughout the summer months, especially in the evenings, beachgoers bundled up in heavy jackets and gloves; beachcombers prevail over sun worshippers.

Jake works his way diagonally toward the harder-packed sand, where the tide licks its chops, leaving a layer of foam and the occasional strand of kelp from the ocean floor as markers to its current ebb or flow state. His footsteps down near the water line sink in as he pads along barefoot, leaving behind narrow footprints with a high arch. The sand spongy and gritty under his feet, each foot strike acts like a mild pumice stone on his callused soles.

He passes by three young boys with plastic buckets and shovels, clambering around their sand castle that's under siege by the sea in an attempt to return it to its original state. Assuredly a losing battle, seeing how the tide marches in with full force and takes no prisoners, yet the trio of sand soldiers fights bravely on.

Less than ten minutes of running south sheds the crowds, his company now the windswept Monterey cypress trees whose twisted branches and evergreens recline eastward along the bluffs, a couple enjoying an extended sunset stroll, and a family atop trail horses from the nearby horse stable. Robyn spotted the horses during a beach excursion earlier in the summer and wished to ride one. "When you're taller," he told her. He didn't think she'd have such patience, watching her measure her height twice a day for the next week, but ultimately she came to the conclusion that some things take time. "Yes, they do," he had replied.

Jake drifts away from the shoreline toward the sand dunes on which he plans to do his "spirited" run. Reaching tall grass, he passes through it and before him lie several square miles of mounds interrupted by patches of indigenous seashore bluegrass, loosely acting like trail markers, defining numerous uncharted paths around the open land devoid of distractions. Private or public land, Jake isn't completely sure, but without signs protesting his presence, he doesn't waste time on the matter, ignoring the token shin-high weathered and broken-down fence he's stepped across many times over the last decade. He swings into motion, legs churning in the sand pit that challenges more than lung capacity or core muscles. Those are the tangibles, the mechanics of conditioning. Instead, Jake embraces the challenge the terrain offers, his mind present and patient in pushing through the slog of the conditions, his body reacting to the ever-shifting nature of the moment, an activity he and Jim performed many times during their three years together in San Luis Obispo. "Builds strong minds and bodies," their coach used to tell them. And so it did.

An intuitive quarter mile later, Jake backs off, now jogging and inhaling large quantities of fresh coastal life, patiently waiting for homeostatic breathing to signal him to get back to it. Again he accelerates, again he recovers, no watch to inform him when to do either side of the equation. Precision is not a quality he subscribes to, or can completely understand, the breaking down to the molecular level an activity that frees the body and mind to greater heights than without it. "The body knows not of distance, but of time and effort, the only measures that truly count," he often counters when Chase and Spencer discuss their data-infused training programs. Technology is handy, but often puts one out of touch with their body, distancing themselves from it rather than connecting them to it, instead relying on what a graph tells them, creating too much dependence on such feedback methods, but to each their own. Jake feasts on the experience—in the moment, barefoot—his body absorbing the effort, free from anything that his day or life may tie him down with; just him—legs, arms, lungs, heart, mind, spirit, soul—moving through space and time of his own volition.

Once the hourglass to the invigorating portion of his workout winds down, Jake has completed approximately four miles, broken up into roughly sixteen quarter-mile repeats. He works his way back down to the shoreline, the sun shrinking on the horizon, and heads back to his truck, his spirit awash in philosophical rhetoric, his audience ebbing and flowing in front of him, passively listening, anointing his bare feet with its salty offering.

Wednesday Evening
Past Catches Present

Dillon's cell phone rings. He peeks at it resting next to his tall glass of beer, the display a number he doesn't recognize. He ignores it, lifts the glass, and savors a sip, his gaze returning to the peaceful evening view from the front porch of the BR&B. Murmurs drift out from the living area as guests from the three occupied rooms enjoy complimentary Beardsworth wine, locally produced cheese, and seasoned crackers. When the phone reaches the fourth ring something about the number nags at him. He sighs at second glance. It's been a while since he's seen *her* number displayed in living color instead of scribbled on a notepad by Terri, which he'd tear off, crumple, and recycle. *How did she get this number?* Up until now if his ex-wife called it funneled through the BR&B's landline, a regulated buffer between him and his past. Now it appears she's discovered his personal cell phone number. He swills his beer around the glass, sips it, and gazes off into the last of the twilight across the property while the phone drones on and slips off to voicemail. He lets out a heavy sigh this time. *Just go away.*

"You wouldn't by chance have another one of those?" Hank, the guest from the Athens Room asks from the doorway, pointing to the Allagash White Dillon holds.

"Oh, sure," Dillon says, setting his down and rising.

"No, no, sit . . . I'll retrieve it," Hank says. "Mind if I join you?"

"Sure. They're in the fridge. Help yourself."

A minute later, bottle in hand, Hank wanders back out to the porch, taking a seat. "Your wine offering is more to my wife's liking. I'm a beer guy, and a fine Belgian-style one like this is right up my alley," the man from Aspen says, raising the bottle toward Dillon.

Dillon raises his glass. "Cheers. You want a glass?"

"Naw. I prefer to keep things simple."

Dillon nods at the older gentleman, whose age is difficult to estimate. Runners often look younger than their biological age, though Dillon has developed a theory, based on the handful of ultramarathoners he's come across since opening the BR&B, that at some point a diminishing of returns for looking younger occurs: the excess miles take their toll on the body, possibly *accelerating* the aging process. Is it the extra exposure to the elements, imparting a weathered exterior? Or extra stress placed upon the body at the cellular level that no amount of time off or recovery can counteract? Dillon doesn't know for sure, only that the extreme side of the sport tends to offset the benefits outwardly.

"Noticed you running around the property earlier. Quite a few laps by my count."

Dillon recalls the one minute hard/one minute easy workout he did for thirty minutes with Miles, not including the easy miles before and after. "Working on leg turnover."

Hank nods as Dillon's phone chimes, announcing a new voicemail. Dillon retrieves the phone, enters the voicemail app, and permanently deletes the call, setting the phone back down. Out of the corner of his eye, he catches Hank nodding again.

"Did you and your wife enjoy Armstrong Woods?" Dillon asks.

"Quite. It's wonderful, and like you said the main trail up to the pond is *very* steep to run in sections. We just hiked those spots. We can't get enough of the old-growth redwoods, the way they tower above the earth. Very different from what we have in the Rockies."

"What are your plans for tomorrow?"

"How far is Mount Saint Helena from here? Wife wants to run to the top if possible."

Dillon turns to his left, the twilight silhouette of Mount Saint Helena in the distance. Previous guests from back east thought at first glimpse of the majestic summit from their Munich-themed room that it was the volcanic mountain that erupted back in 1980. From his four years in the Pacific Northwest, Dillon corrected them, that it was Mount Saint *Helens* in Washington state that spewed volcanic ash fifteen miles into the atmosphere, the largest eruption in the contiguous forty-eight states since Lassen Peak back in 1915.

"I haven't run it myself, but I hear it's ten miles round-trip from the trailhead," Dillon says. "If I recall, it's a half-hour drive over to Calistoga. From there I'm not sure. I'll find out for you."

"Where do you usually run?"

"Sundays up in Annadel with some friends," Dillon says, gesturing toward the east and its rounded summit. "And around here and the vineyards next door."

"I prefer more variety myself. Oh sure, I have a fave I do more than once a month, but beyond it I run a different trail every day. Keeps me from getting stuck in a routine."

"Out here is convenient, and I don't mind repetition. There's a certain comfort and purpose to it."

"You mentioned at breakfast this morning that you run seventy miles a week . . . that's a *whole* lot of laps."

Dillon's attention drifts back to the deleted voicemail lurking in his mind. She never understood the structure, the routines, and, yes, sometimes the repetition; they're an endurance athlete's best friends. That's what made him competitive on the road-racing scene, the very thing that drew her to him. They'd met at the fund-raising Human Race in Los Angeles, where he won the 10K and set a new course record, she a volunteer inside the finishing chute, retrieving timing chips from laced shoes, instantly infatuated with his performance, the promise it held for bigger things to come. From that point on she watched him dedicate those hours not consumed by work and sleep and other of life's obligations to running. He considered it a balanced lifestyle, having cast aside Olympic dreams after college. But that didn't mean he had to give up pursuing smaller dreams: winning local and regional races, setting PRs. At worst he surmised what he did qualified as a hobby, a healthy hobby that satiated his thirst for competition, measuring himself against others. At some point she didn't see it that way: "Sports are for professionals and kids," the ambitious entrepreneur in her often quipped.

"I'm sorry, what was that?" Dillon says, back in the present.

"Quite a bit of running around in circles is all," Hank says.

"I'm sure there's a metaphor in there somewhere." Dillon knocks back the rest of his beer.

"Only if you want to see it." Hank sips from his bottle. "Every man has his vice for dealing with that which he doesn't want to face." His words float in the stillness as the darker shades of night overshadow the lighter shades of evening. Wineglasses clink inside amid muted conversation. In the distance an ATV motors along the dirt path around Beardsworth's vineyards, the headlight rhythmically filtering between the rows of Pinot Noir grapes before disappearing altogether. "It's been my experience that you really can't outrun life, son. It *always* catches back up no matter how far or fast you run." Hank takes another sip from his bottle and rises. "Thanks for the Allagash and conversation. I'm sure my wife is wondering what's taking me so long in retrieving your evening's offerings."

"I'll have the directions and drive time to Mount Saint Helena for you in the morning."

"Much obliged."

Dillon stares down the last of the twilight while the bottom of his empty beer glass magnifies and distorts the table's wood grain. The endorphin rush from his run lingers, though more in memory than body now. The cell phone rests peacefully next to the glass, the beer submerges him under the surface of the past, and the voices from inside remind him of a sense of duty, his higher purpose. Circle or no circle, he feels pretty content, the satisfaction of a fulfilling day.

Thursday Morning
The Writing on the Wall

Jim leans up against the nondescript, checker-patterned fabric wall of the cramped, recently designated Pinnacle Tax Consultants' conference room. All the comfortable office chairs have been taken by the time he wanders into the room a few minutes late, though today he prefers to stand after the hour-plus session he's just wrapped up with the gluten free, cash-flow-inept client who tried to convince Jim that the gazebo in the backyard, where his wife, trained in ashram yoga leads Sunday sessions, should be classified as a nonprofit religious entity.

In front of the attentive staff of local CPAs and admins stands a wall of intimidating personnel from Pinnacle Tax Consultants' *transitioning* team: a human resources lady, two male directors, and the CEO himself, Samuel Solomon, immaculately presented from manicured haircut to pressed black suit to shiny black shoes. The guy hasn't cracked the slimmest of smiles since Jim's arrival despite the current speakers glowing accolades about Samuel.

Jim has walked in on the end of the welcoming preamble by one of the directors who's now animatedly waving his hands and liberally sprinkling the word "synergy" as if it's pixie dust. Jim scans the room, wondering what his colleagues' reactions are. Dinky is sitting prim and proper as if begging for a treat, hands clasped tightly together on her lap. Of all the staff, Jim pities her the most. At fifty-plus years of age she'll be hard pressed to land another accounting job in the area if she's cut. Fred, Ned, and Jed, a trio of hucksters, all sitting together in the front row, appear oddly relaxed, no doubt secure with inside knowledge about their future positions. Darryl and Brendan, the founders of the local firm, stand up front but off to the side in the corner, a symbolic statement that doesn't go unnoticed by Jim. *This is bad, very bad.* The rest of the crowd stands or sits poised in their go-to, under-the-threat-of-being-let-go postures and subconscious tics.

Next, Samuel Solomon is introduced, and the reserved reception from the room, despite the spirited rah-rah preamble, speaks volumes: *Are we going to lose our jobs, or what?*

"Thank you," Samuel says. "I'm a man of few words, so I will address your obvious concerns."

Jim's heart pauses as if the starter's pistol has been raised, the hush around the room ready for it to fire.

"There will be significant changes."

Unlike the start of a race, no one moves, or blinks for that matter. No groans, no sighs, no buts. The dagger is swift. No skirting around the issue with Samuel. No sugar coating the situation, building them up for the bad news. Just *pow!* And there it is. Even the HR lady flinches at the plainspokenness.

After Samuel's words float out, hang over the group like crop dust, and alight on their shoulders, Jim's heart resumes beating. Dinky's head bows. Darryl's and Brendan's expression remains stoic, though Jim reads sadness in them.

"My apologies for the bluntness," Samuel says. "I have been in your very chairs among coworkers, strung along by management, fretting over rumors and uncertainty."

Jim swears that Samuel's gaze, as he scanned the room, landed on Jim to punctuate the last sentence.

"There will be a reduction in the workforce here in Santa Rosa as we subsume many duties in Seattle."

The stiff upper lips across the room wilt. It's one thing to hear "significant changes," but it's another to hear "RIF." Tense body language sags, a collective ripple around the room. Unsurprised, Jim nods and crosses his arms against his chest. *Might as well be "RIP."*

"The details will be communicated tomorrow." And with that statement, Samuel steps to the side, adhering to his "man of few words" motto. Jim appreciates the efficiency in which Samuel has delivered the news, and for someone who is tight-lipped, he said all that anybody needed to hear.

The HR lady lurches with surprised eyes and speaks about the transition process, what to expect and when, though Jim goes inside his own head before she's gotten too far along. *Now what? So many questions. How will they determine who stays and who goes? What duties will be subsumed? I have numerous credentials: EA, CFE, CISA, CBA, CIA, CMA . . . a veritable*

*smorgasbord of acronyms. Between self-service grocery checkout and bagging my
own groceries, I could probably add those skills to my résumé. I've never taken a
sick day, will that count? Naw, they don't care about health with all the doughnuts
they set out each morning; it's medical leave dunked in cholesterol. Will they go by
seniority? I've been here nine years, long enough to know what life was like before
Facebook turned everybody into zombies. Surely that counts for something. I'll
need to update my résumé on LinkedIn, or whatever the next networking site is
that awaits humanity . . . Kluge.net? I should probably listen to what she's saying
lest I'm volunteered for the Mars One project; a one-way mission to Mars, good
grief . . . We have four months in our rainy day—*

Someone bumps Jim's shoulder, bringing him back to the nondescript,
checker-patterned world as the group rises from their seats and heads for the
exit. Jim slips into the stream, exits the bad-news room, and returns to his
cubicle, where he finds Dinky hovering, many quivering questions at the
ready, none of which he'll be able to answer or console her about. He has
worries of his own to deal with.

Jim circles the rogue path that mountain bikers have over time created
surrounding a large oak tree, waiting for Jake, who fell behind on the mile-
long climb due to Jim's *surge*.

"Sorry," Jim says.

"So you find out tomorrow?"

"Presumably."

"Odds?"

"Not good," Jim says, mentally wringing his hands, shortening his stride
to avoid tripping over Jake, who has slowed and slid over to make room for a
trio of runners approaching.

"Hey, guys," Jake says as legs flutter by in the opposing direction.

"Hey, J and J . . . cooking up another fun event?"

"Just for you, Scotty," Jim says. A running, geo-cache scavenger hunt here
in the park."

"Without the use of cell phones or GPS devices," Jake says.

"Cool!"

"No *cell phones?*"

"Can't wait . . ."

"You just make that up?" Jake says after the other group has disappeared behind them.

"It's crossed my mind once or twice."

"We should toss that around some more, when you're not preoccupied. Told Doris yet?"

"Fortunately she didn't call after the meeting. She really wants to buy a house after the wedding . . . jeez, the wedding . . ."

"You'll get a severance package, right?"

"It's not much of one."

"Perhaps it's time to go back to plan A," Jake says, crossing the Lake Illsanjo Dam, choppy water lapping against the concrete retaining wall.

"I don't know; that was before Doris and I got serious."

"Doris will understand."

"She really does need a better studio than our kitchen table. I'd be starting from scratch."

"Back then, yes. I'm sure you can bring some of your current clients over to seed the soil. Mr. Gluten Free would love to follow you."

Jim snorts.

"I'll switch over, and I know Chase will. Dillon's looking for a local accountant."

Jim calculates the number of accounts that can conceivably move with him, though the number is insignificant in swaying his doubt about plan A.

"Think about it at least. Chase can help you market yourself."

Jim replays the dream he had after acquiring his CPA certification, wishing to head back home to Sonoma County, secure a small downtown office, and build clientele. But before he committed to plan A, Bennett Valley Accounting Services contacted him and offered him a job. Despite a partial athletic scholarship, Jim had incurred student loans, which made the offer hard to resist, so he settled into a salaried life.

As his head spins with the idea of plan A, worries spawn, and more worries spawn from those worries, his pace increasing with each iteration as they round the lake and start up the half-mile stretch of Gravel Grind. And the farther he ascends, the more his breathing deepens and his previous thoughts vanish until the summit, where he glances from one side to the other to find Jake dropped again. And again Jim circles in the middle of the fire road, breathing deeply, another apology at the ready.

Friday Noon
Back on Track

Chase pauses at the water fountain by the grandstand for a drink before he resumes the final minute of his five-minute recovery interval. He's already crushed the bulk of his two-part track workout, a grueling inverted pyramid of layered laps, starting with one and stepping up one lap at a time until he reached four, then back down, taking half the distance between each interval for recovery. All told, four hard miles.

A favorite of Chase's, the workout reflects his racing style, the desire to establish a solid pace from the start, run evenly throughout the middle miles, then blast by those at the end who lack a finishing kick or are badly fading, winning him many races on the track and the road. Cross-country events don't always reward him with as many victories, owing to the uneven surfaces and abrupt changes in topography, but his sub-4 mile pedigree is always considered a threat, ensuring that those up front *earn* their spots.

All sports demand specificity to excel at them, and running cross-country is no exception, as Spencer has harped on Chase many times in the past. Chase's current track workout is better suited out on the trails, though not the hilly long climbs and rapid descents of Annadel, but the rolling and technical stretches such as those around Spring Lake or Foothill Park, where Chase lives within running distance of. The ease of translating 400-meter laps into equivalent sections via his GPS watch is easy to accomplish, tackling each section of the course. But Chase prefers the rhythm of the oval track, the consistent surface, the precision each lap holds and the way it can be recorded, analyzed, and compared to previous workouts. It's purity at its finest.

Chase jogs in wide circles near the start/finish line, running out the clock on his long recovery interval, and at five minutes on the nose, he launches—*beep*—into the first of eight 200-meter repeats to stimulate his abundance of fast-twitch calf and quad muscles. In less than thirty meters, he reaches peak speed, each leg a set of various-length levers in motion, extending, recoiling, while tendons store and release energy directed down into the surface and propel him forward like an alternating series of seamless one-legged hops.

Beep. Thirty-two seconds. He glides to a slow 200-meter trot, replicating the sequence like a well-oiled machine—32, 31, 32, 32, 31, 31.

Approaching the start of his last interval, he spots Terri coming out onto the track, dressed in her usual running attire. He waves, but she's too far away to notice. *Beep.* Chase accelerates quicker than on the previous attempts, hitting the desired speed several meters earlier than before. Coming off the turn and onto the backstretch, Chase ratchets up the torque, reaches for another gear, an ingrained habit since high school track—though to discount Terri's presence as additional motivation is naïve—and cruises by the 200-meter mark. *Beep.* Clearly her presence aides in the sub-thirty spilt. His smile mixes awkwardly with a grimace, a sadistic pleasure from completing a tough workout even by his standards.

Passing by the oak tree at the top of the straightaway, Chase scans his oval domain until he finds Terri running in one of the outer lanes 100 meters ahead. He glances at his watch; he has time to join her for a few laps before returning to the office, and if he hurries he can stop by the grandstand, take a quick drink, and swap out his shoes before she circles around. Unfortunately, he hasn't allowed for the dark manifestations that unloop, unswoop, and unpull in his mind upon kneeling, the random details that haunt him: the announcement of his name over the public address system, crowning him state champion in the wake of his coach's condolences, or the reporter who asked Chase how he felt about breaking Olympian's Gabe Jennings's high school state record, replying, "Are his parents—?"

"Hey there, speedy," Terri says.

Chase's eyes fly open. "Hey, yeah . . . just finishing up—" He yanks both shoes off, one with the laces still knotted. "How far you going?"

"Thirty minutes. Care to join me?"

"Absolutely."

He rises once his trainers are laced and falls in step with Terri.

"Thought about what I said last Sunday at the BR&B?"

Chase flushes as he did that Sunday morning, a reaction the workout can't fully account for. "Yeah, I have. But . . ."

"Nervous?"

"Somewhat."

"It's completely confidential, and no one will know your name. It would really help me out."

Perhaps it's the bliss of a superb track workout, or the tight running shorts and black sports bra Terri wears, or her straightforward approach in asking him to participate in her Human Sexuality project; whatever the reason, he agrees to participate.

"Awesome! You'll make a perfect candidate: a tech obsessive athlete not in a relationship."

Chase frowns at this sterile assessment of himself.

"When can we start?"

"I'm crazy busy next week."

"How 'bout the week after?"

"Works for me. Dinner?"

"Sure."

"Your *pace* or mine?" Chase says with a grin.

"And Dillon thinks *I'm* trouble."

Three laps later, Chase realizes he needs to head back to the office. He bids Terri farewell, makes his way off the track and out onto the city sidewalks, waves to Spencer's classroom window, and switches his mind to the latest ad campaign he's taken on: Dillon's BR&B. But a block later his mind drifts back to Terri. *What are you doing? She's a grad student with a psych background; she'll see right through your bullshit. It's just a study, just volunteering to help out, right? . . . Wrong, dude.* Chase shrugs, crossing a street, switching back to marketing ideas he has for Dillon's inn, a much easier task to process, bullshit and all.

Saturday Morning
Willow Hills Invitational: Zac's First Big Race of the Season

Sunlight shimmers off the dewy grass field adjacent Folsom High School as small groups of runners dressed down in team sweats jog through it, the official start/finish area, either heading out or returning from previewing the spectator-friendly, rolling-hills 5K course that winds its way around the Willow Hill Reservoir.

"Enough of a warm-up?" Spencer asks as he and the varsity boys slow to a walk, finishing up their preview.

"Yep," Zac responds. He drops to a knee, retrieves his bright-green cross-country racing flats from his gym bag, and slips them on, lacing them up alongside his teammates on an oversized blanket sprawled amongst dozens of other team blankets against a chain-link fence. "Legs feel good. The trails are bone dry. All systems go, Coach."

Spencer surveys the scene, the first notable high school cross-country invitational of the fall, where teams from all over Northern California are entered. "Race strategy locked in?"

"Cruise the first two miles, green-light the last mile."

"There isn't anybody here that you haven't beaten before. The Mateo twins have improved and will stick with you for a while, along with the usual suspects. And remember—"

"I know, Coach, don't burn off anybody too early . . . got it."

Spencer nods as Zac stands up. "Run a controlled race. The CIF and Footlocker races are your goals this year," he says, turning toward the rest of the varsity squad. "Watch the start. It's crowded and narrows after three hundred yards. Bring it in." Focused nods follow as the team of seven huddle around Spencer in a tight circle. "Never give up on your team, and . . ."

"Quit on your own time," says the charged circle.

"One, two, three."

"Once a Panther, always a Panther!"

"Okay, guys, time to get dirty," Zac says, turning and walking toward the start line, making adjustments to his bib number and the amount of jersey he wants tucked into his shorts.

"Dirty, Zac Man?" Oz says.

"Time to step up, Oz," Spencer says. "You're as important as Zac."

"Right, Coach," he says, displaying a mixture of a sarcasm and thoughtfulness.

Oz is stuck somewhere between the desire to be the class clown and a solid runner. Whether he realizes it or not, he's a vital cog in the Panthers' quest not only to win league, but district and possibly state. Spencer's challenge is to find the right set of buttons to bring Oz to that realization at some point in the next two months.

Then there's Zac, a confident facade atop a bedrock of insecurity, the result of an unstable home life. For the most part talent, dedication, and hard work keep him feet and legs ahead of the others during smaller races. It's at the bigger meets, with more runners in Zac's realm, that the wheels fall off the wagon, testing him early to shake his confidence. Yet another challenge for Spencer to tackle.

Spencer trots along the first quarter mile of the course, around a portion of the reservoir to a short pier, walking out to the end of it, watching the varsity boys assemble at the start line from across the peaceful surface, his cross-country scoring app queued up and a hand ready to start the watch.

The start line stretches thirty yards wide, two runners from each school in front, the rest of the squad lined up directly behind like a television test pattern of colors: blue, dark blue, faded yellow, green, black, navy blue, orange, white and so on. The familiar hush spreads across the field, the kind reserved for separating pent-up potential and realized energy, Rob Shore's arm poised, ready to release it. One hundred and thirty-three stringy-legged bodies clad in loosely fitted team uniforms crouch in anticipation, toeing an imperfectly laid chalk line. First the puff of white smoke spews out from the pistol, the moment Spencer starts his watch, followed by the sound of the distant *crack!*

The runners lurch off the line like a herd of startled deer, their thoughts no more advanced than that, thundering out with short, rapid steps. The previously segmented color band blurs and melds into a kaleidoscope of motion, stretching out like an accordion. Zac has gotten off to a good start, a quick burst of speed off the line then settling in as the pack sweeps around the reservoir toward Spencer.

After the field flashes by, Spencer walks a short distance to a spot where they will pass, beyond the one-mile mark. While waiting he remembers an email from Walter that requires attention, but before he opens it he finds a new one from the school principal with the Subject "Open Department Chair . . ." Spencer virtually performs a backflip. His mind entertains the possibilities: shaping policy, devising curriculum, he can finally enact his "Chalk Is Cheap" program. Sure, there are downsides, dealing with parental concerns, playing den mother to the others in the department, certainly no minor feat, but "department chair!" Maggie's dad might finally get off Spencer's back about running. He opens the email, reading through the specifics, monthly meeting for all chairs, monthly district chair meeting, writing out the yearly teacher class schedule, on call to the principal and vice principal, no small time commitment, but "department chair!"

A cowbell clanks. Spencer peers in its direction, but instead of racers a boy from one school walks by hand in hand with a girl from another school. *That's not complicated.* The cowbell clanks again. Spencer strains his eyes, but he's hard-pressed to make out anything among the teeming spectators and oak trees.

Maggie . . . I can already hear her, "It is not enough to be busy. So are the ants. The question is: What are we busy about?" . . . I don't understand her fascination with Thoreau. . . . Simplicity? Wilderness preservation? . . . The pay increase is meager, pretty much on par with running coach. But "department chair!" Dad could dine on this for years.

A frantic cowbell and shouts return Spencer to his current anthill, catching sight of Zac exiting a cluster of oak trees sixty yards in front of a pack of six runners. "Control, Zac, control," Spencer says as Zac zips by. He's straying from the race plan, laying down an early burn to put the field away sooner rather than later. The trouble is, the field will fall away on its own over the second flat-ish mile. The talent isn't there to sustain the current pace, but Zac's been spooked by the crowd that hung on to him through the first hilly mile and is now taking charge. *Still needs more patience.*

Once the chase pack of six has passed, the rest of the field comes into view and streams by Spencer, his finger tapping fast and furious the scoring app. Spencer doles out words of encouragement to his squad. Even Oz sails by engaged and focused in *front* of the team's fourth man. *Funny to think, but he's the team's future.*

All seven members accounted for, Spencer walks back out to the end of the pier, watching the quiet struggle of anaerobic competition drift along, passing through the dewy start area again, where they'll run a longer second loop and filter back toward the finish. The Panthers sit comfortably in first place based on the initial data from Spencer's app. He resets it for the finish.

"Your boys are looking strong this year," says an approaching man. "Zac looks solid."

"Hey, Tomlin," Spencer says, extending his hand to shake with the Mateo coach. "It's still early, but certainly looks promising. The Labonte twins must've had a good summer of training."

"They did. Now if only they wouldn't burn each other out. Everything is a competition with them," Tomlin says, chuckling.

"It'd be nice if that spilled over to the rest of the team."

"I'm working on it, but the twins like to keep to themselves for the most part. I spoke with their parents and they told me that they have never really been very social."

"Not the best trait for cross-country,"

"Certainly not . . . your club sure surprised Chico at the RERC Open last weekend. Who's the new guy that finished behind Chase?"

"Dillon. Transplant from Southern California."

"Everybody thought Chico would give Agras a run for their money this year. Now it looks like you guys are in the mix as well."

"We'll see. The Agras never show their true hand until the PA Champs."

"True," Tomlin says, turning to leave, "but it should be fun to watch."

"You're looking fit this year," Spencer says, joining Tomlin in jogging back to the start/finish area, discussing his training as well as his club's race-commitment problem, always playing negotiator in convincing enough guys to run each weekend, telling one guy that so-and-so is running when in fact so-and-so hadn't committed yet and his commitment was conditional on some other guy, who would only run if there were already four committed. It sounds like a circus act.

"See you at Ancil Hoffman next week," Spencer says after arriving to the finish area and hearing someone nearby shout, "Here they come!" Spencer turns around as Zac, demeanor possessed, barrels down the hard-packed path along the reservoir. Spencer glances at his watch as Zac flashes under the finish banner; a twenty-two-second PR over last year on this course, and quite possibly a new meet record. Though it's hard to argue with the overall results, Spencer still groans over the *way* Zac accomplished it. *It's time to unleash the Big Dogs on him. It's about the only way to prep him for the bigger meets down the road.*

A commanding thirty seconds passes before the next runner hits the reservoir path, one of the Mateo twins, head tilted back, legs slicing through the crisp air. He's followed shortly after by two more runners, then the other twin, and soon the main field arrives, a grimacing stream of countenances, laborious palpitations, and lactic-acid anarchy, yet dogged determination until the last contested parcel is chewed up and spit out. It harks back to Helsinki's triple gold-medal winner, Czechoslovakia's Emil Zátopek, form and spirit in all his contorted Olympic glory. Torsos flop forward once past the finish line, some unable to proceed, bunching up the chute until a volunteer gives them a nudge, along with the words, "Keep moving." The line flows again, shoulder pats and "good jobs" are added in for good measure as the course empties its harriers.

All seven Panthers accounted for, Spencer reviews the team scoring on his app—Santa Rosa: 32; Mateo 63; Orchard: 98; St. Henry: 132; Windsor: 146. A convincing win, though not the strongest field. The true test lies ahead in a few weeks at the Stanford Cross-Country Invitational. *Zac won't get away with today's strategy on that course against a very strong field.*

Zac flits about outside the finishing chute, waiting for his teammates, cheering them on, giving Oz a high five to celebrate his move up to fourth man on the team. Now the Panthers stroll up to the blanket, all very animated and joking around.

"How'd we do, Coach?" Oz says, flopping spread-eagle on the blanket. "We better have won 'cause I gave my left nut today."

The rest of the guys and some of the girls standing nearby laugh.

"You won, Oz, but you might want to retrieve it. We'll need it in three weeks."

"Not to worry, Coach. I have two—"

"Thank you, Oz, for the anatomy lesson," Spencer says. "Now, get your warm-down in. Awards are in thirty minutes, and the bus leaves ten minutes after they're done."

Sunday Morning
City, County, and State Politics

"Chase, staging a coup d'état," Dillon says at 8:11 a.m. as they begin their run from city-operated Howarth Park, every kid's summer amusement haven with its miniature train rides, quaint carousel, animal farm, and pony rides. "Shirtless no less, à la Putin."

"I'm *not* a fan of horses," Chase says, having beaten Spencer to the punch on his weekly email and rallying the others offline beforehand. "Too big for their own good."

Jim and Jake exchange troubled glances. As benign as Chase's maneuver seemed to them initially, it quickly becomes apparent that repercussions will soon follow.

"Spence, how'd the Panthers—?" Jake starts to say, attempting a preemptive strike while skirting around serene Lake Ralphine, where young anglers cast lines outward and whose only political worries in life are who to invite to their birthday parties.

"Given the GOP's current—" Spencer says.

"Oh, boy," Jim says. "I should've known this—"

"Let it go, Spence—" Jake says.

"Given the GOP's current unrest and fifteen-candidate clown car, the coup isn't surprising."

"Clown car!" Chase says.

"Guys, drop it," Jake says. "Nothing good ever comes from this."

"Like we need a *Seinfeld* character or a *former* First Lady leading the nation," Chase says.

Crossing the border into county-operated Spring Lake and its recreational bounty of water park, swimming lagoon, group picnic areas, and campgrounds, Jim and Jake shake their heads; Pandora's box has flung wide open.

"Trump is leading the GOP polls by a wide margin. Watergate was less embarrassing to politics."

"And another Zippergate is preferable?"

"You do know that Trump is widely blamed for sacking the old USFL," Spencer says, bringing the fight to Chase's affinity for football. "Imagine that on a grander—"

"The what?" Chase says.

"The United States Football League, back in the early '80s. A good example of how knowing history keeps us from repeating the same mistakes," Spencer says.

"I was in diapers," Chase says.

"I'd like to speak to you about the Lord," Jim says. "Do you have a minute?"

"As philosopher George Santayana once wrote, 'Those who cannot remember the past are doomed to repeat it,'" Jake says. "This is why we shouldn't discuss politics."

"Or religion," Jim says.

"Guess Dillon agrees . . ." Chase says.

Dillon has crossed over into state-operated Annadel thirty yards ahead, the gap growing.

The guys adopt a bipartisan stance and pursue Dillon, who says when caught that their political bickering reminds him too much of his parents.

"So, not a fan of politics?" Chase says.

"Runners haven't discussed politics during a run since Carter's Moscow Olympics boycott. It's bad form," Dillon says. "Besides, I don't take sides and I don't vote."

"Yet it was Mr. Switzerland here who incited the whole affair," Jim says.

Dillon apologizes, vows it'll never happen again, and atones for his faux pas on the holiest running day of the week by saying, "Exercise gives you endorphins. Endorphins make you happy. Happy people just don't discuss politics, they just don't." No one offers up a response. "*Legally Blonde*."

"Interesting," Jim says. "I missed that one altogether."

Jake agrees.

"The ex made me watch. That line is the only part I remember."

"Can I say one last thing?" Chase says.

Groans emanate at the Spring Creek/Canyon Trail split.

"I'll allow a one-sentence closing argument from each candidate," Jake says.

An acorn woodpecker lands on a nearby oak tree and goes to work.

"Surely Trump's voice doesn't represent America," Chase says.

"And from the DNC candidate?"

Spence-speak.

"Brilliant!" Jim says. "Never have politics been so concise and informative."

They pass underneath an abundance of alders, bay trees, and redwoods that flank and shade the Spring Creek trail up to Lake Illsanjo. Chase and Jim readily gap the others, more so over the dry creek runoff and up the steeper section of trail. Jake has dropped back to run with a couple of old-timers he hasn't seen in some time. Dillon is caught between Spencer and the duo up front. Two Spence-speaks have no effect on the disrupters, mostly due to the deep inhalations and noisy exhalations imposed by the gradient, and so the faction is resigned to regroup at the top of the climb on the Lake Illsanjo Dam.

Spencer adds one more Spence-speak once he catches up to Chase, Jim, and Dillon, though it goes unacknowledged. Instead they admire the thin layer of fog overlaying the placid lake, ducks floating across the top in various directions and paces while black bass and bluegill dart underneath near the shoreline. A minute later, Jake arrives with the two other runners, who bid him a "good run" and keep on going.

"Do you know everybody in the county?" Dillon asks Jake.

Jake shrugs.

"I have 673 friends on Facebook," Chase says.

"Yeah, that's the same," Jim says.

While the guys debate which way around the lake they want to head, Dale comes into view, shuffling toward them from the other direction. "Running hard, Dale?" Chase says. "Or hardly running?"

"You talkin' to me, wise guy?" Dale raises his arms like a '40s boxer caricature with a grin equally cartoonish.

Chase feigns fear by hiding behind Jake.

"Always in motion, my friend," Jake says as Dale passes by.

"Hurts less than standing."

Jim excuses himself and heads back the way they have just come, cutting his long run short because he and Doris have plans to drive to the city for a wedding expo. The others tell him to have fun, and best of luck with the job decision he's been saddled with.

Still miffed about the coup—and more so at finding out that Jim had planned a shorter run, which undoubtedly contributed to the fast Spring Creek ascent—Spencer expresses his displeasure over the lack of an overall route plan, but his subtle comments are ignored as the rest of the group have a more meandering mood in mind. They do at least decide upon the next segment, rounding the lake clockwise, and off they venture.

Seeking political asylum, Spencer says, "Did you guys hear that Chico beat the Agras yesterday at Garin Park?"

"Really?" Dillon says. "How'd that happen?"

"The Agras switched out their second and fourth men, who weren't as fast."

"That makes things *interesting*—" Chase starts to say before he and the group have to zigzag their way through a horde of birders strewn across the slim trail: some amble side by side, pointing out a possible dark-eyed junco;

others stand poised with binoculars, searching for a Steller's jay or black phoebe; and one who steps back into the middle of the trail without looking to snap off a picture of a suspected Northern flicker and is nearly trampled by the roving mammalian herd.

"How'd the Panthers do yesterday?" Jake asks.

"They won," Spencer says.

"And Zac?" Chase says.

"Broke the meet record," Spencer says.

"Nice!"

"Did he follow the race plan you laid out?" Jake says.

"No. There were a handful of guys with him at the mile and he put them away."

"Sounds like nothing has changed from last year," Chase says.

"Not really."

"What happened last year?" Dillon says, scaling back his effort when no one matches his acceleration at the base of Gravel Grind.

"At CIF, he tried to lose the field too early and almost missed a spot to Footlocker. He has a hard time mentally when there's a group with him. Many of his races are run where he's way out front, so when the bigger meets come up and there are a number of guys just as talented as him, he tries to outrun them early on," Spencer says.

"Only they don't go away," Dillon says.

"Exactly. At league meets and regional invitationals he compensates by running all-out, which makes things worse for him, I think. It gives him a false since of accomplishment."

"What ended up happening at Footlocker?" Dillon says.

"Basically the same thing. Only there the top guys had more championship experience and let him blow himself up early by simply sitting on his shoulder."

"He showed heart, though," Jake says.

"He did. He never gave up despite dropping back twelve spots. He recovered some and finished strong," Spencer says. "He's a fighter."

"Hmmm," Chase utters. "It sounds more like self-sabotaging behavior than simply his *style* of racing. How do you fix that?"

"I'm glad you asked," Spencer says.

"It was bound to happen."

Jake half snorts, half chuckles.

"I'm thinking of going old-school on him, John Wooden–style."

Beyond Gravel Grind's sway and traversing the flat stretch between the Burma South and North Trailheads the other guys glance over to Spencer with the same question, though it isn't clear if the question is "John Wooden who?" or what the late great, ULCA basketball coaching legend has to do with running.

"The 'Wizard of Westwood'?" Dillon says.

"The one and only. He used to have practice sessions where he simulated game day on the road, putting the team through every imaginable scenario using practice squads."

Their footsteps press fallen leaves, accumulating by the week, into the trail like fossil imprints, though Spencer's plan doesn't leave the same impression on the guys.

"So, what I was thinking of doing is setting up a couple race time trials and have as his competition . . . *us*."

"Oh, like having a major-league pitcher throw batting practice to the high school teams," Chase says. "Coach, let's see you bring—"

"*The Rookie*," Jake says.

"What do you think?" Spencer says.

"Do we have to let the kid win?" Chase says.

"Chase . . ." Spencer says.

"I'm just asking; let the kid win or make him work?"

"I'm in," Dillon says, after which Jake confirms his interest.

"I was thinking a good place to do it so we're not bothered by pedestrian traffic would be Percy's Loop. Would that be okay, Dillon?"

"No problem. We'll throw Miles in there for good measure."

"And we can have Terri there to distract him," Chase says.

Someone groans, another utters Chase's name, and Spencer concludes, "He's in high school."

"My point exactly."

"So what's this sex study you're participating in with Terri?" Dillon asks.

Chase stumbles, though he recovers before going down. "What?"

Chuckles sprout.

"Terri mentioned it."

"It was supposed to be—"

"Riiiight. Like she covers anything up."

The guys give Chase grief about his involvement in Terri's sex study, though Dillon admits that the details of the study haven't been revealed to him, so Chase is safe . . . for now.

After pausing halfway down Richardson at the hairpin turn to decide where to go next, they embark up Two Quarry. And though Spencer steered the group decision in that direction, the increase in pace instantly rubs against his controlled Sunday wishes, Chase and Dillon leading the charge, silently egging each other on.

"Don't sweat it, Spence," Jake says as Chase and Dillon disappear around the bend.

"Why bother getting together, then?" Spencer says. "Sundays are meant for conversational pace . . . unless someone has something specific to do."

"You can't control *everything*." Jake deftly negotiates an uphill stretch of loose shale that shifts and grinds against other pieces under his weight, gapping Spencer's steady road marathon stride. "Think of it this way . . . friendly group competition galvanizes the soul. *That's* why we get together."

Spencer considers Jake's comment while bridging the gap back to his heels beyond the slippery slope of shale, the concept not entirely off base: competition does bring out the best in an individual. But midweek hard runs are a better time to "galvanize the soul." Spencer has to admit, however, that the guys seldom run together during the work week, given the fact that they rarely follow the same training plan or train at the same time of day. Despite the logical conundrum, Spencer remains miffed.

Once Spencer is within listening distance again, Jake adds, "Besides, you've occasionally double-booked your Sunday runs with non-conversational paces."

"They're called combo workouts."

"Yours is a nuance of obscurity."

Spence-speak.

Three-quarters of a mile later, Spence and Jake reach the spot where Chase and Dillon have stopped and are talking with another runner, who happened upon them from a connecting trail. Once regrouped, they resume running up the rutty fire road to the outhouse at the Marsh.

"That way you start off your training week with a bunch of miles," concludes the mid-twenties runner, full of enthusiasm, answering Chase's question as to why the guy starts his training log on Sunday rather than the traditional way: Monday through Sunday.

"Calendars don't make sense to me: work and school weeks don't run Sunday to Saturday," Dillon says. "So why are they set up that way?"

"Saturday is considered the Sabbath, the end of the week, making Sunday the first day," Jake says.

"Really?" Dillon says.

"Really . . . it's in the Bible."

"They did much running back then, did they?" Chase says, chuckling afterward. "Still, you shouldn't start a training week off with a long run. Place it at the end of the training week and build up to it throughout the week. It has a better flow to it." Chase petitions the rest of the Sunday crew.

One by one each acknowledges Monday.

"There you go," Chase says, bypassing the Marsh outhouse.

"I like starting off my week with the long run," the young runner says. "That way it's out of the way."

"Tackling the toughest chore first is admirable, especially for procrastinators," Jake says, "but then there's something to be said for saving the best for last: endows one with a greater sense of satisfaction at the end of the week."

"Jake, you're a riddle, wrapped in a mystery, inside an enigma," Chase says.

"The highest of compliments," Jake says.

"What are you training for?" Spencer asks.

"Portland Marathon in October. I've done it three years in a row, and can't seem to break my PR. It's a fast flat course too. I've been trying to qualify for Boston."

"Any ideas as to why?"

"I don't know . . . I put in all these miles, run speed stuff, tempo runs . . . can't break through."

"Where do things go wrong?"

"Usually the last seven or eight miles. When I pick up the pace my legs go wonky."

"Chase has a sport drink for that," Spencer says.

"Pfft."

Upon further discussion and listening to the Boston hopeful explain his fascination with legendary runners, Prefontaine's and Lindgren's balls-to-the-wall approach to training and racing, Spencer informs him that neither of the two great runners had ever run a marathon, and, sure, their approach to a 5K or 10K is tolerable, considering that the race is relatively short compared to a marathon. This revelation doesn't faze the young buck, however, and he prattles on about how he's going to *own* the marathon until they come to the Ridge Trail split, where he bids the group farewell and veers left toward it while the guys stay on course, back through the political gauntlet of the park agency trifecta, albeit with diplomatic immunity.

Back at Howarth Park, the guys slow to a walk, except for Spencer, who continues on, running laps around the parking lot, going in circles like the nearby carousel that has filled with jubilant, wide-eyed children.

"What's he doing?" Dillon says, stepping up to his early-model compact pickup truck. "Twenty not enough?"

Jake and Chase grin.

"He's rounding out the mileage to the next half mile," Jake says.

"Really?"

They both nod.

"They call me data obsessive, but I don't round my distances off," Chase says, mixing up his usual post-run recovery drink. He explains to Dillon the science behind the formula after he inquires about it. "Research has shown that a four-to-one ratio of protein to carbohydrates is optimal for recovery after long or hard runs."

"Whose research?" Dillon says.

"The company selling the product."

"So not independent?"

"Like you always say, it's all about the branding," Jake says.

"Jake over here is eating a Slim Jim," Chase says.

"I go with what my body craves."

"Your body woke up craving beef jerky?"

"My body woke up craving a run. Now it craves beef jerky. Jim treats himself to a Slurpee every Sunday. Fuel is fuel, my friends."

"I'm still hungry," Chase says, his liquid recovery now empty.

Dillon offers him a slice of banana bread, which Chase accepts and samples. "Tasty. You make this?"

Dillon nods.

"Doesn't that throw off the ratio?" Spencer says upon concluding his rounding-off exercise. *Beep.*

Chase swallows his second bite and pauses, mind deep in thought. "Naw, I'm sure they factored that into it." He bites off another chunk.

"Sure, anything consumed ninety seconds before or after should work," Jake says.

"Metaphorically speaking, that is," Dillon says.

	PA/USATF TOP 5 TEAM STANDINGS AS OF 10/4/2015	
	Club	Total
1	Agras (10–9)	19
2	Chico Running Club (8–10)	18
3	Strawberry Hill Harriers (7–7)	14
4	South Bay Striders (6–8)	14
5	RERC (9–x)	9

Week 40 Training Summary			
	Long Run	Mileage Total	Comments
Dillon	20	73	Legs are starting to feel some snap to them.
Chase	19.98	68	Great week on the track!
Spencer	20.50	84	Tired this week . . . mileage?
Jim	10	56	Threat of termination is distracting.
Jake	20	67	Celebrating 25 years of running this week.

Week 6
October 5

Monday Daybreak
Pacing Himself

Clad in gray running shorts, a blue short-sleeved shirt shrouded under a gray longer-sleeved one, Jim exits his home through the back door and heads down the extended driveway flanked by lush rose bushes that Doris spends several hours each week maintaining. Walking toward the street he preps his watch to alert him at specific times, per his scheduled "tempo" workout: fifteen minutes (warm-up), forty-five minutes (tempo pace), fifteen minutes (warm-down). The tempo portion of his workout will be divided into two paces, ten seconds over his lactate threshold pace outbound to Willowside along the creekside path—5:23/mile pace based on his half-marathon race run several weeks earlier—and ten seconds under that pace on the trip home. Taking advantage of a shorter-than-normal Sunday long run, Jim alters his week's schedule by moving this workout up one day to allow for an additional easy day before next Saturday's cross-country meet; he wants his legs *fresh* for the faster race course in Sacramento.

Beep. Out on the street, Jim slips on his gloves and settles into a brisk pace down the middle of the road, past parked cars with dewy windows, some with occupants ready to embark on their commute to the Bay Area. It's 6:10 a.m., the air crisp to his exposed quads and face. He blows on his gloved hands a couple times, drawing pleasure from the quiet neighborhood before excited school children wander to invisible bus stops, awaiting yellow school buses to shuttle them off to a brave new world.

He passes by Juilliard Park, which shows little activity save for a couple of dog walkers, restless vagrants, and Leo, whose stress fracture has apparently reduced him to walking on soft surfaces. This connects him with the easternmost point of the Prince Greenway, paved for multiuse pedestrian traffic, hugging the Santa Rosa Creek that snakes lazily west for six miles to Willowside Road—a journey from downtown Santa Rosa to the outskirts of west county without automotive interruption.

Cruising past the "The Guardian of the Creek," or the "Fish," as locals refer to it, a thirteen-foot-tall mosaic statue depicting a rainbow trout yearning to return to the creek, Jim glances at his watch; ten minutes left in the warm-up. The news had been harsh but swift last Friday when he received an email from HR requesting his presence in their office. The message itself lacked any hint of what was to come, though Jim's mind jumped immediately to the worst-case scenario. The walk from the main open floor down the short hallway stretched longer than previous trips. He spotted details he'd either never seen or had long forgotten since his first day there: Darryl and Brendan actually had the same middle initials, according to their office door placards; the carpet appeared a darker shade of gray, and threadbare down the middle; the walls felt closer together, to the point that should someone try to pass by, personal space would be violated. He spread his arms out but neither hand reached a wall.

He stopped at the one open door in the hallway, lightly knocked on the mahogany door, and peered inside to see the HR lady sitting with her face glued to her computer monitor.

"Jay. Come in and have a seat," she said, waving him in.

"It's Jim," he replied, pulling the chair back from her desk and sitting.

"Oh! Sorry . . . Jim," she said, peering closer at the monitor, "Greyson?"

"Right."

"Could you please close the door."

Jim rose and pushed the door. As he returned to the chair the door clicked into place, and the room emptied like a vacuum, the office din out front doused, leaving behind a suffocating cloud of worry, the movement of office supplies on the desk, and Jim's heartbeat. He took a seat.

"Jim, my name is Norrine," she said, extending her hand to shake his between two stacks of personnel files. "As you may recall, Mr. Solomon stated last week that he is making significant changes here at the Santa Rosa location, which means, unfortunately, layoffs."

Jim presented a passive appearance, though inside a flock of black swans gathered. *Flock or wedge?*

"You've been with Bennett Valley Accounting Services for"—Norrine peeked at Jim's personnel file—"nine years now, correct?"

Jim forced a delayed nod when his voice failed to produce a yes. He wished he'd brought along his water bottle.

"While you haven't been here the longest, you do possess credentials the others do not have."

A glimmer of hope flickered.

"However . . ."

Glimmer extinguished.

"We're not going to be able to keep you on permanently."

Smoldering ash remained.

Permanently? What does that mean?

"We'd like to offer you an eight-week transition period position to assist with the merger, after which you'd be let go with the standard severance package. This will give you an extra eight weeks of paid decision-making time for your next opportunity."

Jim remained nonplused. *Eight weeks . . . standing on the guillotine with a noose around my neck, the rest of the office morbid gawking villagers?*

"What do you think, Jim—?"

Beep.

Jim shakes his arms out, letting the gradual downward slope pull him to a brisker pace without much effort, gradually hitting what he feels is his tempo pace. He'll reassess after a couple minutes and adjust as needed based on his breathing rate and the occasional glance at his watch for validation. Gliding along, his legs fresh after an easy weekend of running, he catches sight of a homeless man stirring next to the pilings that support the roadway above, a common sight at this hour. Jim gives the man a nod, receiving a glassy-eyed response in return.

To his left the creek, flowing with him, low, slow, and narrow, splits into two streams and creates a small island that two ducks wander across. He slides to his right at the sound of a bike bell, which is followed by "Morning," from the fully decked-out cyclist passing by. Jim flicks his left hand up in acknowledgment.

As the cyclist shrinks into the distance, Jim adjusts his pace, a nudge faster, and locks onto the path's vanishing point, letting the world around him, and in him, go quiet. Steady state, the virtue of the tempo run, reflects Jim's tried and true form in life. It isn't taxing enough to command complete mental effort, yet the pace does demand a constant and steady focus, for letting the mind wander blissfully or worrisomely can easily send him off pace. So with a free mind and nothing but asphalt six feet wide stretched out before him, Jim focuses on what matters most: his breathing and the bisecting charms of Sonoma County.

By the time Jim dips under Fulton Road, essentially leaving Santa Rosa city life behind, the warmth of the two shirts he wears turns to a light sweat, the material of the base layer wicking off the excess, though he isn't quite ready to ditch his gloves. The scenery to his left and right changes dramatically, from suburban pockets and business parks butted up against the path, to expansive vineyards and pastoral parcels. In the distance to his right Mount Saint Helena rises majestically. The ability to run from downtown to out-of-town via underpasses and rust-colored truss bridges in mere miles on foot and back chronicles a journey that often takes him back in time, a simpler time, shuttling him from his doorstep through school systems, commerce, homes, vineyards, open space, grounding him to the county, then watching it slowly, and at times imperceptibly, "grow up" on the return trip home.

At Willowside, Jim hangs a left, runs the width of the creek across the county road bridge, and leans into the next left, preparing to accelerate, but he juts wide at the last moment to avoid a dog walker immersed on his cell phone and whose furry companion is six feet or more from its owner across the dirt path and tethered by an all but invisible piece of retractable nylon. Nothing is said by dog owner or runner, just a silent understanding by each party to be more alert next time.

Halfway point, the free energy return from the asphalt gives way to moderately hard-packed dirt as Jim works his way to a faster-than-tempo pace against the flow of the creek. Twenty-four minutes down, twenty-one minutes left at twenty seconds per mile faster than the previous outbound pace, Jim narrows his focus, warding off the temptation to let the mind wander, the pace no longer on the aerobic side of his lactate threshold line, no longer conversational even with himself. This is the unheralded mental benefit that bolsters the modern-day runner, to remain focused on one task for more than a minute or two: multitasking, two monitors on the desk, several forms of communication options, *squirrel!*, all purported to improve productivity yet do the exact opposite. Easy recovery runs and longer runs that lack intensity, both allow the runner to switch between thoughts as needed, but sustained tempo runs expand their attention beyond multitasking temptations and the ever changing daily scroll of life on social media.

Lacking underpasses on this side of the creek, Jim opts to *cross* Fulton Road rather than go through the gymnastics of left, left, left, underpass, left, left, left, the early morning traffic light enough to support his choice. He barely slows, just enough to glance both ways, hopping over the median in short order, reaching the other sidewalk and creekside trail, large oak trees arching over from both sides, framing his route.

Gloves off, each tucked into the front of his shorts, the fingers flopping freely over the waistband, Jim pushes the sleeves of his outer shirt above his elbows as his metabolic engine answers the call he's placed, guiding him along efficiently as signs of suburbia crop back up, home after home whose backyards border the path. He wonders what it would be like living along here, having his backyard on display by all passersby; he doubts he'd ever be able to relax out back with people constantly flowing by, peering in.

Attention momentarily diverted, he refocuses, approaching another road crossing, this time Stoney Point—more business-park traffic than Fulton, but with additional stoplights, opportunistic gaps in traffic often form—he glances left and right and dashes across, the last of such inconveniences. The scenery remains unchanged, the dirt path less packed yet not overly uneven. He peers up ahead, surveying the small encampment that litters the approaching underpass. The smell of pot assaults his respiration. This is one section, the outskirts of downtown and along depressed real estate, where unsavory activities occur. He holds his breath, passing by three men huddled around a halved wine barrel, one or two who grumble and bark gibberish Jim doesn't try to understand. Beyond the nauseating stench he opens his mouth, captive air bursting out, now short of breath, heart rate further elevated. He gulps in what air he can, restoring tempo stasis.

Beep, beep, beep.

Great timing!

Grateful for the reprieve, he slows to a jog, holds it several minutes to catch his breath, and picks back up for the easy trot home, where the downtown area shows commuter life in various modes of transportation and commerce coming to life, yellow school buses making stops and filling up.

What do I think? Do I basically take a temp position for a company I've worked at for nine years, training new people to take my position? That sounds logical. I say yes; then what? Spend eight weeks walking the plank while looking for another job locally? The others who are let go before me will have first dibs. I suppose there are more opportunities and better pay down south. Commuting . . . ugh. Like I don't have better things to do with my time than sit in a car on the freeway with the rest of the rat race. I can run faster than traffic half the time. The new SMART train is coming to town. The cattle car would be faster, and less stress. Still, a couple hours out of my day. My training would be affected. They should put a treadmill on the train: the rat race collides with the hamster wheel . . . Doris won't like not being able to call me during an extended commute. She knows I hate talking on my cell phone in public, everybody eavesdropping on the call: my responses are too easily taken out of context, then I'm explaining myself to strangers. It's a whole thing. Opposable thumbs not withstanding, having a conversation via text message is worse; so tedious . . . Severance package is pretty basic: nine weeks, plus job placement courses. He shrugs his shoulders. *Plan A?*

Too much stress? Jake and Doris might be right, though. I could work from home until I build a client list before hanging a shingle on an office door. I don't know. Could be risky. Maybe I should simply suck it up and take the transition position for the next two months and give this some more thought.

Jim cruises into his driveway, slows to a stop—*beep*—and then walks the rose-bush gauntlet toward the back door. Shaking out his legs, he wonders what answer he'll give to the HR lady in a couple hours. But for now no matter what answer he gives at least he has started his day off on the right foot.

Monday Night Football
San Francisco at Green Bay

Chase has just set out bowls of tortilla chips, salsa, and guacamole as well as his Packer Cheesehead platter layered with a couple different Wisconsin cheeses and accompanying crackers when the doorbell rings, the first of many guests to arrive. If tradition holds, Chase knows who it is. "Come in, Dale!"

The door springs open and in walks the RERC's eldest member, his lunch-sized cooler in hand. "Hey, hey, Chase," he says, shuffling in like a man with more miles on his legs than Chase can ever imagine running himself or keeping a car around long enough for its odometer to compile.

"Greetings and salutations. You're the first to arrive. Make yourself at home." Chase returns to the kitchen to grab napkins.

"Meow."

"You get near the food tonight, Dogma, and I'm going to grill *you* instead of the chicken," Chase says, nudging Dogma out from under his feet. "Cat kabobs, I'll call it."

Dogma's expression shows no concern.

"Nice place, Chase," Dale says, taking up residence on the couch. He opens his 49ers cooler and pulls a beer out, flipping the can's tab open. "Don't think I've been here to watch a game."

"The guys only let me host when the Packers are playing."

"Why?"

"I make them watch the commercials."

Dale chuckles. "That explains the early start time."

"Millions of dollars in advertising flushed down—"

"We can't decide," Jim says, entering the condo with Doris, Jake, Linda, Robyn, and a couple other club members on their heels, "if you'd rather watch the game or the commercials."

"Commercials heighten the suspense of the game. Certainly better than watching the sportscasters pick their noses while filling dead air time."

"I love Gruden," Linda says.

"He is entertaining, I'll give him that," Chase says. "Bottom shelf in the fridge is empty. Toss your grub on it."

"Chasey," Robyn says, handing him a bag, "Mom and I picked these from our garden."

"Thank you, Robyn with a *y*," Chase says, accepting the bag and finding it filled with fresh vegetables for the grill.

Robyn skips back out to the living room, planting herself on the plush beanbag in the center of the living room, where Dogma had taken up residence. "Hello, there," she says, stroking him. "What's your name?"

"Dogma," someone nearby says, causing a round of laughter.

"Dogma is a funny name for a cat," Robyn says. "I shall call you . . . Kitty."

"Meow."

As pre-game images and hype fill Chase's made-for-sports TV, the volume low, the room begins to fill with the usual crowd of eighteen who gather every Monday night throughout the football season, each bringing a grillable dinner item and an adult beverage or two.

"Hey, Doris," Chase says while he draws lines across a blank piece of paper, filling in the team names at the top with brief instructions for anybody who wants in on the action, a tub of Red Vines Original Red Licorice Twists, perhaps the most coveted raffle prize among club members.

"I didn't recognize you without a shirt," Doris says.

Chase lifts his shirt, flashing his washboard abs.

"Chase!"

"Doris," Jim hollers from the living room, "come have a seat."

"Okay, anybody who wants a shot at the Red Vines here's the sign-up sheet," Chase says, waving the paper around. "Guess the total score for the night, and the closest person to it, over or under, wins."

"I'll help, Chasey." Robyn springs into action, clutches the scorecard, and walks around the room, stopping at each attendee and pointing to where they should write their name.

"Red Vines?" Dillon says, entering the room. "There's got to be a story behind that."

"Hey, you made it," Chase says. "There is. Corty raffles them away at the race he directs every year, the Valley Ford Relays on Presidents Day weekend.

"You diaper butts don't know your history," Dale says, entering the kitchen, eyeballing the communal banana bread on the counter that Dillon has brought along. "It was held on Labor Day weekend the first year, so red was the theme. The next year he moved the race to Presidents Day weekend, and it also happened to be Valentine's Day that year, so Corty made it the grand prize for its sweet and red theme."

"A Red Bouquet of Sweet Affection," Chase says, his creative side bubbling forth.

Dale mumbles and shuffles back into the living room with slices of banana bread.

"In college we clipped the ends of Red Vines and fashioned them into straws," Dillon says.

"Creative. Stash your grub down here." Chase leads Dillon over to the fridge and points inside it, noticing Dillon's non-carnivore fare. "Nothing for the grill?"

"I only eat meat on occasion, mostly when dining out, which is rare these days."

"Ah, a flexitarian."

"A what?"

"Someone who's a semi-vegetarian."

"That doesn't make any sense."

"Of course it doesn't. Nothing like a label to make people feel good about their nonsensical choices, though." Chase laughs. "Someone wrote a book about it, a '*mostly* vegetarian way to lose weight' or something along those—"

"Kick-off time!" someone shouts.

"Go, Packers," Chase says, walking into the living room, beer in hand, Dillon alongside.

"Go, Niners," Linda shouts in response, decked out in an oversized Joe Montana 49ers jersey, her long brown hair streaming out from underneath a team cap.

"Really, Jakey, you had to bring her?"

"You're in Niner country, Chasey," Linda says. The rest of the room backs her statement up with cheers and jeers.

"This is going to be a long night," Chase says, nabbing the chair alongside the crowded couch.

Robyn giggles as everybody settles down into various spots, all pointed toward the TV. "Can I wear your hat, Chasey?"

"Sure you can." He hands her his official Packer Cheesehead hat. "You can be a honorary Packer fan."

She giggles again as soon as she places the yellow wedge on her head. "Go, cheesy!"

"Now you're *stinky cheesy*," Jake tells her, and afterward she pinches her nose.

The game kicks off, and after two first downs by the home team they have to punt, and upon the conclusion of the play the first series of commercials airs, which prompts groans of "Skip 'em."

"We're live, baby!" Chase says. "Hey, Spence and Maggie, come on in."

"But I don't need a new twenty-ton truck," someone gripes from the peanut gallery. "Especially one that has ten times more horsepower than the space shuttle. What am I hauling . . . the Kennedy Space Center?"

"Commercials are *literally* interruptions in my life," another peanut gallery member tosses out.

"They're an *opportunity* to a live a fuller life," Chase counters before turning his attention behind him.

"What'd you decide, Jim?" Jake says, downing a handful of salted peanuts. Chase and Dillon turn their attention toward Jim.

Jim bobs his head a couple times. "I passed on it."

"Sweet!" Chase says. "You don't need those yahoos anyway. I'll switch over."

"Me too," Jake says.

"I'm looking for a local guy," Dillon says. "Count me in."

"Thanks, guys." Jim raises his beer bottle to them. "Between the three of you, I should be able to buy a new pair of running shoes every six months."

"What about you, Spence?" Chase says. "Let Jimbo do your taxes?"

"He likes to do them himself," Maggie says as Spencer ducks into the kitchen with their food.

"He might find some extra deductions now that you own a home. Jim did for me, and it easily covers his fee. Heck, Spence! Getting married will give you additional tax benefits."

"Chase!" Doris says.

Spence-speak.

". . . self-publishing route," Chase overhears Maggie say to Linda.

"You should," Linda says. "There's no reason not to. The odds of finding an agent are long—"

"That's an understatement," Chase says. "I had a buddy in New York who spent two years"—Chase holds up two fingers—"trying to find an agent. He said it was a lot like online dating, profiling agents, trying to make a connection with them with one of those . . . what are they called?"

"Query letters," Maggie says.

"Yeah, and you may or may not hear back from them."

"It's very subjective."

"I say go for it," Chase says, rising to his feet. "But steer clear of the vanity presses. My buddy says they're piranhas."

"A lady in my writing group mentioned her experience," Maggie says. "They charged her eight grand, promising that her book would be sold in bookstores, and that they'd market it; all false promises. And now she doesn't own the rights to her book."

"If you need any marketing ideas let me know."

"Is that all you think about, Chase?" Doris says.

"Who you going to call?" Chase says with his arms spread wide.

Jake leads the chorus from the room, "The Chasester!" to which Jim adds, "*Ghostbusters!*"

Nearing halftime, Chase heads out onto the balcony and fires up the gas grill. In the kitchen, he sets out various condiments, plates, and utensils until a roar of dismay goes up. He drops what he's doing and dashes into the living room to see his player performing the Lambeau Leap. "Woo-hoo! Go Packers, go Packers . . . high five, Robyn." She reaches up and taps his hand, holding on to her cheesy hat with the other. He picks up the Red Vines score sheet, scanning it over. "All right, Arthur, you're out and so is Peter." Both men groan. "Grill should be ready in a minute."

Once the final seconds tick off for the second quarter, the hungry crowd rises and like a unionized job site, everyone grabs their dinner items—chicken breasts, a salmon filet, sausage links, oversized vegetables, a veggie burger—and jockey for position on the Lynx 36-inch gas grill. Some hang around the grill with beers in hand, discussing the latest race they ran, or are about to run, and the training they're doing in preparation for it. Some comment about the ongoing drought in the region and what effect it'll have long-term. Robyn hands out paper plates to anybody who needs one, "Kitty" following her.

At some point Chase and Dillon are talking about life in Sonoma county as compared to the bigger metropolitan areas they moved from. Linda wanders over, joins in on the conversation and when the topic turns toward the singles scene, she asks Dillon if he's seeing anyone.

"Too busy with the inn."

"Well, I have a friend who—" Chase rolls his eyes and Linda shoots Chase an exasperated look. "There's just no pleasing this one, Dillon, so ignore him. What I was about to say is that I have a friend who I think you'd like. She moved here from Florida last year and she's real sweet. She's a triathlete."

"Thanks, but I'm pretty busy these days."

"What about the hottie from the RERC open?" Chase says.

"Kate? I really don't need any distractions right now."

"If you change your mind, let me know," Linda says, squeezing Dillon's shoulder on her way to the kitchen.

The second half commences, the Packers with the ball and holding a three-point advantage. The Monday-night crowd returns to their viewing positions, grilled food in hand, the conversations no less animated or varied, while Robyn feeds Kitty bits of food off her paper plate; Chase turns a blind eye on the messy matter and instead watches Doris hunt through his music playlist queued up on the stereo tuner.

"What are you looking for, Doris?" Chase asks, biting into a strip of chicken breast.

"Checking to see if you have 'Free Bird.'"

Breast not yet swallowed, Chase chokes. He lets out a cough to clear his throat. "Yeah, it's in there somewhere. Why?"

The room erupts with shouts of "*Go, go, go . . .*" Chase misses the key moment, but based on Linda jumping up and down, a Niners player intercepted a pass and was still running with it. By the time he catches sight of the TV, the player has crossed into the end zone, dancing around. Chase scratches the back of his head while the celebration continues, restraining a couple choice vocal cuss words in Robyn's presence. *Damn Niner fans.*

After the ensuing kickoff and a couple plays have been run, a red challenge flag ends up on the field by the Niners coach for a ruling on the spot of the ball, which if overruled will leave the Packers inches short of a first down. As soon as the official makes the impending instant replay announcement, the telecast segues to commercial.

"Ugh, instant replay," a peanut gallery member bemoans. "It slows the game down so much."

"At least they get the calls," Linda says.

"Not always," Dillon says.

"Hey, the technology is there, why not use it?" Chase says.

"Journalist George Hill once said football combines the two worst elements of American life: violence punctuated by committee meetings," Maggie says.

"Which makes instant replay 'governmental oversight,'" Jim says.

"Must everything be analyzed down to the microscopic level? Is it still a sport or simply talking points?" Dillon says.

"The essence of sport is lost once it's broken down so finely," Jake says. "You lose touch with the game. The conversation becomes more about the extraneous—the technology, the cost, who has what and its advantage—and less about the athleticism. Might as well have robots play on a *real* gridiron that is wired to make fair play a reality. Humanity would prefer that anyway, I surmise; take away the human element altogether."

"What about Socrates, Jake?" the peanut gallery says. "An unexamined life is not worth living."

"He's like Play-Doh," Robyn says.

"'The unexamined life is not worth living for a human being' is the correct quote," Jake answers. "This hardly qualifies as humanity."

"Certainly creates more opportunities to air commercials. Heck, when a player goes down, injury timeout, no problem, straight to commercial," the peanut gallery jokes.

By the time the official comes out from underneath the hooded replay booth to announce the results of the gridiron inquiry, the group quiets enough to hear that upon further review the ruling on the field stands, which is followed by boos in the room and another minute of analysis by the sportscasters, supporting the ruling, which is backed by numerous replays from an equal number of angles. That single moment in time is replayed again and again, and gobbles up more air time than the previous ten downs, allowing beer to warm, food to cool, Dogma to lick himself, Dale to fall asleep, trivial conversations to take place, and several commercials to attempt to convince the group that *their* product was the best choice because, as one preached, they support worm removal from an endangered species in Antarctica; yes, they truly cared, Chase reminds everybody.

As the game clock ticks down to zero, the Niners' losing fate sealed several minutes earlier, the crowd gathers up their belongings. Robyn is ready to adopt Kitty until Chase announces that she is, miraculously enough, the winner of the Red Vines for her total score of fifty-eight points.

When asked why she chose that number, she responds that she added up the placings from the guys' last cross-country meet for a bonus math homework project.

Tuesday Noon
BR&B Landscaping

Conversing with two female guests on the porch at the BR&B, Dillon turns his head toward the rumble of Jake's truck and black-mulch-filled trailer rolling across the gravel driveway. The engine sputters to quiet, the passenger door opens, and Robyn jumps out, then reaches back in the open cab and pulls out a small suitcase plastered with sunflower stickers.

"Hi, Dilly," Robyn says, marching toward him. "Where's Miley?"

"*Wooooowooowooo Wooooowoooo,*" Miles says, coming out from the house.

"Let's go, Miley. We have work to do." Robyn scales the steps like a mountaineer and tromps into the house, Miles on her heels. "Terri! I'm here."

Dillon and his two guests share a smile.

"Could she be any cuter?" Dillon asks.

"Probably not, and I sure hope she stays that way," Jake replies, climbing the porch steps.

Dillon introduces Jake to his guests, a female couple, Lydia and Jamelle, who hail from Coeur d'Alene and have been in town for the fifty-mile ultra race on the trails around Lake Sonoma over the past weekend. The taller of the two women, Jamelle, won her 30–34 age group. They're now on their way out to go kayaking on the Russian River, dropping in at Johnson's Beach in Guerneville to head upriver and enjoy a picnic in one of the secluded coves along the way. Dillon gives them last-minute advice on where to park in the small, liberal, west county town that holds events like Lazy Bear Weekend, Polar Bear Weekend, and Women's Weekend, gatherings Lydia's and Jamelle's permissive expressions suggest they're familiar with.

"Ready to get your hands dirty?" Jake asks Dillon after the women set out.

"Always," Dillon says. "This is very nice of you, but are you sure I can't at least pay for the material?"

"Wouldn't think of it. I see you've already cleared the old vegetation and dug the holes for the plants. How's your back?"

"Sore . . . very sore. After the sixth one, I regretted not taking you up on having your crew use the auger for them."

Jake chuckles. "The soil in this area is clay, and after a long, dry summer . . ." He chuckles again, walking to the back of the trailer.

"I'll call it my one upper-body workout for the season."

"I've never been one for lifting either. In college the coach had Jim and me in the weight room. Never did like it. I walked from one station to next, looking busy, but rarely did anything."

"I never found it very functional."

Jake opens the trailer, pulls out the weed-cover roll, and tosses it down onto the ground. He and Dillon cart it over to the 800-square-foot area that comprises the bulb-shaped portion of the circular driveway's island. What stands as a brown patch of dead grass, gopher holes, plants in the wrong place, and mounds of dirt will soon be transformed into a living garden full of colorful perennials and shrubs to accent the front of the inn.

"Spencer's the one up on the latest this and that in the training world," Jake says, cutting long strips from the roll. "He has the kids doing pre-run routines. And twice a week he has them do core workouts."

"That's pretty standard these days," Dillon says. "I go through phases when time permits, and do things like planks and other balancing exercises." Dillon laughs. "It's like having a part-time job."

"I read somewhere that running is one of the few sports where we don't practice proper mechanics. We simply *run*, since it's a natural behavior. Other sports spend hours practicing batting skills, jumping skills, throwing skills. We just lace up and go."

"Might explain why the injury rate is so high among runners. We end up practicing whatever *natural* form we possess, even if the mechanics are less than ideal."

"Ever since the book *Born to Run* came out, Chase and Spencer have pushed the shoe angle as the culprit, but if you ask me, people simply run *too much* for their needs. Chase regularly lifts weights. Spencer does dynamic core training, and both stay healthy, but they also train smart. Jim does short hill bursts after his workouts three or four days a week; it's supposed to be dynamic weight training for runners. Kind of crazy in theory, but he does seem pretty injury-proof." Jake shrugs. "Landscaping does all that *and* I earn a living."

Dillon nods, squats several times, and positions the weed fabric around the edges of the island. "My coach in high school spoke a lot about listening to your body during heavy bouts of training: 'You're only as good as what your body can absorb. Anything beyond that is inviting injury.'"

"I like that. The blanket training programs in magazines and online are meant as templates, but too many take them as absolutes."

"That's where an *actual* coach comes in handy."

Once the weed cover is laid, and holes cut out where the plants and shrubs will go, the guys fill the holes with a variety of indigenous vegetation and set up the drip system, laying out a maze of black tubing with tiny nozzles positioned where needed.

"Did Chase come up with any ideas for the inn?" Jake asks, shoveling mulch into the wheelbarrow that Dillon stands by.

"And then some. He had Zac come by to revamp my website and it looks professional now. We snapped off a bunch of pics, especially of the vineyards in full bloom, and put them up. And the ad and article in the club newsletter gave the place a lot of exposure. In fact, the two women you met earlier heard about it from someone they knew in the club."

"Great. You going to try to finish off that last room anytime soon?"

"Next spring when I've built up some reserve. I've only had a few nights with a full house, so it's not urgent."

"I had an idea that might help out."

"Yeah?"

"I thought about bringing up a motion at our next club meeting for sponsoring the room in the name of RERC."

Dillon ponders the generous thought but uncomfortable burden as Jake shovels more mulch in the wheelbarrow.

"The club gives back to the community in many ways, college scholarships, park initiatives, and the like. And with all the running events this county has, it might be a great way to provide the club some exposure. Think about it."

Tempting . . . Dillon pictures the inn's exterior, the money and labor he's already applied to it, the personal and even therapeutic nature to it, his and his alone: *Man is his own star* . . . "I'll mull it over."

"How much do you think it'll take to finish it off?"

"Not more than eight hundred," Dillon says. "My labor is free, and Dale only works for breakfast and beer, not always in that order."

"Eight hundred shouldn't be a problem. We spend several thousand every fall on cross-country. I'll give Spencer a call."

When enough mulch has been dumped onto the weed tarp, Dillon rakes and spreads it around, making adjustments to the thickness per Jake's recommendations. Jake continues shuttling mulch until the formerly drab and lifeless island pops with reds, greens, yellows, and oranges, tall and short, surrounded in a sea of rich black mulch, the oak tree an inviting beacon of shady respite.

Nearly five hours elapse from the time Jake arrived until he and Dillon are leaned up against the truck munching on banana bread and drinking lemonade that Robyn brought out to them, admiring their handiwork. Lydia and Jamelle return from their day on the river and join in on viewing the transformation.

"Great job, guys," Jamelle says.

Jake and Dillon nod.

"Nice day kayaking?" Dillon asks the two lovebirds, who each have an arm wrapped around the other's waist.

"Perfection," Lydia replies. "Now we're in the mood for a run before heading into town for dinner."

"Jake and I are headed out for a few easy miles in the vineyards if you'd care to join us."

"Sure. We'll change and be right out."

Jake and Dillon marvel over the revitalized view one last time before Jake shows Dillon how to program the new irrigation control panel, then they both change into running gear. Dillon arches his back in different ways to loosen it up, resigning to call Nicola, the masseuse, to see if she'll be available later to sort things out. She says she'll come by at nine. *Excellent!*

Miles escorts all four out to the vineyards, the sun setting over the distant hillside. Twilight bathes the group who no longer cast shadows, running within themselves, and sharing the magic of a day well spent.

Wednesday Night
Monthly Club Meeting

As Spencer stands behind the podium, his stomach swirls with butterflies, nervous about his first club meeting as president, his former vice president position recently upgraded when the elected president unexpectedly quit over "a lack of support for his visions for the club." True, Walter had many new ideas, fresh ideas, ideas that were in keeping with the evolving running world as a whole, but ideas that cost money, a lot of money, and despite a healthy balance sheet, the club's more conservative and traditional history resisted Walter's charismatic charms and visionary dreams that often lacked adequate detail to seriously consider or budget for. "We have the money, let's build something with it!" he had said during the last meeting. The vote didn't go his way, and so he decided to go his own way. Last anybody heard from him he'd moved to Modoc County, bought property, and was raising alfalfa.

Since joining the club as a kid, Spencer longed to preside over it, to keep up its traditions and commitments to the community. The club sprung up in the early '70s as a grassroots movement, answering the call of a number of local runners in Sonoma County who united to compete. As with most such movements from that era, the few-and-hearty crowd embodied a competitive bent, their charter measured more or less on how well they performed at races and who was willing to bring the post-run beer. While they didn't shun others from joining—the running boom in full bloom enticed many to do so when news of the club spread—their more *race-minded* attitude scared off the run-for-fun types clad in velour sweats and clean shoes. A typical meet-and-greet at Howarth for a group run basically resulted in seven or eight guys bolting out from the parking lot at speeds that left newcomers far behind in short order and fending for themselves. They were often never seen again, and the club's membership languished for many years until the mid-'90s, when that "competitive" perception was overhauled with a social one.

As Spencer pores over the agenda, he hears Robyn's voice over the din of La Vera Pizza's small back room filling with gathering club members.

"Dilly!" She jumps up from her seat, runs over to him, and grabs his hand. "Come sit with me, Daddy, and Chasey." She guides him through the small crowd who nod, smile, and offer heys to him.

"Chase, Jake," Dillon says, sitting where Robyn points to.

"Hey, Dillon," Jake says. "Slice?"

Dillon accepts the slice and bites into it.

"Okay, I think we can begin," Spencer says, the clock's hour hand pointing straight up like an arrow on the wall behind him. "We have a full agenda this evening, so let's dive right in." Spencer has the meeting minutes read from the previous meeting, receiving unanimous approval for them. He has the treasurer read her report on the fiscal health of the club, including money paid in and out for various events and benefits over the last month. He proceeds to introduce himself until Dale voices, "Everybody already knows who you are, so get on with it, will ya?"

"Okay, new business," Spencer says, conceding to Dale's quip. "Item one. Chase."

"Thanks, Spence," Chase says, standing. "One aspect missing in the sport of cross-country is the ability for spectators to assess how clubs are doing *during* the race. Unless they use an app like Spencer has, they don't know who's winning." Nods follow Chase's line of thought. "Cheering is done solely for the individuals, when cross-country is much more about teams competing against one another. Track and field has up-to-the-minute team scoring after each event is completed. The Olympics report medal tallies. So my proposal is to upgrade our existing timing system by adding chip mats in various spots throughout our home course and adding chip timing to the mix."

Between beverage sips and pizza consumption, the crowd murmurs at the notion before someone speaks. "The Renegades used chip timing a couple years ago. They had some problems with it."

"That's true, but they were using it as the de facto race timing. I'm not purposing to replace how we judge and time races today. The chips would only provide in-race team scoring. I've spoken with Zac Critton, and he would write the software for it, so besides chip mats and chips for the runners we'd need a scoreboard of some sort. An inexpensive flat screen should work, and it could also serve to display messages, race results, et cetera. The other benefit for doing this as a prototype is that the software can be patented and potentially licensed out to other cross-country meets that might be interested in it; a potential revenue stream for the club."

"Thanks, Chase," Spencer says. "Let's take a quick vote to decide if we want to explore Chase's 'real-time' team scoring proposal."

Once the count has been tallied—in favor—Spencer makes a note. "Item number two. Jake has proposed that we donate upward of eight hundred dollars to Dillon's bed, run, and breakfast inn in order to renovate his last room. Dillon, this would be a good time for you to discuss your plans."

"Thank you, Spencer," Dillon says, walking up to the podium. "My name is Dillon Percy for those of you who I haven't met yet. As some of you know, I opened up the BR&B out off Hall Road this past summer. I spent the spring and summer fixing up four of the five guest rooms. Basically, I blew through my renovation budget before I could get to the last room. Now, when Jake brought up the idea earlier this week, I was hesitant in accepting such a generous donation, even with dedicating the theme of the room to the RERC. But after some thought, I decided I'd be good with it if I could give something back. So I'd like to propose the following: One, offer the room up for RERC members on a first-come, first-serve basis, at a discounted rate. Now, this could be for themselves or visiting family members. Two, donate a percentage of any bookings for the room back to the general fund of the club." He pauses as his proposal percolates in their minds—Dale leans toward the gentleman to the right, whispers in his ear, lifts a slice of pizza from the gentleman's plate, and sits upright; a seated woman hikes up a leg, rests its heel on the other leg's thigh, and leans forward over the supporting leg, stretching her piriformis; Robyn jots in her notebook. "Are there any questions?"

"How'd you come up with a bed, *run*, and breakfast?" the piriformis-stretching woman asks.

"I needed a place to sleep. I love to run. And my favorite meal is breakfast. Might as well make money off something I'm already doing."

The room collectively chuckles.

"Seriously, I attended many camps in high school and college—even had a small business running a summer running-camp series for high school students—and really loved the lifestyle. So as I was preparing to leave Southern California, it seemed like a good time to try the same concept out for adults. I offer morning runs before breakfast on the property and out in the vineyards next door along with other amenities. I also would like to have guest speakers on occasion who discuss various running-related topics."

Robyn has her hand up. "Yes, Robyn."

"Does Miley chase the bunnies in the vineyards?"

Members titter as Robyn resumes munching on her pizza slice.

Dillon smiles. "She tries, but they're too quick."

"How'd you come up with the themes for the rooms?" the gentleman with one less pizza slice on his plate asks.

Dillon grins. "Runners think in Olympic years and venues."

Nods and smiles follow.

"Any other questions?" None come forth. "Okay, thanks for hearing me out." Dillon returns to his spot next to Robyn.

Spencer summons another vote on Jake's proposal and a unanimous in-favor decision is reached. From there Spencer fulfills his new role as president with the same precision and command he doles out throughout the school week. At times he can't believe he's actually there, a wonderful dream unfolding before him, and at any moment he'll awaken, still trying to support Walter's dreams, yet talk him down from his often lofty visions. It isn't until he wraps up the meeting and Robyn approaches him to inform him that he makes a better president than Walter because Walter didn't allow her to call him Wally that Spencer knows *he* is the club president.

Thursday Night
Tweet, Tweet, Tweet; Buzz, Buzz, Buzz

Jake coasts his truck to a stop in the driveway at the homestead, catching sight of Robyn in the picture window with her arms crossed; he's late for dinner. There had been a car accident ahead of him on his way back from the coast that tied up Highway 16 for an hour until tow trucks could remove the wreckage. And of course, as with many rural parts of Sonoma County, cell reception was sketchy at best. Once moving again, he pulled over when his cell phone showed life and let Linda know he was on his way.

"Hi, sweetie," he says, entering the house.

Robyn conveys her displeasure, a blend of sternness and pouting, still learning the subtleties of when to show which at what times.

"I'm sorry I'm late."

"Miss Jenners makes us do extra homework when *we're* tardy," Robyn says, unfolding her arms. She grabs her *Agent Carter* notebook and makes a couple entries.

"I can do that."

"She also makes us stand in the corner and wear a funny hat."

"Are you sure about that?"

"Okay, it was me. I saw it on TV once." Her stern, pouty expression loses all potency. "It was pointy and went way high." She's now on her tiptoes, demonstrating how high with her hand above her head.

"A dunce cap."

"Like an ice-cream cone."

"I see, funny-looking."

"Dinner's ready," Linda says, carrying a serving bowl of mashed potatoes into the dining area.

The Dearborns settle into their chairs, say grace, and fill their plates with tossed salad, chicken cacciatore, steamed vegetables, and mashed potatoes. Jake explains the details of the accident—two cars collided around a blind curve—and the new project he started for a client that involves a waterfall in their backyard. Linda's day has been long—getting Robyn to and from school, running errands—and will extend on after dinner as she is scheduled to cover a half shift at the hospital. Robyn talks about her school day, which involved a kid in her class who was caught texting; Robyn thinks the boy rude for doing so, as Miss Jenners is teaching them about listening and respecting others while they're speaking.

"Do babies come from hospitals?" Robyn says, scooping more mashed potatoes onto her plate.

Stunned, Jake and Linda glance at each other before addressing Robyn, who nibbles on a carrot, her eyes shifting back and forth between Mom and Dad.

"Did someone at school say something?" Jake says.

"No . . . I was curious. Shelby's older sister had a baby, and they drove to the hospital to visit her and bring the baby home. Do they have babies at your hospital, Mom?"

"Yes, they do, sweetie."

"If someone wants a baby do they fill out those little forms like we do when we order sandwiches at the deli?"

Jake and Linda barely restrain their shared laughter. "No, sweetie," Jake says. "It has to do with the birds and bees."

"Oh!" Robyn says and starts singing, "*Tweet, tweet, tweet, and buzz, buzz—*"

"No singing at the dinner table," Linda says, still harboring a lurking laugh.

"Then Terri will tell me," Robyn announces after finishing up the last of her meal. "She says I should be informed on these things."

"We can talk about it later, sweetie," Jake says. "Why don't you go read."

"Okay." Robyn scoots off her chair and heads for her room.

"Lord love a duck."

"Her little mind just won't shut down . . . for a minute," Linda says, consolidating Robyn's dinner plate and place settings with hers.

"I'll talk to her."

"That should be entertaining. I vote for Terri at this point. Are you racing on Saturday?"

His mouth full, Jake nods.

"Where?"

"Sacramento. Should be back by three if we stop to eat afterward. That work?"

"Don't forget my birthday date night. I'm dropping Robyn off at Shelby's for their sleepover at four." Linda rises and makes her way into Jake's lap, wrapping her arms around his torso and kissing him.

"Wouldn't miss it for the world," Jake says once their kiss ends. "Dillon's offered up a few free nights at the inn. I say we take our date night on the road."

Linda's eyes light up, squeezing him. "See if the Athens Room is available. I've always wanted to visit Greece." She delivers a passionate kiss.

"*Tweet, tweet, tweet and buzz, buzz, buzz,*" Robyn sings, skipping back into the room. "*I see Mommy kissing Daddy, tweet, tweet, tweet and buzz, buzz, buzz.*" Her voice trails off as she passes through the living area and into the family room with a book in hand.

Jake and Linda laugh, like teenagers caught making out in the back of a car by friends.

"We could always tell her that babies come from Mommy kissing Daddy," Linda says. Jake moves his fingers to her stomach, tickling her. "That should"—she squirms and giggles—"hold her for . . . a while." Her laughs are now uncontrollable. "Stop!" she pleads as tears begin to form.

Linda leaves for work, and after a couple tweet, tweet, tweet and buzz, buzz, buzz epilogues, Robyn is down for the night. Jake pulls up a chair to Linda's computer, brings up her email account, and finds Spencer's weekly email, this week's edition regarding the car pool for Saturday's race.

From: Spencer Lingard <MarathonMan@gomail.com>
To: Team Thirsty Boys <SundayRunDL>
Subject: Saturday Race Carpool . . .

Dear Sirs,
This Saturday is the Renegades XC Challenge at Ancil
Hoffman in Sacramento. Race time is 10:30 a.m. so let's meet

at the usual spot, Montgomery High School's parking lot, and hit the road by 7:15 a.m. It's my turn to drive.

We'll stop in Davis to eat at our usual spot on the way back.

Okay, so we leave Montgomery at 7:15! Yes, Jim, that was for you.

Signing off,

Spencer

I will reply to your email after I've had sufficient time to reflect on its content.

From: Linda Dearborn <LDRN@gomail.com>
To: Team Thirsty Boys <SundayRunDL>
Subject: RE: Saturday Race Carpool . . .

Spencer, congrats again on your new club president position. I know this has been a dream of yours since your first RERC event as a kid. And thanks for bringing up the motion for sponsoring a room at Dillon's inn. While I know it doesn't technically benefit the community at large, it's nice to afford the club various perks.

Happy Trails,

Jakey

Jake sends off his email, or at least he thinks he has. The updated interface of the web email site confuses him, revamped color scheme, task buttons placed in new locations, new social interactive functions added, and he'd only *mostly* gotten used to the last version. After poking around, he finds a reply from Jim, who made a sarcastic remark concerning the extra message about the carpool departure time, and in the body of the email, Jake spots his message to Spencer.

Satisfied, Jake strolls outside, zipping up his / Sisters Trail Race jacket in the crisp night air. He retrieves his journal from the glove compartment, sets it on the hood of the truck, and writes:

His sleepy body slowly shakes off the remnants of a long night's sleep, recalling Sunday's morning ritual with the same autonomic response as breathing. His effort varies throughout the early miles in tandem with the terrain, the heart shunting blood to legs where the trail soars above his sightline; then, reaching a plateau, diverting it back to other extremities, warming hands against autumn's nip.

He rereads and rereads, refining here and there before turning to the page for the current week's training log: twelve miles peppered with eight miles of hard and easy effort along the coastal trail.

He replaces the journal and walks back toward the house, humming, "Tweet, tweet, tweet and buzz, buzz, buzz."

Saturday Morning
Renegades XC Challenge, Ancil Hoffman

Sunlight filters through the tall eucalyptus trees that surround Montgomery High School's parking lot like flames crackling under kindling. Jake pulls into a slot next to Chase's BMW as Spencer's car enters the lot, Dillon's car behind his. It's 7:07 a.m. and the air has a bite to it, a California fall bite to it, an opportunity for Chase to tease the others about the heavier clothing options they've sported while standing outside their vehicles.

"Where's Jim?" Spencer says.

"He's on his way," Jake says. "We're fine."

"You okay?" Chase asks Dillon, who's arching and twisty his upper body.

"Stiff back," he replies.

"Two hour car ride should loosen that up," Chase says. "Spence . . . TP?"

"Yeah, but we don't have time." Chase has to tilt his head to the side and purse his lips before Spence tosses him the roll.

"If you didn't drive like an old church lady, we could leave a half hour later and still arrive in plenty of time," Chase says, heading off to the back side of a building, where the shrubs provide cover. He chuckles at Spence's retort about Chase's aggressive driving skills.

"You're an excellent driver," Jake says.

"*Rain Man,*" Spencer says, checking his watch—7:14—as Doris arrives with Jim, witnessing their goodbye kiss.

"Dad lets you drive slow on the driveway every Saturday. But not on Monday, definitely not on Monday."

"*Rain Man,*" Jim says, waving goodbye to Doris.

"Okay, let's roll," Spencer says once Chase returns.

The five guys load their gym bags into the trunk and pile into the cramped confines of the Prius, Chase calling shotgun.

After settling the obligatory debate over the best route in getting to Interstate 80, with a couple different options, or "shortcuts" as Chase refers to them, the nod, as always, goes to the driver's preference, thus the guys drive *through* the town of Sonoma on their way to the interstate.

"Slow boat to Sac it is," Chase says. He glances to the backseat and tilts his head toward Jim, who is fast asleep. "How he does that, I have no idea."

Squished between Jake and Jim, Dillon turns toward the slumbering Jim. Spittle has already formed. "I take it he does this often?"

"Since childhood," Jake says. "As soon as his parents put him in a car seat and started driving, he'd go out like a light."

"Lucky him," Dillon says. "What's the course like today?"

"Fast," Chase says, sipping from his cloudy water bottle.

"There's one good hilly section toward the end, but yeah, pretty flat and fast," Spencer says.

"The start and finish are around the same large grass field," Chase says. "It's three quarters of a mile around it. After that it heads out onto narrow trails. It's six kilometers."

Jake tells the story of last year's unusual race circumstances where on the one good hilly section a swarm of yellowjackets descended on them, many of the runners getting stung, and many more finding yellow hitchhikers on their jerseys after they finished a mile and half later. At first it was thought to be an unfortunate coincidence, but after a while evidence mounted that painted a different picture: the host club for the race didn't suffer any such yellowjacket welts; during pre-race warm-ups along the stretch in question no one showed any such attacks; one person swore that he witnessed the home club spraying themselves before the race with what was later assumed to be some type of repellent; and the host club won four of the eight team races on the day, a higher winning percentage than normal for them. It became known as "Beegate."

PA officials were forced to investigate, the first such "–gate" action they could ever recall. After several calls, interviews, and a run-through on the course that included an apiarist, it was determined that not enough evidence could be found to support any wrongdoing by the host club, and therefore they didn't achieve any advantage. They chalked it up to an odd act of nature.

Dillon takes the story seriously until Chase and Spencer break composure and laugh. "Wackadoos."

Surrender to the Pain, Like a Moth to the Flame . . .

Spencer's latest mantra. He invokes it as predicted right near mile two, when the course (flat and fast) and competition (simply fast) impose their will on him. Neurologically speaking his leg turnover has had all the ease of a log-rolling lumberjack until the frenzied start simmered down. Cardiovascular-wise, however, his strong heart and enlarged lungs remain unfazed by the effort, expanding and contracting as if by professional courtesy. Such is the paradox of the marathon-training, cross-country runner.

Out on the course proper and away from the start/finish hub, the race meanders along trails that flirt with the Sacramento River, at times coming up for air and crossing over bike paths toward lush fairways, but only long enough to connect to the next trail that juts away from the golf course and back to the river's westbound flow. Spencer doesn't catch the mile-one marker, but a glance at his watch at mile two infuses him with satisfaction, offsetting the discomfort the pace has imparted—10:32.

Despite his romantic fondness for cross-country, it inflicts challenges he's not always physiologically able to meet effectively or efficiently, not since college anyway, after which he switched to full-time marathon training.

Where Chase embraces the short and sweet anaerobic effort, Spencer prefers the long and slow burn of his resources, negotiating the tightrope between the aerobic and anaerobic states.

He loses sight of Jim up front once the course weaves its way toward and along the wooded riverbank. Positioned in the top twenty-five Spencer can conceivably work his way up a few spots when the course moves into the hillier section and away from the current speedway. But with just over half of the race completed, his brain intervenes:

Psst, History Man. I know you can hear me.

Surrender to the Pain, Like a Moth to the Flame.

Yeah, yeah, that's a good one, but listen, I'm getting some pushback on the pace. The short-twitch units are up in arms. Get it, up in arms? They work in the leg branch. Nothing? Okay, not in the mood, got it. I'll get right to the point: over half the race is over, but we're still running away from the finish line. Do you see the problem? Let me spell it out for you: the anaerobic guys are worried that we're going to come up short at this pace. They recommend slowing down.

Surrender to the Pain, Like a Moth to the Flame.

You do know what happens to the moth in the end, right? Spoiler alert: Zap! Look, you have no idea what I have to deal with up here while you're gallivanting over hill and dale. I mean the grumblings from the stomach are incessant. You really should eat before a race. Whoa, whoa, what are you doing? You can't pass him now, don't do it, don't you dare, there's no . . . room . . . the right ankle would like a word with you after the race. Now, look, I'm not asking you to stop, just ease off the pace a little. We have things to reflect on. We can't mull over life's mysteries if I'm putting out fires from head to toe. Seriously, you're out of your element at this pace.

Surrender to the Pain, Like a Moth to the Flame.

Quiet down, stomach! You'll get nothing and like it! Get it? Jake would. He's probably not far behind. Ease off just a bit and let's join him. No? Okay, I didn't want to bring this up, but you've left me no choice: the bladder seeks relief. I know, I know. I tried to quell him, but you know what he's like. Worse than the id, and don't get me started on his current runt. Okay, to sum up, pace too fast, moth ends in fiery explosion, ankle disgruntled, stomach hungry, bladder about to burst.

Surrender to the Pain, Like a Moth to the Flame.

Now, don't make me . . . wait . . . what's going on? Oh, man, I should've seen this coming. Okay team, listen up, we've reoriented, the horse smells the barn, time to suck it up. I'll be back, History Man. You know I will.

At the farthest reach from the start, skirting along the perimeter of the golf course's back nine, an undulating section through deep foliage, Spencer works his mantra past three runners, using the top of each rise to gather additional speed until he's out into the open and heading for the great Beegate area of '14.

The approach to Beegate is a mother of a hill, short but so steep that it can stand a runner up, including the leaders. The pace bogs down and Spencer doesn't force anything, can't force anything, leaning as far forward as he can to counter the incline and mitigate the accruing discomfort in his quads.

Surrender to the Pain, Like a Moth to the Flame.

Through arguably the slowest portion of the course, Spencer focuses again on regaining his previous pace on the subsequent rollers that greet him, maximizing as much of his downhill speed to push him up and over the next rise, repeating rhythmically for more than a half mile, staying in sync with a string of seven others coupled by competitive desire.

One by one the runners dump out onto the large grass field, past the three-mile marker, cheers from respective clubs' members follow each one. A glance at Spencer's watch registers 15:57, the hills contributing to his slowest mile of the morning. His mind calculates his projected finishing time as it always does in the final stages of the marathon, especially if his mile splits are increasing. *19:40. That'll be a PR on this course.*

Surrender to the Pain, Like a Moth to the Flame.

The group he's been hitched to splits up and spreads out, Spencer coming to terms with the fact that his legs are at their peak for the day, and with three-quarters of a mile left he needs to milk them for the remainder.

Surrender to the Pain, Like a Moth to the Flame.

Spencer watches those up front churn through the spongy grass, imagining them being more tired than himself. He reaches a worn dirt groove that gives his legs more leverage, approaching the first of two final right turns, keenly aware of footsteps and erratic breathing pressing upon him from behind. He wills his body to go faster, which more or less translates to *not* slowing down.

Surrender to the Pain, Like a Moth to the Flame.

The first turn, Spencer's shuffling form maintained, he outmaneuvers a Chico runner and gains several steps on him.

Surrender to the Pain, Like a Moth to the Flame.

With one turn remaining and a long approach to the finish, Spencer digs in, fixating on the next runner in front, an Agras jersey affixed to him. Spencer draws abreast with the sponsored competitor, attempting to go by, but the Agras runner summons an answer. Now they're in a dog fight, the two running side by side, stride for stride, labored breath for labored breath, rounding the last turn with nothing but 300 yards of spongy grass and a gentle upward slope to the finish, where a stream of runners are crossing.

Surrender to the Pain, Like a Moth to the Flame.

Oxygen jettisons into his lungs and CO_2 expels a fraction of a second later. Pumping madly, his shoulders and biceps stiffen. His etched grimace pleads for submission, but the Agras runner hasn't gained an inch, so until all hope is lost . . .

Surrender to the Pain, Like a Moth to the Flame.

The finish line grows rapidly as the duo sprints up the incline, shouts from opposing clubs urging the two on, Chase's voice the loudest.

Surrender to the Pain, Like a Moth to the Flame.

Nearly to the line, Spencer wants to lean, but his neck is too strained to perform the maneuver, so an awkward chest heave suffices with the last of his reserves.

"RERC! Agras!" barks the PA official once the runners have broken the plane and their forms deteriorate, colliding with another runner bent over with his hands on his knees. Spencer gives the guy a pat on the back, and the runner responds by righting himself and continuing on. Still out of breath and spittle smeared across his face, Spencer extends his hand behind him to the Agras runner, who returns the congratulatory handshake, both too physiologically stressed to form words.

Chase, Dillon, and Jim greet Spencer with high-fives through the chute;

only one lands correctly. Once semi-composed and sensing no raisin in his throat this week, Spencer turns to see Jake coming into the finish area farther back than expected.

Spencer trundles toward the team blanket ahead of the others and plops down, spending several moments to gather himself before changing out of his racing shoes. Though dazed, he feels particularly happy with the effort, all things considered; marathon training, though it gives him strength and stamina for cross-country racing, does not prepare him for the intensity and the surges necessary to compete properly. Yet he recognizes a certain appeal to the short-and-sweet aspect that isn't part of marathons, letting go and letting loose, not controlling and conserving every ounce of energy.

"Surrender to the Pain, Like a Moth to the Flame" appears to be a suitable mantra for him.

"Could we have a couple tables pushed together on the patio?" Spencer asks the hostess, arriving to Sudwerk Brewery, the club's standard post–Sacramento race lunch stop outside downtown Davis, nestled underneath an overpass alongside I-80. "We have more coming along."

"Sure, just a minute," she says, turning to leave, summoning another staff member to follow her.

"Could you fill this with ice?" Spencer presents her with a large Ziploc bag.

The hostess pauses, does a double-take at the bag, and takes it, handing it to the other employee. "Sure."

The guys mill around in the waiting area, all hungry, discussing a little about this and that, nothing important until their seating arrangements are accommodated. They no sooner sit than voices from the women's team fill the patio, heading their way. Beverage orders are placed and various discussions crop up as if a seminar has been split into small groups to carry on with the main topic of the day.

"How'd you guys finish?" one of the women asks after answering Spencer's same question of the women, who finished third in the open race and second in the masters race.

"Second," Spencer says, taking the ice bag and applying it to his bare ankle. "Fifteen points behind the Agras." He wraps a shirt around it to hold it in place.

"Sprained?" Dillon says.

Spencer shakes his head. "Ankle flick."

"I fell apart on the grass," Jake says. "No legs today."

"It was those hills repeats on Wednesday," Chase says. "Sapped your legs."

Jake shrugs. "Or it was simply a short fast course. Speed has never been my strong suit."

"You always round into shape by November," Jim says.

"It took a mile before my back relaxed enough to forget about," Dillon says, rolling his shoulders. "Couldn't catch Chase at the end."

"Pfft. Excuses, excuses . . ." Chase says. "We're gaining on them. Might be able to make a run at them next week."

"Where's next week, again?" Dillon says.

"Crystal Springs," Spencer says.

"Now, that's my kind of course: hills, hills, and more hills," Jake says, smiling.

Jim nods in agreement.

"That's a tough one for me," Chase says. "Hard to get any sort of rhythm—"

"Pffffft," Dillon says. "Excuses, excuses . . ."

The various drinks arrive and a communal "cheers" rings out from the group. The waiter takes their orders, which based on his surprised look may have just as well been for twenty-four people instead of the twelve seated.

"Nice job today, Dillon," a female voice says from behind him.

"Hey, Kate," Dillon says after stiffly looking over his shoulder. "Thanks. How'd your day go?" He angles his chair in her direction.

"Good. I placed eighth," she replies. "The team won."

"Nice."

"You guys are making the Agras nervous. I overheard them talking about your third- and sixth-places finishes today." Her eyes shift from Chase's to Dillon's."

"That's good to know," Chase says.

"Chase, Kate. Kate, Chase," Dillon says.

"What am I, chopped liver?" Jim says.

"When you crack the top ten, buddy," Chase says. "Twelfth doesn't cut it."

"*Pfffft,*" Jim says. "Forgot to tell you the IRS called. You're being audited."

"You guys are doing it wrong," Chase says to Dillon and Jim. "Pfft! Say it, don't spray it."

"I should head back to my group," Kate says. "You guys racing Crystal Springs next weekend?"

Dillon nods. "You?"

"You know it. Interested in hanging out in the city afterward? There's a free concert in Golden Gate Park that starts at one."

Caught off guard, Dillon hesitates long enough to see a shade of disappointment flicker in her eyes. Even Chase casts a questioning *What's wrong with you?* look his way. "Well . . . I never know how busy the inn might be, so it's hard to plan too far in advance."

Her expression softens. "Here's my number in case . . ." She retrieves a pen from her purse and jots it down on Dillon's napkin. "Hope your back feels better." Tuning to walk away, her hand grazes his shoulder. "Good job today."

"You too."

"Dilly," Chase says, channeling Robyn with a *y*'s voice, "why are you 'fraid of commitment?"

Dillon grins at Chase, wondering if an appropriated Spence-speak would be out of order before noticing curious glances from around the RERC table in his direction. "It's just pity attention."

"Pity isn't so bad," Chase says. "That must've been one hell of a breakup. Metaphorically speaking, that is." He elbow-bumps Dillon.

"Cavorting with the Gazelles?" someone farther down the table says. "Our women folk not fast enough for you, Dillon?" Those who have been listening break out into laughter.

"They're having fun with you," Jim says. "The Gazelles are like the rock goddesses on the PA series."

Dillon notices furtive glances his way from the Gazelles table upon Kate's return. *Work, run, and forget, that's all I want.* He consumes a healthy dose of beer as food plates arrive.

Hungry bellies full, race stories told, and club gossip spilled, the group sorts out the one-check tab, Jim acting out the part of accountant. They head for their respective carpool rides, bidding one another good races and goodbyes, and travel home. The guys discuss what the rest of their Saturday looks like, and what time and where they will meet for the Sunday run. Dillon suggests that they make a new tradition on their post-race Sunday runs by running at his place with breakfast afterward, bringing along their significant others. No one balks, including Spencer, and certainly not Jake, who jokes that he'll be there for breakfast but can't guarantee he'll make the run. Chase asks why, but all Jake says is, "Tweet, tweet, tweet, and buzz, buzz, buzz." Dillon smiles, reminding Jake that checkout time is one p.m., even in Athens.

Sunday Morning
Tough Enough

"So you think Western States is tougher than the Tour de France?" Chase says, as he, Jim, Spencer, Dillon, and Miles circle the vineyards. Joining them is a guest of the inn from Switzerland, Derrick, whose wife is strolling around Percy's Loop.

"When you factor in the preparation for it, yes," Spencer says, adding to his argument comparing the big three world-class events, Western States 100 trail race, Tour de France, and the Hawaiian Ironman.

"*Wooooowooowooo Wooooowoooo.*"

"Sorry, girl, no four-legged Iditarod comparison today," Dillon says.

Miles groans.

The notion floats in the crisp morning air, hanging in deliberation as they stride by rows and rows of vines slowly changing color, from summer green to autumn yellow. In the distant sky an unusual sight captures their attention: an immense flock of starlings that has the appearance of a dark cloud and constantly morphs into fantastic shapes with dimension. "Murmurations," Derrick calls it when asked about the visual anomaly. Jim reclassifies it as an aerial Rorschach test.

"As an event alone, the Tour is longer than the Western States, which is longer than the Ironman, but prior to race day there's more to consider," Spencer says a minute later, after the pulsating aerial spectacle has been taken in and commented on—butterfly, twister, mushroom, bear, explosion.

"Hmmm," Chase mutters. "I don't know. The Tour is twenty-one days long. And each day averages, like, over one hundred miles. Western States is only one hundred miles for one day."

"Two counterpoints," Spencer offers. "First, most of those miles on the Tour are in a pack—"

"Peloton," Derrick corrects.

"Peloton," Spencer says. "They're not taxing themselves all day, every day."

"Still, it's a grind," Jim says.

"Two, they're on bikes, which makes the effort non–weight bearing. The Western States athlete has to bear the load and without a peloton."

"They are allowed pacers after sixty miles, but you're right, it's unlikely they benefit from the draft effect," Derrick says.

"In that case my vote is for the Ironman," Dillon says. "They have to juggle training for three very different disciplines. The lack of specialization has to count for something."

"Except two of the three Ironman events—"

"Ironman is the *event*," Derrick corrects. His running form befits his long-course triathlon participation: upright posture, stiff arm movement, minimum knee lift, fast cadence, but unlike Spencer's shuffling form, Derrick flicks his foot out in front of his body and appears to glide over the ground like a cross-country skier. It looks less dynamic, but highly efficient, especially over flat terrain.

"What?"

"It's an Ironman; it combines three sports. It's not a long swim event followed by a century event followed by a marathon event."

"That sounds exhausting when you put it that way," Chase says.

"The endurance athlete's equivalent to *Planes, Trains, and Automobiles*," Jim says.

"Like biathlons combine cross-country skiing and rifle shooting events?" Dillon says.

"Exactly."

"Okay, two of the three sports are still non–weight bearing," Spencer says.

"So your argument is based on the physiological toll the body takes on, and running is harsher than swimming and cycling?" Chase says.

"Basically."

"With regards to automobiles, cyclists must contend with them while training, and they're on their bike approximately three times longer than runners are running," Derrick says.

"The recovery is quicker on the bike than from running," Spencer says.

"I don't know about that," Jim says, yawning and catching sight of the BR&B in the distance, many, *many* rows of vines to pass before reaching it. "Fatigue is fatigue."

"Think of it this way, if you're tired on the bike you can coast. If you're tired while running, no matter how slow you run, your legs still have to support your body weight."

"Coasting while swimming equals drowning," Jim says.

"Point goes to Jim," Chase says.

"But it alone doesn't make it tougher than the Western States."

"Headwinds on the bike for the Ironman," Dillon adds, "can be harsh without the benefit of a pack to—"

"Peloton."

"*Peloton* to draft behind, especially in Kona."

"But they finish where they started, so a tailwind aids them at some point," Spencer says.

"Western States has a net drop in elevation," Dillon says. "It's essentially a downhill race."

"Downhills are harder on the body than uphills, more stress to the quads," Spencer says.

"Cycling a ten-percent grade works the quads—" Chase says.

"Gears offset the load considerably," Spencer says.

"You've really thought this through," Dillon says.

"How'd we end up on this topic?" Chase says.

"Derrick asked if he could run with us," Jim says.

"I'm sure he regrets it now," Dillon says.

"No, no, you guys are quite entertaining, and your arguments are valid, although you did forget to mention that Tour riders wear ear pieces, and are continually informed on what is going on throughout the race. Of the three events the Western States ranks lowest in regards to the technology utilized. Not to mention the support aspect needs to be factored in. The Tour has a support team throughout the event. The Western States has minimal support from their crew: at the aid stations and their pacers later on. And the Ironman athlete has some technology, but no team or support crew that can assist other than cheer them on. They are truly solo, the ultimate endurance time trial."

"Other than the bike, the Ironman allows drafting on the swim and run," Spencer says.

"In terms of *tough*," Derrick says, "I submit the triple crown in Olympic running, five thousand, ten thousand, and marathon by Zátopek, winning gold medals in all three, and the marathon was his first attempt at the distance."

"Technically not a sport," Spencer says.

"Man, his form was atrocious," Dillon says.

"I don't know," Jim says. "It had a kind of distorted poetry to it."

"I agree, Spence," Chase says, "but think about what he had to do based on your model for toughest: all weight bearing, accomplished over several days, each event intense *and* against fresh legs, crossed different race disciplines, not to mention it's never been duplicated."

"Speaking of tough," Dillon says. "How's the ankle?"

"Merely a flesh wound," Spencer says.

"Finally a *Monty Python* reference!" Jim says, slowing to a trot near the

BR&B's front porch, wrapping up their feeble weight-bearing nine miles, breakfast's aroma wafting out from inside.

The kitchen is in full swing by the time Jake and Linda join the breakfast festivities: Dillon fills and refills breakfast plates; Terri has Doris, Maggie, Derrick's better half, and the Idaho couple, who extended their stay the rest of the week, deep in conversation about *something* Dillon chooses to ignore; Spencer is lost in the media lounge with Derrick; and Chase and Jim are discussing options for promoting his new accounting services.

"There they are," Jim says when Jake and Linda emerge from birthday date night, both dressed in sweats and long-sleeve shirts with different trail race logos stretched across them.

As Jake and Linda take a bow, Dillon launches a rendition of "Happy Birthday" for Linda, and the entire kitchen joins in, including Miles.

As the collective serenade rings out, Jake guides a surprised, blushing, and laughing Linda to a stool decorated with a birthday-themed cushion while Dillon places before her a quadruple stack of birthday-cake French toast—plain yogurt mixed with Funfetti cake mix and spread between layers of bread and topped with sprinkles and maple syrup drizzled across the top. He centers a candle on it and lights it.

"*And many morrrrrrrrrrrre,*" the chorus concludes.

Linda pauses a moment, smiles, and blows out the candle. "Thank you, guys."

"You missed a good run, Jakey," Chase says after the celebration subsides.

"I'm sure he got his heart rate up," Terri says on her way out of the kitchen.

"Hey, Jakey, who was that guy you were talking with after the race yesterday?" Chase asks. "The unattached runner who started off strong, dropped back halfway in, and finished ahead of you?"

"Salvador," Jake says, while settling into his coffee and sharing Linda's birthday plate. "I paced him during the Leadville 100 a couple years back. His brother lives locally and connected us."

"Where does he live?"

"Sacramento."

"No club affiliation?" Chase says. "They have a strong club there."

"He's an ultramarathoner and occasionally runs the shorter races," Jake says. "Their club wanted more commitment than he cared for."

"With his talent it wouldn't hurt to recruit him for the PA championships—"

"Nope," Spencer says, entering the kitchen. "We don't recruit from out of the area."

"We thought you got sucked back in time," Jim says.

"Why no recruiting?" Dillon says.

"Here we go," Chase says, bowing and shaking his head.

"Our club is a local one. Not bits and parts strung out all over the region."

"Quite the purity standards we have," Jake says.

"What are we, the Whole Foods of the running community?" Chase says.

"What if I move to the city?" Jim says.

"That's fine, you started here first," Spencer says.

"So were an organic club; attention, Whole Foods shoppers."

"Dillon moved in from out of the area. What about him?" Linda says.

"He lives here now."

"So no quarantine period?" Jake says.

"What if his heart is still in Southern California? He could be a GMO, transplanted to Sonoma County to act local, but isn't," Chase says.

"Dude."

"I rest my case."

"If anybody is genetically modified it's you, Chase," Jake says. "With all the sport product you consume, you're like a science project."

"It's quality stuff. I don't shop at CNG."

"That place is like an arms dealer for nutrition contraband," Dillon says.

"No shit. I do eat real food. I'm not a complete lab rat."

"You're my lab rat, though," Terri says, after which Chase turns beet red and goes quiet.

"Chase speechless?" Doris says. "Now, that's a first!"

Belly laughter fills the kitchen.

"You guys suck," Chase grumbles.

PA/USATF TOP 5 TEAM STANDINGS AS OF 10/11/2015		
	Club	Total
1	Agras (10-9-10)	29
2	Chico Running Club (8-10-8)	26
3	Strawberry Hill Harriers (7-7-7)	21
4	RERC (9-x-9)	18
5	South Bay Striders (6-8-4)	18

Week 41 Training Summary			
	Long Run	Mileage Total	Comments
Dillon	13	68	Need a better kick! Back is tight.
Chase	12.35	51	Dillon is knocking on the door.
Spencer	12.50	81	Good solid week.
Jim	12	48	Unsure about decision to leave the firm.
Jake	0	64	Enjoyed my first BR&B experience.

Week 7
October 12

Monday Morning
Greyson's Accounting Services
CPA, EA, CFE, CISA, CBA, CIA, CMA

"How's it feel to be a free man?" Doris asks Jim, walking into their home office at a little after seven a.m.

"Like I jumped out of a plane and forgot my parachute."

"So . . . splat!"

"Pretty much," he says, setting up new clients on his computer.

"How many switched from Pinnacle?"

"Eighteen indicated they would, but only sixteen have committed so far."

"What'd Chase want so late last night?"

"He gave me a number of a college buddy of his that lives down in San Rafael. He farms out overflow accounting and bookkeeping work."

"That was nice of him."

"I'm going down to meet the guy this afternoon. Not looking forward to the traffic on the 101, though."

"What time?"

"Three."

"Oh . . . could you go for a run first before heading home, after the commute runs its course?"

228

Jim considers the idea. China Camp State Park is nearby and a nice place to run, and it will be the site of a cross-country meet in a couple weeks. "Sure, that might work."

Doris wraps her arms around Jim, kissing him on the neck. "Stop worrying so much. This will be fun, you and me working at home together." She nuzzles his neck. "There'll be plenty of time to buy a house."

"I'm not sure we can even—"

"I've already come up with an idea for the honeymoon."

"What, two nights of camping in a REI outlet store?"

"No, Doomsday. Dillon sent me an email last night, asking if I'd be interested in selling him my breakfast cobblers. The ones I bring to the Sunday brunch at the inn."

"They are good."

"Instead of exchanging money, I offered him two months' worth for our honeymoon!"

"And he agreed?"

"He gave us three nights with some cool perks." Doris is now on her computer scouring the BR&B website, viewing the inn's amenities.

"That could be fun."

"He has a sauna, and a hot tub, evening wine and cheese, and a masseuse . . . masseuse . . . maaaaaasssseusssse. Masseuse, masseuse, masseuse—"

"You goof."

"Have you guys decided what you're doing on your bachelor weekend in Tahoe yet?"

"We've kicked around a few ideas," Jim says. "Some trail running, kayaking, hiking . . . the usual like we did for Jake's."

"No backpacking?"

"Not enough time, and it's getting cold up there at night."

"Reno?"

"Maybe for dinner."

Jim closes out of the software he purchased to manage his new clients, and prints off the legal documents he needs to sign and mail out.

"And to answer your question we're not going to a 'tapas' bar this time."

"With Chase on the trip . . . riiiiight."

"You know I won't spend money on that sort of thing."

"Ha! I know *you* won't, but I'm sure Chase will buy you a few lap dances."

"I'll close my eyes and think of you the whole time."

"Now *you're* the goof," she says, rising to her feet, turning away from him and shaking her moderately padded butt like a hippo in a conga line, chanting, "*Masseuse my caboose, masseuse my caboose, masseuse my caboose . . .*"

"Riiiiight . . . still you," he says, chuckling.

Forty-five minutes after leaving for San Rafael, driving under a thick blanket of clouds that ripple across the sky, Jim finds a parking spot and turns off the engine. He gathers up his old but sturdy briefcase—a graduation present from his parents—from the passenger seat, exits the car, and makes his way to the office of Chase's college buddy, Monroe, who is situated in the heart of downtown San Rafael. The tall front window with Monroe's name and CPA designation stenciled across it reminds Jim of *his* post-college plan A.

"You must be Jim," the tall, stout gentleman says from the small back office.

"That's right . . . Monroe?" Jim says, closing the door behind him.

"Bingo. Come on back." Monroe greets Jim with a hearty handshake that nearly yanks his arm out of its socket. "Nice to meet you. Chase says you guys run together? You must be fast to hang with him. I know he beat the pants off everybody back east. Have a seat. Coffee?"

"Coffee works," Jim says, taking a seat and setting his briefcase on the floor. "Chase is still fast; faster than me."

"We roomed together for a year," Monroe says, pouring a cup of coffee and passing it off to Jim. "Though you wouldn't know it by looking at me now"—he happily pats his paunch—"I played basketball, power forward. I joined him for a run once. I figured with all the running back and forth on the court, I'd be able to hang with him." He guffaws. "A few minutes in and I was gasping for an oxygen mask, and he's running and talking away as if we were shooting the breeze over a beer." He laughs again.

Jim chuckles. "That sounds like Chase."

"I haven't talked to him much since I moved out here last year. Still the funny man?"

"Annoyingly so."

"That's good to hear. It was a tough thing about his grandparents' passing, then his parents. And after all that, his best friend."

"I didn't know about the friend."

"Ah, well, probably not. He never talked much about him with me either, just the usual Chase: chipper exterior, joking around. I heard about it through the grapevine. They roomed together for two years. Then over the summer the guy was killed in a horseback-riding accident. That's how I ended up roommates with Chase."

Jim nods. Chase mentioned at some point on a past Sunday run about his family's early demise. While Chase didn't joke about it, he did put a silver lining spin on the matter, though Jim can't recall what it had been.

"So, Chase mentioned that Pinnacle bought your old place."

"That's right."

"They seem to be gobbling up all the mid-sized accounting firms, bringing their brand of accounting to the masses. They're like the big-box retailers of the accounting world. It's one thing to make a cheaper toaster, but accounting and tax services still require someone knowledgeable, and without pimples and attitude. After all, you can return a defective toaster for a refund, but a bad tax return nets you a visit from the IRS. And don't get me started on those online tax-return sites."

Jim grins. "I've had clients try that route and came back to me."

"Okay, so Chase said you'd been with Bennett's for a number of years. I've worked on a few projects with Darryl and Brendan; they're good people. I often farm out clients whom I call 'ankle biters' because they require excessive handholding. Generally, it's because they're terrible with basic bookkeeping skills, and call me like I'm their wet nurse. I consider myself a people person, but not when they're nipping at my heels all day long. My wife implores me to be more patient." He laughs at his obvious lack of patience for developing patience.

"I have experience with those types, so that won't be a problem."

"I assume you're starting off by working at home?"

"That's correct, until I can gather a steady stream of clients."

"Well, you know the accountants' credo: take care of the short term and the long term will take care of itself. Oh, and in the short term, add another phone line for the ankle biters," he says, shaking his head. "They. Will. Call. At. All. Hours!"

Jim scribbles a note about calling the phone company.

Over the next thirty minutes, Monroe gives Jim a list of clients to start with, their contact information, and any files he has on them, giving Jim a brief overview of each client. Jim takes notes and asks the occasional question. By the time Jim thanks Monroe and leaves his office, heading for the car, Jim feels a sense of relief, now with another two dozen clients added to his first day as a free man.

The relief is short-lived, however, until he reaches the 101 Freeway on his way over to China Camp State Park. It isn't so much a single point of worry that derails him, though canvassing for new clients for his financial survival, setting aside the new-house purchase, and the scaled-down honeymoon gnaw at him. As the sun filters through broken clouds and the road to the park whisks him away from the bustling Marin city life, past strip malls, homes, the financial uncertainties up north, and along the San Pablo Bay with its salty marshes and wonderful vista on one side, and many miles of wooded trails and wildlife on the other, Jim dials in on the nagging feeling that leaves him out of sorts: It's three thirty p.m. on a Monday afternoon, and instead of being shackled to his desk at work, answering one of Dinky's many questions about nothing in particular, or talking with a client, or sitting in a meeting, Jim is changing out of his workday attire, donning running shorts and shirt, lacing up running shoes, locking the car, and heading out for a run. It still feels like he's jumped out of an airplane sans parachute, but at least the view is nice . . . for now.

Wednesday, Late Afternoon
Running with the Big Dogs

"Three minutes until the start," Spencer says through cupped hands. "Three minutes. Please report to the starting line."

Dillon, Chase, Jim, Jake, and Zac are performing strides out from a crudely drawn start line in the gravel in front of the BR&B's porch, Miles overseeing the proceedings. Spencer performs his strides after making the announcement. A couple minutes later he cups his hands again and summons all racers to the start line, and as they assume their starting spots, the elder runners enact the roles Spencer has assigned them. Dillon adds one more short stride and upon returning he steps in front of Zac and turns around, effectively pushing Zac off the start line. Zac tries to squeeze up front, but both Chase and Jim have blockaded the line, so Zac searches for a spot, eyes wide and darting while Spencer shouts fifteen seconds to go, and moves down the line, Jake sliding over to let him in, placing Zac to the right of Jim, whose patented arm idiosyncrasy will come as an unwelcome surprise.

Spencer's discussion with Zac about today's run entailed "running with the big dogs" to simulate conditions he may not see until the end of the season at the bigger meets. Having older, faster, and race-experienced runners in the mix should prove both taxing and intimidating to him. So far, merely settling on the start line stresses him out.

Standing behind Zac, Spencer shouts, "On your marks," then places a coach's whistle into his mouth and positions a hand near Zac's back, ready to give him a mild shove off the line. The shrill of the whistle pierces the brief moment of quiet, sending Miles back into the BR&B.

Everybody lurches from the line, Zac nonplused over Spencer's shove, though several yards later the fling of Jim's right elbow repeatedly catches Zac's left arm, disrupting his form. Meanwhile, Jake has drifted to his left, pressing close to Zac, leaving him boxed in with little room to maneuver. Thirty seconds later, Chase and Dillon with sizable leads, Spencer blows the whistle. All case to a stop and regroup.

"What happened, Zac?" Spencer says.

"I got boxed in, Coach."

"You also were bumped off the start line. Did you notice the subtle move Dillon did right before the start?"

"Yeah, he did a quick stride and stepped in front of me. He boxed me out like in basketball."

"Exactly. And you were nice enough to let him take it. If you want *that* spot, then you need to protect it. If someone goes out for a last minute stride and heads your way, step out in front of the line to dictate what happens. Got it?"

"Got it."

"It's a psych-out move," Chase says. "Lets everybody on the line see *him.*"

"Sly dog," Jim says.

Dillon puts a finger to his lips and winks.

"Now, at the bigger meets they'll have your starting spots marked off, so it won't be an issue, but always beware." Zac spits into the gravel. "Now, what happened after the start?"

"Jimbo hammered me."

"You need to spread your elbows out, just like in basketball. Protect your space."

"Got it, Coach."

"Okay, let's reset and go in thirty seconds."

The group moves around the start line, mixes things up, and settles into their spots. Again the pre-start silence. Miles pokes her head out from the front door, then retreats from the whistle's shrill.

Off the line, sandwiched in the middle of the small field, Zac lets his elbows wander, making a beeline for the narrow path toward Percy's Loop, Chase and Dillon leading the way. The guys lock into formation once they hit the Loop, Dillon and Chase side by side, Jim a half stride back and to the left of Dillon. Jake runs to the right of Zac, and Spencer positions himself to Zac's left a couple steps back, keeping a watch on how Zac reacts to the race tactics, and providing a lurking presence.

Consulting his watch, Spencer allows their bodies to adapt to Zac's 5K race pace—a couple ticks under 4:50 per mile—and the crucial two or so minutes it takes the body to switch from its autonomic anaerobic response to a race start before switching over to aerobic—before initiating another command via a Spence-speak.

Approaching a left-hand turn that crosses a dry creek bed, Chase surges, catching Zac off guard. Chase buys a few yards on the guys, slides into the inside lane in front of Dillon, and rounds the corner, accelerating out of it and across the rocky depression, adding more yards on the group. Dillon responds, closing the gap, while Jim moves up on Zac's shoulder and establishes enough of a position on the inside that Zac has to allow room, diverting his attention just enough to slow him down around the corner.

"You need to bridge the gap now, Zac, or they're gone," Spencer says patiently.

Zac works his way by Jim, who responds, matching Zac's stride. Jake comes up on the other side of Zac and the three race after Dillon and Chase. Spencer lets the group run the simulated midrace move for sixty seconds, then blows the whistle. The group slows, breathing hard, particularly Zac.

"Nice adjustment after the turn, Zac . . . but you need to stay alert when approaching a turn. You're accustomed to being out front and navigating them on your own terms. If you're in a pack, you'll need to position yourself so that if someone makes a move on a corner, especially a blind one, you're already responding to it. If you have to slow down it's like an accordion effect, as the leaders round the corner they're accelerating while you're slowing until you're around it."

"Also," Jim says, "if you go wide around a turn, be sure to watch for guys on the inside who might bump you out further, like they did to Billy Mills on the last lap of the Olympic ten thousand."

"Or," Dillon says, "if the course is wet, make sure you have an escape route should someone lose their footing, because they'll end up taking you out if they go down."

Zac nods, processing the doled-out wisdom.

"Okay, let's start back up in three, two, one, go," and off they go. By this time they're on the backside of Percy's Loop, where the trail zigzags through a tree-lined enclosure, the big dogs behind and flanking Zac. They hold this formation until they arrive back at the driveway, sweeping through it and headed for another loop. Spencer tests Zac, running him at race pace for several minutes with a close group surrounding him, a situation that Zac is rarely exposed to. He handles it well until Jim edges up on him. Zac changes gears. While Zac focuses on repelling Jim, Chase surges from the other side of Zac, who catches sight of the move and responds, staying a step ahead. Jim makes another run at Zac, and Chase follows suit until Zac finds himself redlining. Spencer half smiles, half shakes his head, blowing the whistle, the Chase/Jim battle all too familiar.

The guys slow and regroup.

"Zac, you were—"

"I know . . . Coach . . . controlled until . . . they started coming . . . at me."

"That's a good instinct to have at the end of the race, but not in the middle, not when you're a speed guy. They're going to know you're a kicker and try to stretch you out during the middle miles. Don't make it easy for them."

"Got it."

"Ideally, running with these guys should make you comfortable running in a pack, so at CIF and Footlocker it'll be no big deal."

"What about position, Coach?"

"What about it?"

"What if there's a turn coming up and they're trying to get a better position by going by me?"

"Depends on what you lose by letting them go. If you have them pinched hold your position, but other than that what *you* were doing was racing two guys by trying to hold them off. You really shouldn't be leading the race. Let the others do the work, jockey for position, make the mistakes. Have confidence with what you possess. Come the last six-hundred yards you'll be tapping on *their* shoulders. Patience is your best asset with your long finishing kick."

"And, for God's sake," Jake says, "whatever you do, don't . . . ." He drifts back and chats with Chase.

Zac glances back a couple times.

"*Ocean's Eleven*," Jim says, running alongside Zac.

"Coach mentioned you guys were a riot."

Wednesday Evening
House of Mirrors

"Zac, you want something to eat?" Dillon asks, walking into the media lounge carrying a food plate.

"I'm good, thanks," Zac replies, performing maintenance on the BR&B's website.

"You sure? You haven't eaten since the big dogs run."

"Not that hungry, I guess."

Dillon nods, watching over Zac's shoulder. Dillon had attempted the updates himself after listening to Zac's instructions the last time he was there setting it up. But somewhere between update this and update that he'd messed it up. Not so bad that he couldn't repair some of the damage, but enough that the site lacked the polish Zac had originally applied.

"Thanks for fixing it."

"No problem, Mr. Percy. You mostly had it back to normal."

"You can call me Dillon if you want."

"Cool."

Dillon pays close attention to Zac's handiwork in order to perform his own updates in the future, so much so that he's forgotten to set down the egg sandwich and chips he's brought in for Zac. "Just in case."

"Can I ask you a personal question?"

"Sure."

"Coach mentioned you're divorced."

The hairs on the back of Dillon's neck prickle. "That's right."

Zac hits a number of keys, and refreshes the webpage. "Do you still talk with her?"

Dillon wants to reprise the "metaphorical death" joke, but it doesn't seem appropriate for Zac; it's more a personal coping mechanism than advice. "Not really."

"That's what I'm afraid of."

"Why's that?"

"That my parents' divorce is going to be more than a logistical split, but a *complete* split."

Dillon ponders the comparison. "In my case we didn't have children . . . so it was easier to maintain a permanent split."

"*Wooooowoooowooo Wooooowoooo.*"

"Does she understand us?"

"She likes to think so."

Zac seems to consider Dillon's comparison, though it's just as likely that he's focusing on the code he's writing for the online reservation system. "I'm glad they're not living together anymore. They argued *all* the time and often threw things at each other. But now I feel in the middle, and it's like I need to pick sides."

"My parents split when I was in high school, and you're right it does feel like a side needs to be staked out. I told them I wouldn't choose one over the other."

"Did it help?"

"Not really, but I received many retail bribes out of it."

Zac grins, pauses from his work, and bites into the sandwich.

"It's a like a bad storm; you just have to weather it and keep in mind it has nothing to do with you."

"Yeah, I spend my free time at Donna's place. Her parents have been cool about it."

Dillon relives *his* coping skills from back then and the actions he took to weather the storm. Running was one of them. So was staying out late at libraries and coffeehouses, reading until the establishments closed for the night and shoved him back out into the storm. The discussion also reminds him of the letter his high school coach had written him. "Be right back."

"I could use something to drink, if you don't mind, Mr. Percy."

"Sure."

Dillon walks to his small quarters off the back of the kitchen, or "keeping room" as the real estate agent had excitedly referred to it during their first walk-through, regaling him with the Colonial reference. "It's *fabulously* unique, don't you agree!" He didn't know what to make of it. For one it had no door. And only one small window, with no view to speak of. It was larger than a laundry room but smaller than a child's bedroom; certainly not suitable to charge guests a premium for. After four more listings he circled back and decided the "keeping room" would be his bedroom *and* laundry room. At some point he intended to hang a door to it for privacy, but he rather liked the openness and felt less claustrophobic without one.

From the one makeshift wall shelf he pulls down a plastic crate filled with old Christmas cards, letters, and important personal documents, fishes deep in the stacks that have seen better organization prior to his move north, finds what he wants, and replaces the box. Kneeling on hardwood floor, he opens the handwritten letter and scans it until he reaches the pertinent section, rereading it for the first time in years.

> *. . . you have as much potential as I have ever seen in my twenty years of coaching, Dillon. To consider international levels at 10,000 meters and the marathon is not unrealistic. Having said that, I feel the biggest drawback for you that I can see is you may not be selfish enough. Recognizing that what is best for you may sometimes conflict with what others want or expect of you is difficult. Selfishness is also a component of winning the big races. Winners are possessive of championships, believing they belong to them and want them more than anyone else in the race that day. Furthermore, achieving goals is neither a physical nor an intellectual activity. It is a total experience demanding an integrated approach using all your faculties. Your situation on the home front is an element you'll need to emotionally address in order to realize what I (and I believe you do too) feel you are capable of.*
>
> *All my best,*
> *JW*

Dillon rereads the passage twice more, emotions mixed in reviving old issues and lost dreams, yet hopeful they can provide guidance. He replaces the letter to its envelope, walks out to the kitchen, pours a glass of orange juice, and returns to the media lounge.

"Here," Dillon says, setting the juice glass down and handing Zac the letter. "Give it a read. Might help."

"Thanks . . ." Zac takes the letter and gives it a long stare while turning it over a couple times. "How old are you?"

Dillon chuckles. "My coach wrote it before everybody had email. His handwriting is better than most fonts."

"Okay, I'm all done here. Can I stay a little longer and watch some of the World Cross-Country videos?"

"Do your—" Dillon hesitates, staring at a younger version of himself. "I mean—"

"I'm staying at my mom's place these days and she knows I'm here. Coach vouched for you. I just need to be home by eleven, is all."

"Sure, knock yourself out."

"Cool. This place is awesome."

"Dessert?"

"Oh yeah, that'd be great," Zac says. He cues up an old videotape, jokes about the old technology, and sits on the couch and hits Play.

Dillon strides back into the kitchen to assemble a dessert plate of banana bread and mango slices. He pulls out his cell phone, sending a text message to Spencer to verify Zac's story and situation. By the time Dillon creates the dessert plate, Spencer replies: "It's okay. Not ideal, but okay. Thanks for helping out today with the race simulation."

"No problem," Dillon replies. After delivering the dessert plate to Zac, Dillon unwinds on the couch in the living room, where Miles is now curled up, tasting the beer he opened an hour earlier; no longer cold but good enough. He composes a text message to Kate about her offer to hang out in the city. The phrasing has to be just right, something that gives the impression of "I might want to keep the door open, but not now." Her eyes had tugged at him during lunch the previous weekend when she first asked him about staying, or perhaps the brush of her hand on his shoulder had fleetingly breached the wall he'd constructed. He starts typing, stops, deletes, sips beer; starts again, further along, stops, deletes, sips beer. More typing, more deleting, more sipping. He stares into the kitchen, empty and quiet. Another sip, stroking Miles's white-and-black coat, her eyes opening and closing, before Dillon types, "Thanks for the offer, but can't hang out afterward." Message sent he tosses the phone across the couch, downs the last of his beer, banishing the disappointment he envisions Kate's eyes will hold upon reading the text; or is it his own disappointment for the message he's sent? He's not sure.

Thursday Night
Too Hot to Handle

Chase holds the door open for Terri upon their arrival to Exotic Tandoori, a popular Indian restaurant just north of his condo on the 101 in Healdsburg. The midweek crowd bustles with the energy of tourism, a township burdened with an excessive amount of success for its citizens' tastes. Surrounded by valleys of vineyards on three sides, Fitch Mountain perched like a dais east of town, casting long shadows across the signature downtown plaza square and its wine-tasting caves and trendy fashion boutiques, and the Russian River dancing along the eastern and southern confines, Healdsburg annually lands on one or another top-ten smallest towns in America lists, all but suffocating its livable charm.

Inside, their senses are instantly treated to the rich exotic aroma of cumin, warm ghee, and sweet, fragrant cardamom. The wait will be ten minutes the hostess informs Chase when he has his name placed on the list. Though Indian cuisine isn't at the top of his regular dinner choices, he finds the food flavorful enough on the rare occasions he's partaken. Unfamiliar with the Exotic Tandoori, Chase had asked a coworker about the place, who sang its praises, but it was Terri's high recommendation that really sealed the deal, and who was he to argue with her tastes?

Tonight's dinner with her has weighed on him since last Sunday when they shored up the details during the BR&B post-run brunch. Not so much the dinner, but the reason for the dinner: her human sexuality study. Dating is Chase's forte, an art he'd honed while living in New York City, on par with speed dating without the formal structure, sizing up the other in the blink of an eye and moving on to the next if necessary. But is this a date? It had never been clearly established. Ostensibly it's just a meeting to discuss the study he'd agreed to participate in. Unfortunately for Chase, Terri's coy demeanor with a side of slyness and liberal dose of sex appeal leaves him off balance. And if he thinks she can't look any more appealing than what she normally wears for running and work, he's wrong: proud shoulders and long neck exposed in an orange strapless dress that gently kisses her knees. Gracing her neckline is a simple pendant, an artistic rendering of yin and yang.

"You look nervous," Terri says, standing close to him among the other waiting patrons.

On the track she seemed shorter. With black high heels on she stands eye to eye with him, her pupils scanning his intently.

"No, no, I'm good," he says, breaking her gaze and glancing in the hostess' direction. "I don't have a complete handle on the scope of your study."

"Think of it this way: as society moves toward a technological way of life, the *human interaction* experience is affected in ways that we're not equipped to handle on an emotional level. The ability to develop and show empathy is one example research has shown among children. Texting is not the same as talking, and reading differs from listening. The *conversation* is altered dramatically."

Chase recalls Jake holding forth about this very same topic. "Sure, I can see that part; we rely on technology for many things, but I'm not sure how it relates to"—Chase lowers his voice a notch—"human sexuality."

Terri smiles and nudges him with her elbow. "One of those levels is how we relate and communicate with one another through touch. Technology creates a buffer between the physical and the techno-physical, an actual hug versus the 'hug' emoticon. It literally removes us from the world of touch, replaced with the perception of touch—a less than satisfying emotional experience." She slides her arm through his, her hand gently squeezing his arm. "There are those who find it quicker and easier to achieve instant gratification with technology, forgoing the messy interactions that come from dealing with real people. It's easy to lose yourself in technology, pretending it's better than real relations."

Chase's attention shifts to her hand, the subtle warm and physical sensation it imparts. "Yes, I can see how touch appeals to the senses better than a text message."

"Our table is ready," Terri says.

Chase glances up, the hostess standing in front of them, motioning to follow her. "Of course . . ."

They are seated at a table for two along the back wall, its saffron hue blushing under the diffuse sconce lighting. After Chase seats Terri and settles into his own chair, he strives to regain control. "I worked on a campaign for the Brazilian restaurant across the street last year. They wanted to promote their takeout window during the lunch hour. So I suggested that they offer—" Chase freezes, mentally fast forwarding to the rest of that sentence: Brazilian bikini waxes to women while they waited for their order. It's a story best left for Sunday runs with the guys, but now Terri's focus bores through him, awaiting its conclusion. His mind scrambles for an alternate ending, to no avail. He immediately feels juvenile in her presence despite the six years he has on her.

Terri cackles with laughter. "I'm pretty sure I know how that one ends."

Thankfully the waiter stops by, taking their drink and appetizer orders. Chase composes himself and orders a bottle of German Riesling, a highly recommended pairing due to its slight sweetness, which balances out the spices inherent to Indian cuisine, a detail he learned while researching Grogger's Box Wine campaign. Chase can't tell if Terri is impressed or not with this knowledge.

"Sorry, I suppose I *am* nervous," Chase says, a moment after the waiter left. "So technology creates an unnatural buffer between how people interact physically with each other, and over time . . ." Chase pauses a moment, catching sight of the painting on the wall behind Terri, a caricature of a Indian man and woman intertwined in an exotic dance pose. The light bulb flickers on in his mind. He smiles.

"Very good," Terri says. "You catch on quick."

"Not quick enough, apparently."

Chase relaxes after the wine has been poured, tasted, and approved. Terri explains her thesis in more detail: understanding the impact that technology, more specifically social media and electronic forms of communication—emailing, texting, instant messaging—has on how people relate to one another physically, especially when it comes to intimacy. She offers up a "panacea" by incorporating the teachings of the Kama Sutra in American culture as more than "the sex manual" as it's often labeled, but as a way to increase intimacy—through touch and conversation—with one's partner to develop deeper relationships in a technological world. Terri has been recruiting various subjects to answer a series of questions and grant interviews about their lives, tracking certain aspects of their sex lives as well as their engagement with technology on a day-to-day basis. To date, Terri has worked with a married couple, a gay couple, and a heterosexual couple who've been dating for some time, but not living together. Chase will represent the single male not currently in a relationship.

"So, Chase Brandon, tell me what's the longest relationship you have been in?" Terri asks, sipping her wine, her eyes never straying from his.

Chase contemplates her opening question as the appetizers arrive. "Six months, spanning the last month of my senior year in high school and into freshman year at Ithaca."

"How did it end?"

"She attended Marquette, so after the summer ended, I didn't see her that often. It naturally faded by Christmas break."

"Do you keep in touch with her?"

"Not really. We exchanged a few emails while I was working in New York, and we're connected on Facebook, but that's about the extent of it."

"Any significant relationships during college?"

Chase sips his wine, washing down the spicy appetizer, and uses a napkin to wipe away the residue. "Nothing significant . . . nothing lasting more than five or six weeks. I was pretty busy with school and running. I was on scholarship and primarily focused on competing."

"What about after college?"

"This is making me sound aloof, isn't it?" Chase says with a smile, though inside he's wishing for the peever.

"On the contrary," Terri says. "I'm not here to judge. Everybody has a different path. That's why I'm fascinated with this study, to understand how people deal with relationships in today's socially challenged world. Humankind has enormous capacity to achieve many things, but the speed at which they are achieved puts humanity on their heels, scrambling to adapt."

Chase stops fidgeting when their dinner arrives. He muses at what most assuredly will go down as the worst date ever if this is an actual date, talking about past relationships. He once went on a date in New York City, shortly after starting his first job, where ten minutes in she started crying over a recent ex; the check was summoned posthaste.

"How'd you become interested in human sexuality?"

"Ah, a diversion," Terri says with a grin.

"Perhaps, but I am curious."

"So was I, curious, that is. I find people *fascinating*. I love watching how couples interact in public. You'd be surprised how often two people having coffee together are checking emails, texts, the Internet and not actually interacting with one another. Simply having a cell phone on the table during conversation creates a distraction that inhibits the depth of their conversation. After my bachelor's degree, I wanted to delve deeper into how relationships are affected by technology, and, more specifically, how it affects intimacy in relationships."

"So how does a single guy factor into your study if you're studying relationships?"

"It provides another dimension to the question. Just because you're not currently in a relationship, it doesn't mean your past experiences aren't valuable to study, as are your current lifestyle choices, and how they shape future ones."

Beads of sweat form on his forehead despite cautiously eating the pork vindaloo dish.

"Spicy?"

"Good for the immune system," Chase says, and takes a gulp of water.

"How regularly do you have sex on a first date?"

Half the helping on Chase's next forkful returns to the plate. He smiles. "Perhaps we should've ordered in." He eats what's left on the fork and swallows. "Only a few times. I never expect to." He gulps more water.

"How far do you usually *expect* to go?"

"Twenty miles," Chase says, and adds a cheesy grin.

"Cute."

"A kiss at the door is generally the protocol."

"In your experience do you find a woman more or less intriguing the more dates you go on before having sex with her?"

Tough question. A woman intrigues him more or less the same no matter when they actually make it to the bedroom. True, he often finds himself losing interest after the sex, though he isn't sure why exactly. What he does know for certain, or feels he knows, is that sowing wild oats is not his modus operandi. Having the same conversations over and over with someone new bores him. He longs for a connection that lasts beyond the tit-for-tat dialogue the early phases of dating burdens him with. It just seems to elude him.

"I would say . . . sex doesn't change their intrigue."

"Just haven't found the right woman yet?"

"Exactly. The guys joke about my dating adventures, but they're having fun with me. I really don't treat dating or sex as if it were a sport."

Once Chase makes the connection that Terri's questions are based on relationships rather than sex itself, he relaxes, opening up about certain aspects of his social life. And, yes, he loves technology, but as far as he's concerned it doesn't prevent him from searching for a real connection with a woman. By the time dinner has been consumed and their dessert plates are whisked away, Chase realizes that he's essentially engaged in pillow talk about his life, sans the pillow, the result of which brings on an uneasy exposed state. Fleeing seems like the immediate response.

"Ready?" Chase says after the check has been dealt with.

"If you are."

Chase rises and waits for her to pass by him, again noticing how much taller she appears.

The drive back to her place is quiet except for comments Terri makes about the dinner, if Chase enjoyed it, asking him where they're racing on Saturday, and again thanking him for participating in her study along with setting up two more meetings for the questionnaire and interview portions. Pulling up in front of her place, Chase sits lost in thought about the nature of the evening: date or study kick-off. It seems improper to think of it as a date, yet the flirting feels real. And he can't recall ever simply having dinner with a woman who *wasn't* a date. Before he has time to consider it further, Terri laughs.

"What?"

"You think too much," she replies. "Kiss me or don't kiss me good night. You're not on the hook for anything, Chase Brandon." She leans in halfway to him and smiles. "The Inuit have a hundred ways to describe snow."

Sandalwood and May blossom waft into his nostrils. "So I've heard."

"How many ways do you imagine the Kama Sutra has in describing a kiss?"

"I'm going to go out on a limb and say more than a few."

"There's the Contact Kiss," Terri whispers, lightly, but briefly, grazing her moist lips against his.

A hint of musk crashes the olfactory party. "I . . . I like that one."

"There's Kiss to Ignite the"—Terri tilts her head and presses her supple lips against the corner of his mouth, lingering for a moment—"Flame."

Mesmerized, Chase can't move.

"All told, thirty variations," she says, leaning back.

He gazes into her eyes, lost in a world of lust, confusion, and paralysis. "That's . . . that's a lot of kisses to explore."

"Until next time, Chase Brandon," she says, and with that she exits.

Friday Night
Homestead Faith

"Robyn, what are you doing?" Jake hollers as he taps out the details on the invoice spreadsheet situated on Linda's computer monitor in his usual manner: key tap, quick peek at the monitor, key tap, quick peek at the monitor. "You're supposed to be taking a shower."

"I already did," she says, walking into the room, carrying a small pail filled with water.

"I didn't hear the water running for very long." Jake recalls the sound of water turning on and off several times.

"I took a boat shower. See?" She bows her damp head for inspection.

Jake sniffs her head, the shampoo's fragrance apparent. "Boat shower?"

"Like grandpa used to do: rinse, soap, rinse, soap."

"Ah, a *navy* shower."

"He called it a boat shower. I like that better."

"So do I, sweetie." Jake returns to his task: creating client invoices, involving more time and effort than he cares to think about. He'd much rather spend the day laying river rock or planting trees than itemizing them. Linda generally handles the lion's share of the administrative side of his landscaping business, but on occasion he steps up. And despite Jim's best attempts at streamlining the invoicing process, Jake hasn't completely grasped the automation. "What's with the pail?"

"I saved the extra shower water for the plants."

"Did the TV news story about the drought scare you?"

"I don't want to run out of water. Sometimes I get thirsty in the middle of the night."

"I'll make sure you always have water."

"Okay." She watches him hunt and peck his way through the invoice. "Daddy?"

"Yes, sweetie."

"Why do you keep peeking at the screen?" She points to the half-completed invoice on the screen.

"Daddy's slow, sweetie."

"Can't you type as fast as you run?"

Jake chuckles. "Sadly I cannot."

Robyn observes Jake's progress several more moments. "You have to have faith!"

"Yes, I do," Jake says. "I'm better with emails, but Jimmy's program confuses me sometimes so I have to pay close attention."

Robyn seems to consider Jake's comments, or perhaps she wants to use the computer herself; if the latter, she doesn't say anything to that effect. "Can I teach you something?"

"Of course."

Robyn sets the pail down and wiggles her way in between Jake and the desk. "Use this key"—she points to the Tab key—"to change to a different square." She then points to the cursor that's moving between the different cells on the invoice as she repetitively presses the Tab key. "And type without peeking."

"How'd you get so smart on computers?"

"At school, and Mom lets me play . . . *learn* on the computer. It's the future, Dad!"

"My future is making sure you have a future with water."

"I like that future too," Robyn says, leaning her head back and grinning at Jake.

"Your near future is getting ready for bed."

"It's still early."

"It's nine."

Robyn glances at his wrist. "But you're not wearing—"

"Your futuristic computer told me." Jake points to the time display on the task bar.

"Oh. Why don't you wear a watch when you run like Jimmy and Spencey and Chasey and Dilly?"

Act one.

"Mom bought you a real neat one for Christmas last year. I helped pick it out."

"It's complicated." He immediately regrets the word choice when Robyn's expression challenges him. "Not that kind of complicated. The watch is hard to understand, like Jimmy's program. Besides, when I run with the guys they all have watches and tell me how far I've run."

Robyn tilts her head, considering Jake's rationale. "Like when *you* wake me up in the morning instead of the alarm?"

"That's right."

Robyn nods, watching Jake's mildly faster typing. She's either getting sleepy or is in deep thought.

"It seems silly to let a clock tell you to eat or stop learning, right?" Jake says.

"Then I could stay in the classes I like longer?"

"That's right, and if you want me to wake you up in time for class you need to go to bed."

"After I water the plants."

Act two.

Robyn hugs Jake, picks up her pail, and walks out of the office. "Come tuck me in!"

"I will, sweetie." He pecks the Tab key until the cursor rests in the correct square. He strives to focus entirely on typing, but after a few keystrokes he peeks. So far so good, so he continues typing, and before long, though long enough that Robyn has hollered for him, he completes the invoice.

Saturday Morning
Agras XC Open, Crystal Springs

Hunched over, gazing downward, the trail narrowing to a fine point, Jim clears his mind after one last key-pocket check. Overhead, the blazing sun singes his exposed shoulders as the arid San Mateo County air hangs over the barren swath, like kindling awaiting a spark.

Crack!

They thunder off the wide start line, a cloud of dust trailing them, plummeting from the highest point on the course, the emphatic pitter-patter of soles generating momentum until the slap, slap, slap of foot strikes against the hard-packed surface signal optimal speed for a controlled half-mile descent, whereupon heels dig in and quads contract fiercely, all but bringing them to a screeching halt and releasing them right back up from whence they came along a parallel trail.

Welcome to the Crystal Springs first mile.

Jim's favorite venue by far, the fabled course—one of only a handful in the United States dedicated solely to cross-country—has tested the mettle, at one time or another, of nearly every Northern California high school and collegiate runner since its inception in 1971. So true of a cross-country course, Crystal Springs has hosted many national-caliber races whose alumni include Mary Decker, Linda Somers, Frank Shorter, Gary Tuttle, Marty Liquori, Don Kardong, and Nick Rose racing around various configurations—2.95 miles to 10K—of the desolate venue. Today's configuration: 4.19 miles.

To the naked eye, the surroundings lack visual appeal: lifeless, resting high on a plateau overlooking Interstate 280 and the Upper Crystal Springs Reservoir to the west, and butted up against Belmont's western suburban sprawl. Yet the course itself, when physically experienced, embodies historical reverence, never forgotten, much like riding an old wooden roller coaster along a famed boardwalk: anticipation before a sharp drop; a long, dusty grind back up; an extended winding, often jarring, descent; a handful of punishing ups and downs until the finale: a spirit-crushing uphill slope to the finish line and dashing under the permanent finishing structure, its inscription memorized by few, cherished by all.

Jim starts out particularly well, leveraging the rare downhill start to gather "bonus seconds" while his leg muscles are fresh and lactic acid–free, a strategy Spencer emphatically argues against with his marathon-biased mind-set, owing to the fact it unduly taxes the system and saps one's finishing push. But Jim uses the start of every race he runs to set the tone for his effort. Though there was a time when Jim did it purely to mess with Spencer's controlling nature, Jim learned long ago that changing gears during the race was not his forte. His is a one-speed constitution, save for the modest surge here and there. A slow or cautious start results in a slow or cautious performance. A fast start, throwing caution to the wind, bordering on reckless, nets him a better race. That it irks Spencer is simply a guilty pleasure.

Down and back up, one mile in and the field splintered like kindling because of it, Jim rolls over the start summit ready to take on the Outback, free from the white and starchy-collar confines of his business week, instead ready to grind it out and get it done with a blue-collar work ethic: no frills, no watch, simply dig in and don't give in until the finish line.

Dillon's out good with the leaders and has gapped Jim enough to disappear from constant view. Surprisingly enough, Chase remains behind Jim this far in. His aggressive starts generally force Chase to play catch-up, but on this course it gives Jim a longer leash to run with. He's beaten Chase only once, a 12K road race that ran across the Golden Gate Bridge years ago. Chase jokingly claimed he'd suffered vertigo during the bridge crossing. He did buy Jim a beer that night, a nod to Jim's feat, though during the toast Chase tossed out the jab, "Enjoy it while you can because it will be the last."

While Jim took the good-natured competitive ribbing in stride, he did feel a certain pang, dropping from the club's perennial number-one open cross-country runner to number two when Chase arrived on the scene. At longer distances, Jim can take Chase, but he stays clear of anything longer than 12Ks. Jim remembers that first defeat, the passing of the torch, the race where Jim had thirty yards on Chase going into the final quarter mile, only to hear, feel, and see Chase roar by like a shiny new sports car. And now with Dillon's arrival, Jim again feels the further slide from the top spot.

The one "easy" section of the course allows those with wheels to roll with abandon down the moderate slope, making up for the jarring first mile, and soon enough, as Jim settles into his own pace, the not-so-shiny, not-so-new sports car races by with a determined face and glance at his watch, trying to manage the greater damage that Dillon has imposed today. Inter-squad competition adds depth and dimension to the equation, each wanting to do well, and rooting for the other to do just as well. It's said that competition breeds peak performances, but perhaps none greater than chasing down one's own teammate.

The respite concluded and only one spot lost, Jim focuses his attention on those within shouting distance. Turning back toward the start/finish some two-plus miles in, Jim sizes up two runners in the foreground, both strong in form until they hit the first hill after the long gradual descent, a temptress that lulls the legs into a false sense of vigor, but pulls the rug out from underneath where the terrain rises unmercifully.

With a mental cord attached to Chase as he's cresting the top, Jim leans into the hill, shortens his stride, and punches the air with his fists as if shadowboxing. Both competitors' heads sag subtly, the one nearest Jim glancing over, expression defeated, while the other adjusts his effort and stays abreast with Jim. But by the time they reach the top a hundred yards later, Jim has weighed, measured, and found the pursuer wanting.

Over the top and hurtling downward again, Jim scopes out a trio of guys lined up like dominoes ready to be knocked over. Jim works his way up to the catalyst, tucks in for a momentary breather, and swings wide around the curve where the trail juts up. Two of the three respond and keep pace with Jim, one to the side and the other directly behind. Jim doesn't waver at the challenge. He's here for the challenge. Throughout the last half of any race, road or cross-country, Jim absolutely hates getting passed. Hates it! He'd rather pass a kidney stone than let someone get by him. What's the purpose of training every day, week after week, year after year if he doesn't "throw down" on Saturdays? What's the point to merely show up and go through the motions? May as well make it his own personal Olympic moment. After all, what repercussions will come from getting beaten? Nothing. No endorsements lost. No disappointed coach. Doris will still love and marry him. Jake will continue to meet and run with him on Thursday evenings. There will still be Spence-speaks to chuckle at. So why not make the most of it? He has only himself to answer to, and it's much more pragmatic to leave it out on the course than to live with the worrisome pain of wimping out.

The summit looms. With nose to the grindstone, Jim manages to crack the guy behind him, but the one alongside holds tough, just off Jim's shoulder. Jim surges, nothing long, fifty yards, to test the guy; he doesn't budge.

Another surge, this one longer on flat terrain with three-quarters of a mile to go, the finish line a disturbing thirty yards off to their right. Still the guy pursues.

The pace changes push them past two guys, whose forms hold steady though disengaged, merely hanging on, perhaps too fast too early, or perhaps, as Dillon observed during the warm-up, the sight and proximity of the finish line creates a mental paradox, the brain fighting with itself, between what it can see and what it knows is not the finish line, easily disengaging, especially when weary and additional hard running left on the horizon.

Jim remains stoic; he's combated the potential paradox before. The bigger matter lies behind and alongside him, footsteps and forceful breathing, a visceral reminder of his hatred of being passed. Yet perhaps the *bigger* incentive unfolds farther up, the sight of Chase sitting three spots *behind* Dillon. The club order teeters on the brink of disruption again.

Back in the trenches, Jim spots Chico and Agras jerseys ahead, summons his game face, and bears down. It doesn't feel good, of course, digging for more; it never does. His legs protest, sometimes twitch, sometimes wobble on an uneven step or two. Dust from foot strikes ahead clogs his expanded lungs. He licks his lips, attempting to generate moisture in his mouth to overcome the chalky taste building up as he reaches the sweeping U-turn that directs them toward the infamous uphill finish.

Closer to the Chico and Agras runners, but farther than he likes, Jim digs deeper into the bedrock of his Saturday throw-down, the spade piercing granite, a meager but precious haul, hitching him to their heels and gapping his pursuers.

The finish line comes into view, two fifteen-foot poles with three horizontal planks fastened up high, with CSM CRYSTAL SPRINGS, CROSS COUNTRY, FINISH etched into each plank. The Chico runner switches gears and accelerates. Jim responds, legs on the verge of staggering, unsure if he can hold on, but damned if he will throw the towel in now. This is when things get good: face muscles strain in the barrenness of the incline; eyes squint at the rising sun; his right elbow lashes out; his thinly covered feet burn against the Earth's unyielding thick crust.

With one eye locked on the Chico singlet, and one ear listening to footsteps fading behind him, Jim strides in tandem with the Chico runner, and as they approach the line both slip by the Agras runner, who has tied up badly, his body lurching toward the line.

"Single file, men. Single file!" a deep and unsympathetic voice hollers as Jim, the guy in front, and several runners behind him bunch up in the chute.

"Nice job," Dillon says from alongside the chute, giving Jim a hand to slap.

Muscles depleted, mind weary, bones weighed down by gravity, all Jim can do is grimace and trudge forward.

"You beat their third man today," Chase whispers from the end of the chute, subtly nodding toward the Agras runner one spot behind Jim.

Jim doesn't have to look. His burnt neck, scorched legs, and encrusted salt ring around his neck and chest tell him as much.

Spencer soon passes through the chute, arms raised high and both hands cradling the back of his head. He spits forcibly but it doesn't make a clean exit. Too tired to care, it coagulates on his dusty lips and chin. "Great job today."

Jim nods, then turns his attention toward the finish line. "Come on, Jakey!" he hollers, his voice hoarse, as two speedier runners go by Jake near the line.

"I wish he'd join me on the track," Chase says. "He could use the speed training."

"Good luck," Jim says. "He hasn't been on the track since high school . . . nice job." Jim gives Jake a hearty handshake.

The guys mill around the finish area for some time, talking amongst themselves and other club runners who wander by, sipping water from paper cups filled from scuffed-up Gatorade containers as well as biting into quarter slices of oranges laid out by race organizers, the Agras. Seduced into lethargy by desolation and post-race depletion, it takes some time until the guys rally for a warm-down, motivated by their solid outing: Dillon beat Chase for the first time, and both took down Agras's second man; Jim's effort gave them a slight edge, but Jake didn't fare as well, finishing several spots behind Agras's fifth man; even Spencer's consistency in whom he beats from week to week plagued them. All in all, though, their second-place finish to the Agras on *their* home course shows promise as the point spread continues to drop.

As for Saturday throw-downs, Jim gives his day a thumbs-up. And though he doesn't take great satisfaction in Dillon unseating Chase, Jim does enjoy it a little bit; a guilty pleasure.

Sunday Morning
The Winds of Change

"Wait, what?" Chase says as the guys cruise around Beardsworth's vineyards, the trellised vines stripped clean of the dark-skinned grapes used in the current season's crush.

"I think, and correct me if I'm wrong," Jim says, "I think . . . Spencer said he's *changing* training plans."

"Really?" Dillon says. "Skip CIM? I thought—"

"Yeah, it was going to be my Olympic trials qualifying attempt."

"Lord love a duck."

"I didn't think hell could freeze over during a drought," Chase says, shirtless under the sunny October sky.

"The PA series is heating up," Spencer says. "This is the closest we've ever been to the Agras this far into the season. My marathon training isn't going to help us; I need less weekly mileage, and more cross-country-oriented workouts."

"I don't know," Chase says. "That's a slippery slope. First it's your training, then next thing you know you're buying an engagement ring."

Spence-speak.

Chuckles follow.

"Seriously, though," Spencer says, "we're knocking on their door, and with the Agras' loss to Chico two weeks ago all we have to do is run the table at China Camp, Presidio, and the Championships, and the grand prix is ours."

"Would you like fries with that?" Chase says.

"We could conceivably help our chances by running an extra race," Spencer says. "The Slug invite in Santa Cruz is on a Sunday, November eighth. Historically, the Agras skip that race—"

"That's my wedding weekend," Jim says.

"That's right . . . but on Saturday though—"

"Not happening."

"And it's too far out for me to commit right now," Dillon says.

"And I'm on post-wedding cleanup duty at the homestead," Jake says. "We'll just have to make do with the schedule we have."

"But since you're into *changing* things up, Spencer," Jim says, "why don't you join Dillon and me on Tuesday for a track workout with Chase."

"On the track?" Spencer says. "What are you doing?"

"Noah's Ladder," Chase says.

"Intriguing."

"Two of everything," Chase says. "Thousand meter, eight hundred, six hundred, four hundred, three hundred, two hundred."

"Hummmm. What's the rest interval?"

"Two minutes until the three hundreds, then only sixty seconds."

"Robust. I wouldn't be able to run until after school, or *very* early in the morning."

As the guys work their way around a second time on the vineyard path, the sun behind them, long sinewy shadows dance out front, cartoonish in nature, a fluid funhouse mirror reflection.

"You going to join us in Tahoe next weekend?" Jim asks Dillon.

"So far it shouldn't be a problem," he replies. "There aren't many bookings yet. I'll know for certain on Thursday."

"It's going to be epic!" Chase says.

Spence-speak.

"Hey, Spence," Chase says. "You're the history buff. How much more technologically advanced do you think the world would be if the Dark Ages had never occurred?"

"We'd certainly have flying cars by now, I'd imagine," Dillon says.

"Maybe we wouldn't have to fly, just teleport," Chase says.

"So you're saying Facebook would've been around a thousand years earlier?" Jake says.

"Cavemen and -women were posting on 'walls' long before that," Jim says.

"Don't tell Zuckerberg or the Winklevoss twins," Dillon says.

"I'm sure Bitcoin would be the world's currency and render accountants obsolete," Jim says. "It's impossible to audit someone's Bitcoin stash."

"Would there be any unanswered questions left to ponder?" Jake says.

"I'd have one outstanding question," Dillon says. "What's Bitcoin?"

"Probably not, guys," Spencer says. "Many historians refrain from calling it *that*, but rather the Middle Ages. A poet coined the term 'Dark Ages' for what he viewed as a lack of quality Latin literature after the fall of Rome, not because it lacked progress in other areas."

"Francesco Petrarch," Jake says.

The others glance at Jake, their group shadow shifting to the left on the next turn.

"The Italian poet who coined 'Dark Ages,'" Jake says. "Also, Petrarch's rediscovery of Cicero's letters is thought to be an important reason the fourteenth-century Renaissance emerged."

The guys offer a moment of silence in deference to Jake's broad knowledge beyond horticulture.

"So no flying cars?" Dillon says.

"There were plenty of technological advancements in China and India," Spencer says. "The general consensus is that the supposed Dark Ages didn't inhibit the world's current technological state."

"Interestingly enough," Jake says, "technology upsets the world order, undermining its authority, which is why powerful entities tend to oppose its use and suppress advancement. Gutenberg's printing press was strongly opposed by the Catholic Church in the fifteenth century, whereas Protestants championed it to spread *their* word."

"Makes sense," Chase says. "Today Airbnb challenges the hospitality industry, and Uber challenges the transportation industry, both calling themselves 'technology companies or marketplaces,' which allows them to undermine both industries' traditional operating policies and stranglehold."

"Explains why they're both being sued left and right," Jim says.

"Technology allows writers to self-publish, challenging the traditional publishing world," Spencer says.

"Giveth David a new tool and Goliath shall falleth," Jake says.

"Did Jake just give a biblical thumbs-up for technology?" Chase says.

"Speaking of self-publishing," Spencer says, sidling up alongside Jim. "Maggie is considering self-publishing her book. We'd like to know how best to go about setting it up from a tax perspective."

"Sure, there are a couple things to consider. Let's get together some night and I can show her some of the available tax breaks."

"Great. We'll have you and Doris over for dinner."

Having turned back toward the BR&B, their group shadow now dances in front of them again, all five fanned out.

"How's the sex study with Terri coming along?" Jim asks Chase. "Getting much studying done?"

Despite chuckles from the others, Chase boldly returns an answer. "Well, my unenlightened and deprived friend, it's not *about* sex. It's actually about how technology inhibits social interaction and intimacy."

With the exception of Jake, who smiles, the rest of the guys show mild shock at Chase's mature attitude.

"Let me ask you this," Chase says without any semblance of mockery to his tone. "Do you think social media brings us closer together?"

A moment of silence envelops the guys as they glide through a chilly pocket of vineyard air, rounding a corner. A jackrabbit, caught by surprise, bolts some fifty yards down the path, stops, glances back, and sensing the guys' encroaching presence, bolts another fifty yards, stopping for another quick peek back. Still fearing pursuit the jackrabbit veers down one of the hundreds of rows and disappears for good.

"I sense an Oprah moment upon us?" Spencer says, the group slowing at the fence line.

"This," Jake says with a broad smile, spreading his arms wide, symbolically encompassing the group's collective shadow, "is what brings people together: community, conversation."

"I like how I can stay connected with my friends back east," Chase says, "without spending hours talking on the phone."

"Social networking allows me to easily connect with other educators around the country."

"People, people, people," Jake says, the run concluded. *Beep, beeeep, beep.* They climb the stairs into the BR&B, where breakfast percolates for four sets of overnight guests, one couple off in the nook and the other couple and two single guests seated around the kitchen island. "You're confusing *connections* with conversations. They're not the same. Sherry Turkle suggests that connections have replaced conversations, a change that represents less interest in conversing and more interest in being loosely connected. I'm not convinced it brings people *closer* together."

"Sherry Turkle?" Chase says.

"Media scholar at MIT," Jake says.

"Above your dating pay grade," Spencer says wryly, and Doris laughs.

"Pfft."

"Like the difference between a person who is book smart versus street smart," says one of the guests seated at the island, a woman staying in the Athens Room and in town for the Wine Country Half Marathon.

"Laura, the Algonquin Round Table; Algonquin Round Table, Laura," Dillon says, shifting into host mode, preparing meals from the prep work Terri has completed.

Greetings and nods follow as the group, including Linda, Doris, and Maggie, catch up with the conversation the guys have brought in from the vineyards.

"True. Book-smart people spend their time reading through a filter, that of the book's author," Maggie says. "They don't experience real life, simply the one that is presented to them."

"My point precisely," Jake says. "They aren't involved in the discussion about it. It's one-way communication."

"Much like a person's online social media presence: it's an idealized and controlled narrative of themselves," Maggie says. "It's practically a must these days."

"What about résumés?" Jim says. "They're a controlled narrative about oneself."

Jake contemplates the nuance. "Applying for a job is different than applying for *life*."

"And street smarties *read* people," Doris says, "by interacting, and having *actual* conversations."

"What do you think, Chase?" Jake says with a rhetorical grin.

Chase, who initially launched the conversation, is now lost in his run data. He pauses and addresses the group. "Yeah, conversations certainly suffer when"—he returns his attention to his watch as it syncs with an app on his cell phone that's now on the counter next to him—"they're online."

This brings amused chuckles.

"That's true," Spencer says. "When someone posts a discussion topic on Facebook others simply chime in their two cents' worth, but the discussion doesn't evolve like it would if the posters were sitting around a table, drinking coffee. It often devolves."

"Just random streams of consciousness, each person talking over the other," Jake says. "There is no listening or empathy taking place."

"Get this," Dillon says. "They call that downward social media spiral 'Godwin's law': the longer an online discussion goes on over a single topic, the probability of a comparison involving Nazis or Hitler grows significantly."

The group laughs and nods, some having experienced it.

"I call it the loony bin," Spencer says.

"Hitler?" Chase says, reengaging with the conversation, which spawns a bout of teasing.

Terri, on her way back with dirty dishes from the couple in the nook, nudges Chase and tilts her head in the nook's direction. Chase turns and views the scene, where both are talking *while* engaged with individual cell phones.

"Looks like they're talking," Chase says.

"Are they?" Terri responds.

Chase shrugs. "I can't hear them from here."

"They're sharing what they find on their cell phone, *not* discussing or expanding upon it."

"They're merely commenting and then moving on to something new and shiny that captures their attention," Jake says.

"I see that in the shortened attention span of many of my students," Spencer says.

"They're *pretending* to be engaged with each other when in fact they're engaged in a self-amusing, solo activity," Terri says, giving Spencer a wink. He shifts uncomfortably on his stool. "They're sharing what's on their phones, not their minds."

"What about Dillon here?" Chase says.

"More waffles?"

"Sure," Chase says. "He chimes in from time to time, but he's distracted while serving breakfast. Awesome waffles, by the way."

Dillon takes a bow.

"Certainly," Terri says. "But it's an *activity*, not a task that prevents him from having a conversation about the topic at hand. His brain isn't processing or distracted by *other* information that is off topic."

"Does anyone else find it ironic that we're having a conversation about *conversations?*" Jim says.

"*We* are," Jake says. "Chase is communing with his Garmin."

As Terri passes by Chase, she confiscates his cell phone from the counter and replaces it with a glass of apple juice.

"At least I know more about my run than the rest of you."

"Thirteen miles in less than ninety minutes," Dillon says.

"Less than fifty feet of elevation gain," Spencer says.

"*Conversational* pace," Jim says.

"Vineyard rabbits are skittish creatures," Jake says.

"What was the average temp?" Chase says.

"Chilly." "Cold." "Nippy." "Brisk."

"Troglodytes," Chase says, shaking his head.

PA/USATF TOP 5 TEAM STANDINGS AS OF 10/18/2015		
	Club	Total
1	Agras (10-9-10-10)	39
2	Chico Running Club (8-10-8-8)	34
3	RERC (9-x-9-9)	27
4	Strawberry Hill Harriers (7-7-7-5)	26
5	South Bay Striders (6-8-4-x)	19

Week 42 Training Summary			
	Long Run	Mileage Total	Comments
Dillon	14	62	Finally beat Chase!
Chase	13.11	48	Need to amp up my training to keep pace with Dillon.
Spencer	13.50	73	Switching to XC training.
Jim	13	54	Strong XC race.
Jake	13	Around 70	This group is really gelling.

Week 8
October 19

Monday Night
Forget Me Knot

"Shoot," Spencer says, sitting upright in bed upon reading an email from Jim.

"What?" Maggie says seated alongside him, pausing a moment from typing on her laptop.

"I forgot to RSVP to Jim and Doris's wedding." He climbs out of bed and goes to the living room to retrieve it.

"Uh-huh," Maggie mutters, resuming work on her manuscript. "Mr. Organization. And you want to be the department chair . . ."

"Do you want lasagna or cheese ravioli?" Spencer says, returning with invitation in hand.

Maggie pauses again, hazel eyes fixed on him.

"What? Lasagna?"

"I won't be here."

"Why not?"

"I'm heading to L.A. for the writers' conference that weekend," she says, typing again.

Spencer stands motionless, pondering her words before crawling back into bed. "That's right." He stares at the invitation, undecided on which food choice to make.

"They're more your friends than mine."

"I know. I forgot about the conflict." He pulls a pen from the nightstand, circles the cheese ravioli, and pensively pens in "1" guest attending. It somehow feels like a guess to a test question he isn't sure about, the kind one should skip and come back to. He seals the RSVP envelope and moves on to grading student essays, this one from Conrad entitled "Today in *1984*." *Clever . . . for a jock. Perhaps too clever.* Spencer reads through the first paragraph and instinctively knows Conrad hasn't written it. First of all, it isn't in his voice. Secondly, the insight exceeds Conrad's interests. He generally uses football in some capacity to narrate his points. Big Brother and the New England Patriots' Spygate incident would have been his likely go-to, not Edward Snowden's revelation of illegal domestic surveillance operations in the United States.

Spencer launches the TurnItIn website, one of many plagiarism-detection sites for educators. Despite his gut feeling, he needs data to confirm the deceit. He copy/pastes Conrad's first paragraph into a text box and clicks the Search button. It takes all of three Orwellian seconds to find a match among the 24 billion web pages, 300 million student papers and 110,000 publications the site has canvassed. Conrad hasn't even bothered to alter the title.

Spence-speak.

"What?"

"Sorry."

Maggie leans over and views Spencer's laptop. "Busted."

"Uh-huh."

"Conrad?"

Spencer nods.

"What are you going to do?"

"Report him to the department chair. I don't have a choice."

"Talk about irony," Maggie says, returning to her own literary conundrum. "Big Brother takes down an essay about Big Brother. I sense a ripple in the space-time continuum."

Spencer cracks a wry smile, typing "See me after class" in large, bold red letters across the top of the essay. He initiates an email to the department chair, summarizes the situation, and all but seals Conrad's fate when a thought strikes him: Why not challenge Conrad with the very concept he's plagiarizing? Point out that his narrative is not *original*, that many others have previously covered the Orwellian nightmares of macrosurveillance, and instead make him choose a more personal, microcosm example where *anybody* with an Internet connection can dredge up information on another, even a humble US history teacher checking up on the goings-on of his students. Spencer's wry smile turns sardonic.

"Still considering department chair for next year?" Maggie asks, powering down her laptop.

"I've given it some consideration." Spencer puts his teachable moment into motion, granting Conrad's football dreams a second chance. "Thoughts?"

Writing hat retired for the night, she curls up and says, "It's *another* leadership role for you." She adjusts her pillows. "And you could put your Chalk Is Cheap program in place." With this she pokes his shoulder. "Assuming anybody has chalkboards. Dry Erase is the new chalk."

Spence-speak. "Writing out information on a board of any kind engages students more than presenting a PowerPoint and pointing at it with a laser. Besides, chalk is less toxic. LPs are making a comeback, so why not—"

Maggie leans over, kisses him good night, snuggles up under the covers, and closes her eyes.

Is it too much, another leadership role to take on? He doesn't think of it that way. Simply another opportunity. Perhaps not all opportunities are equally weighted? Not *simply* a time slot to make room for?

Spencer shrugs, finishes off two last essays, and opens up his fall training schedule. Though it pains him to scrap the marathon at the end of the year, he acknowledges the once-in-a-lifetime opportunity *and* unprecedented feat for the RERC to beat the Agras in the Open Division. With the way the guys are rolling, improving each week, it's too good of an opportunity to pass up. Jake will still be a wildcard with his less race-oriented training, but he tends to *race* his way into shape throughout the season. And Spencer knows he himself may not round into much better shape by switching so late, but simply reducing his high weekly mileage will pay small dividends, and that alone is worth the change.

Week by week, he adjusts the schedule, pulling out the extra ten easy miles he runs on those post-race Sundays, adding to his morning vineyard mileage at the BR&B with the guys, surplus they probably don't know about. Next on the chopping block, the sixteen to eighteen miles he runs on Thursdays up in the park, reducing it to a refreshing eight or nine. The quality workouts are altered dramatically as well: tempo runs are replaced by hill repeats or 500- to 1,000-meter intervals on the RERC cross-country course with less and less recovery time each week; his long progressive road runs, where the pace drops from marathon pace to 10K pace, are replaced by fartlek runs on trails. If it isn't run faster than 5K pace, it's scratched for workouts that push him into the red, and his marathon training to date provides ample base and strength to handle the faster efforts.

As the weeks morph into training cycles he might create for his high school squad—though with more volume and interval quantity—Spencer warms to the idea of jumping into the mix with Dillon, Chase, and Jim for their Noah's Ladder workout the following day. The workout that day for the high school team is easy mileage, which the assistant coach can oversee. Getting back on the track will hurt, no doubt about it. But Spencer opts for the long view over the immediate discomfort factor.

Surrender to the Pain, Like a Moth to the Fame.

Tuesday, Late Afternoon
Competition Breeds Competition

Beep! Chase passes by his crumpled shirt on the back side of his favorite training oval one second ahead of Dillon, who led the entire thousand meters until the final straightway. Jim follows ten seconds later, Spencer four seconds after that.

"One down," Chase says, drifting out toward lanes five and six.

"Damn milers," Dillon says, forming a partial smile.

"This workout would be better suited on our cross-country course," Spencer says.

"The track gives us consistent rhythm," Chase says.

"You have oak trees, leaves to crunch through, errant footballs to leap over, and wildlife in uniforms," Jim says, gesturing to each. "How much more cross-country do you want?"

The follow-up Spence-speak comes with a grin, which lightens their strained expressions.

Chase frequently glances at his watch, and when the midpoint of their two-minute recovery nears, he makes an about-face to head back to the start/finish line, the others following his lead like ducklings.

"Who came up with Noah's Ladder?" Spencer asks.

"I came up with the workout," Chase says. "Jake named it."

They swing a wide U-turn at the start line, now facing counterclockwise and inching forward, all four staring at their watches as the recovery interval winds down, and with a rolling start they embark on the second 1,000-meter interval, Dillon sprinting to the front in lane one, Chase directly behind him. Based on the long dual shadows Chase can see to his right, Jim and Spencer are side by side and latched to Chase's heels until a gap forms 150 yards in.

Chase peeks at his watch at the 200 mark, concerned that it's a second under his goal time, but Dillon has altered his start strategy on this interval attempting to take the sting out of the "damn miler's" legs, and Chase feels the call to action.

At 400 and 600 meters, Chase lets Dillon extend the gap precious meters at each point, struggling to stay within the extreme bounds of his goal pace. But damned if sitting back and watching Dillon best him doesn't eat away at Chase's competitive disposition. It's time to go. And as Chase accelerates on the back stretch with less than 300 to go, a shadow creeps up and passes him. Based on the form, Chase surmises it's Jim, which it is, breathing hard, his physical form approaching Chase's shoulder.

Chase lifts his self-imposed mental governor regulating his effort and holds Jim off, though his shadow lingers close by. Rounding the final turn, Chase launches into an all-out kick much to his chagrin so early in the workout, but Dillon has laid down the gauntlet. Between Dillon's fast start handicapping his finish and Chase's kick, the gap closes quickly, but not completely. Chase leans, jabs the Split button on his watch—*Beep!*—and glances at the damage: 2:56. "Damn non-milers," Chase grunts, and chuckles.

Jim comes through a couple seconds later and Spencer several seconds after that.

"See, Spencer," Jim says when Spencer comes up alongside him, "I'm not the one that pushes the pace; Chase is, and now Dillon."

"Hey," Dillon protests, "I'm trying to find Chase's weakness."

"You'd better watch out there, spider legs," Chase says, turning back to the start line. "We're dropping down to shorter and shorter intervals . . . can't stretch me out forever."

They trot to the start line and at two-minutes on the nose they surge forward. Dillon moves to the front, though at a slower pace than the previous interval, which irritates Chase on this interval because it's *shorter* by 200 meters. But before Chase can respond and go around Dillon, Jim goes by them both and takes up the charge. *What the hell! Are they teaming up on me?* Dillon's double-take, however, nullifies the conspiracy theory.

So there it is, the desecration of Chase's sacred oval. It's been a long while since he's run intervals with someone other than his Garmin, and online Strava friends. Another disgruntled glance at his wrist confirms that Jim has led them through the first of two laps faster than desired. From that point on Chase ignores the splits that leave him conflicted about staying put or chasing down the rabbits. And the rabbits win out as Chase abandons the governor once and for all and takes up pursuit.

Into the backstretch where football players lampoon the guys' efforts off to the side by running circles around a football, Chase moves up on Dillon, intending to go by him, but Dillon's prompt acceleration says no, relegating Chase to the back of the rabbit's shoulder for the moment. Rounding the final curve, racing down the straightaway, they both overtake Jim, Chase creeping up alongside Dillon at the finish line, Chase's watch beeping first.

"No turning back . . . now," Dillon says when they decelerate sufficiently enough.

Chase glances over, eyes Dillon suspiciously, and grimaces. "You know . . . this is going to hurt."

"Oh yeah."

"Pain is your friend, your ally, it will tell you when you are seriously injured," Jim says in the victors' shadows. "But the best thing about pain is that it lets you know you're not dead yet."

Running up on Jim's heels, Spencer utters, "*GI Jane*," followed by what sounds like a Spence-speak.

"You wanted faster training," Chase says. "This is what it looks like . . . no more marathon pacing. You're all in now—"

"It was a cough . . . you don't need to convince me . . ."

Another 800 meters, a pair of 600s, followed by two 400s, every meter contested, each runner sizing up the other; times, though recorded, less and less a talking point. Breathing becomes the new conversation, punctuated with hocked loogies, an occasional grunt or two or three, the scuff of a tired foot dragged across the track during the recovery interval, a chorus of beeps and "check these track geeks out" from the infield bookending each respite.

A certain gloom flitters in Chase's mind after fending off a hard-charging Dillon on the first of two 300s: a slim sixty seconds of recovery awaits them; half of what they've luxuriated in up until now. What a body and mind warp. He takes an extended gaze at Dillon, gauging his state. The "new guy" had taken Chase down at the last cross-country meet. The roller-coaster hills and uphill finish at Crystal Springs did Chase in. But now, on the track, flat and fast, Chase can see the animal lurking under the skin, rounding into shape.

"Ugh," Jim says as all their watches beep in unison.

Yet it's Jim who gets the drop on the guys and leads them through the first turn, where Chase and Dillon work their way by him and barrel along until the line has passed underneath, both deflating like popped balloons, beyond uniforms taking knees, footballs in hand and fascinated expressions.

A moment later, Chase strays from his initial path and bumps into Spencer, who bested Jim at the line.

Chase's startled look prompts Spencer to say, "Hurts less when they're over quicker."

Chase isn't sure about that logic but takes Spencer at his word, circling back to gear up for a pair of 200s.

Beeeep!

This time Chase grabs the inside lane and rides it hard around the turn, a shadow lurking alongside that edges up on him. Out of the turn, Chase lifts his knees, but no extra speed emerges, and it's all he can do to maintain his starting pace, the shadow extending beyond him and crossing the finish line first, but not its owner. *Be-beep!*

Awash in newfound gridiron respect, they stagger like Rocky Balboa before his final punishing round. Chase conjures up images of elite training meccas around the country—Mammoth Lakes, Flagstaff, Eugene, Portland, Boulder, Minneapolis/St. Paul—runners going out and pushing one another throughout their workouts, forging that unbreakable bond: shared grit and determination.

Beeeep!

One more, the last one.

Chase has the inside lane again, but Dillon is mere inches alongside, both sharing the lane like a pair of high-performance motorcycles on the freeway. The shadow outside them belongs to Jim, who straddles the white line between lanes one and two, while Spencer's shadow lurks between Chase's and Dillon's.

Despite rousing shouts from shoulder pads and cleats, Chase knows he doesn't have another gear to finish this one off. Dillon isn't making any sudden moves either. But Jim, well, he follows his shadow out of the turn and down the interminable straightaway, moving a half stride on the front two over the final meters, his breathing as loud and resonant as that of a locomotive.

Be-beep . . . beep!

The four deflate to a jog, each giving the others plenty of space, as if a bystander witnessing an accident has shouted, "Stand back . . . give them room to breathe."

They shadow one another in a state of silence, save for hard breathing that is slowly coming to order, painfully so, their pace about as limp as possible without it being considered a walk until the magic sixty-second recovery interval has elapsed. And with four distinctive beeps they stop, pivot around, tip their figurative caps toward the SRJC Bear Cubs and mosey back to where their extra clothing and shoe options await. Handshakes are extended and received all around, exhausted smiles shared in lieu of conversation. That will come later, during the warm-down. For now the effort burns in them like a ring of fire, stoking competitive camaraderie, the sun dipping in a brilliant October sky, where contrails streak across the vast blueness.

Tuesday Evening
Run to the Top

Jake's leg muscles flex and slacken, a symphonic duet in harmony, crescendoing up the old rutted ranch road toward the summit at Shilo Park, briefly defying gravity with each movement. His impassioned breathing signals to hikers ahead to move aside, giving them a subtle nod, gesturing his silent appreciation, their conversations diminishing with his next breath.

The long day out on Chalk Hill Road planting two dozen Santa Rosa plum trees places him close by Shilo for a short yet intense run before heading home, on the type of hills he loves, the kind that others whimper on or complain about, privately or out loud. Jake never understands why. Hills are an absolute engaging physical and mental experience: the labored breathing reminds him he's alive; it tests one's mettle against gravity's daunting force: press forward or relent; leaves you breathless at the summit with a reward beyond compare. He doesn't comprehend why so many runners hate hills, even curse them. Such a negative attitude perpetuates their difficulty, setting runners up for failure long before the first rise.

Others often disassociate from the experience, conjuring "happy" thoughts to endure the climb, or tune out to music on the go. Not Jake. He embraces it, craves it in fact, deliberately savors it, absorbing it viscerally, forever inscribed in him. His love started with the "butterfly effect," though not Edward Lorenz's version regarding chaos theory—change one thing, change everything—but rather the spring day he found himself running up this very same hill. On that day as a teenager, enjoying the sun as it bore down on him, shirtless, a butterfly flitted out from the side of the trail and joined him. He glanced at it once or twice when it drew parallel with him, floating near his hip; he expected it to swerve away at any moment. But the butterfly stayed true, and as Jake pressed or lightened the pace so too did the butterfly. For the next minute, he glided along with nature, discovering the secret to running hills: float up them. Driving and pressing hard only robbed the body. Jake learned to relax and glide up the hills, which in turn ultimately quickened his pace without sapping his energy. Only when Jake reached the summit did the butterfly break formation.

Rounding the last bend to the summit, the steepest pitch of the climb, a turkey vulture drifts overhead on the currents, exerting little energy to hover, glide, and dive. At one point the brown plume stalls and floats motionless a mere thirty feet above Jake like a kite at the end of a string before dipping a wing and soaring onward. As if the incline isn't challenging enough, the sun meets Jake head-on. He squints, lowers his head, and follows the narrow band of brilliant sunlight reflecting off embedded rocks and pebbles that guide him the rest of the way until he can feel the incline lessen, his body naturally accelerating, cresting the hill.

Clear of the hill's dominance, Jake hooks left, slows to a trot, and walks over to the hitching post whose dedication placard honors Clyde Dearborn, Jake's grandfather, who had hiked every day to the summit well into his eighties. Jake developed his love of the outdoors as a youngster on their shared hikes in Shilo. It was on those hikes that his restless energy found walking too sedate, and he would scamper on up the trail, get several hundred yards out front, turn back, and reconnect with his grandfather, repeating the process over and over again.

Jake leans against Clyde's tribute, catching his breath, raking in the same panoramic view his grandfather had basked in: a grape cluster–shaped county dangling off the nurturing vine of the pacific ocean, enriched with organic diversity—rivers, creeks, valleys, hot springs—an intimate, unrushed confluence of viticulture, pastoral grasslands, bucolic and spacious, rural city life that beckons neighboring counties to the south on the weekends, offering refuge from the claustrophobic confines and harried demands of the business week. The view permeates his being through the hard effort of running to the top, visceral permanence a photograph can never capture; embedded in his soul, in expanded lungs, in muscle memory, never forgotten, encompassing all senses beyond simple sight.

Fall has imposed its will on the county's colors. Out-of-staters often quip how seasons don't change in California, that there's summer and then one day the rains and cooler temps mark winter until the temperatures warm and summer returns. The plethora of vineyards laid out on the valley floor with their changing foliage, from summer green to post-harvest yellows, purples, dark blues, and oranges indicate otherwise.

Jake draws in the air deliberately, chronicling the moment, and exhales, striding off and veering away from where the trail brought him up. The terrain falls away, his stride lengthens, his face slackens, eyes wide, smile broad. Tax-free running, Clyde called it, downhill running. Let gravity do its thing, pull you down, and enjoy the ride. If running uphill makes Jake feel like an animal, every fiber of his body fully engaged, then running downhill makes him feel free of any worldly force, flying without wings, a free fall that requires only a line of faith to follow.

Back at his truck he retrieves his journal. Thoughts form with ease, sensations converted to words spill across the page:

Unlike city sidewalks that lack variation from one concrete slab to the next, the park unfolds like an obstacle course of dry riverbed crossings, elongated etchings across trails left behind by snakes seeking warmth, narrow wooden bridges, steep climbs and precipitous descents. Meanwhile fawn nibble on wild grass, clover, and twigs unaware of mankind's fabricated existence. It doesn't take long for his body to wake up out here.

Jake rereads the passage several times, each time further validating the internal beauty he's experienced and internalized since his last creative storm. Satisfied, he creates an entry in his training log that reads: *Shilo, Run to the Top.* That says it all. No additional description necessary. No need to write in the thirty minutes it generally takes him.

Wednesday Afternoon
Muscles He Doesn't Know He Has

Any reservation Jim has about someone other than Doris giving him a suitable massage evaporates in a flash when Nicola's knuckles dig deep into the knotted muscle tension submerged between his shoulders: it's both painful and cathartic. It had been Doris's suggestion, setting up an appointment with Nicola through Dillon, a pre–bachelor party weekend gift, her version of a lap dance, she joked. Now it seems like a cruel joke, a punishment even.

"You okay?" Nicola asks.

Jim grunts what he hopes sounds like "yes," but whatever comes out will have to do. With the weight of her body pressed down on a fulcrum the size of her bony knuckles, Jim has little control over what he can utter.

"You're very, very tight up here," she says as if she's spilling the latest gossip. "You carry your stress in your shoulders." She shifts her knuckles farther between his shoulder blades. "It's important to break it up."

Jim grunts again, though he really wants to scream, "Owwwwwwwwwww." Instead it's swallowed up in the vortex of yet another "trigger point," as she calls them. This is going to be a long sixty minutes. Hill repeats with Jake at the beach after a long day of landscaping sounds more appealing.

Sports massage, that luxury enjoyed by elites, generally gratis, or those lazy/busy runner's unwilling to stretch their own muscles, so Jim has theorized at some point. After hard runs, Jim rubs out his own calves and quads, the workhorses to his running game. For those less accessible muscles, Doris lends a hand, though more times than not it leads to a "happy ending." Scar tissue, fibrous connective tissue, adhesions—terms Nicola tosses out as if everyone should know what they mean—soar over Jim's head as she explains them. He recalls Jake and Dillon once extolling the benefits of massage some time back, or in Jake's case Rolfing, which screams torture with its "structural integration" theory and fascia-manipulation techniques, designed to better align the body in gravity. Or as Jake once put it, "Rolfing is penance for poor posture." Jim paid them little attention, uncomfortable with the thought of letting a stranger touch him, let alone *manipulate* him, especially wearing nothing but running shorts and loosely covered by a towel.

"We'll move to your hamstrings once I make some headway up here," she says, working her way around his upper back. "Often times a tight upper back can affect lower extremities like your hammies."

Jim skips the grunt this time and bobs his head as it rests facedown in the cradle that extends beyond the table. During Nicola's first plunge into his "stress zone," Jim had closed his eyes, grinning and bearing it, and when that didn't work he searched for his happy place. But then he realized he didn't have one; he prefers associating to pain, especially throughout hard running, not disassociating from it as some runners choose to do. Opening his eyes, fixing them on the pattern of the carpet—tan squares with dark-brown overlapping circles that he imagines as Olympic rings—Jim finds a suitable distraction exterior to him. Occasionally as Nicola switches positions her bare feet enter his limited view, toenails painted purple. Doris occasionally paints hers yellow; he once called her banana foot.

"Been running long?" Nicola asks.

Jim wants to laugh but instead lets out a gust of air. Questions asked under duress remind him of sitting in the chair at the dentist's office, mouth wide open, sharp, barbaric instruments probing around inside, the dentist asking Jim if this or that is deductible. *You're kidding, right?* Jim bobs his head again, the eucalyptus-scented sheets infusing him with a mentally cooling and refreshing sensation.

"I'm not trying to push my services on you, but with as many miles that you and Dillon run, periodic massage can be beneficial. Helps increase blood flow for muscle repair."

Jim can't imagine a world where he'll subject himself routinely to the torture that bears down on him at the moment, though as the session wears on and Nicola works her way down his spine to what he initially requested to have worked on, a certain pulverized bliss emerges: He feels too beat-up to care about anything else. The frustration over one client's loose taxation morals . . . gone. Next up, the concern over quitting his old job and venturing out on his own . . . dispatched. The nagging thought about a frugal existence for him and Doris in the near future as they embark down matrimony lane . . .

vanquished. It will all work out somehow—

A new pain-threshold bubble bursts, summoning Jim's attention. He winces as Nicola buries her elbow in the meat of his left hamstring. When the sensations plateaus he says, "I guess my hamstrings are tighter than I thought."

"Well, the dirty little secret is that all runners have tight hammies. Yours aren't as much tight as they are shortened, and they're bundled up and not striated. That comes from sitting at a desk all day, and from many miles of training." She kneads them in a manner that seems to separate and lengthen them. "Running basically creates micro tears, and as they heal they adhere to one another but not in the same way they originally were. Over time they operate less efficiently. Most runners don't notice it, but if you train enough it adds up, and as you get older your muscles become less elastic."

While she works her way down into his mildly knotty calves, Jim contemplates the notion of micro tears, the cumulative effect they may have, not unlike paying taxes over several years and the eventuality of a visit from the IRS.

Twenty minutes later after Agent Nicola has wrapped up the audit of Jim's life, he lies motionless, searching for a tax break.

"Sorry if I was too harsh on you today."

"No worries." Jim remains still after Nicola steps out of the room, letting his mind wander, tuning into the ambiance, water streaming over glass rocks in the ceramic bowl atop the marble stand off in the corner. The gurgling reminds Jim of Annadel after a hard rain, the park's creeks coming to life: peaceful, soothing. And *that's* a tax loophole he's never considered.

Friday Early Afternoon
Tahoe-Bound

"Tahoe, baby!" Chase says as soon as the group crests Brockaway Summit, Truckee behind them and Lake Tahoe beckoning to the south.

Seated in the midsection of Linda's minivan, Dillon leans forward, ready to take in the immense blueness of the massive lake, but the experience is short-lived, temporarily blanketed by the thick sierra forest flanking the road, sequestering the lake at 7,000 feet elevation.

"The view is better up ahead," Jake says.

Dillon catches Jake's eyes in the rearview mirror, nods, and leans back, excited to make the trip with the guys for Jim's bachelor party weekend. With lean bookings Dillon feels comfortable in leaving Terri and Miles in charge. Maggie and Doris have offered backup should Terri need it.

"Well, hello, Bachelor Boy," Chase says as Jim stirs to life from the last row, leaned up against a pillow drizzled with drool. "Ready for some fun?"

Jim stretches out and yawns. "Define 'fun.'"

Chase laughs. "No, no, it won't be like that. I promise."

"No tigers, babies, crazy little men, Elvis weddings, or Tyson sightings . . . Doris's orders."

Everybody laughs. "*The Hangover!*"

"Yeah, right. We're runners," Chase says. "Need I say more?"

"While you were sleeping we actually *defined* fun," Spencer says. "We're going to settle into Jake's cabin, hit the grocery store, and hike up to Mount Baldy—"

"You'll get a great view of the lake, Dillon," Jake says.

"It is pretty sweet," Spencer says. "We'll eat lunch, then hike back down. If anybody has the need for a short run there's time before dinner."

"I'm in the mood for Indian cuisine," Chase says.

"Tomorrow's tee time is at 9:10 a.m. If you want to run do it early, but remember, we're going around three hours on Sunday. After that we'll hit the lake and kayak a couple hours, regroup at the cabin, relax, and head to the south shore for dinner. On Sunday after the run we'll have breakfast at the Log Cabin, and come back to Jake's place, clean up, and head down the mountain."

"Sounds organized."

"Tee times for Frisbee golf?" Dillon says.

"That's Spencer's doing," Chase says.

"Let's push it to 9:15 so I can stretch my rectus abdominis," Jim says. Spence-speak.

"Hopefully we won't get booted from the course this time," Chase says.

"Booted from playing disk golf?" Dillon says, amused by the notion.

"It was regular golf," Jim says, "for Jake's bachelor party weekend. It didn't go well."

All laugh but Dillon.

"Jake doesn't golf, so he's sharing my golf clubs," Chase says, answering Dillon's silent question. "First hole, he gets ready to tee off, rears back, and swings. *Whoosh!* Nothing but air. But on the return swing he makes contact with the ball and it caroms into these old geezers' cart who were waiting off to the side. *Smack!* Hit the Plexiglas. They were not pleased. We're all laughing except Jake, who is profusely apologizing to them. We're not sure when, but the old geezers ratted us out for each player not having their *own* set of clubs. Anyway, someone from the front desk came out and booted us before we started the back nine."

"I think you telling the one geezer's wife to 'waggle' her hips did us in," Spencer says.

"*Tin Cup*," Jim and Jake say together.

"I swear she looked like his daughter," Chase says.

"Sure, that makes it better," Jake says.

They find their way to Jake's family three-bedroom, lakeside cabin in Kings Beach. Alongside it a short pier juts out from the shore. While the others lug their belongings inside, Dillon walks out to the end of the pier, drops his baggage, and gazes out at the 180-degree, panoramic view. "Epic" is the word that comes to mind, just as the couple that stayed at the BR&B had said. The majestic rim gives the flat, blue expanse dimension, rising anywhere from 1,000 feet to over 2,000 feet above the surface. But it's the way the lake's surface reflects a mirror image of the adjacent mountains and the color of the sky that strikes Dillon the most, a portrait within a portrait within a portrait, all but luring him into it.

"Takes your breath away," Jake says, coming up alongside Dillon.

Dillon nods, gaze uninterrupted.

"You good? You seemed quiet on the drive up."

"Other than running, this is the first time in a long while that I've felt . . . unencumbered."

"Tahoe is literally above the din of life."

"Hey, guys," Spencer's voice hollers from behind them. "Let's get going."

Both men extend their admiration a few more minutes before responding to Spencer's call.

Once they've gathered supplies from the grocery store—a humorous event that entailed five hungry runners deciding what they want, amusing the clerk at the checkout stand—unloaded them at the cabin, and filled up day packs, the guys climb back into the minivan and head to the Brockaway Trailhead. Parked, geared up, and ready, they embark up the trail that steadily gains in elevation.

The first mile of switchback trail meanders through thick forest whose resinous sierra pines offer a different olfactory experience from the dry oaks and musty redwoods back home. The next mile presents the guys with an inspiring glimpse of Lake Tahoe as it stretches south toward a thin snowcapped mountainous layer beneath a blue sky dome as majestic as the lake itself. The section of the TRT they are on—formally known as the Tahoe Rim Trail—marks the absolute northernmost point of the route. Dillon pauses, hypnotized by the immense view, still and quiet. He finds its vastness difficult to fathom.

Dillon rejoins the others and inquires about the lake, so Jake and Jim regale him with noteworthy factoids: At a depth a little more than 1,600 feet, it's the second deepest in the United States, behind Crater Lake; the TRT they're hiking circumnavigates the lake, a 165-mile excursion once run by famed Spanish endurance athlete Kílian Jornet in less than forty hours, the only sub-forty time to date. There's the legend of Tahoe Tessie, the region's version of the Loch Ness Monster, though dubious by design. And lastly the numerous stories of gamblers dumped in the lake, presumably for welching on debts, their bodies never to be seen again due to the vast depths and steep drop-offs along the northern shores.

After an hour of uphill hiking over soft forested trails, rugged jeep routes, loose shale, and then crossing state lines into Nevada, the guys reach the summit, Mount Baldy, 9,200 feet above sea level. They find flat-ish boulders, unload their grocery bounty, and dig in, though Spencer and Chase first capture the moment with their SLR cameras, discussing the overhead sun and its effect on the exposure this time of the afternoon. Chase also includes a couple shirtless selfies with his phone's camera that he wants to upload to Facebook but can't without a signal.

Dillon munches on trail mix, half taking in the view and half listening to Jake, who's enjoying a large piece of beef jerky, and Jim, who's eating a muffin that Doris sent along, recount the movies that have been filmed in the region, each man one-upping the other in turn: *Into the Wild* and *Wild*; *The American President*; *Smokin' Aces*; *The Bodyguard* and *City of Angels*; *The Deep End*; *The Donner Party*; *Godfather II*, with its infamous "horse head" scene; and not a movie but the TV series that debuted color television to the masses, *Bonanza*, showcasing more of the lake than all the others combined with a fully functioning Wild West theme park for filming and tourists.

Dillon tires of their cinema knowledge and focuses his attention on the lake itself, recalling the Ponderosa ranch his parents had taken him and his sister to back in the '90s. It was where they filmed some of the scenes for *Bonanza*, and where they offered wagon trail rides, western-style breakfasts, stunt shows, and more.

"Is the Ponderosa ranch up here?" Dillon asks.

Jake nods and Jim points in the general direction, toward the northeast corner of the Tahoe basin, though Jake comments that the ranch no longer exists. It turns out that Dillon had been to Tahoe long ago. He hadn't recalled the lake's name, but what he does recall is how the trip had been the last time his family *was* a family. After that they merely pretended to be one, though eventually the pretense was dropped and life became fractured.

Once the photogs rejoin the group, the conversation and internal thoughts centralize.

"Jim," Chase says, holding up a water bottle filled with a translucent mixture, "to one last weekend getaway as a single man."

"Cheers," everybody chimes in, raising various beverages.

"You're next, Spence," Chase says. "We can finally climb Mount Whitney for your bachelor weekend."

Spence lets out a delayed Spence-speak as a bulbous woman huffs and puffs her way along the trail near them, wearing tight running apparel that accentuates her curves. She has music streaming through ear buds, a large fitness-tracking device wrapped around her thick upper arm, a watch around a wrist, and an oversized water pack on her back. Auditory, respiratory, and visual cues divert her attention away from the guys.

Chase has barely opened his mouth after she moves farther up the trail before Spencer shakes his head. "Don't say it."

Chase feigns innocence and lowers his voice. "I was only going to say she's packing a *lot* for a run."

Spencer doesn't look convinced, and the others are caught between grins and grimaces.

"I'm just saying if she hauls ass it's going to take two trips."

It's hard for the rest of the group not to at least chuckle, though individually they chastise Chase's subtext.

"We're at nine thousand feet elevation, and she *ran* by us," Spencer says.

"She looked fit and healthy to me," Jake says.

"Certainly outlast your skinny ass in a race across the Serengeti," Jim says.

"What is wrong with you?" Dillon says.

"The list is long and distinguished," Jim says.

"*Top Gun*," Spencer and Jake say together.

"Solving the mystery as to why Chase is single," Dillon says.

"Certainly not for a lack of opportunities," Jake says.

"Or skills," Jim says. "What's this oral anthem I've heard about?"

Jake bursts out laughing while Dillon and Spencer stare at Jim and Chase, whose stunned expression spawns laughter from the rest.

"Jake?" Chase says.

Jake holds up his hands. "That sounds like *womenfolk* gossip."

"Why do you ask?" Chase says.

"So," Jim says sheepishly, glancing at the others, returning his focus to Chase, "Doris heard about it and was wondering . . . what all the fuss was about."

"Maggie also mentioned it once," Spencer says.

Chase searches through his day pack for an energy bar, partially covering up the shade of embarrassment flushing his cheeks.

"If it's what I think it is . . ." Jim says. "When it's comes to anything south of the border, I feel like I'm trying to do someone's taxes who hasn't saved their receipts."

Any embarrassment Chase has, or uneasiness within the group, soon fades into communal nods. So Chase proceeds to explain his musical and lyrical training anthem, which came about one night back in college when he, too, was floundering as to what to do south of the border, even chastised by his girlfriend at the time in the moment. Just then Lynyrd Skynyrd's "Free Bird" started blaring in another dorm room down the hall, and he followed along with the melody, finding the results quite dramatic. Over time he perfected the routine and achieved a glowing Yelp-like status.

The guys are all laughing by the time he finishes explaining it.

"You're going to thank me," Chase says, bringing the discussion to a conclusion, and motivating the guys to pack up and head back down the trail.

Saturday Morning
9:18 Tee Time
Tahoe Vista Course

Chase lets out a long elated whistle as he and the guys watch the flight of Dillon's Frisbee soar 250 feet and gently slice left—or as Dillon officially terms the movement in disc-golf parlance, hyzers—and lands near the first hole, or again in disc-golf parlance: the basket. "Boys, we have ourselves a disc-golf ringer."

"I feel hyzered," Jim says.

"This is a par three?" Spencer says. "He almost holed it with one toss!"

"I'm glad we choose the shorter of the three pins to play from," Chase says.

"Son of a beach boy," Jake says.

"I did play down in Newport," Dillon says.

"You think?" Spencer says. "You're up, Jake."

Jake lets loose a long throw that wobbles but soon levels out and skips along the rough grass toward the basket. Once Jake's Frisbee lands, they gather up their day packs filled with an assortment of rental discs and walk toward their respective tosses.

"Do you have your own disc set?" Chase says.

"I sold them before moving up here," Dillon says.

"We tried playing speed disc golf last year like they do with speed golf," Jim says. "But we kept running up against those playing in front of us. After a few holes it was too frustrating starting and stopping our watches, waiting for the others to finish their play."

"You think regular golfers are slow, try hanging out with disc golfers," Chase says. "Like dudes, just throw and go! No need to line everything up."

"Elevation makes the game trickier," Dillon says. "Different Frisbee weights come into play for long drives or putting."

"They actually call them that?" Chase says.

"Seems more like big tosses and flipping," Jim says.

The guys locate their discs and make their way to the basket, where, after waiting out the rest to finish play, Dillon birdies with what he calls a "straddle putt." Nobody can resist laughing during said putt, and Dillon takes a bow when his disc rattles the chains of the basket.

They hike out from the cluster of trees and skirt along a small pond where several ducks roam freely to find the next tee, another weathered rubber pad to assist the discer in propelling his Frisbee.

"And they have actual tournaments?" Spencer says.

"Oh, yeah. All over the US. I had my PDGA card for a while."

"Don't tell me—"

"Professional Disc Golf Association."

"You're kidding."

"Had to pass a rules-proficiency exam."

So much laughter.

"The perfect exhibition sport for the Olympics in Rio," Jim says. "Pair it up with beach volleyball: Frisbees and volleyballs!"

"Where the hell is the hole?" Chase says, using his right hand as a visor and peering off into a vast tree line.

"Drive it between those two trees and it'll be in line with the basket," Dillon says, pointing the direction out.

"Sure, *no problem*," Chase says. "After you." Chase sweeps his arm dramatically to allow Dillon access to the tee.

Again Dillon backhand flips his disc with little forward movement, and like a laser it slices through the air, running a straight course between the trees he pointed out moments earlier.

"Hmmm," Spencer says.

"Damn! I don't think I could drive my car that straight," Chase says, stepping onto the tee and taking a couple practice arcs. He steps to the back of the tee, thrusts forward like a javelin thrower, and sends the Frisbee aloft. He cringes a moment later; the flight path severely hyzers and disappears into a bank of trees.

"Lumberyard," Jake says.

"*Caddyshack*," Jim says.

"It's going to be a long morning," Chase says.

"I'll show you some tricks," Dillon offers as Spencer unleashes a toss that sails down the gully and lands short of Dillon's.

Jake and Jim fare somewhere between Chase's off-the-beaten-path and Dillon's and Spencer's direct flight. While Chase pays a visit to the lumberyard, the rest gather up their discs and advance until they all hole out, conserving time by bypassing certain etiquette turn taking, which spawns a discussion, led by Dillon, about the proper etiquette for returning text messages.

"In general or for dating?" Spencer says.

"I sense a *Swingers* moment upon us," Jim says, which causes Jake to laugh.

"You two," Dillon says, shaking his head. "Does it matter?"

"Chase once told me he lets a woman sweat for at least four hours, more for the needier variety," Jake says.

"If I'm not busy, I generally reply right away with Maggie, though she rarely sends one during school hours unless it's important."

"If I don't respond within a couple minutes, Doris calls me."

They stand around debating and extending the topic further while waiting for Chase—Dillon and Jim complain about how frustrating it is to send out emails only to have portions of them replied to, often leaving important questions unanswered; Spencer cites their concerns as *benefits* in controlling emotional topics and rash responses, the method allowing for thought before sending a reply; and Jake, after listening to all of this, postulates that electronic forms of communication are disjointed at best and unproductive at worst. Not to be ignored, Chase's Frisbee whizzes toward them, crashes through the branches overhead, and ricochets off a nearby tree trunk, sending the guys for cover.

"Forrrrrrrrrrrrre!" Chase says, returning from the lumberyard. "Do they say 'fore' in disc golf, Dillon?"

"Heads-up. 'Look out' works too. Some shout 'clear on' and the hole number." Dillon shrugs. "It's a plastic disc, not a golf ball coming at you at a hundred miles an hour."

"A Titleist smacked me once during a run," Chase says. "I'm on the sidewalk alongside the golf course in Rohnert Park and I hear this little *skipping,* and before my mind can process that it's a golf ball bouncing off pavement it glanced off my chest and shot across the street. Left a mark for a week." He rubs the area as if it's still there

"Wouldn't have left a mark if you'd been wearing a shirt," Spencer says.

"Pfft."

"You keep using that word," Jake says, facing Chase. "I do not think it means what you think it means."

"*Princess Bride,*" Jim says.

They wrap up the second hole and work their way through the next several scenic ones tucked away among trees surrounded by a bed of fallen pine cones and squirrels busy stashing away seeds and nuts for the winter, meadows with the occasional family of black bears frolicking a healthy distance away, and stream crossings where mountain whitefish and Kokanee salmon dart about, Dillon's lead growing each time his disc rattles the chains. At some point the others declare Dillon has doped to gain an unfair advantage. They speculate over the secret ingredient in his BR&B banana bread, which he confesses is sour cream, and as punishment handicap him two strokes for every future toss as well as making him toss-off from the back pin. This causes his lead to widen more slowly, as does his assisting the guys with their technique where they landed a par here and there. At one point Dillon sends the guys into fits of laughter when he demonstrates the "Jump Putt," which looks awkward at best, jumping straight up and flipping the Frisbees in midair, though his disc sails right in for another birdie.

As the sun reaches the noon hour, they have completed the eighteenth hole and are milling around the shack where they first checked in. Spencer is going over the scores, double-checking the finishing order—Dillon, Spencer, Jake, Jim, Chase. Off to the side, Chase and Dillon discuss the merits of weight training for runners while Jim and Jake discuss a new J&J event.

"A 'persistent hunt' in Annadel," Jake says when Spencer inquires about it. "We're imagining a similar concept where runners track other *runners* instead of prey for food."

"Mountain bikers might fulfill the role of food," Spencer says half-jokingly. "In a hilly environment with rocky terrain they're less agile."

"Food?" Chase says, now in the mix. "I'm starving."

"Me too," Dillon says. "I don't think I can hold out for a persistent hunt, though."

"I doubt modern-day man would survive very long if they had to rely on it," Jake says.

"Is it similar in concept to the Dipsea?" Spencer asks as they head to the minivan, pile in, and venture off for lunch.

"I hadn't thought of it that way," Jim says, nodding in agreement at the analogy.

"Dipsea?" Dillon says.

"You know, the *Dipsea*," Spencer says.

"Sorry."

"It's only, like, the second oldest race in the US, behind the Boston Marathon," Jim says. "Oldest trail race by a long shot. It's age and gender handicapped, and the first person to go from downtown Mill Valley to Stinson Beach wins no matter what wave they started in."

"How many black shirts do you have, Jake?" Chase says.

"Fourteen and counting," Jake says. "I've been running it every year since high school," he adds, directing his comment toward Dillon.

Working their way back to Kings Beach and settling into lunch out on Jason's Beachside Grille's patio, Jake speaks of Dipsea lore: a mangled, convoluted trail race with treacherous shortcuts and certain disaster awaiting at every turn as thousands of runners vie for precious spots—top thirty-five receive the coveted black shirt with their finishing place boldly printed on the back—shouting, "Left, left, left," and bumping and rumbling by those who don't heed said commands. The past June's effort had been Jake's best finish, placing second, while his inaugural year netted his lowest rank: ninth. When asked his secret for navigating the crowded course so swiftly, he simply smiled and said, "I run like there's nothing in my way."

Full bellies supported by tired legs—trail hiking and disc-golf walking pose more challenging than running twenty miles in Annadel, they all agree— the guys amble back to the minivan to collect their packs. After redistribution of contents, they stop in the kayak shop, where Spencer has made reservations for five single, top-sitting kayaks. There they sign liability forms, purchase paddle gloves, and spontaneously yawn a time or two before they wander down to the lake proper, where scuffed-up kayaks from a long summer of use await them.

Seated and ready to go, they shove off, which sets off chuckles when Chase starts his watch—*beep*—and begin their journey east along the shoreline before pushing out beyond the swimming areas and boat moorings, though not for too long. The late-afternoon breeze on the lake creates a choppy ride, encouraging them to paddle in closer for better shelter and calmer waters.

What Chase lacks in Frisbee golf skills he more than makes up for in leading the hard plastic yellow flotilla against the chop and steady breeze, his upper-body strength from weight lifting no longer ridiculed by the others as they tuck in behind his wake when the going gets tough.

"My arms are already sore," Dillon says.

"Sure," Chase says, "you can chuck a Frisbee a mile, but paddle a plastic boat and you come up lame."

While the lake ripples under the group's efforts, the shoreline lies in quiet repose, left to recuperate under a fall sky, no longer hosting tourists from around the world. Locals sparsely dot the sandy beaches segmented by short private piers and the occasional longer municipal one. Children splash around in the chilly water near shore, their conversations and screams of excitement carry out several hundred yards across the water.

"Dillon," Jim says, paddling up alongside him.

"Nevada, baby!" Chase shouts, raising his paddle above his head.

"We're crossing the state line," Spencer says on the other side of Dillon. "He's easily entertained."

"I heard that!" Chase sends water flying behind him with the aid of his paddle. Only the spray reaches the trio.

"Chilly," Jim says, returning his attention back to Dillon. "Doris wanted me to let you know that she mailed out your wedding invitation on Friday."

"Thanks."

"And she made me promise to tell you *not* to get us anything. The nights at your place are more than generous."

"I'll try, but as a formerly married man it's hard *not* to show up with something for any invite. You'll see." Dillon smiles at Jim and turns his head toward Spencer. "Right, Spencer?"

Spencer smirks. "What's Chase doing, setting a new kayak speed record?"

"Everything's a competition with him," Jim says.

"The return trip will be a breeze," Jake says, paddling on by them.

Rounding the state-line point exposes them to harsher conditions, but the views along the cliffs towering above more than offsets the extra effort. Houses jut out and teeter from the rocky cliffs, each with long, convoluted staircases that switchback their way down to docks with boats moored to them, jostling in the chop that laps against their hulls.

They paddle for an hour and pull ashore, an empty strip of beach that becomes their personal *Cast Away* moment when Jim finds a partially deflated volleyball in the high grass. With kayaks secure, they prop up Wilson up on Jake's kayak, hunker down on flat rocks, and stare out toward the lake, where a parasailing company's boat cruises several hundred yards offshore, towing a parachute that bellows above a dangling soul.

"What do you think, Dillon?" Spencer says. "Tahoe suit you?"

"Words fail me. I've heard many things from my guests, but none do it justice."

"We should do the relay up here next summer," Chase says.

"That'd be fun," Jim says. "Jake, think we could tempt you into a road race up here?"

"Up here, sure."

"Don't race on the roads much?" Dillon says.

"Not if I can help it. Don't ever feel inspired by it. I enjoy the trails, getting lost amongst the trees, not negotiating intersections and ingesting carbon dioxide."

"I like how the big road races shut down city streets," Chase says. "Move over, mankind, here comes the runner! Boston shuts down three major routes for their marathon, and the San Diego Rock 'n' Roll Marathon shuts down one side of a freeway. A *freeway*!"

"You run them?" Dillon asks.

"Too long for me. A buddy of mine did 'em. I prefer anaerobic races. I like to hurt for a short period of time, not torture myself over miles and miles. Besides, the recovery is way too long for my taste. I like to move onto the next race as soon as possible."

"Spence's done a number of marathons," Jim says. "Won one too."

"Just a local one," Spencer says.

"Still," Dillon says. "Not many people can say that. What others have you done?"

"Boston '08 is the biggest. Also my PR: 2:19."

Dillon's eyes bulge. "Whoa."

The rest of the guys nod reverently.

As the sun drifts west and clouds move in, with precipitation forecasted for later in the night, the wind and chop kick up, encouraging the guys to leave behind their sandy getaway and head back. And despite a couple Spence-speaks purportedly lost in the wind, Jim, Chase, and Dillon exert stronger and stronger pulls with their paddles until they have significantly gapped Jake and Spencer.

Chase clearly has the upper hand, but Jim and Dillon aren't letting that stop them from working together to keep pace with Chase, who catches on to what they're doing behind him: "drafting like pussies," as he puts it.

"You guys suck!" Chase shouts, and proceeds to launch paddle-sized scoops of cold water behind him, then powering on while the guys laugh in his wake.

"Here's to Jim's impending nuptials," Jake says, raising his glass of beer, sitting outside on the covered deck, a stone's throw away from the lake at the Beacon Bar & Grill. Nearby heat lamps provide warmth against the chilly mountain air and light drizzle.

"Hear, hear," Chase says, which is followed by various forms of similar salutes by the others, glasses all raised before they clink.

"How'd you two meet?" Dillon asks.

Jake laughs. Jim smirks. And Chase and Spencer chuckle.

"That funny?" Dillon says.

"Jake set us up back in college . . . or so he led me to believe."

"This ought to be good."

"Sophomore year, end of the school year, and we're out having dinner off campus at Charlie's Place. It's Saturday night and we've had a couple beers and are feeling pretty mellow. The place is hopping and Jake leans over, taps me on the shoulder, and points to a girl sitting across the way with a couple friends. I tell him I don't know who she is. Jake goes, 'Her name is Annie and she sits in one of my classes. She asked about you the other day.' I go, 'Really?' and he nods. So I look back over her way and she's cute and all and she's talking, waving her hands and sort of bouncing up and down in her stool, like it's one of those hippity-hops. Odd, but no big deal; she's telling a story, I don't know. Of course, I'm working on my third beer so who knows, right? So Jake nudges me and tells me to go talk to her. 'I'll go with you,' he says. So after much deliberation, I decide to at least say hi. I'd PRed in the five thousand on the track earlier that day so I'm feeling good about myself. I stand, assuming Jake is right behind me, but he isn't."

The smiles around the table grow with each sentence.

"I stroll up to the table and one of the girls spots me and the table goes quiet. Annie looks up at me and says, 'Yes?' I say, 'Hi. My friend Jake—' and I turn to introduce Jake but he's not there; instead he's laughing back at our table, so I already look stupid. And at that moment I know I've been duped for what I did to him back in high school. Jake's never seen her before; doesn't have a class with her; her name's not Annie, I'm guessing."

The guys are all laughing now.

"So now I'm stuck and Annie says, 'This is, like, the worst pickup attempt ever!' And she and the girls start laughing. All I could think of at the moment, besides turning around and going back to punch Jake, was to say, 'If I'm going to go crash and burn, I might as well go down in style,' and so I start to sing 'You've Lost That Lovin' Feeling.'"

"*Top Gun!*" the others shout, followed by belly laughs that draw stares from nearby tables.

"So . . ." Dillon says.

"She starts laughing, begs me to stop singing, and tells me her real name. I tell her mine and she invites me to sit with her and her friends. I look back at Jake, who gives me a 'bravo' salute, and sit down. We ended up having a good time. I asked her out before the night was over."

"And that was that . . ." Dillon says.

"Not completely. We dated for a month before she left school early to go back to Alaska and take care of some family issues. She told me she didn't have time to deal with that *and* carry on a long-distance relationship, so she encouraged me to move on. I did, though she and I kept in touch periodically. A year ago I was single again and Doris and I got to talking. Things had settled down with her family drama, and she invited me up for a visit. I went, and *that* was that."

"What happened in Jake's case, back in high school?" Dillon says.

"The girl squirted ketchup on him and he walked around the rest of the day looking wounded."

"Here's to Jake's revenge plan gone wrong," Chase says.

They all clink their glasses just as a platoon of servers with dinner plates and side dishes arrive.

"Might as well go around the horn . . ." Dillon says, casting an eye toward Spencer.

"She was stalking me," Spencer says with a grin.

Puzzled, Dillon says, "Seriously?"

"Yes and no. I thought she was stalking me because she'd keep 'running into me' and talking to me like we'd met before, but as far as I could remember we hadn't. I didn't know who she was. I was spending the summer up in Portland with some friends after college. A couple runners from school had a place there and I wanted to get some serious marathon training in with them for the Athens Games Olympic trials. Anyway, sometime in July, I'm running laps in Pier Park, going easy after my crash on the trails up in Forest Park the previous weekend that landed me in the ER. And this woman running in the opposite direction waves, says, 'Hi again,' and turns around and starts running with me. She's asking me these out-of-the blue, follow-up type questions and I have no idea what she's talking about. It was too weird, so I politely move on, and as I leave she says to call her. I don't have her number so now she's coming across as bizarre.

"Two days later, I'm at a farmers' market and *wham*, her again. I try brushing her off, but nothing is working, so I ignore her until she leaves in a huff. The next week she shows up again as I'm getting out of my car at home. Now I'm freaking out, and she's actually getting mad at me, telling me 'what my problem was,' et cetera. And somewhere in all of this she keeps referencing a run we did together and I ask her when it took place. She stares at me like I'm high but tells me a couple Sundays ago up at Forest Park. The only thing I can think of is that I *had* met her and shortly after we parted ways is when I tripped, went down hard, and suffered my concussion. I tell her this, almost excited about it, and she just stares at me like I've told her the lamest brushoff story in history. But I say, 'No, no it's true, see?' and I show her the stitches on my ear and noggin, but I can tell she's not buying it. She gets *really* mad and starts going off on me and I'm like, whoa, whoa. Anyway, she eventually simmers down and I tell her I'll make it up to her by taking her out . . . and I did."

"Maybe she *was* a stalker and that was a cover story," Dillon says. "She hangs out around hospitals, waiting for pale, skinny runners suffering from short-term memory loss."

"Was it love at first sight?" Jake says.

"Maybe you're actually married and don't remember!" Jim says.

"Remember when we first met . . . nope!" Chase says.

Spence-speak.

"Jake?" Dillon says.

Jake gives off a big smile. "Spencer ditched me in the middle of nowhere and a nurse rescued me."

The rest of the guys chuckle, though Dillon has no idea what Jake means, but as Jake begins recounting the story, Chase's cell phone chimes the arrival of a text message, which he reflexively views, and begins replying to, announcing it's from Terri, which spawns ribbing about him not adhering to his "let them dangle" rule. A moment later, Spence's phone rings, and because Chase has already introduced technology into their sacred conversation, Spencer takes Maggie's call. Chase returns his attention to the group to find Jim answering a call from Doris, who, he has warned the others, would likely call to "check in" on their whereabouts, to which Chase says, "Man, she runs a tight ship." Jim concedes as much and adds that she doesn't let him gain any weight or watch Woody Allen movies, which spawns more laughter. Before long the bill arrives as Dillon responds to a text from Terri about a BR&B question, and, moments later, Kate. Wallets open, the bill divvied up, leading them from the restaurant, Jake's story lost in the shuffle of connections.

Sunday Morning
Rarefied Air

"Altitude training . . . good for the lungs," Chase says, reaching the first appreciable level section of jeep trail after a 1,450-foot ascent thirty minutes into their run that began at the Tunnel Creek Café off Highway 28, east of Incline Village. "Hell on the metrics, though," he adds, glancing at his

Garmin that shows they've averaged 8:32 throughout the more than three-mile climb.

"What is it . . . up here?" Dillon says.

"Are we on the . . . Flume Trail yet?" Spencer says.

"It's off to the right at the next trail juncture," Jake replies, pointing ahead to where three trails intersect. "See?"

"We're at 7,674 feet," Chase says after glancing at his watch. "We'll hit 8,800 at Marlette Peak."

"The views from there are spectacular," Jake says.

"I always forget how gorgeous it is up here," Jim says.

"Eight thousand, you say?" Dillon says. "It's been a while since I've been this high."

This spawns chuckles.

"Let it come to you," Jake says. "You'll adapt soon enough."

Mind and body primed, they embark on arguably one of the finest trails around Lake Tahoe, a flat ribbon of single-track traversing a cliff whose sheer drop-off toward the lake appears as daunting as it feels magnetic. If the distant lake views don't take your breath away, the vertigo may, as Chase mentions a time or three when the guys let their gaze drift uncomfortably long downward. The vertical mountainous rise on the opposing side of the trail exasperates his discomfort, especially where large boulders jut out and force him closer to the abyss.

The sun filters down through the trees overhead, glistening off droplets from the previous night's modest rain that has wetted the trail, leaving it muddy in places as well as creating shallow puddles to either navigate around or tromp through. Jake and Jim are the mudders of the group, reveling in splashing their way along the trail, much to the ire of the others, though eventually the effort to avoid the puddles proves more work than necessary, and they all end up displacing pooled-up water off to the sides.

"I feel like a Kenyan training up here," Dillon says. "I can see where training like this gives them an edge."

"You need to balance your time at altitude with lower-elevation training when it comes to speed workouts," Spencer says.

"Why's that, *Coach*?" Chase says.

Spence-speak. "You can't achieve the absolute speed at altitude that is required to compete well; therefore you wind up training your body to race at a slower pace."

"Won't it feel faster racing at sea level?" Jim says.

"At first, yes, but if you're racing at, say, sixty-five-second quarters, but you've been training at a sixty-eight quarter pace, eventually the faster pace will prove too tough since your neuromuscular system is trained at the slower pace. It will feel uncomfortable despite a lack of cardiovascular strain."

"Ah . . . got it," Jim says, passing by three hikers enjoying a snack and feeding a grateful chipmunk. They are seated on an overhang, their view over Jeffrey pine and white fir treetops Sandy Harbor, Lake Tahoe's eastern artistic palette: turquoise with hints of sandy beige hug the shoreline and transition into a dense cobalt blue with the colder and immense depths of the lake that spreads far and wide.

"That was part of my argument during our discussion about which is tougher, Western States, the Tour, or the Ironman: neuromuscular adaptation," Spencer says. "Case in point, and many, *many* apologies for referencing him but he makes a good example, however infamous: Lance's first attempt at running the marathon. He barely broke three hours despite having arguably one of the best cardiovascular systems ever."

"I'd say Kílian Jornet has the best cardio system with a 90 VO$_2$max," Jim says.

"Pikes Peak legend, Matt Carpenter, tested at 92," Jake says. "It's no wonder he held the course records on *both* the ascent and descent events."

"VO$_2$max is certainly advantageous at altitude," Spencer says, "but at sea level if you don't train at a high percentage of your VO$_2$max you're not going to win many races. Frank Shorter only tested at 71 but won gold at the Munich Games."

"Should've won at the Montreal Games four years later, too," Chase said, shaking his head. "Damn 'Pinski."

"And who knows how much of Lance's cardio was manufactured," Dillon says.

"True."

"Think he doped for the marathon?" Jim says.

That'd be pathetic if he had," Chase says. "I'd feel hollow afterward if I took shortcuts like that. Besides, my grandfather would've kicked me nine ways to Sunday if I ever cheated."

"As John Wooden once said, 'Sport doesn't build character, it reveals it,'" Spencer says.

Wooden's prophetic words linger in the crisp, clean air of the Sierras, the guys deftly making way without pausing for a string of mountain bikers flowing toward and past them, with "Hey," "Hi," "Thanks," "There's one more," exchanged along with chain clatter.

"I'm glad we haven't had any doping issues in the PA," Jim says.

"Except for Regina Jacobs, but she was a world-class runner, so . . ." Spencer says.

"Ever come across anything down south, Dillon?" Chase says.

"Does the name Davis Litton ring any bells?" No bells ring. "He kind of jumped onto the scene one year, winning many of the local races—you know, the ones that have a little prize money, but not enough to attract the elites?" Nods follow, as does the "there's-one-more" mountain biker, who looks displeased about his friends dropping him. "There were some rumors, but since he wasn't winning *big* races, there was never any race-day testing, and it wasn't worth the USATF's time to test guys like him out of season. One day after a race one of his club mates spotted needles and paraphernalia in Davis's gym bag and confronted him. They told him to turn himself in or they'd do it for him."

"What an idiot," Jim says. "He carried the crap around with him?"

"I recognize that name now," Chase says. "He won the Bakersfield 10K. I remember because I was fourth, one spot out of the prize money."

"You should contact the race director to see about getting your money now," Dillon says.

The notion amuses the group, though it does spawn a brief but somber discussion about the true cost of cheating in sport in general: robbing legitimate athletes of their day in the sun.

As the Flume Trail nears its southern reach it sidles up alongside Marlette Lake, whose pristine surface reflects the fall foliage in invigorating fashion: tall aspens descend the hillside in groves to the shoreline with yellow and orange shades interspersed among greens not yet ready to leave summer behind.

Chase frequently consults his watch, the much slower "oxygen-deprived" pace messing with his sea-level averages. And now that they're climbing again up toward the TRT at an 8:49 pace his unease rises.

"You're still getting in a good run," Jake says. "Don't worry about the pace. Enjoy the scenery."

"I know, I know," Chase says, "the body only knows time and effort . . . not mileage."

"And besides—" Spencer says.

"And the *time* on my feet is one of the benefits of the long run . . . yes, guys, I get it."

"Mr. Technology is just concerned his weekly TPS report is going to be thrown off," Jim says.

"*Office Space*," Jake and Dillon say together.

"What was it you said to me once, Chase?" Spencer says. "Step off the train once in a while."

"Thanks for the medicine, Dr. Spence."

"No matter what . . . pace we run . . . this is still more taxing than back home," Jim says.

"No deductions?" Chase says.

Jim snorts, conversation no longer feasible, and manages the precipitous rise against the Carson Range. Eyes cast downward, up they creep with short steps, legs stabbing at the trail, each exerting force disproportionate to the amount of forward progress, lungs bellowing in protest against an unsympathetic atmosphere deprived of oxygen and pressure, false summits taunting them with every upward glance.

Dillon is the first to speak once the ascent softens and their breaths slacken. "Speaking of technology, Chase . . . how'd your Tesla test drive go?"

"Awesome!" he replies. "I'm really, *really*, tempted to buy one. It has these—" Chase's last word hangs in the air much like his body for a split second, eyes dilated and mind in suspended animation, his unsuspecting frame unprepared for the impending thud.

Chase's toe catches a root, barely visible, camouflaged by the dark color of the dampened trail. Briefly anchored, forward progress disrupted, his body lurches forward and downward, arms reflexively reaching out. The moment is quick, too quick for him to roll left or right to avoid a belly flop. He glides through the air, the top half of his body dipping while the other half rises until like a seesaw, the plane of his body reverses itself with no intention of swinging back.

He grimaces, eyes shut tight, bracing for impact. First his torso hits the brownish rainwater, and like a bad dive from the side of a lake into shallow waters the rest of his body follows suit; the puddle splays outward. The slick bottom allows him to slide forward, shooting him to the end of the puddle, where he comes to rest, his lower leg extremities extending beyond the puddle's ragged edge like an overgrown child in a small bed.

Ahead of Chase, Jake and Jim turn and stop at the yelp Chase makes. Dillon, who is right behind Chase, juts to the side to avoid trampling him, and Spencer, who is behind Dillon, reacts and skids to a sudden stop at the puddle's edge, straddling Chase's shoes. For an agonizingly long moment those upright hover, staring down at the fallen, waiting for some movement. The silent questions echo throughout the sierras: Is he hurt? If so, how bad? How far away are they from medical assistance? Runners spend the majority of their activity in flight, both feet in the air, and only brief moments connected to the ground, but it's those fleeting earthbound seconds that cause the most havoc.

Chase's right arm rises out from the muck, water and mud dripping from it. He angles the arm over to the other equally stretched-out one, the hand finding its counterpart, and a finger reaches for the wrist. *Beep.*

Chuckles follow, along with a collective sigh of relief.

"You okay, buddy?" Spencer says.

"Good thing you had a shirt on," Jim says.

"What a *beee-yooo-tiful* day for a mud bath!"

"*Bruce Almighty*," Jake says.

Jim snaps his fingers and points toward Jake. "Nice."

Chase pushes himself up from the puddle, flips over, and flexes everything from head to toe, assessing damages. The impact points, chest and knees, the right one more than the left, appear no worse for wear. The landing zone is forgiving, more so than it would've been a day earlier, when the same acrobatics would've left redder marks, trail rash, and *severely* bruised impact points.

After he rights himself, walks up the trail, and breaks into a deliberate trot twenty yards out and back, testing the body's reaction to involuntary flight, Chase feels confident that the run can continue—*beep*—though his Tesla story is left submerged in the muddy puddle behind them, the new conversation now centering on epic and not so epic falls each of the guys has endured at one time or another. And even with Chase's latest Superman-style spill added to the list, Spencer's amnesiac event continues to top them all, though they admit that Dillon's Zuma Canyon Trail adventure, where he failed to duck under a broken tree branch on a stormy winter day, thunked his forehead, landed flat on his back, and slid off the trail into a creek is a pretty entertaining close second, especially when he mentions the capper to the story: he received a citation from park officials for going off trail.

Week 43 Training Summary			
	Long Run	Mileage Total	Comments
Dillon	22	65	Loved the trails in Tahoe. Must go back!
Chase	21.42	45	Biffed it in Tahoe. Some bruising and soreness but runnable.
Spencer	21.50	59	Sore from first week of XC training.
Jim	20	54	Fun hanging and running with the guys in Tahoe.
Jake	22	70	The family cabin always takes me back to childhood.

Week 9
October 26

Monday Evening at the BR&B
Wedding Invitation

Dillon stares and *stares* and stares! at *it*, the formal, cream-colored envelope addressed to him. When he concludes it will not spontaneously combust he slashes it with a letter opener, pulling out the multi-papered contents that announce the impending wedding between Doris Brown Harrington and Jim Ronald Greyson at the Dearborn Homestead on November 7, 2015. It requests the pleasure of his company to witness their special day. He draws in a long breath through his nostrils, holds it, and lets it flow out. Miles peers up from her slumber with hypnotic blue eyes, an old soul gazing back at Dillon in the emptiness of a guestless BR&B. She licks her lips, yawns, and rests her head on the area rug in the main room, drifting back off to sleep to the distant sound of linen from last night's guests tumbling over and over in the dryer.

All the physical miles put between him and his ex, all the road and trail miles tallied trying to move on and forget have left him right back where he started from, staring at a wedding invitation. Though Dillon isn't a principal actor it does little to comfort him. The fleshy images continue to flash before him, the parting words echo around him. At the sound of a branch scraping the side window, Dillon half expects the apparition of a former guest to appear and say, "I told you so, son."

The invites had been sent out shortly after Jim had proposed to Doris, two months ago, to accommodate the short run-up to the wedding, before Dillon became a part of the group. Now immersed in the community of runners and their respective mates, the group has opened their lives to him. Thus the invite, late as it is. Dillon's hope to miss out was a faint one. After bartering with Doris for honeymoon nights at the BR&B it was only a matter of time when *the* envelope would arrive. Jim had confirmed it during their kayaking excursion in Tahoe. And now it rests in the palm of his hand, not conveying the hope and promise that lies ahead for Jim and Doris, but the broken promise from Dillon's own marriage turned divorce. He's more than happy to offer the newlyweds his place for their honeymoon bliss. He just isn't sure he can stomach the ceremony and reception alone.

Dillon scans the rest of the invitation, noting that La Vera Pizza will cater the reception meal. Dillon remembers the owners and RERC club members, a married couple, Martin and Maureen, where, after a cross-country meet, the guys stopped in for lunch. He circles the lasagna instead of the meatless choice of cheese ravioli. That's easy enough. The next question, however, pains him: "_____ Persons Will Attend."

He reaches for his beer from the coffee table, leans back on the couch, sips from the frosted mug, and ponders his options. He'll leave Miles at the inn, though Robyn will ask about her. His sister will be off on some wild adventure. Inviting Terri will raise too many questions and suspicions.

Wedding gift! Dillon thinks about it a moment, despite Doris and Jim telling him not to bring one. He figures as much, but despite that he's learned never to show up empty-handed to any invite of any kind. Marriage taught him certain things he can't ignore or forget in divorce, like the importance of making the bed upon rising, cleaning out the dryer's lint trap, and tidying the kitchen after a meal, especially dinner. His ex didn't like waking up to dirty dishes in the sink. He'd never given these domestic chores a thought until he met her. He scratches the back of his head and sighs, the "persons will attend" question still taunting him. He really should pick out a commemorative procrastination coin to reconcile such deliberations. Perhaps with Douglas Adams on it. Or Truman Capote. Or Margaret Atwood. . . .all reputed procrastinators.

Kate? He replaces the beer with his cell phone, scrolling to the last text message from her after he'd declined her invitation to meet for dinner over the last weekend because of the Tahoe trip: "No worries. There'll be other opportunities to catch up." She'll probably want to dance. Women like to dance at weddings. He can suffer through a few dances if it means someone to talk to. Chase will undoubtedly bring someone. Spencer has Maggie. Jake, Linda. Dillon starts to pencil in the number "2" but pauses. *The grapevine will want to know who I'm bringing if I write "2." Who is she? Where'd you meet her? Is she a runner?* Dillon runs fingers through his hair and massages the back of his head. *Women ask so many questions.* He catches sight of Miles staring at him again. "Okay, girl. I know, I know." He writes "2" on the invitation, places it in the envelope, seals it, and flips it back onto the coffee table. He picks his mug back up, raises it toward Miles, and chugs the remainder, rising at the sound of the dryer's buzzer. Miles lowers her head and dozes off.

Tuesday Night
Socializing

Sitting at home, Chase scans the laptop screen intently, scrutinizing the data he's uploaded to the Garmin Connect website from his workout that afternoon: six 1-mile repeats ranging from 5:02 to 5:11. Chase altered his workout from its original plan—600-meter repeats—to take advantage of the no-race week with hopes of boosting his long-course race stamina. He likes where his speed is for this time of the year, but with two regular season cross-country meets left—and the finale a mother of a hilly one at that—Chase doesn't like his current fitness for its ability to sustain long climbs *and* have a kick at the end. This'll be especially true in three weeks when the race distance jumps to a full six miles at the PA championships. Dillon has already bested Chase now that "the new guy" has settled into the cross-country season. And if keeping pace with Dillon looks grim, staying ahead of the Agras runners he's already beaten is paramount if the RERC wants a shot at winning the series title, a goal Chase's competitive nature can practically taste, adding a PA Championship plaque to his collection of other surprising accomplishments in his career: Wisconsin high school state championship and athlete of the year, Ithaca College's team captain of NCAA Division III's track-and-field champions, the only division III athlete to break four minutes indoors, and, of course, his individually glass-encased, sub-4 track spikes from both indoor and outdoor feats.

Today's workout data looks good, hitting the right splits with less recovery than previously taken, his heart rate data consistent with summer workouts at shorter distances, though he doesn't place much stock in it, given that cardiovascular exertion is easily skewed by variables beyond the pace itself, such as ambient temperature and hydration levels. To heed rising heart-rate levels throughout a workout by *slowing down* negates the workout's neuromuscular goals. It's simply another dashboard metric for him to track.

"Meow."

"What, Dogma?"

"Meow."

"Not any clearer." Chase turns his attention to the next day's workout, bringing up its history for reference, three ten-minute intervals with one minute of recovery, his Achilles' heel.

A moment later his iRobot Roomba 880 vacuum comes to life, whirring from the living room, where its docking station resides. Chase pauses from calculating the tempo pace he'll need to run, contemplating why the unit has activated so late in the day.

Chase rises from his chair and pokes his head out from the office. Spinning around and around and shooting off toward the kitchen sits Dogma atop the iRobot.

"Meoooooooooow."

"You piss on that and I'm going to use up one of your lives." Chase catches up with the erratic device, nudges Dogma off it, and presses a couple buttons that send the robot back to its docking station.

"Meow."

"Food. My bad." He prepares Dogma's dinner and commences with boiling water for the wild rice that will go along with the baked salmon and fresh asparagus he plans for his dinner with Terri.

Rice simmering, Chase returns to his office, switches over to Strava's website, uploads his day's workout, and checks in on how his friends have fared with their efforts. He notes no PRs for the day, but makes a comment on a former college buddy who's getting back into running after a long layoff: "Great job, Toby! Keep at it. Nothing worth doing comes easy."

Chase summons Facebook next, posting a link to his workout for the day with the caption: "Awesome track workout. Mile repeats, never my forte, kicked my ass but know I'm better for it. We'll see how my legs feel on my thirty-minute tempo-style run tomorrow. Got to love back-to-back toughies."

Within minutes comments and Likes pour in on his post as Chase scans the latest scroll of social media on his wall.

Likes: 12.

Bobby: "You rock, Chase Dog!!!"

Chase reply: "You rock, you crazy ultra dog. What's your next event? 1000 miles!"

Likes: 25.

Rachel: "You're my hero."

Chase reply: "You're too kind, Rachel. When's your next event?"

Matt: "What was your HR at the end of each recovery interval? Mr. Data wants to know. Nice job, man."

Chase reply: "88, 89, 91, 90, 95, 97."

Matt: "Of course you'd know them. What was I thinking?! LOL."

Likes: 38.

Liz: "You going to be in Green Bay this Thanksgiving? We'd love to see you. It's been too long."

Chase reply: "Would love to, but crazy busy with work and running. Tell Anthony hi for me."

Chaz: "Green Bay? Not that frozen tundra. Come back to NYC for New Year's. We'll rock the place."

Chase reply: "Which twin are you dating now? LOL."

Likes: 49.

Blair: "5:02 mile? Is that the best you can do, old man? You ran sub-4 in college, for crying out loud. Just kidding. I haven't run in five years, so who am I to say."

Chase reply: "Ran 4:20 this summer. I haven't focused on the mile since college. What are you doing these days besides getting fat? Just kidding! How are the wife and kids? Still crunching numbers on Wall Street?"

Likes: 71.

Joel: "Ah, the DOMS principle . . . nicely done, my friend."

Chase reply: "Yeah, the hard/easy/hard/easy days are a thing of the past."

Nik: "As in Dom Perignon? What does champagne have to do with running hard?"

Chase: "Google 'delayed onset muscle soreness.'"

Joel: "Fit runners don't experience muscle soreness from a hard effort until forty-eight hours later so they can sneak in a second hard run the following day. Less fit runners often *feel* their workout within twenty-four hours."

Judy: "I had an entirely different take on DOMS. Wink, wink . . ."

Likes: 101.

Chase smiles while his post garners the results he expects, often craves, closes the laptop, sets the table, and decants the wine. Terri arrives shortly thereafter with the study questionnaire portion of her project, and after settling down on the couch, sipping wine, Terri begins.

"Answer yes or no to the following tech items that you own." Dogma snuggles up with her on the chair. "Desktop computer."

"Yes."

"Laptop."

"Yes."

"Tablet."

"Yes."

"Smart phone."

"Yes."

"Digital camera, digital camcorder, webcam."

"Yes. Yes. Yes."

"GPS enabled sport"—Chase is smiling—"Of course. Any other electronic devices used to engage with others or control your environment?"

Chase sits in deep thought, gazing around the living room. "Robot vacuum . . . digital thermostat, and . . . oh! My newest toy: a digital doorbell."

"Really?"

Chase pulls out his iPhone, queues up the Skybell app, and shows it to Terri. "When someone rings the doorbell it sends me a notice. That way I can see who it is from my phone, and even video chat with them."

"Wouldn't it be easier to answer the door?"

"Not if I'm not at home or don't want to deal with a door-to-door salesman."

Terri smiles and jots on the questionnaire. "Okay, now your online presence and social activity level."

"Let's take a break. Dinner is ready."

Terri smiles. "That's not convenient at all."

"No, no. It really is ready."

Seated and eating, they discuss various topics: where he's racing on Saturday and how it feels weird to no longer be the club's lead runner, which Terri suggests he not worry about and instead focus on what he can do to regain his former status as well as support the team; Jim and Doris's upcoming wedding, Terri commenting on how cute a couple they make; whether Terri is going to attend Dillon's Halloween party on Saturday, to which she says "yes," citing her costume of choice, which gives Chase an idea about what he can wear to complement hers, especially if they arrive together, both laughing and agreeing afterward.

Dinner consumed and chocolate mousse savored, Terri continues with her study questions in the living room, Dogma again by her side, first focusing on Chase's current social media profiles (Facebook, Strava, Garmin, Google+, LinkedIn); his online community activity (viewing profiles, reading blogs, listening to podcasts, posting messages, photos, videos, or run activity data); and lastly his use of electronic forms of communication—email, text message, instant messaging, Twitter.

The questionnaire wrapped up, Chase asks, "Where do I rank?"

Terri smiles politely. "It's not a competition."

Chase crosses his arms against his chest, expression hurt, a puppy full of energy told to lie down and stay still.

"You are certainly *very* technologically engaged," she says.

"I knew it!"

"I'll pair your overall technology score with your intimacy score to get a better idea on how you *really* stack up," she says with a wink.

After she has gathered up her study material she bestows Chase with three new Kama Sutra inspired kisses to ponder, which leaves him dazed long after the door has closed behind her.

"Meow."

"You wouldn't understand."

Wednesday Afternoon
Olympic Dreams

"Sorry I'm late," Dillon says, exiting his pickup truck at Cobblestone. "My sister's flight arrived later than expected."

"You have a sister?" Spencer says.

Dillon nodded. "Ready?"

The two start trotting up Channel Drive. *Beep. Beep.*

"Where does she live?"

"She calls Whidbey Island home, but she's rarely there. She travels extensively for work."

"Doing what?"

"She leads adventure tours to places like Peru, Alaska, South America . . ."

"Rough job."

"I'm sure if we ever want to go on an epic running adventure she'd be able to hook us up for cheap."

"I've always wanted to run in Viren's hometown of Myrskylä, Finland, and in the Great Rift valley of Kenya."

"Running is certainly in your blood."

Spencer chuckles. "Up in Portland I made it my life. Everything revolved around it. I lived with these guys who were part of the Nike Elite Project. It was practically like living at a training camp."

"Reminds you how simple life can be, only focused on one thing: eat, sleep, run; repeat twice daily."

"Like a Bed, Run, and Breakfast."

"The subconscious wants what the subconscious wants."

"So true . . . my biggest problem, or I should say the biggest challenge, was *not* racing all the time. Every weekend, one race after another. I didn't have much in the way of sponsorship, so I ended up racing quite a bit to make a few dollars in prize money. But it hindered my marathon training."

"I would imagine. In college, racing seasons are fairly structured: cross-country in the fall, indoor track in the winter, and outdoor track in the spring. But after that it's a wide-open field for racing . . . like you said, year-round. Too many temptations."

"Hey, Dale," Spencer says, rapidly approaching the octogenarian.

"Slow down before you hurt yourself," Dale says, chuckles gurgling afterward.

"What was Pheidippides like as a training partner?" Spencer says.

"Wise guys!" Dale stretches his arms out as if to hold back the youth movement. "Enjoy it while you can, kiddos," he says when they sweep past. "Nature's your friend when your young; after that it's nothin' but nurture."

"Wise beyond your years."

Dale grunts and veers right, taking the shortcut to the base of Richardson's trail. "Wise guys, them two."

"He's like the traveling gnome," Dillon says. "I see him everywhere."

"If there's a race to be run, or free food to be had," Spencer says, "Dale will appear."

At the end of Channel, Dillon veers right to catch the start of Richardson's Trail, but Spencer stays the course.

"Where're we going?" Dillon says after he readjusts his route.

"Out through Oakmont." He points up ahead, where the road ends and a short dirt path connects to another road into an entirely different world, one filled with townhomes, manicured lawns, and elderly citizens walking small often manicured dogs.

"What is this place?"

"A retirement community. I use it for long tempo runs. It has a big loop with modest grades up and down to keep things honest."

Dillon's fish-out-of-water expression morphs into disappointment. "Tempo run? My legs are still cooked from Tahoe."

"Mine too. Nothing hard today, just easy. I don't want to run hills, so this is our best option from where we parked."

"Got it."

"Anyway, I realized after training full-time and constantly racing, and after I missed the trials qualifying time by forty-three seconds, that I couldn't continue living that way. Imagining myself running alongside Kempainen at the marathon trials, making *the* team, coming out from the tunnel and into a packed stadium, a gold medal around my neck . . . no longer seemed worth the effort. And somewhere in the back of my head I kept hearing my dad's voice: 'Running is a great activity, but it's just that, an activity. Get on with the real purpose to your life, teaching.' I'd met Maggie by then too. Honestly, I think part of me realized I didn't have it in me to make the team anyway, and I certainly didn't have the support systems in place to make an honest go of it. I wanted to move back here and Maggie was cool with it, so . . . here we are."

"Running through a retirement community."

"Oh, the irony."

"We *all* have that defining moment," Dillon says wistfully, turning onto a four-lane roadway.

"What was yours?"

"This place is bizarre. Is that a polo field?"

"Uh-huh, and they have a golf course. It's for active senior citizens."

"I guess so," Dillon says, watching cars putt along. "Now I know where all the old people I see on Channel come from. So my defining I'm-not-going-to-the-Olympics moment was my last year at U-dub during the Pac 10 track championship in Eugene—10,000 meters. I'd been racing well all season long, ready for a peak race, and I remember thinking during the last mile that this was my last collegiate race. I don't know why the thought popped into my head, but there it was. I was in a small group at the time, three of us, primed for a strong finish. I'd beaten each of the guys at least once earlier that season. Then, I don't know, the next three laps blurred by and we're on the last one, the crowd is standing in the grandstands on the backstretch like they do at Hayward Field, chanting for one of their own, and I felt like I was watching the race from afar, not even in it. That's when I realized that I didn't have the extra big game drive to bring it home. In a way I'd known that I'd never had it and it took me eight years to figure it out. I was fast enough to win a lot of races, but not the ones that counted."

"Where'd you end up in the race?"

"Second."

Much like the introspection an athlete encounters when relegated to runner-up near the end of a contest, compiling a list of excuses, a quiet moment ensues; Spencer ponders Dillon's quandary: perhaps a "fear of success" holds him back, the responsibility and vulnerability associated with climbing atop the winner's pedestal for all to see and take shots at. The pressure of success often exacts its toll on those not properly grounded at keys stages in their life.

"Well, one of these days, I'd still like to qualify for the trials," Spencer says. "That would make my career. Doesn't help that they keep lowering the standard. I mean, it's great that the times reflect quality runners in this country again, but still . . . tough standards . . . always just out of reach."

"Is that why you don't want to get married? Unfinished business?"

Spencer shoots an alarmed look Dillon's way, the face of commerce receding behind them and sturdy, squat homes lacking front porch steps flanking them.

"Sorry, Jake once made a comment about your goals, and the thought clicked in my mind. I often wondered when I got married if it would slow me down, not only with running but in other pursuits I had."

Spencer doesn't say anything, but his pace does increase up the wide, sweeping curve in the road.

"Also, Jim's and Doris's wedding invitation arrived this week, so there's that too."

Spencer continues to push the pace on the incline. Dillon opens up his stride to draw abreast, though it doesn't look easy, comfortable, or wanted.

"Forget what I said," Dillon says a minute later as his breathing becomes more pronounced. "I wasn't trying to pry . . . just a bubble thought."

Spencer relaxes the pace halfway up the incline. "Normally Jake's the one with wisdom over wisecracks."

Dillon laughs. "He kind of rubs off on you. Plus, I have been married."

"You're not too far off, I suppose. I do worry that tying the knot will impose certain expectations that aren't there now. I'm afraid the change will alter things too much for me . . . or us."

"Change for runners really is like a four-letter word. We definitely thrive on stability. But the way I've always viewed change is that it took change to arrive at this moment, the current routine."

Spencer rolls his shoulders and shakes out his arms, passing by the Quail Inn Restaurant and Bar, whose marquee invites the community in for "Weekday Happy Hour 3PM–5PM." Three hopeful cars troll the packed parking lot.

"Think of it from a coaching perspective," Dillon says. "The same workout done over and over doesn't promote improvements in racing fitness. *Changing* up the workouts is a good thing. Makes the body stronger."

"Jakeism?"

"My sister's influence."

"Aside from Rob de Castella, whose coach had him doing pretty much the same training program year after year throughout his career, you're right about changing things up, giving the body new stresses to adapt to."

Nearly identical low-maintenance front yards and white posts spaced every other driveway with black mailboxes attached to each side flank the roadway, giving the impression they are running on a concrete treadmill.

"You and Maggie coming to the Halloween party on Saturday?"

"We're coming. Not sure as what yet. You bringing someone to the wedding?"

"Kate, if I get around to asking her," Dillon says, staring at a caravan of golf carts whizzing by without golf clubs hanging off the back, driver and passenger staring back with blank expressions.

"Maggie is out of town that weekend, so I'm solo."

"Bummer. Too bad Dana is only here for a few days. You two could hang out. There's always Robyn with a *y.*"

"*Great!*"

Dillon chuckles and attempts a Spence-speak when Spencer picks up the pace again, but he fails to capture its essence. Dillon then asks Spencer how his transition to cross-country training is going.

"Not bad. A little sore from the intensity, but all manageable . . . and expected. Reminds me of my cross-country days in college."

"Speaking of college, why history?" Dillon says, the pace still brisk as they hit the farthest point from their cars, now zigzagging through neighborhoods, working their way back. "I slept through it most of the time. Too much memorization of dates and facts."

Spencer backs off the pace. "Yeah . . . the curriculum often doesn't make history relevant, and it really is. I read quite a bit of dystopian fiction in high school: *Lord of the Flies, Brave New World, Neuromancer, Animal Farm, The Running Man, 1984* . . ."

"I read *Iron Heel*. Politics, capitalism . . . too depressing for me."

"Very dark, especially since it fostered the genre. For me, I enjoyed the sense of reading about the future as written from a historical perspective. It started me thinking about how much of the future depends on our history. I also recognized similar patterns in distance running success, how modes of training philosophies influenced success at the international levels. Hard-core running in the '60s and '70s brought the US success, but when it morphed during the '80s into 'Train, Don't Strain,' it ushered in two decades of decline. Often the answers to modern-day issues are right behind us if we simply turn around and look."

"You definitely are meant to teach," Dillon says as they set retirement aside and return to the jungle, cruising along Channel Drive back toward their cars, their tired Tahoe legs partially revived from the gentle run, and talk of past and future running dreams, so much so that the pace quickens, the pull of Cobblestone too tempting, Spence-speaks left checked at the door.

Friday Early Afternoon
RERC Therapy Room

Jim wanders into the BR&B to the sound of a skill saw in action upstairs. He's immediately greeted by Miles, who gives the briefcase in Jim's hand a quick sniff, sits, and lets out a questioning, "*Wooooowoooowooo Wooooowoooo?*"

Formally attired, Jim feels the need to state his business. "I'm here to see Dillon—"

Miles rises and pads toward the stairs. She pauses at the base, glancing back at Jim, who remains stationary. "*Wooooowoooowooo Wooooowoooo.*"

"Right." He follows her up the stairs and to the room where the skill saw's buzz wanes.

"Jim!" Dillon hollers.

Jim nods, the skill saw too much to compete with.

"What brings you by?" Dillon says, removing a face mask and goggles.

"I have those papers for you to sign."

"I could've come by your place."

"I needed to get out of the house."

"Let's go downstairs." Dillon fans the dust that circulates around them.

Miles leads the guys downstairs and peels off for the front door at the sound of a car pulling up in front.

"Hungry?" Dillon says.

"I'm good," Jim says, setting his briefcase on the kitchen island.

"You look so official."

"Old habits."

He pulls out the documents Dillon needs to sign for setting up the BR&B with Jim's accounting service. Dillon signs each page where Jim has stuck a yellow Post-it "Sign Here" arrow. Papers neatly stacked and placed back in the briefcase, Jim snaps it shut.

"What's next on your schedule?" Dillon says.

"Nothing really. Other than an easy run to loosen up before tomorrow's race, that's about it."

"I have about four more hours of work. Then I was going to head out for an easy eight if you want to stop by later."

Jim considers it. "Need an extra hand?"

Dillon glances toward the staircase, then the front door when Miles pads in. "Well . . ."

"It's the RERC Room, right?"

"Yeah."

"It'd be nice to help out on it."

"*Wooooowooowooo Wooooowoooo.*"

"You know, I could use an extra hand."

"Wise dog."

Dillon prepares a food plate, shares it with Jim, checks in two guests to the Tokyo Room—apologizing to them in advance for the construction noise, discounting their room rate and giving them a pair of tickets to a comedy show at the LBC (Luther Burbank Center)–and ventures up to the RERC Room. Jim slips on the sweatshirt and an old baggy pair of overalls Dillon offers him to protect his old-habit work clothes.

Dillon works the skill saw when Jim shies away from it, preferring instead to nail up the sheetrock along one of the remaining bare framed walls. Work gloves snugly fitted, Jim tentatively picks up the hammer, adjusting his grip to the weight. It has been many years since Jim wielded a hammer, or any home-improvement tool for that matter. Junior high, to be exact. He wanted to take wood shop at the time but his dad said no, worried that it was "too dangerous of an activity with simple public education supervision." So Jim compromised, deciding to build a tree house in their home's backyard where his dad could supervise.

Young Jim excitedly drew up the plans, but from day one, the less-than-perfect design gave rise to many questions from his dad. Would the tree support the weight? What would the maximum occupancy be? Did he allow for the growth of the tree? Had he considered permits to build the structure? Jim simply wanted to build *something*, anything. Instead it was the Pinewood Derby all over again: dad taking over the project that was meant for Jim, fretting over the minutiae.

Eventually they did start on the tree house, all initial questions and concerns addressed adequately enough, if not profusely. After playing "Dad's little helper" in setting up the platform frame and laying down the flooring, Jim exercised his will to do some real work. His first task was to cut the 2 x 4 studs to the proper length for the wall framing. Enter the skill saw. Jim watched his dad demonstrate; one then two then three then four studs were sized before Jim got his chance. He aligned his body as his dad had once the skill saw was in hand, but as Jim readied to fire it up his dad offered additional advice. "Stand a little closer. Now, angle your arm like this. Bend your right knee more. Okay, focus on the mark I penciled. Nice and smooth." As the tweaks and adjustments overwhelmed Jim, his dad had actually taken the skill saw from Jim's eager hands before he had a chance to turn it on, and demonstrated again, and again, and again, until all the studs had been cut.

Next, the hammer. Jim watched and listened to his dad give detailed instructions on how to hammer a nail into the framing. Jim felt confident in his ability, grasped the hammer in one hand, readied the nail with the other hand, preparing to swing the hammer downward until he noticed his dad cringing, ready to dole out additional corrections.

"*Wooooowooowooo Wooooowooo.*"

"What?" Jim says, catching Dillon's stare.

"You okay?"

Thwack! The nail pierces the sheetrock and into the stud "All good." *Thwack! Thwack! Thwack!* And just like that the nail rests perfectly indented, ready for drywall compound to give it a smooth finish once painted.

Dillon cuts the remaining sections of sheetrock and Jim hammers them up. Once taped and mudded, they move on to installing two new windows, hanging a thicker door than what was previously there, and laying down new tile in the bathroom. Though Jim's un-callused office hands develop blisters toward the end, he doesn't mind or complain one bit. The manual labor feds his inner desire to move about freely, offsetting the career that has little creativity to it and shackles his body to a chair.

The room structurally complete and lastly in need of paint and Sonoma County ambience, Dillon and Jim knock off for the day, whistle for Miles, and head out to Percy's Loop to shake out their days, discussing the next day's race, Jim citing Jake's love of the course, which can possibly push them over the top in beating the Agras.

Saturday Morning
Dipsean XC Challenge, China Camp

Crack!

The start reminds Jake of the Dipsea stairs in Mill Valley: bodies scrunched together, all vying for the precious feet that exist from left and right. As a Dipsea scratch runner, Jake contends with dozens of handicapped waves ahead of him. And now, on a fire trail no wider than a park ranger's truck, Jake finds himself jostling for space in much the same manner as on the 688 Dipsea stairs, following the rest of the RERC squad across the start line and moderate upward slope, which further compresses the hundred-plus starters.

Jake shows no concern, however. Many years of running the Dipsea has seasoned him; he simply assumes the role of Zen master, letting the pent-up energy around him burst like the Big Bang, and waits for the contraction. With their speed, Dillon and Chase have gotten out clean with the leaders. Jim is sandwiched in the middle of the thick bunch, though his right-arm flair creates a little space on that side. Years of marathon training regimen leaves Spencer without much explosive speed, so he cruises mere rows up on Jake as they reach the picnic area, where the race will ultimately conclude, a cacophony of cheers from fellow club members greeting them.

While some surge to improve their position toward the short single-file bridge up ahead, Jake remains passive, waiting until the *real* portion of the race begins, just beyond the bridge. And with that, a quick left onto and right off the wooden structure, Jake reaches into his Dipsea bag of tricks and skirts along the edge of the single-track trail, more times than not just off-trail, crunching through dry leaves and other autumn debris, slipping by a string of runners caught completely off guard, those in lockstep with the person in front of them, as if riding a crowded escalator.

By the time his first ramble ends, slipping back onto the trail proper, he's moved up some twelve spots, his sights set on the next pack. With the trail rising it doesn't take long to catch them, and once again, where the trail curves, Jake slips to the outer edge while others hug the inside line, establishing position and working on the next *trammel*, as Jake refers to the runners he approaches and passes.

"Trammels?" Chase asked quizzically the first time he'd raced with Jake. Yes, trammels: fluid variations in nature impeding freedom of movement. Of course Chase didn't quite understand, despite Jake patiently explaining the concept during a Sunday run.

After dispatching a handful of trammels, Jake reaches the summit and stretches out his made-for-downhill-running legs, keeping pace with the next trio who probably think they have their current positions secure where the course shunts to the right onto a tight, partially overgrown trail that dumps out into a parking lot. But before they reach the pavement, Jake deftly bushwhacks his way by all three men, his momentum, once on solid and unobstructed asphalt, gaps the three trammels with little effort.

Minutes along flat asphalt, the one blight to the nearly perfect course, Jake floats, uninspired, neither moving up nor falling back. With a vast expanse of visibility, Jake regards those farther up where the road winds and disappears back onto the trails, spotting Jim battling a small pack of runners. Spencer isn't in view; most likely a trammel victim.

When the asphalt gives way to trails, Jake regains harmony with nature and slips by trammels here and there, around blind corners, over fallen tree branches strewn just off the trail, down log steps. They cross another wooden bridge and head up the hardest and trickiest section of the course, the switchbacks, where rhythms stutter, except for Jake who uses the tight 180-degree turns to his advantage, practically flinging himself around them by grasping tree branches or the occasional thinner tree trunk rooted in the turn's crease, his legs churning to keep up. Each switchback, utilizing what's available to assist in his ascent, he gaps those on the tiers below him and beats a path to those in front.

Jim once told Jake his trail running style captures the essence of parkour, the art of displacement, constantly in tune with his surroundings, using anything and everything to maintain constant motion with minimal slowing. It embodies freedom, playfulness, adaptability. Truer words have never been spoken on the section of the course Jake now journeys along, several minutes of hard-banking left-hand turns laid out like creases on a ruffled curtain, skirting along the base of a ridge, putting philosophy into practice and adding precious yards on the trammels behind him.

Over and over, Jake plays this out until the course reconnects with the outbound section, now heading back to the finish. What Jake lacks in speed he more than makes up for in embracing lactic-acid buildup. The broad grin people often speak of on Jake's face toward the end of races is nothing more than anguish that he revels in, so Spencer surmised a time or two. It's truly remarkable that someone can take such great pleasure in anaerobic debt. Thrive on it, really: air rushing through the lungs, burning sensation in the leg muscles, racing perilously toward utter exhaustion. "Envious" is the word Spencer has expressed regarding it.

The last summit reached and nothing but downhill remaining, Jake channels the final minutes of his Dipsea experience, blinders intact, scenery beyond trammels blurred, leaving nothing on the course. At a trailhead crossing stand fellow club members.

"Way to go, Jake!"

"Get that guy!"

"You have fifty yards on Agras's fourth man!"

"Come on, Spencer! Hang with Jake. You guys can win this!"

Sweeping swiftly in a state of near free fall past another trammel whose short legs plead no contest in matching Jake's longer ones, the first rambunctious sounds of the finish area filter through the trees to his left. The last wooden bridge comes into view, Jake's approach visualized in his mind, and with fluid motion he crosses the dry creek bed, the finish line in sight.

"Kick, Jake! Only fifty to go!"

"Dig, baby!"

"Wooooooooo!"

The urgent *crunch, crunch, crunch* of gravel crescendos behind him above the cheers as his earthly limitations bring him back to reality, lacking a kick, though it hardly matters, bliss written across his face despite two runners, then Spencer, slipping by him right before the finish line.

Jake comes to a complete stop, eyes bulging, and wheezing like a steam-engine whistle. He grabs the string of flags flanking him for unsteady support and proceeds along. Between gasps he hears someone behind him quip, "Good thing we only run this course . . . once a year." The guy pats Jake on the shoulder.

"Awesome performance, my friend!" Chase says as Jake stumbles out from the chute.

Dillon grabs and steadies Jake, guiding him off to the side, where Spencer is hunched over, furiously spitting.

"How'd you . . . guys do?" Jake asks, voice raw, glassy eyes on Dillon and Chase.

"Second and fifth," Chase says, pointing to Dillon then himself.

"You and Spencer finished twelfth and thirteenth," Dillon says. "That includes unattached, though."

Jake raises his eyebrow toward Jim.

"Eighth."

"You're moving up," Jake says.

Spencer hacks, and hacks again. "Our score will be tough"—another hack for good measure—"to beat today."

This brings smiles and a subtle swagger to the group's gait as they saunter over to the table where the host club, the Dipseans, passes out commemorative glass mugs that will be filled with a local brew once their warm-down has been completed to go along with stories about their respective races, trammels and all.

Saturday Evening
Trick or Tweet and Buzz

"Come on, girls," Linda hollers from the front door of the Dearborn homestead. "We're going to be late."

"*Tweet, tweet, tweet,*" Robyn sings, skipping though the living room in full costume.

"*And buzz, buzz, buzz,*" her friend Shelby says in concert, decked out as well and skipping right behind Robyn.

"Let's go, Mom," Robyn says, passing through the front door, careful not to clip her wings.

"We don't want to beeeeeeee late," Shelby says, performing the same acrobatics and giggling.

"Jake?! Where are the keys to the minivan?"

"Right here," Jake says, sauntering out from the kitchen.

Linda can't contain her laugh as Jake strolls up to her attired as Tom Sawyer, chewing on a dry reed of grass.

"Why, Becky Thatcher," Tom says in a drawl that sounds less Tom Sawyer and more Sean Connery, "don't you look all fetching and whatnot."

"Why, thank you, Tom," Linda says as she curtsies. "We best get a move on if we're to make the dance on time."

"I reckon you're right, Bessie." Tom juts his elbow out so that Linda can slide her arm through. "Shall we? Later let's wander into a cave and see what kind of trouble we can get into."

Staying in character, Tom professes his love for Bessie and implores her to marry him while Robyn and Shelby work on their trick-or-treat routine as the minivan shuttles them over to Dillon's Haunted BR&B party, a small gathering of the Sunday crew, guests staying the night, and other RERC members with little ones. Once parked, the cast of characters pile out, clambering up the steps to the porch, where Miles stands, her neck adorned with numerous glow necklaces and gazing at the decorative scarecrow sitting on the nearby rocking chair. Miles turns her attention toward the arriving guests.

"*Wooooowoooowooo Wooooowoooo.*"

Robyn spies Miles's multicolored neck and bends over to examine it. "Oh, cool! Shelby, check out—"

"Howdy!" shouts the decorative scarecrow as it jumps up from its seated position.

The girls scream and reel backward, which sends Miles running into the inn, while a laughing Linda buries her face in Jake's chest, who stands bemused at the sight of Dillon the scarecrow.

Dillon laughs like Jake has never seen him laugh before: unfiltered, unrestrained.

"This way," Dillon says, gesturing ahead of him and strutting in stilted fashion, entering the Haunted BR&B that has transformed from a country inn into a spooky affair, complete with cobwebs hanging from the ceiling timbers; candlelit, carved-out pumpkins glowing throughout; and furniture draped with white sheets.

Robyn and Shelby's initial start morphs into giggles as they follow Dillon inside, taking in all the Halloween decorations with plenty of oohs and ahs.

"Let me guess," Dillon says, placing a hand on his chin and rubbing it theatrically while he views Robyn, "Rudolph the Red-Nosed Reindeer with wings, and you're"—he tilts his head toward Shelby—"a yellow marshmallow Peep."

"Nooooo!" Robyn and Shelby say in unison.

"Okay, okay, let's see . . . I know, a red tomato and a bruised banana?"

"Nooooo!" the girls say, a pitch higher than before.

"I'm a red *Robyn*." Robyn says, flapping her arms like a bird. "Get it?"

"And I'm a bumblebee," Shelby says, twirling around to show off her pear-shaped, yellow-and-black-striped costume.

"We're tweet, tweet, tweet, and buzz, buzz, buzz," Robyn proudly announces.

Dillon chuckles and gives Jake and Linda a scarecrow look, scratching his floppy hat.

Jake returns a Lord-love-a-duck nod.

"Birds and bees, oh my!" Dillon says, turning to pour them each a glass of sweet red liquid that foams. "Here's some ghoulish nectar for you."

"What do you say, girls?" Linda says.

"Thank you, Dilly," Robyn says after she's stuck her nose near the concoction and taken a whiff.

"Thank you," Shelby says after she's taken a slurp. "What is it?"

"The blood of an Englishman!" Dillon says, raising his scarecrow hands into the air and waving them up and down.

"Ewww," the bird and bee tweet and buzz.

"Muah-ha-ha-ha," Dillon belts out. "And what can I offer Tom and Becky?"

"Something stronger than the blood of Englishman," Jake says.

"Right this way."

After Dillon proffers Jake and Linda their adult beverages, he leads them and the girls over to the kitchen nook, where diffuse moonlight sheets the windows. Miles tags along.

"I want you to meet someone special," Dillon says, stepping up to the backside of a tall woman peering out the window, her pale shoulders exposed in a tattered white Victorian dress. "The witch of the place."

The woman spins around, shooting a fleeting pasty-faced frown behind a white veil toward Dillon before her eyes twinkle and greet the rest.

Shelby steps back, bumps into the adults, and squeals.

"*Wooooowooowooo Wooooowoooo.*"

"You don't *look* like a witch," Robyn says. "Daddy, she doesn't look—"

"Pleased to make your acquaintance, Miss Havisham," Jake says, tipping his straw hat.

"Charmed, I'm sure."

"And this is my soon-to-be-wife, Bessie."

Linda curtsies.

"And who do we have here?" Miss Havisham bends down toward the bird and the bee.

Shelby takes flight and buzzes from the nook.

"But Daddy, she doesn't look like a witch!" Robyn tugs at the handkerchief dangling from the back pocket of his tatty overalls.

"She could be the Good Witch," Linda says.

"In a scary dress?"

"Is your spirit filled with guardianship, vengeance, or repentance tonight?" Jake asks Miss Havisham.

"She antagonizes me *like* a witch," Dillon says to Robyn, whose return look of pursed lips and furrowed eyebrows casts doubt on the scarecrow's brain activity.

"You nixed my Norman Bates and Jack Torrance costume ideas," the woman retorts, her hands on her slender hips.

"Scary movie motel references . . ." Jake says. "I like her."

"See, Sawyer gets it," the witch says.

Robyn decides the self-amusing adults are a literary buzzkill and takes flight to track down Shelby.

Dillon introduces the witch/not a witch. "Jake, Linda, this is my sister, Dana."

"Nice to meet you," Linda says. "I didn't realize Dillon had a sister." She turns toward Jake. "Did you?"

Jake shrugs.

"Men!" Miss Havisham shouts, chortling.

Jake grins while Dillon rolls his eyes.

The adults rejoin the growing crowd in the main room to find Jim and Doris dressed as Raggedy Ann and Raggedy Andy. Much teasing and joking ensues until the front door flings open and a warlike rebel yell ripples through the room.

"Look!" Dillon says. "It's Tarzan and Jane!"

"Of course Chase wore a shirtless costume!" Doris says, shaking her stringy red hair.

"You know, I didn't realize it until now, but they make a cute pair, he and Terri," Dillon says. "Neither one of them ever wears much clothing."

"Lord love—" Jake says of Jane's costume, catching an elbow to the ribs from a jealous Linda.

"A duck—" Jim ekes out before his ribs, too, endure a blunt force from a not so raggedy Doris.

"They're minimalists!" Dillon proclaims, handing Chase an adult beverage and Terri a ginger ale.

"Chase wears more tech than clothes half the time," Jim says.

"And they say people resemble their pets," Chase says of Jim and Doris. "But in your case . . ."

More couples arrive with their children and the scarecrow introduces them to his wicked sister while the rest mingle and Robyn and Shelby perform their tweet, tweet, tweet, and buzz, buzz, buzz routine several times, flittering in and around the guests. The guys discuss their race that morning with other club members, making mention that with today's narrow margin of victory they are on track to possibly beating the Agras for the grand prix series. All agree that would be impressive. At some point Spencer and Maggie make an appearance as Paulie Bleeker and a very pregnant Juno; the irony is lost on no one. Of course Dale shows up, dressed as nothing in particular, though soon enough Chase dubs Dale "Father Time."

"Hey, Dillon?" says the Athens Room guest, standing under the arch to the media lounge.

"Yeah, Dean," Dillon says, interrupting his conversation with Dana and Jake.

"I think I found an old YouTube video of you racing in the state championships from high school. Did you race for Corona del Mar High?"

"Go Sea Kings!"

"Come take a look."

"This should be interesting," Dillon says, following Dean, along with Dana, Jake, Chase, and others nearby who've caught the conversation.

Paused on the TV screen is a middle-distance shot from the grandstand alongside a collegiate-grade track with two runners doing battle some fifty yards in front of the rest of the field.

"Yep, that's me"—Dillon lowers his voice to a whisper that only Jake hears—"about to place second yet again."

Dean rewinds the feed sixty seconds and hits Play. Loud voices shriek across the media lounge to shaky images. A bell rings shortly before the two front-runners cross the start/finish line, signaling the final lap for the 3,200-meter CIF event from 2000.

"Look at that hair!" Spencer says, howling as laughter shakes the room.

"Man, you were so skinny back then . . . like a scarecrow," Chase says, spawning more laughter as Dillon flaps his straw arms wildly around.

Everyone watches as Dillon and the other runner, Eric, a Laguna Beach standout who hadn't lost a race all season, hit the back stretch side by side, Dillon on the outside and starting to nudge ahead. The crowd and camera elevate while the two runners duke it out, gliding into the final turn, the noise level rising with louder and louder frantic screams.

Confident and in command, young Dillon has a step on the other runner, but as the final fifty yards play out, Dillon fades, and when the duo reaches the line, the Laguna Beach runner leans forward and nips Dillon for the state championship title.

The room doesn't exactly fall silent, but a subtle collective sigh ensues, a certain expectation unmet. Jake turns and notices Dana rubbing her brother's back.

The video doesn't end right away, and it follows Dillon for another couple minutes as he congratulates the winner, who pats Dillon on the back and moves on to celebrate and take on the news media circling him. An out-of-breath and defeated Dillon mills around the finish line area, shaking hands with the next several runners who cross the line. He works his way toward the camera, giving a halfhearted smile upon noticing the camcorder. He gives a Siskel & Ebert–style one thumb up, one thumb down and says, "Wish I could say 'there's always next year,' but I can't." The feed cuts out.

"Tough race," Chase says, breaking the subdued mood. "What were you guys's times?"

"It was 8:49."

"Holy shit!" Chase says.

"Chase!" Doris says.

"Sorry. No need to be ashamed, buddy"—he gives Dillon a backslap—"your hair probably slowed you down like a parachute during the kick."

"Runner-up isn't always a bad thing," Dillon says. "Buzz Aldrin was the second man to walk on the moon."

The majority of the group vacates the media lounge. Dillon follows the crowd and resumes his hosting duties while Jake hangs back with Dana.

"It seems Dillon's more animated tonight than usual," he says. "Either he loves Halloween or he's glad you're in town."

"Probably a little bit of both," she says. "He's generally reserved when he's not taking care of others. I'm glad he found the club. He does love being a part of a team."

"I thought perhaps the divorce weighed upon him."

"It did," she says, watching her brother as he chases the bird and the bee around the living with a broom. "Our parents never wanted kids, so when Dillon came along the grandparents ended up doing a lot of babysitting. I popped out a year later, and the grandparents sat our parents down and told them they needed to raise us. That was a disaster. Dillon was more than just a big brother to me. He felt the need to take care of me, often at a sacrifice . . ." Her voice trails off, glancing at the TV screen that is now blank as Dean cues up another video.

Jake gazes out into the living area, where Dillon refills drinks and entertains guests, sensing a communal family that fills a deep hole in his life. "I was referring to him and his ex."

"Oh! He told you about *her*?"

"A little, not much."

"Yeah, that sent him *running* for sure," Miss Havisham says with a vengeful smile.

By midnight the cast of costumes has departed, inn guests have retired, and the BR&B rests hauntingly quiet after hours of ghoulish activity. Dillon works his way around the living room, picking up cups, bottles, and half-full bowls of snacks while Miles follows in hopes of dropped leftovers, ready to call dibs. Dana attempts to clear items from end tables but Dillon chases her off to go get cleaned up and relax. When she returns, her natural long hair and Scandinavian complexion replacing her costume, the living room is reverted back to normalcy except for the glowing jack-o'-lanterns.

"Get enough hot water?" Dillon says.

"Plenty," she says, carrying dishes from her room. She loads them into the dishwasher.

"Hungry?"

"I'm *fine*, Dillon." She leans up against the counter. "You have some nice friends."

"They're a good bunch."

"Jake said you're racing well."

Dillon hands her a bowl of Neapolitan ice cream, motioning for her to follow and take a seat on the couch in the living area, where Miles has given up on her scrap-food hunt and retired to the floor rug. "I put in a lot of miles over the summer while working on this place. Then I ran into Jake one day at the park and . . . well it's been nice." The first scoop numbs his lips.

Dana samples the three-flavored frozen dessert. "Just like when we were kids. You always gave me an extra scoop."

Dillon smiles. "But you could never finish it and *I'd* have to."

"I knew what you were doing," she says. "But I liked it."

"Do you have to head out tomorrow?"

Her mouth full, she nods before answering. "I'm leading a hike to Machu Picchu next weekend."

"You can always move here and help me if you're *bored* with the adventure world."

"We did always talk about teaming up to do something epic," she says, glancing around the room. "Your idea for staging summer running camps around the country had potential . . . but this place certainly suits you; more entertaining, less babysitting."

Spoons clinks near-empty bowls and Miles lets out a vocal yawn.

"You ever going to call her back?"

Dillon places his bowl on the coffee table, gazes at a candle whose shrinking wick flickers in a pool of hot wax, and fiddles with his costume, removing the floppy hat. "Don't see the point. Everything is final. Time to move on."

Dana leans forward and hands her bowl to him with a scoop of childhood memory still left in it. "I know she screwed you over the way she did, and there's no excuse for it, but . . ."

Dillon pauses mid-scoop. "But . . ."

"*But* ignoring the problem is only making it worse."

"What problem? I don't have a problem."

She peers at him, the same confrontational expression that drove him crazy as a teenager when he would duck out during intense parental squabbles.

Dillon splits the remaining ice-cream scoop in half, spooning and nursing it.

"You need to recognize you had a hand in the marriage's demise, or at the very least forgive her for cheating on you so you can *really* move on, because running away to a remote town, throwing yourself into a huge project, and racking up tons of miles isn't allowing you forget, now is it? I mean really, 'metaphorical death'?"

"*Wooooowoooowooo Wooooowoooo.*"

Dillon stares at Dana, wondering who gave him away. "Chase? Jake?" When she doesn't answer, he polishes off the rest of the ice cream, sets one bowl in the other, and sighs. "Yeah, I know."

"And what's with the scarecrow costume?"

"You know, out in the country, scaring people off."

"It is pretty *country* out here."

"I like the simplicity; less stress than back home."

"Until it becomes the new norm. Even in simplicity lies complexity and new things to *run* away from."

"Yes, Confucius."

"Who's this Kate I heard about?" Dana says with a coy tone.

Dillon rolls his eyes. "This is why friends are a bad thing," he says with a hearty unbridled laugh.

Sunday Morning
Go Big or Go Home

"Did I hear someone say back at the inn that you're a running coach?" asks Jeremy, a thirtysomething guest staying in the Helsinki Room. He has joined the guys—minus Dillon, who's preparing breakfast with Dana—on their Sunday run under a foggy canopy. And though the sun breaks through here and there in mystical fashion it doesn't provide enough warmth for Chase to go shirtless. Jim remarks that he's surprised to see Winter Chase before Thanksgiving; Summer Chase must be getting soft. Chase ignores the comment.

"High school cross-country," Spencer says.

"Very cool. Hey, I had a—"

Spence-speak.

Chase and Jim have pulled on the rest of the group after they crossed over into the vineyards. "Sorry. You were saying?" Spencer says once the pace has been reined in to accommodate Jeremy's slower pace they *all* agreed to run for the early miles to show him around.

"Oh, yeah, so I started running a couple months ago and my goal is to run the Walt Disney World Marathon in January."

Spencer's placid expression masks his attitude toward the notion, a beginning runner shooting for a marathon so quickly, just ten weeks out. It's too ambitious for someone with no endurance background, and is moderately overweight to boot. Best to get lean, build a foundation, and shoot for a reasonable distance like a 5K or 10K before moving up to longer distances.

"I found two training schedules online but I can't decide which one to use."

"Doesn't matter," Spencer says, anticipating Jeremy's question, the group running through a sunlit patch of ground until fog envelops them again. "I wouldn't get too wrapped up in complex training details right now. *Any* running you do will make you faster at this point. How many days are you running?"

"Three to five, depending on work."

"Keep it simple. Make one weekend day your long run, like you're doing today, another day during the week where your pace varies, such as fartlek, and the rest easy. Do that for several months to let your body adapt, adding a mile each week to your long run."

Jeremy plods along, his breathing more labored than it should be for a long run, but he's keeping up. "Will that get me ready for a marathon? What about tempo runs and base and speed workouts and—?"

"Those are effective for runners who have more experience behind them. Call them advanced workouts, if you will, a goal to work up to, not jump into right off the bat. That invites injury."

"But the online schedules say that I need to run a twenty-miler before I can do a marathon."

"Do you want to just *do* a marathon and check it off your bucket list, or do you want to make running a part of your life?"

"I want both?"

Spencer wishes he had a Spence-speak for unrealistic goals. He vows to work on one. "I wouldn't recommend starting off with a marathon. Enter a 5K or 10K and work your way up to a half marathon, *then* a marathon. Let your body—"

"The marathon is where it's at," Jeremy says. "Telling my friends I did a 5K or half of something isn't going to sound as impressive as 'I ran a marathon.' I want one of those '26.2' stickers for my car."

"I heard some running stores won't sell those stickers unless you can prove you ran a marathon," Chase says.

"Really?" Jim says. "People who aren't racecar drivers buy sports cars."

As a high school teacher, a high school running coach, and a long distance runner, Spencer has patience in spades. But Jeremy's not-uncommon mindset vexes him.

"In that case, I'd recommend joining one of those team-and-training or paid training groups back home. They'll provide a rudimentary and basic approach that should get you through your first marathon."

"Naw. I'm a do-it-yourself kind of guy," Jeremy says, and explains what he knows about the two online training methods, asking Spencer which one is best.

"I really can't, in good conscience, recommend either one for you, Jeremy."

"I see. But if you *had* to choose between them . . . which one?"

Spencer sighs. Chase and Jim snicker up front, holding their pace in check purely for entertainment reasons. Even Jake, running on the other side of Jeremy, has a grin going.

"What do you like about running?" Jake asks the guest runner, his first words of the morning as the fog thins and sun rays filter through stronger and brighter.

"Being able to tell my friends I ran a marathon."

"Follow your bliss, my friend—"

"I'd choose the one that suits your personality the best," Spencer says, hoping to wrap the conversation up. "If you like very specific, complex things in your everyday life, choose the method that appeals to that. If you prefer less structure, go with that one."

"Oh, okay. I like that! Thanks."

And with that, Chase and Jim pull again, and instead of objecting, Spencer bids Jeremy "good luck" and shuffles forward, content that Jake will show Jeremy around the property in Dillon's absence.

"Hey, Coach," Chase whispers, sun rays unfettered and his shirt wrapped around his waist, "my name is Forrest, Forrest Gump. I want to run across the country . . . do I need to train for that?"

"Why people want to *go big or go home* is beyond me."

"Marathon or bust," Jim says. "It adds nobility to the pursuit."

"Naw, it's binge mentality," Chase says. "Millennials have the attention span of gnats."

"Not us," Jim says.

"Of course not."

"Can't forget peer pressure," Spencer says.

"Whatever you call it, it does invite injury," Jim says. "I like Jake's theory that ninety-nine percent of all running injuries stem from doing *too* much."

"Did you know Linda buys Jake's running shoes from Redwood Shoe Emporium, the discount place?" Chase says. "They're not recognizable brands."

"They set themselves up for failure from the get-go. But hey, if it makes them feel like rock stars, then, like Jake said, 'Go for it,' I suppose," Spencer says with a certain amount of resignation, turning in the direction of the BR&B, the fog completely lifted, forcing him to squint into the rising sun.

"Koala Tracks," Jim says. Chase and Spencer glance Jim's way. "Jake's shoes."

"Koalas don't run. They sit around and eat all day," Chase says. "That's terrible branding."

"But cute," Jim says.

Chase shrugs. "Good point."

"Last month I was talking with a new club member," Spencer says, still grinding an ax about training misconceptions, "and he asked me to draw up a 2:45 marathon schedule, as if I were a doctor writing a prescription. Here you go. Take one daily and drink plenty of water."

"They're idiots," Chase says. "I occasionally run into this guy at the track on Tuesdays and he goes on and on about all the stuff he does *beyond* what his training program calls for. I finally had enough and told him he lacked discipline, and he got all defensive and went on about how he ran every day and lifted every other day, blah, blah, blah, 'I'm the most disciplined guy I know.' I told him that's not discipline . . . that's dedication. Discipline is sticking to what is called for."

"I blame ego," Spencer says. "Just because you *can* do something, it doesn't mean you should throw caution to the wind."

"*Spider-Man*," Jim says.

"That's a stretch," Chase says.

Jim shrugs.

"That's the biggest issue I see with newbies," Spencer says. "They go out and do too much too early. Everything seems fine at first, but after a month or two problems crop up and they're like, 'Everything was fine then this or that started aching.'"

"Whatever happened to the guy who raced for us a couple years ago?" Chase says.

Jim and Spencer express no recognition.

"You know, the one who had, like, five different sports doctors on speed dial?"

"*That* guy . . . he's a cyclist now," Spencer says. "He shredded his hamstrings."

"Not to poke holes in your theory, Spence," Chase says, "but sometimes it takes throwing a dozen eggs at a wall to find the one that doesn't crack."

Spencer can appreciate Chase's summation in pushing the envelope for human endurance limits. And certainly at the world-class level athletes constantly straddle the tenuous line between extreme fitness and injury, perpetually a day away from breaking a world record or nursing a stress fracture. But, and this is what frustrates Spencer to no end, it's not the mentality that should drive the recreational runner, risking injury and being left sidelined, unable to participate. Wearing an injury badge of honor holds no honor—or long-term health benefits, for that matter.

The trio returns to the BR&B to find Jeremy showing Dillon the online marathon training schedules spoken of earlier, asking him which one he'd recommend. Spencer shakes his head, catches Dillon's eye, and gives a silent and consoling Spence-speak, which puts a smile on Dillon's face.

Seated around the kitchen island, food streaming from prep table to place mats, Spencer finds himself embroiled in another annoying conversation about online information for runners, this time about predictive models that show runners what times they can run at certain distances based on past race performances at other distances.

Posed by a guest from the Tokyo Room, the question drifts around the kitchen while Spencer chews a bite from his oversized cinnamon roll, melted butter dripping onto the plate. He glances around at the Algonquin Round Table, eyes pleading for backup, but they enjoy watching Coach Spencer sit in the hot seat.

"So, there are many assumptions left out of those models," Spencer says.

"You're saying I *can't* run a sub-2:35 marathon based on my sixteen-minute 5K?"

"Hard to tell, since I don't know anything about you, but what the formulas leave out are the runner's genetic or physiological makeup. Every runner has one, maybe two, 'distance sweet spots.' And those can be mental, physical, or both. If the 5K is your sweet spot, your body, or your mind, may not be suited to run a 2:35 marathon. Doesn't mean you *can't* run a marathon, just that *that* time goal may be unrealistic."

Spencer slices off another chunk of cinnamon roll before a rebuttal forms, and somewhere in the mix Dillon offers backup. "I would use those calculators as incentive to try other distances, but keep in mind that the absolute times aren't specific to *your* circumstances."

"How about those guys who've run a sub-4 mile *and* a sub-2:10 marathon," Jim says. "Talk about two *sweet* spots."

"It's a small club. Twenty, I think," Spencer says.

"Twenty-one if you include Quenton Cassidy," Dillon says.

Smiles and nods follow from those recognizing the cult classic, fictional character from John Parker's three novels.

"Lost in translation," Jake says. "The real issue with the Internet is that it only provides information sans context. It should be the start of a larger interpretive conversation."

That quells or confuses the stream of questions from the inquisitive lot around the island, allowing Spencer to enjoy the rest of his cinnamon roll in peace.

"At the end of the day . . . 'Just Do It,'" Chase says with an ear-to-ear grin that cracks everybody up except for Doris.

"Why's that funny?" Doris says.

"Let's go, Doris," Jim says.

"But it's *not* funny . . ."

	Club	Total
	PA/USATF TOP 5 TEAM STANDINGS AS OF 11/01/2015	
1	Agras (10-9-10-10-9)	48
2	RERC (9-x-9-9-10)	37
3	Chico Running Club (8-10-8-8-x)	34
4	Strawberry Hill Harriers (7-7-7-5-7)	33
5	South Bay Striders (6-8-4-x-8)	26

Week 44 Training Summary			
	Long Run	Mileage Total	Comments
Dillon	15	54	Getting stronger every week.
Chase	12.23	48	WE BEAT THE AGRAS!!
Spencer	12.50	52	Better leg turnover this week.
Jim	12	55	Sleeping better these days.
Jake	8	61	The colors around the county are majestic.

Week 10
November 2

"Whoa!" Zac exclaims as he, Spencer, and, from time to time, Dillon, watch video in the BR&B's media lounge of other high school cross-country meets from around the country, focusing on likely contenders for the top ten at CIF and Footlocker. "That guy *buried* them on the hill."

"Yes, but how did he do it?" Spencer says.

"Wicked surge."

"The other two surged, but where did Manny drop them?"

"Oh, at the top . . . he didn't slow down and the others did."

"Exactly. Always, I mean *always*, accelerate at the top of a hill and let the summit pull you over. While they're taking a few seconds to recover you'll gap *and* dishearten them. Manny does it very well."

"Gotcha, Coach."

"You guys want anything to eat?" Dillon asks, wandering in. Before Zac can say anything, "Yes, there's more banana bread."

"Sweet!"

"Thanks, but Maggie texted me and has dinner ready to go."

"Sounds good." With the inn's cordless phone in one hand, Dillon strikes a flamingo pose, standing on one leg and using the free hand to stretch the hip flexor of the other leg, folded up behind him.

They'd finished up another "Zac vs. the Big Dogs" run around Percy's Loop an hour earlier. This time Zac showed signs of a seasoned runner, became physical where he needed to, read the moves the others made, adjusting accordingly. His speed had improved since the last time as well, surprising both Dillon and Chase when they made a move to drop him and a hundred yards later Zac said, "Is that all you got?" He received his fair share of smirks and comments from the group, but Zac's playful cockiness pleased Spencer.

"Now, this guy from West Virginia . . . you remember him from last year," Spencer says, pointing to a runner in a purple jersey gliding down a hill, passing the two front-runners as if they were standing still. "He's been beaten twice this year. Had a knee issue early in the season so he's going to be there in the beginning and middle parts of the race, but he won't have the same finish he had last year."

"So watch him, but don't get sucked into his game early on," Zac says.

"Exactly."

"I wish I'd had you for a coach in high school," Dillon says. "My coach was knowledgeable, but cross-country strategy wasn't his forte, track was. So I chased anybody who looked like a threat."

"Mr. Percy, did you run Footlocker?"

"Yep, '99. Runner-up."

"Nice!"

Dillon scrunches his lips and scratches his nose. "You win some and lose some. I'll get the banana bread."

Spencer watches Dillon wander off, stop to greet and check two guests in, gaining a better sense of what makes Dillon tick as a runner, and he understands why Zac has connected with Dillon on some level. The video Spencer watched during the Halloween party of Dillon's second-place finish illustrated a reoccurring theme. And once a theme takes root in a runner's mind it's often hard to shake, like a dormant infection waiting to present when their defenses are down.

"What about Marty, Coach?" Zac says, pointing to a runner who has a huge lead on the field running around a golf course in Florida.

Spencer sizes up the tall, lanky Floridian and peruses his tablet device containing notes on the best high school runners in the country. "He's stronger than last year, but still not a big race guy yet. He runs away in the local and regional meets, but at two big invites this year, Mt. Sac and Greensboro, he finished out of the top ten."

"So don't let his early tactics bother me either?"

"Exactly," Spencer says. "Racing really comes down to this: you can make all the sacrifices you want, put in all the hard training your body can handle, but come race day if you aren't confident in your ability . . . then everything is for naught. Runners often let matters that don't matter creep into their minds during the race if it's not going their way. Some psych themselves out long before the race while watching others warm up. The champions are the ones who set all the mental noise aside and focus on nothing other than competing and the desire to win. Yes, it's going to hurt, but the hurt is what makes it great—"

"*A League of Their Own*," Dillon says, arriving with a half loaf of banana bread in hand, which he passes off to Zac, and a thick slice to Spencer.

Spencer grins. "That's a great coach's speech."

"My coach used to tell me"—Dillon glances at the ringing cordless phone, gives it a disapproving glare, and ignores it—"that we all have a little bit more to give when things are on the line, like squeezing the last bit of toothpaste from the tube. You have to be willing to go inside and find it," he says, doing flamingo pose on the other leg, phone on the floor.

"Seek, and ye shall find," Zac says. "I read that on a bumper sticker once."

"Sure, that works too." Dillon shares other race tactics he's learned over the years—biting his lip when the racing intensity reaches unbearable levels, diverting attention to the new pain—though Spencer tunes out for a moment, mulling over the "tube of toothpaste" metaphor, wishing *his* high school coach had at some point helped him with that aspect. He can tolerate pain and discomfort for many miles, marathon miles, layers upon layers of fatigue stacking up on themselves without respite, but in the final miles he finds it impossible to leave his comfort zone. The qualifying standard dangles like a carrot on the horizon of his mind, taunting him, begging him to break free from his cozy confines, a stepping-stone that can make all the difference in the world in getting to the next level. But he just can't do it. It often nags him, and he lets it get the best of him every time. In workouts, he'll test the waters in a safe environment, peeking into the dark abyss, but at every juncture an impenetrable brick wall stares back at him. Post-race analysis leaves him feeling the would've, could've, should've blues; perhaps next time he'll dive in with both feet. The mind-set, once it takes root in a runner's mind . . . it owns him.

"Late into a race, if someone tries to pass speed up a little, just enough to challenge him without digging too deep. Little surges like that can throw them off and make them doubt themselves," Dillon explains.

"That's what all those mystery fartlek workouts have been about, Zac," Spencer says.

"I love those workouts," Dillon says, now seated on the floor and stretching each piriformis in turn. "It's like a running chess match."

"I've been dying to ask you what method of training you follow," Spencer says.

Dillon grins. "You know, I still consult with my high school coach."

"Really?"

"Yeah, I know that sounds funny, but after college I didn't have an interest in reading up on all the training philosophies out there."

"Do you happen to know what method he follows?"

"I don't. I've never enjoyed the details of training. I like having the workouts given to me, and get to it. I have a conceptual idea of what I'm doing over the course of the season, but I never give it much thought beyond that."

This puzzles Spencer. He has high school runners who hold the same attitude, but they also aren't accomplished runners like Dillon. He clearly runs off guts and intuition.

"What type of intervals would you run?"

"Tons of quarters"—Dillon pauses to take a call, assures the caller it's no problem that their flight has been delayed, he'll be around at midnight when they arrive, and hangs up—"but he'd change up the recovery interval, shorter and shorter as the season progressed. Half-mile repeats. Hill repeats. Lots of hill repeats . . . two minutes' worth of effort. And fartlek."

Spencer can't put a specific label to Dillon's training. It has all the key ingredients, including the all-important Sunday long run, along with a healthy weekly mileage total.

"I'd say he puts together a hybrid plan for me these days. Keeps me in good fitness throughout the year, like on simmer, and when I want to get ready for a series of races he brings me to boil as it were."

"Nice analogy. If you wouldn't mind sharing them, I'd like to review some of your training logs."

Dillon doesn't respond right away. And when he does it shocks Spencer and, to a lesser degree, Zac.

"You've never kept a training log?"

"Nope," Dillon says. "I don't dwell on the past like a *history* teacher . . ."

"Nice one, Mr. Percy!"

Spence-speak.

"Though if I may be so bold, Mr. Percy, one could argue it's you who is stuck in the past," Zac says. "No offense, Coach, but I'd don't see myself seeking your advice when I'm an adult."

"None taken. That's how you grow."

"A little offended," Dillon says.

"He's like that guy you told me about, what's his name, who held the American 10,000-meter record way back when?" Zac says.

"Mark Nenow. He never tracked his training either."

"Less offended," Dillon says. "What about you?"

"I've tracked every mile I've ever run."

"Impressive. A lifetime mileage count might be interesting to have."

"As of last Sunday, I'm at 62,248."

"You've run around the Earth . . . about two and a half times, Coach," Zac says.

"That sounds exhausting. What training plan do you follow?"

"I've tried a few, but I like the Hudson training system. It suits my style of running better than the others. He stresses *progressive* miles where the pace quickens over the course of the run. It's ideally suited for longer races like the marathon."

"The pace *changes* . . . interesting?"

Spence-speak.

"What about Chase? Seems like he's always doing some *very* specific workout that needs to be done at certain times and under specific conditions"—Dillon rises when a couple stops by on their way to the sauna and requests additional towels—"like a Tuesday full moon."

Spencer chuckles and waits for Dillon to return with fresh towels. "Chase loves the Jack Daniels system . . . vDots and all that. He often comes up with his own modified workouts as well. I read the book and found it, like you said, so specific that it seemed too obsessive and compulsive for me."

"That's Chase in a nutshell!"

"Chase is an animal on the track," Zac says.

"*Wooooowooowooo Wooooowoooo.*"

"This dog is *awesome.*"

"I developed a theory that, in many ways, training plans reflect a runner's personality," Spencer says.

"I can see that. If you're going to commit to it for a long period of time you'd better enjoy it." Dillon answers the inn line again, informs the caller that he *can* cater to their vegan dietary needs, hangs up, and sighs. "It's hard to hate something so physically demanding."

"You're like a circus ringmaster," Zac says.

Dillon nods. "Step right up, the *tastiest* breakfast on Earth: asparagus tofu omelet!"

"Add enough salsa . . . perhaps," Zac says.

"I also think some plans work better physically with some runners more than others," Spencer says. "Each runner is different in what they bring genetically to the table, so it's the coach's job to figure out what's best. Most training plans share certain components: long run once a week, two or more quality runs along with easy mileage each week."

"Jake's too good of a runner *not* to follow some kind of plan, but what?

He certainly isn't concerned with mileage and splits."

"Jake doesn't like reducing life down to fine print. He's *loaded* with natural talent and leaves some of it on the table. He does follow a plan, loosely anyway, and keeps a journal of sorts. It's the Lydiard method. Tons of aerobic mileage. And he tosses in burly workouts on the hills, like the sand dunes. He gets his leg speed from downhill running. We joke with him that he's the descendant of Luther Burbank."

"Not familiar with him."

"Really?" Spencer says.

"The russet Burbank potato? Developed during the Irish potato famine?" Zac says.

"Southern California, remember? Fish tacos, palm trees, surfing."

"Babe city!"

Dillon shrugs.

"You've probably seen the name around town on buildings," Spencer says. "Luther Burbank was a prolific horticulturist, among other things, who wasn't interested in spending his time recording the details of what he did. As you can imagine, it frustrated the scientific community."

"Just like Jake. And Jim?"

"Jim probably knows himself better than the rest of us know ourselves, so he puts together a composite of various training plans that suit him. If I had to sum it up, I'd say he runs very few miles at an easy pace. Beyond the warm-up and warm-down he's all business. And as much as I hate to encourage it, it does work for him."

"Goes to show how many ways"—Dillon fetches his ringing cell phone from his pocket, groans, utters "shrew," silences it, and stows it back in his pocket—"there are to be good." He lies flat-out on the floor with his hands behind his head, half leaned up against the couch.

"Coach always likes to say that 'in a group of runners training together, one is doing the correct workout and the others are not,'" Zac says.

"That's right. There are no magic training plans, just a right one for each of us. That's what I love about coaching: finding the right plan for each athlete."

"I received a Facebook message from a coach in Minneapolis today who said I should be doing more hill repeats, long ones, like half mile or more," Zac says nonchalantly while watching the CIF finals from 2014.

Spencer strokes his chin as if he had a goatee, displeased at the need to defend his training program against armchair coaches. *What good do they think it will do, questioning Zac's training, getting inside his head, creating doubt? Call me if you have concerns or advice.* "It's easy to make that type of assessment when they don't have the full picture. Trust in the program and block out the *noise.*"

"Right on," Zac says, finishing off the last of the banana bread. "This stuff rocks, Mr. Percy."

"Yes, Mr. Percy, this *stuff* rocks," Spencer says.

"*Woooooowooowooo Wooooowoooo.*"

"Can I have your dog?" Zac says.

Wednesday Late Afternoon
Sand Dunes

Beep. "How did I let"—Chase lets out a dry cough that sandpapers his throat—"you talk me into this?" He gasps for more oxygen at the top of the sand dune when Jake joins him two seconds later. Both men turn and trundle back down the 18 percent graded slope.

"Track guys, running around artificial surfaces all day long," Jake says, his breathing back in check after the first, roughly hundred-yard, uphill spurt. A gentle breeze off the glimmering ocean under an intense blue sky cools them. "Hills are your friends."

"Too shifty for me."

They reach the base, turn, and charge back up—*beep*—Jake getting a jump on Chase for the first twenty yards until Chase powers by, though near the top he falters, allowing Jake to close the gap.

Beep. "Ack!" Chase hunches over at the top. "Two down." He straightens and joins Jake on the descent. "Thirteen to go."

"You're muscling your way up. You're sapping yourself."

"How else do you work a hill with no firm footing?"

"On the next one don't try to race me. Focus on moving smoothly instead. Get a feel for the terrain and go from there."

"Not. *Race*. You?" Chase says, though inside he's searching for any excuse to scale back his effort. *These are killing me!*

Jake chuckles, performing a U-turn over Chase's foot-drawn line at the bottom that is beginning to blur, much like the one at the top. "Suit yourself," he says, launching into another repeat, leaving Chase behind.

Damn him.

Chase doesn't heed Jake's suggestion, catches Jake and passes him halfway up, assuming the retching pose at the top.

"You'd better pace yourself . . . or you'll never make it to the end. We're not breaking this up into sets like a *wimpy* track workout."

Chase wants to laugh but coughs instead. "Nice try, Sandman . . . but seriously . . . how can you run these . . . and *not* run faster in races?"

"I've never had good speed. I'm more of a mountain goat. The natural terrain, hills, trails, this"—Jake gestures to the surrounding seaside—"they sing to me."

Chase nods subtly, conserving energy.

Again the turn on the beach, another assault up the hill, Jake plants each foot as if he knows a secret path of solid footholds to the top. Meanwhile, Chase restrains his pursuit of Jake, attempting to "find" his way up the hill with less power, and though he catches Jake at the top, he still hunches over and shakes his head. *Beep.* "My quads!"

"Yeah, you're going to feel this workout," Jake says, descending once again. "Any repercussions from your tumble in Tahoe?"

"Not much. Some minor trail rash, stubbed toe, and a sore right elbow, though that could be from Frisbee golf."

Jake chuckles.

"Why aren't you timing these?"

"No need to. It's hard. I'm tired afterward. Job well done."

Chase frowns. "How do you know if your fitness is improving?"

"Don't you *feel* fitter from one season to the next? You don't need data to tell you that."

"Well, sure, I can feel it, but workout data tells me by how much, and motivates me to run the same workout faster in the future, *and* tells me how much faster I should do it."

"Sounds like you're seeking validation."

Beep. They move up the hill, Chase allowing Jake to lead the way toward the clear blue sky.

Beep.

"Is that . . . why you're rarely . . . injured?" Chase says.

"Perhaps. I love running too much to risk injury by extracting every last ounce of fitness so I can race a few seconds faster. If, as they say, sport is ninety percent mental then I can use my mind for those few extra seconds, not my body. No need for fancy workouts, just the basics will suffice."

"Back in college as I was closing in on my first sub-four-minute mile, my coach and I were reviewing my workout and race data and noticed that I had a stronger kick when I backed off on the third lap. Up until that point I always worked the third lap hard, since historically that's where milers tend to lose time. Next race, I eased back two seconds and it allowed me to run four seconds faster on the bell lap, and under four minutes. It became pretty routine after that."

"Sometimes taking a step back allows you to take two steps forward. Nicely done."

The two runners with very different approaches to training work their way through several more binge-and-purge cycles, Chase finding a rhythm that allows him to conserve energy *and* run alongside Jake from bottom to top, though his quads and lungs continue to burn after each repeat, but not enough to complain about.

"How'd Linda's latest date for you go?" Jake says.

"I canceled it," Chase replies as sweat beads transfer from his forehead to his sunglasses. "Too busy." He removes the blurry eyewear, dries them on his shorts, and glances over to Jake. "You ever feel funny with Linda . . . after, say, revealing things about yourself that are personal?"

"Not since we first met. Why?"

"Nothing really . . . I know the guys tease me about my *social* life, but I can't figure out why I wig out after telling a woman personal things about myself."

Beep. Up they charge while young children behind them ask their parents why two grown men are running up and down the hill, the answer left wanting as their legs push them closer to the top and heavy breathing drowns out the curiosity.

Beep. "I hate having the . . . same conversations over . . . and over with someone new."

"Like these hill repeats?"

Chase laughs between deep breaths. "Something like that."

"Vulnerability is tricky. Perhaps you haven't found someone that makes you feel comfortable."

"I keep telling myself that, but I've met some pretty nice women. It makes me wonder."

"And this has something to do with Terri?"

Chase stumbles at the base of the hill. "She does throw me off balance." *Beep.* "One moment I'm cool, revealing a little personal anecdote, the next thing I know, I'm spinning . . . and want to run and hide, but . . . with her I can't seem to . . ."

The hill pushes their conversation aside, reminding them that sand coupled with gravity is a bitch, as Chase puts it.

Beep. ". . . run and hide . . . I find myself reeling when we're together . . . always going back for more. We haven't even slept together."

"Is the sex study contributing to it?"

Chase shrugs. "I don't think so . . . at first maybe."

"Sounds like you're falling for her, and old issues are flooding you with fear."

"Could be. I'd like to know what those *old issues* are."

"You don't have any data on that?" Jake says, turning around at the bottom for their last ascent, waving to a small group that has formed to watch, and in one case, videotape them with a cell phone. No doubt Chase's shirtless torso holds the young woman's attention in the group, the one with the video camera.

Chase grunts at Jake's "data" comment, accelerates past him, and pays for it dearly near the top where Jake cruises by him like an animal that has boundless strength and energy.

"If you . . . say . . . fifteen more . . . I'll unfriend you," Chase spits out, turning to run back down.

"You need to embrace the real world once in a while and leave the watch behind." Jake gestures around him and toward the group at the bottom, where one person has lit up a cigarette. "Technology at the beach is as unnatural as smoking on it."

Puff, puff.

Beep.

Thursday Afternoon
The Client

In his home office, Jim lets the client sitting before him continue unabated with his convoluted rationale about how he should be able to write off his daughter's wedding as a tax deduction because he had invited several important business associates to it, and there had been talk about business-related matters over the course of the afternoon and evening. After the client has made his case, Jim remains quiet, studying the man formally known as Monty, though was informally referred to as "Mr. Let's Make a Deal" back at Bennett Valley Accounting Services. Monty has followed Jim from the old accounting firm, and though Jim wishes at times that Monty hadn't, Jim has to admit that he's heard worse pleas. Like a woman Monroe had passed along. One of the "ankle biters." She felt that since cats had been ruled a legitimate tax deduction in keeping snakes and such from a business owner's property that her dog should be allowed the same deductions—food, care, lodging—by virtue of the same logic because her precious Kismet protected her from intruders while she worked from home. Jim didn't say it out loud but he wondered how protective a miniature Chihuahua could be. *Sic 'em, Kismet. Snag his socks.*

"Okay, so, Monty," Jim says, "that's not going to fly with the IRS. Big red flag."

"But—"

"You can't justify piggybacking a business meeting on your daughter's wedding. Sorry."

Monty sits dejected and genuinely hurt. "I thought since you were on your own you didn't need to follow the firm's rules anymore. You'd have more flexibility."

The Firm . . . Tom Cruise . . . quick, think of a quote . . . I got nothing.

"Actually the IRS is considered 'the firm' in the end, and it's their tax code that I follow."

Monty doesn't look pleased, and based on past encounters, Jim waits for it.

"How 'bout the food and drink and dessert . . . business meal?"

Right, the negotiation. Jim lets his placid expression answer the question.

"Weddings are so damn expensive, you know?" Monty says, exasperated. "Of course you know. You're getting married this weekend. Congratulations on that, by the way. I didn't mean to put a damper on the mood."

"They don't have to be," Jim says, fending off the financial black swans that have swarmed him since striking out on his own. Doris seems at ease and accepting of their situation, a cavalier attitude that is refreshing and comforting for Jim, but at the same time disconcerting. Perhaps she doesn't fully comprehend the situation, though he's painted her a pretty straightforward picture of it, including spreadsheets and a couple PowerPoint presentations with pie charts and projections. She teased him during the presentations, cracked jokes, made him chuckle now and then. Hopefully she understands that things are going to be lean for the foreseeable future. And as if she's been eavesdropping on his thoughts, she appears at the door, making a silly face before she knocks and enters. She says hi to Monty, passes Jim a Post-it note, and hurries out of the office, making yet another funny face at the door. Jim half expects the note to be a message from Jake about their Thursday-evening run, but instead it reads: "Smile. You haven't lost that loving feeling." He does smile, affixing the note to his desk, and readdresses Monty, back on point

"So the wedding is out, but we can write off your gluten-free groceries since it's a medical condition, but not from restaurants, unless you're entertaining clients, then that's a basic business expense."

"Excellent! Where'd we land on deducting my Cessna?"

Jim shakes his head, updating Monty's grocery expense sheet. "It's for personal use. It's not—"

"But I read where a couple justified the purchase of their plane as a means to oversee their rental income condo in another state."

"Do you have rental income or business affairs several states away that I'm not aware of?"

"Well, no, but I'm sure there's wiggle room in there somewhere . . . one of my barns or storage units?"

Jim wants to sigh, but refrains. "Some things do have *wiggle* room, but your Cessna isn't one of them. My job is to maximize your deductions *and* avoid an IRS audit. Items like wedding write-offs and pleasure flying are no-brainers that will land you an audit faster than you can blink, which means they can go back several years . . . before I started doing your taxes. Probably not something you want, based on what you showed me at Bennett Valley Accounting Services."

Monty clasps his hands, eyes cast on them, his expression attempting to negotiate a win for the day.

Jim pulls out his ace in the hole. "But good news. We can write off the babysitting expense for you and your wife's weekly volunteer work at the MS Society. Its nonprofit status allows for it."

"That's great!" Monty exclaims. "What about the pet sitter?"

Jim grins, masking a sigh on the inside, catching sight of the clock on the wall; another hour until he'll be free of Monty and running with Jake. Jim has *The Shawshank Redemption*, *Dave*, and *Midnight Run* movie references ready to go; accountants do win in the end. Sometimes.

Thursday Night
The Shoe Drops

"Back in my day there were two kinds of shoes," says Kinney, the local shoe guru in a mock old-geezer voice years beyond his actual age. "The left shoe and the right shoe."

The small crowd of sixteen in the main room at the BR&B laughs at the fiftysomething balding gentleman dressed in shorts and a crisp running T-shirt, with a deep sun-kissed tan standing up front with various shoe models surrounding him like a harem.

"Needless to say for those of you who are new to running, or are under the age of thirty, running has evolved immensely over the years. When I started running back in '72 there were basically only a couple choices, and those choices would be considered minimalist shoes by today's standards." He pulls out a pair of well-worn shoes, blue with a white crisscross emblem on the side, and holds them up. "These are them, my first training pair, the Onitsuka Tiger Marathon. As you can see, there isn't much to the sole, and as far as structure is concerned . . . forget about it. Ain't none to speak of." He leans to one side and picks up another shoe that resembles an overly inflated clog. "Today," he says, placing his first pair next to the modern pair, "this is what many train in. These are called Hoka One One, the Stinson model. Quite a difference, right?"

The group nods, points, and mumbles.

"So how did we go from this"—Kinney raises the twentieth-century model—"to this?" He raises the twenty-first century model.

Chase glances around the room, and when no one speaks up he says, "More consumers began running whose bodies weren't as efficient as the early adopters to the sport."

Kinney has a stunned grin on his face. "You must've read the book *Born to Run*, or you're a time traveler."

Chuckles circle the room.

"You're mostly correct," Kinney continues, "though running has been around much longer than the '70s, so 'early adopters' is somewhat misguided.

But to your point, those who get involved in any new or obscure activity are often better suited for that activity. And as that activity catches on for whatever reason, when the masses join in, the early equipment no longer meets everybody's needs, and by everybody I mean their bodies. Hence the changes that occurred in the '80s onward by shoe manufactures, after the running boom took hold." Kinney discusses research that employs video analysis and force plates to study running form, how the pendulum swings from one extreme to another in terms of shoe structure and padding, the exceedingly high injury rate among runners no matter where the pendulum is at any given time, and how important it is to receive expert advice when choosing running shoes lest you end up with the wrong type for your feet.

"Is this shoe taken?" The soft whisper of a voice catches Dillon's attention, who stands in back toward the kitchen overseeing the guest speaker's lecture. He glances to his side and smiles.

"If the shoe fits," he says to Kate.

"I'll be the little shoe if you're the big shoe," she responds with a smile and shoulder nudge to his arm.

"What brings you up here?"

"I noticed the banner on your website about the 'shoe guru' speaking tonight. Couldn't miss it."

"He is pretty knowledgeable—" The crowd breaks out into laughter while Kinney has his nose buried deep in a shoe, inhaling a big whiff as if it's a rare bottle of wine. "Not to mention entertaining."

Kate nods and smiles, turning her attention back to Dillon. "Did you see the updated PA standings?"

"Spencer filled me in."

"A win at Presidio next week and it'll be a showdown at the PA Champs between your club and the Agras."

Dillon scratches a cheek, oddly comforted *and* patently distressed over discussing racing with Kate. It's not a topic that went over well with his ex. "We'll see. How's your club doing?"

"First place . . . of course."

Dillon smirks. "Hungry?"

"What are you offering? Is it too late for breakfast?"

"No breakfast, but there are crackers, cheese, and wine."

"Appetizers it is then."

Dillon prepares a plate, pours her a glass of wine, and turns around when he hears his surname. "Hey, Zac. Grab a seat anywhere."

"Do you have any banana bread left?"

"Sure." Dillon goes over to the counter and retrieves a thick slice for the always-hungry teenager. "Here you go." He slices off two more chunks. "Pass these along to Chase and Dale."

"Awesome! This stuff rocks." Zac works himself into the cozy crowd, where outstretched legs recoil as he passes by, and sits alongside Chase and nearby Dale.

"A little young to be a guest, isn't he?" Kate says.

"Local high-schooler . . . *very* talented, like national-champion talented."

Kate nods while sampling a cheese slice laid across a cracker.

"Parents are going through a nasty divorce, so he hangs out here some evenings."

She sips her wine.

"He built the inn's website and keeps it up to date."

Kate smiles, mixing and matching another appetizer from the offerings.

"He's a running junkie and spends a lot of time in the media lounge." Dillon points it out to her across the crowd of attendees. He picks up a slice of banana bread and nibbles on it. He's run out of things to say, so their attention drifts back to the shoe guru, who has wrapped up his talk and is now answering questions from the attendees, one about the difference between road shoes and trail shoes—more aggressive tread, water-resistant material, and generally heavier, the off-road variety—and another about the life span of a shoe, which Kinney states is 300 to 500 miles depending on the person's body type and surface run on. Dale scoffs at this, citing that he keeps a pair of shoes until the uppers no longer hold together, some 2,000 miles or more, which spawns a wiseass comment from Chase, who always wondered what that smell was that followed Dale around.

With no further questions, Kinney thanks the crowd for their time. Those from the audience who are not staying at the BR&B file out to the front porch as Miles gapes like a kid seated along a parade route.

"Thanks, Mr. Percy," Zac says, pausing where Dillon and Kate stand. "Did you know your name is the same as that famous Australian coach from the '50s?"

"Yeah, though Percy was his first name."

"Very cool. Coach mentioned him once about his training methods . . . very hardcore dude . . . made his team run up and down sand dunes all day and eat next to nothing," he says, holding his hand out for Miles to paw, which she does. "This dog is so cool. Thanks for the bread, Mr. Percy." Zac strides out from the inn behind the last of the guests.

"You're famous," Kate says.

Dillon smiles sheepishly. "My high school coach told me about Percy Cerutty and the training camps he held at Portsea, Australia. During the summers, I'd drive over to the Balboa Peninsula and pretend it was my own little Portsea."

Kate smiles. "I should go. Thanks for the appetizers," she says, putting on her jacket and leisurely searching for her car keys.

Dillon wants to ask her *the* question he's been putting off for over a week, but he struggles with the delivery queued up in his mind as he has before, despite rehearsing it several times. He'd assumed he'd ask over the phone, or leave a voicemail, or not ask at all, not a face-to-face request. Her answer one way or the other doesn't worry him. Yes or no appears equal, all things considered.

"So . . . this weekend, Saturday actually . . . some friends, well, you know Jim from the club . . . anyway they, well, I was invited—"

"*Wooooowooowooo Wooooowooooo.*"

"I'd love to be your plus-one," Kate says, scratching Miles's head.

Dillon's cheeks flush.

"Chase mentioned it while you were introducing the shoe guy."

"Of course he did. Sorry for the late notice. I didn't want to—"

"I get it," she says, giving him a hug and kiss on an embarrassed cheek. "Text me the deets and I'll be here with bells on." She gives Miles a pat on the head and exits.

Saturday Afternoon
Wedding Day

The Dearborn homestead bubbles and fizzes with wedding-day anticipation: Robyn walks around and introduces herself to arriving guests, announcing that she and her best friend Shelby with a *y* are the flower girls; the weather holds, owing to the ongoing drought, allowing for the wedding to take place outdoors in the gazebo hand built by Jim and Jake as originally planned; Jim paces around inside the house worrying that *something* will happen, though nothing remotely has presented a potential dilemma thus far—in fact, the only worrisome thing that some feared was Jim's last "single" run with the guys in Annadel that morning, but other than dusty shins, all survived; Doris's mom arrived from Skagway, Alaska, in decent health and cheery spirits, happy that her eldest daughter is marrying a "good egg" as she puts it, a passive-aggressive comment, Jim explains to the others, aimed at her two younger daughters who've already been married and divorced, twice each; and Jim's mom has reeled in Jim's dad's concern about *something* that is never fully revealed, letting it slide for the duration of the ceremony.

"Sixteen minutes until 'I do,'" Chase says, striding into the side room, giving Jim a pat on the back. "Ready?"

"Some men are born ready, Jim was born worried," Jake says, performing preening duties on Jim's tuxedo as Dillon and Spencer look on.

"I'm ready," Jim says with a crackle in his voice. Dillon hands him a water bottle. "Thanks." After a quick chug, he returns it. "I'm good, guys."

"Speaking of ready," Dillon says, reaching into his jacket pocket and pulling out a key. "No need to check in."

"I meant to ask," Chase says to Dillon, "can I take you up on your offer for a night next Wednesday? They're shutting the water off at my place for twenty-four hours."

"No problem."

"Everyone keeping well in here?" the person performing the ceremonies says, poking his head into the side room.

"I see no Federal Express trucks out front," Jake says.

Jim chuckles. "*Runaway Bride*, and thanks for that."

"Good, good. It's almost time. Best wishes," the man says with a smile, and disappears.

"Was that a Kiwi accent?" Dillon asks.

Jim and Jake nod.

"He used to run for us before you joined," Chase says. "Moved back to New Zealand two years ago."

"Well, all right," Dillon says. "Nothing like a little international flair to add to the ambience."

"Okay, let's get seated, guys," Spencer says. "Good luck, Jim."

Spencer leads Dillon and Chase out from the room.

"You look great, buddy," Jake says. "I can't say enough how happy I am for you and Doris. You two complement each other perfectly."

"Thanks," Jim replies. "And thanks for keeping me grounded all these years. Not sure what I would've done without you."

"That's easy . . . worry."

"No, I mean it. I never said it but you were a tremendous influence on me in college. My focus was so singular: run, study, run, study, run, study . . . you balanced me out. And for that, I thank you."

"If I'd known you were going to go college speech on me, I'd have come up with a quote from *The Graduate*."

"It's not too late."

"Mrs. Robinson, if you don't mind my saying so, this conversation is getting a little strange."

"Touché."

Outside, Dillon spots his plus-one, Kate, talking with Linda. Dillon wonders if that's a good or bad thing. At this point he's given up on thinking too much about it; small-community gossip is what it is.

"Where's Maggie?" Linda asks Spencer when the guys approach.

"She had another commitment today," he says, scanning the outdoor seating area.

"Everything good?" Kate says.

"Stellar." Dillon turns his attention to Spencer. "Come sit with us."

Spencer accepts the seating invite, following Dillon, Kate, Linda, and Chase to their seats among the fifty-five or so guests. Once everybody settles in, wedding music begins playing, creating a stillness in the air, not unlike the start of a race—a much longer race, though. Dillon's wedding had been a beach affair, in Malibu, the sound of the surf drowning out the wedding music. The hour delay in the proceedings also allowed the tide to come in enough to wash out the sand castle that he and the groomsmen had built at low tide for the bride and groom to stand behind. Those should've been signs.

Robyn and Shelby parade down the grass aisle, tossing flower petals aimlessly, both waving at Dillon and the guys. Next, Jake escorts Betty, Doris's youngest sister—who oscillates between appearing inconvenienced by the affair and responsibility, and beaming with pride from the associated attention directed her way—toward the gazebo.

Shortly after, the wedding anthem commences, and everybody rises, catching the first glimpse of the bride. Dillon hasn't ever seen Doris dressed up before. In fact, he can't recall Jim having been dressed up either, beyond work clothes. But here he is, decked out in a tux, not running gear. Even the sight of the other club runners in attendance in regular clothing is an odd sight, though Dale more than makes up for it by wearing a running-themed tie over a short-sleeve polo shirt with an ancient race logo across the left breast pocket.

The ceremony proceeds as planned with no drama beyond the emotions embraced throughout a wedding. At one point Dillon wonders what's going through Spencer's mind: he looks like he's forgotten to prepare a lesson plan for class. As for himself, Dillon takes pleasure in the simplicity of the homespun ceremony: held in a friend's backyard, presided over by a friend, catered by yet another club-member friend, and the newlyweds spending their honeymoon at a new friend's place. Seated next to him, stunning in an azure dress that hugs her slim frame, Kate dangles one leg over the other, showing her defined runner's calves. Twice she nudges him and smiles, catching him staring at them, though his thoughts are less lusty than she may have assumed.

They hypnotize him, and he harks back to his wedding day, stuck in L.A. traffic while sitting in the limo on the way to the airport for their honeymoon in Maui.

Soon the I-dos and till-deaths are expressed and echoed, the Kiwi pronounces them husband and wife, Doris's veil lifts, and the newlyweds kiss. Chase leads the cheer, whooping it up, snapping off pictures with one of the many disposable cameras sitting out as the happy couple strolls down the aisle. Dillon spies a sly grin on Jim's usually serious face when the couple passes his row, which begets Dillon's smile. *Happy endings start with happy beginnings.*

"Where's Maggie?" Chase asks Spencer, sitting down to decorated picnic tables.

"Previous engagement," Spencer says more gruffly than he intends, but by this, the fifth time the question has been asked, he's a little more than irritated by it. After the fourth inquiry he about called it a day and left the event, but that plan didn't last long.

Chase gives Dillon a quizzical glance, but doesn't say anything more on the matter when Dillon subtly shakes his head.

"I'm hungry," Chase says, sifting through the breadbasket on the table.

"You're always hungry," Spencer says.

"It's all those protein shakes," Jake says, stepping up to the table. "They don't satiate your inner carnivore."

With a mouth full of bread, Chase shrugs.

"I think Jim smiled when he and Doris walked down the aisle," Dillon says.

"He's pretty happy," Jake says as he watches Jim hug his mother and father. "He's going to stop by when things settle down to say hi."

"When's dinner?" Chase asks.

Everybody laughs.

"Soon." Jake hands Chase a hunk of beef jerky from his tux pocket.

Chase studies it, chews off a piece, and gnashes on it. Between chews he says, "This is a lot of work. I'm burning more calories than I'm consuming."

Jake chuckles and moves away from the table.

Chase's caveman-like approach to eating Jake's primitive offering garners its requisite amount of teasing but soon Dillon turns his attention to Kate, and Chase splits his time between texting with friends back east and flirting with Doris's cousin, who has driven down from Reno. Spencer listens in on Dillon and Kate's conversation, learning that Kate is director of product development at Fitbit, the company known for its activity trackers and wireless-enabled wearable devices he often sees on neighbors walking around his neighborhood. Counting steps is a good start, of course, but what about measuring intensity? Pseudo-exercise, tracking what they already do and telling themselves it's exercise? Does the reality of data motivate or discourage? Always a tricky and touchy subject . . .

He diverts his attention away from his table, observing the wedding festivities as if through a telescope while holding on tight to his half-full bottle of beer. The one table that has other fifth-wheelers are club members he doesn't know beyond facial recognition from the trails. Despite his club presidency credentials, he doesn't see the need to drum up club business on Jim and Doris's special day. The cross-country series may be an acceptable topic, but the key players for that discussion are preoccupied. He munches on bread, watching Robyn circulate among the guests with her notebook, scribbling entries now and again, her friend Shelby listening but not saying much.

Spencer shifts his mind to the cross-country series, the various scenarios for the open team's efforts to win it all with one regular season race left— Presidio—before the PA championships: *If the Agras don't show up it would be an easy win for us, putting us 1 point behind them. Then it's winner take all. If the Agras do show up and we beat them, the same scenario exists. But if they beat us at Presidio, then in addition to beating them at the championships, Chico or another club would also have to place ahead of them. . . .*

Spencer ruminates over the unfortunate position of the team *not* running an earlier race, or tomorrow's race in Santa Cruz, where the Agras would've been unlikely to show, giving the RERC a likely win and more points to make things less complicated. But even if they win next week, the Agras's propensity for bringing in new guys, better guys, than what they've seen all season causes him to shake his head at what amounts to the futility of the situation.

"Spencer, you're starting to look like Jim," Dillon says, tapping him on the shoulder.

"Jim passed the torch on to Spencer," Chase says.

Spence-speak. He longs for his plus-one, but instead settles for dinner when his table is summoned to serve itself at the buffet.

Jake bursts into laughter when Doris, upon selecting one of the four varieties of wedding cupcakes, mashes it in Jim's unsuspecting face. Robyn hands Jim a clean napkin. Doris had baked the cupcakes herself, an assortment of chocolate, vanilla, strawberry, and pumpkin. Like a teenage prank on Halloween, smashed pumpkin bits drip from Jim's face.

"Looks good on you, Jim," Chase says, the guys huddling around the groom once the tradition has played out and guests are clamoring around the cupcake tree for one of their own.

"I joked earlier that I was going to smear one on her and she told me that I'd better not. I honestly wasn't going to, but she didn't take any chances," he says, still wiping, licking, and using his hand to remove frosting on his eyebrows.

"What a great idea to serve cupcakes instead of a cake," Kate says. "Gives everybody a choice."

"I'll grab us two," Dillon says. "What flavor?"

"Surprise me," she replies as the beaming bride steps up to the group. "What a lovely wedding, Doris."

"Thanks," Doris says with a smile that is as radiant as the late-afternoon sun that presides over the reception.

Doris hears her name called and excuses herself just as Dillon returns with two cupcakes, strawberry for Kate and chocolate for himself.

"One down," Linda says, leaning against Jake.

Jake smiles.

"Who's next?" she says.

Part of Dillon's cupcake drops to the ground.

"Clearly not Dillon," Chase says, which spawns laughter from the group.

"You, buddy," Dillon says.

"He's in a relationship with his Garmin," Jim says.

"Pfft."

"I say Spencer," Jake says, watching Spencer meander and mill around various groups, working his way toward Jake and company.

"I think so too," Linda says.

Chase gives a doubtful expression while Dillon manages to eat his cupcake without further spillage.

"Attention! Can we gather all the single ladies over here?" a voice calls out. "It's that time!"

"Kate, that's you," Linda says.

Dillon's eyes open wide, and Linda and Jake laugh.

Kate works her way over to the singles crowd, awaiting the toss of the bouquet from Doris. The bride turns her back toward the hopefuls and heaves it straight up in the air, where it hovers for a brief moment and lands a foot from where she stands. Laughter rises from all around, with hollers for "redo" shouted out and a "you goof" from Jim. But before any of the adults can collect the bouquet a little girl stoops over and retrieves it, holding it up for the crowd to see, whereupon cheers ring out. The little girl has no idea what's happening, but she smiles nonetheless.

"Oh, Magdalene," the little girl's mother says, bending down to pick her up. "Look what you found!" Magdalene buries her head in her mom's shoulder, clutching the bouquet. The rest of the crowd cheers, accepting the fate of the next person to get married . . . in twenty years' time.

"What happened?" Spencer says, rejoining the group.

"The little girl ended up with the bouquet," Jake says.

Linda lets out a laugh and promptly stifles it.

"What?" Spencer says.

Everybody, including Kate, who rejoins them, acts puzzled except Jake, who smiles and says, "Wishful thinking."

Dancing breaks out when the DJ starts up the music again with "Hold My Hand," by Hootie and the Blowfish. Jake guides Linda out onto the patio, followed by Chase and Doris's cousin, and Dillon and Kate. A song later, Jake hollers to Robyn, who comes out to him. She nods when Jake whispers into her ear, marches over to a stag Spencer, takes hold of his hand, and pulls him out on the patio, dancing to Billy Ray Cyrus's "Achy Breaky Heart."

When the DJ switches gears to Celine Dion, Jake gathers Dillon, Chase, and Spencer and leads them to the front of the homestead. "You guys can help." He opens a large bag that contains old running shoes. The smell wafting out is a mixture of dried sweat caked in dust and salty leather, canvas, and mesh.

"These have seen better days," Dillon says, tying stained and frayed shoelaces to two six-foot ropes that Jake has attached to the back of Jim's Subaru.

"Dale would think these still had life in them," Chase says.

While the guys tie ancient shoes to the ropes, Jake pulls out another bag that contains energy gels and condom packets, liberally littering the inside of the car with them. He tops off the traditional shenanigans by spraying JUST MARRIED across the back window. Once all the shoes are secured they return to the reception until Jim and Doris announce they're about to leave. Goodbyes expressed many times over, the happy couple navigate the gauntlet of well-wishers, ducking birdseed that showers them. At their adorned Subaru soap bubbles grace them, courtesy of Robyn and Shelby.

Once seated in their chariot, the crowd converges, and as Jim guides it out the driveway he shakes his head at all the shoes that bounce wildly behind them while Doris waves excitedly back to the crowd. When the last of car and shoes have disappeared from view out on the road, Jake wraps an arm around Linda, and with the crowd turns and strolls back inside the homestead while Robyn and Shelby stay put, continuing to blow bubbles at each other.

"What's this?" Doris says when Jim hands her a small gift-wrapped package.

"Don't know," he says, steering their car toward the BR&B, receiving the occasional congratulatory horn honk from other motorists. "Chase slipped it into my jacket as we were leaving. Open it."

Doris shreds the wrapping instantly like a wood chipper.

"You goof."

Doris smiles, and laughs, louder and louder.

"What is it?" Jim fears the worst, coming from Chase, but with Doris laughing, Jim holds out hope.

She shows him the disc cover to the CD: Lynyrd Skynyrd. Jim turns beet red as a car of teenagers passes by, honking and giving the couple thumbs-up.

"His note says there's an extended version of 'Free Bird' on it," Doris says. "Hope you're not planning on running with the guys tomorrow."

"Hadn't planned on it."

Sunday Morning
Accidental Discoveries

"What'd you buy now?" Jake asks Chase, watching him attach a small oval gadget to the back of each running shoe at the Cobblestone Trailhead.

"runScribes," Chase replies, tugging on the devices, ensuring they are securely attached. "They track all my foot movements throughout the run. Pretty cool, right?"

Dillon scratches his chin and stares. Spencer reads through the device's manual. Jake presents a dubious expression.

"And that's important why?" Jake says.

"I can tell how my foot moves in any running shoe over different surfaces," Chase says. "They analyze my running form using kinematics with a nine-axis sensor . . . stride length, turnover rate, what type of foot strike I have—forefoot, midfoot, heel striker—"

"'Kinematics'?" Dillon says. "I think I failed that course."

"I can tell all that by watching you run and inspecting your shoe soles," Jake says.

"But I can't upload and chart your humble observations."

"Does it replace your Garmin?" Dillon says. "It sounds like it can calculate your mileage and pace too."

"It does," Spencer says, his nose now in the features section. "But it's not real-time. It needs to be uploaded *after* the run."

"Plus, my watch gives me metrics that these don't," Chase says.

"Like what? A deeper understanding of the universe?" Dillon says.

"Forty-two," Jake says.

"My universe," Chase says.

"*The Hitchhiker's Guide to the Galaxy*," Dillon says.

Jake grins.

"The motion of objects independent of the cause of the motion," Spencer says.

Dillon and Jake stare at Spencer with blank expressions.

"Kinematics. Geometry of motion."

"Definitely failed that."

"You're one step away from becoming an astronaut," Jake says. "All you need now is one of those self-contained space suits to run in and you'd never need to stop. Just *go* on the run."

"Do they make a shirtless model?"

"Running used to be so simple," Dillon says. "Lace up and go."

"Astronauts are passé," Spencer says. "Body hacking is the next frontier."

"Like implantable RFID chips that hold encrypted information?" Dillon says.

"We've been implanting pacemakers for sixty years," Jake says.

"Let's get rolling before Chase needs to reboot," Spencer says.

"I'm ready," Chase says, grabbing the instructions from Spencer and tossing them into his car.

Dillon, Jake, and Spencer begin running. *Beep, beep.*

"You and Kate looked pretty cozy at the wedding," Jake says.

"Yeah, she's pretty cool. I'm thinking of asking her out to dinner some night."

"Whatcha waiting for, Chase?" Spencer hollers, glancing back.

"I need to stand still for ten seconds for the devices to initialize."

"Lord love a duck. Soon you'll need to be certified in order to go for a run. 'I'm sorry, sir, but you're not qualified to run today.'"

"Should we wait?" Dillon says.

"With all that technology he'll catch us soon enough."

"Weird not having Jim with us," Dillon says.

"I know. I have a movie quote about astronauts ready to go."

"What's that in your hand?" Spencer asks Jake.

Jake doesn't say anything.

"Is that what I think it is?" Dillon says, checking out Jake's partially concealed item.

A large grin forms. "Okay, let's have it. Bring it on."

"Bring what on?" Chase says, rejoining the group.

"Jake's running with a cell phone," Spencer says.

"What?!" Chase hollers. "Say it ain't so. Oh, lord love a duck!"

"I never thought I'd see the day, Jake carrying technology on a run," Spencer says.

"I still remember the grief you guys gave me when I brought mine along on a run," Chase says. "Never again . . ."

"I don't know," Dillon says. "Does it qualify as technology if it's a flip phone?"

"Still waiting for a call from Beverly D'Angelo?" Chase says, reminiscing. "Very harsh. It was a harmless boyhood crush . . ."

"He's going to Skype with Jim during the run, give him a virtual tour of Annadel," Spencer says.

"Does it even have a data plan?" Dillon says.

"Data plan?" Jake says.

"He wants a firsthand report on how things went on Jim's wedding night," Chase says.

"Did you really give him a "Free Bird" CD?" Jake says.

"The gift that keeps on giving." Chase takes a bow.

"Or in case a client calls about a flat tire on their wheelbarrow," Dillon says.

"Yuk, yuk, yuk," Jake says. "Linda is on call this morning, so I may need to cut my run short."

"What would you have done before cell phones?" Spencer says.

"Run later in the day, of course."

"So what you're saying," Chase says as if he's a well-heeled trial lawyer on the verge of cracking a key witness during cross-examination, "is that technology has freed you to commune with society on your own terms. Is that correct, Mr. Dearborn?"

This brings on laughter, at which Jake grins, inviting further teasing for another half mile until they reach North Burma, where Jake ratchets up the pace on the first incline. Nobody seems too concerned about the gap that opens until a minute later. Chase quickens his pace to match Jake's. Dillon falls in behind Chase. Spence vents a couple of Spence-speaks to no avail and loudly mumbles, as the trio steadily gaps him around the dry creek bed and up the "Twitter ascent."

They regroup on the fire road a mile and a half later, but the pace changes begin again, this time with Chase leading the charge, presumably as a data-gathering exercise so he can test various paces with his new runScribes. The problem with that guise is Dillon's response to each of Chase's surges, closing it and at times driving it once the gap has closed. Not to be outdone, Jake pushes the pace on the hillier sections, and soon enough Spencer, buying into changing things up in his own training, tosses in surges on the rolling segments that suit his ability. Five miles later, and pent-up energy from a no-race weekend expended, they return to the normal Sunday run at conversational pace.

"So these runScribes," Jake says, "what do you plan on getting out of them?"

"Not entirely sure. But once I see the data, I'm sure something valuable will present itself."

"Like shelves in the garage," Spencer says. "Build them and you'll fill them."

"*Field of Dreams*," Jake says.

"He *really* misses Jim today," Dillon says.

"Nice analogy, Spence," Chase says. "Any insight I can gather is worthwhile."

"Won't that raise more questions than answers?" Jake says.

"Data *is* only useful if it's understood," Spencer says.

"Fine, you caught me," Chase says, chuckling. "I'm an early adopter. I like to explore . . . some of the coolest things have resulted from discoveries that at one time no one knew what to do with."

"Penicillin is an obvious example," Dillon says.

"Also the microwave," Spencer says, "by a man named, get this, Dillon: Percy Spencer."

"No kidding."

"Teflon," Chase says.

"Viagra," Dillon says.

"Velcro," Spencer says.

"Slinky," Chase says.

"Waffle cones," Dillon says.

"Plato said, 'Science is nothing but perception,'" Jake says as the group descends Canyon and works their way through Spring Lake and back to Channel Drive.

"Play-doh too," Chase says. The others cast dubious glances his way. "Seriously, Google it."

"I read recently that Febreze was an accidental discovery," Dillon says. "Good thing too: it's a godsend around the inn."

"Back in New York, I was kicked off the Febreze account."

"This should be good," Jake says.

"Febreze . . . when life stinks."

"I can't *imagine* why they kicked you off," Dillon says, approaching their cars.

"They actually liked—" Chase stops short at the shimmer of light reflecting off glass on the ground next to his BMW. "Oh shit!"

"That doesn't look good," Dillon says.

The front driver's-side window has been smashed in, marble-sized pieces of glass strewn over the driver's seat and floor mat. Chase rushes to unlock the door, his trembling hand making it difficult at first. "They stole everything. Dammit! The Nav, my cell phone. Even my . . ."

"Wallet?" Spencer says.

"No, that was locked up. They snatched my radar detector."

The guys survey the area as Chase fumes, assessing his losses, finding the trowel used to breach the vehicle.

"Jake's truck is wide open!" Chase says, flipping the tool back into the truck parked next to the BMW. "Shovels, rakes, hoes, gloves . . . free for the taking."

"They require manual labor," Jake says, handing him a short-handled broom from the back of the truck bed.

Chase uses Jake's antiquated flip phone to call the police, and cleans up the mess in his car as best he can while the guys mill around and console him. Eventually Jake receives a call from Linda and has to leave. Spencer has brunch plans with Maggie and leaves when Jake does. Dillon hangs out a while longer until the officer arrives, but leaves Chase to file a report with the officer in solitude.

Week 45 Training Summary			
	Long Run	Mileage Total	Comments
Dillon	20	68	I feel in great shape.
Chase	18.90	60	New running toy is crazy cool.
Spencer	19	61	Marked improvement in leg turnover.
Jim	0	45	Officially married.
Jake	19	72	Godspeed, Jimbo.

Week 11
November 9

Monday Morning
Honeymoon Bliss

"Morning, Dillon!" a chipper Doris says as she and Jim settle at the kitchen island. "What's for breakfast *todaaaaay?*"

"Well, *today*, I'll start you off with plain organic yogurt mixed with a berry medley."

Doris claps her hands and sports a huge smile, like a giddy kid celebrating their birthday.

"Then, a made-to-order omelet." Dillon points to the variety of options they can choose from.

After scanning the platter, Doris selects everything.

"Jim?" Dillon says, setting their yogurt-filled parfait glasses before them.

"Toss in everything, but hold the bell peppers and mushrooms."

"You got it." Dillon cracks eggs into a bowl and readies them for the omelet pan.

"*No shroom for the groom, no shroom for the groom,*" Doris chants, wiggling on the tall stool.

"You goof. I'm not a groom anymore."

"I couldn't think of anything that rhymed with hubby . . . you're definitely *not* chubby."

Dillon chuckles.

"I knew Kate was going to be your plus-one," Doris says.

"Oh, yeah?"

"Chase said you guys hang out after all the races. She's real smart. So are you two dating?"

"Doris," Jim says. "I told you not to say—"

"What? It's just a question. They looked like they were having a great time at our wedding."

Jim rubs the back of his neck, eyes apologetic while Dillon refills their orange juice glasses.

"No, we're not dating. Besides, she lives in Frisc—the city."

"That's nothing! I lived in Alaska, and Jim and I dated."

"We'll see. The masseuse will be here tonight at seven if that works for you two."

"Oh yes, that'll be wonderful," Doris says. "Where does she do it? Can we get naked?"

"Doris . . ." Jim says, bowing his head and massaging his temples. *This can't be happening.*

Dillon grins. "There's a private room next to the sauna, so you can figure things out with Nicola."

Doris's bubbly mood continues, rendering Jim red and speechless at times, and transforming Dillon's chuckles to laughs and ultimately a spit take, at which point Miles joins in. Even the reserved non-runner couple from Dayton, occupying the Helsinki Room, who've joined them for breakfast, can't help but laugh. Jim accuses Dillon of serving Doris mimosas, which furthers Doris's happy state. Doris launches into "*Santa Mimosa, Santa Mimosa, we're honeymooning in Santa Mimosa*" until their omelets are served.

"Sorry about Doris this morning," Jim says, running with Dillon and Miles out in the vineyards as daylight announces last call, having left Doris to enjoy wine and cheese with that night's houseguests and regale them with details from the wedding.

"No worries. I figured she still had 'Free Bird' humming through her head."

Jim tries to execute a Spence-speak, but croaks instead.

"Sorry, couldn't resist."

"Chase is a genius, all right."

"Besides, that's what women do . . . they're always trying to fix single guys up."

"True."

"And Kate and I *were* having fun at the wedding."

Jim nods, unsure what else to say on the matter. Doris will want more details about Dillon and Kate, but Jim doesn't have the meddlesome gene.

"How was zip-lining?" Dillon asks.

"Doris screamed like a howler monkey . . . eight hundred feet on one line."

"I'm surprised her voice isn't hoarse."

"She loved it. Thanks for the tickets."

"Speaking of which, I have tickets back at the inn for tomorrow at Safari West."

"She's going to love that."

"After the tour they put on a big barbecue on their deck, which has a nice view of the giraffes."

"When Doris insisted that we cancel our honeymoon to Kauai, I felt horrible. It was worth it to me to put it on the credit card and deal with it later. And I'm an accountant!"

Dillon chuckles. "Hawaii isn't all it's cracked up to be."

"Between the sunset horseback ride yesterday at the beach, zip-lining through the redwoods today, and the safari tomorrow, it's like a vacation without leaving the county. So, many thanks for making a special honeymoon for us."

"Don't mention it. It's my pleasure. Or as Chase would say, 'Who's your Dylster?'"

"*Wooooowoooowooo Wooooowoooo.*"

"Doesn't really work that well," Dillon says.

"No. No, it doesn't."

"Purely a Chase thing."

"And you'd have to take your shirt off."

"Too cold for me."

"*Wooooowooowooo Wooooowoooo.*"

"No, not for you, girl," Dillon says.

Tuesday Night
On the Couch

"You didn't bring Dogma," Terri says, closing the front door behind Chase.

"He doesn't travel well," he says, standing with a bottle of wine in Terri's very small "cottage," as she calls it, in, of all places around Sonoma County, Sebastopol. The warm confines and scents that embrace him have a familiar appeal, though he can't put a finger on it, only that the rich Italian aroma wafting from the kitchen carries him back to childhood; perhaps his grandparents' Italian neighbors on Lake Michigan who had a pair of ski boats and hosted waterski parties all summer long, including sleepovers out on the deck under the stars and an abundance of food beyond imagination. "*Eat, eat, eat! You need meat on your bones*" rings through the distant memory.

"This is Freud," Terri says, picking up a black cat with white streaks across his thick fur coat. "He's a little shy at first." She scratches the back of Freud's ears as he casts a watchful eye on Chase.

"I'm sure Freud and Dogma would have a lot to discuss," Chase says, offering his knuckles to Freud for inspection. Freud sniffs Chase's offering and licks it several times. "What do you know, I'm psychoanalytically approved."

"We'll see. Hope you're hungry. Dinner is ready." She sets Freud down, and he scampers off behind the couch.

Chase opens the bottle of wine he brought, telling Terri the story about the Grogger's Box Wine campaign he worked on while she serves up a homemade dinner of lasagna, antipasto salad, and garlic bread laden with butter. The smell intoxicates Chase's senses, to the point of forgetting about the caloric content the hearty meal contains. He muses to himself as to how she stays so thin with cooking like this. Her at-home attire differs dramatically from the revealing minimalist way she normally appears at the BR&B: baggy Prana yoga pants and a loose-fitting T-shirt, her feet bare and toenails painted turquoise.

Chase keeps the conversation going by explaining in great detail the data he's gathered from his new runScribes, elaborating on all the valuable info derived from it until he senses a lack of interest from Terri. He mentions the fact about his car getting broken in to, but the upside is that insurance will replace and upgrade the stolen technology, which excites him.

The discussion turns to some of the highlights from the wedding, Chase commenting on how jubilant Doris looked the entire afternoon and evening, adding in the story about Jim's dad, who spent thirty minutes thoroughly inspecting the gazebo, expressing his concerns over its structural integrity to Jim's mom, who politely listened and reassured him that everything would be fine.

"They complement each other nicely," Terri says between bites. "She has this bubbly, creative persona and he's this reserved guy who bears the weight of the world in his daily expression."

Chase swallows the bite he's taken halfway into Terri's observation. "Jim can be a tough read, but trust me, he was very happy that day. She's good for him."

"She was so funny at breakfast the other morning. She went on and on about the gift you gave them."

Chase chokes on a piece of bread and lets out a couple throat-clearing coughs. Terri laughs at his expense. He gulps from the water glass, washing down the embarrassment.

"Better?"

"Glad my stay at the inn isn't until tomorrow night."

"I noticed the reservation. Why?"

"The HOA is repairing a crack in the retaining wall by the fire hydrant. They need to shut down the complex's water main for twenty-four hours."

Dinner consumed, Chase offers to clear off the table and clean up the kitchen while Terri sets up the video recorder for the final interview. When Chase finishes, he takes a seat on the couch, lying back as if ready for a therapy session; he chuckles. Freud doesn't look amused, sitting atop the chair next to Chase.

Terri readies her interview questions, sits next to Freud, and flips the video recorder on. Chase gazes at the red light, drawn to its illumination until Terri's voice breaks the spell.

"This is Terri Day's human sexuality subject interview with Chase Brandon, a thirty-two-year-old male, endurance athlete. He is currently single. Thank you for participating, Chase."

"My pleasure," he responds stiffly.

Terri begins with basic questions about influences in his life throughout his young-adult years—ages ten to eighteen—people he considered role models, whom he respected and guided him when he needed guidance. He cites his parents and paternal grandparents, before their early departures while he was in high school. When asked who had the "sex talk" with him, he replies that his father had, in eighth grade, though it wasn't a sex talk as much as it was about women and dating.

Chase laughs. "He basically said, 'Chase, just ask them if they want to go out. The worst thing they can say is no.'" He laughs again. "I told him *that* was what I was afraid of!"

Over the course of the interview as Terri asks open-ended questions surrounding Chase's history of intimacy with women, connections and references circle back to the loss of his grandparents, and subsequently his parents. Chase's straight-up, honest, and jovial answers soon turn poignant. The interview stirs internal struggles he's dealt with in years past, or so he thinks. His posture, which started off as relaxed, leaned back against the couch with an arm draped wide over the back, has transformed to hands in his lap, fingers massaging the palms of each. His speech takes on a distant, gravelly tone, and his gaze becomes hypnotized by the red light on the video camera. He doesn't know how much time has passed since the interview started, and only becomes aware that it's been halted when Freud's tongue scrapes across his knuckles. He looks down to see that he's petting the cat, who's now sitting in his lap.

"Here," Terri says, handing him a tissue to dry the tears that have streamed down his face.

Chase accepts the tissue, blotting the salty past away. Several minutes pass before he can look Terri in the eye.

"Chase, I'm so sorry." She rises from the chair, moves beside him, and gives him a hug. "I didn't mean for the interview to go this deep."

Chase sniffles, drawing in through his nostrils Terri's perfume, a subtle lavender scent.

"I'm good," he says, pulling back from her, striving to regain a modicum of composure. The vulnerability that sweeps over him leaves him exhausted and exposed. But it's not so much the exposure that bothers him, at least not in Terri's presence, though a side of embarrassment has been served up by it. No, vulnerability isn't what holds him back in sleeping with someone and finding faults in them so he can reasonably and logically move on and away without remorse. What hovers over him now, through the painful journey back to the losses in his life, is a very basic fact: he's afraid to get close to someone for fear they'll leave him. Not leave him in the breakup sense, but in the dying and abandoning sense. That recurring pain spurs him to build walls to protect himself from that kind of disillusionment again, despite the greater pain of *not* finding someone to spend his life with, or understanding why he moves on and on, from one woman to the next. Identifying with brand names instead comforts him, always there, forever, like a favorite old sweatshirt that substitutes for a warm hug on a cold winter night. Or the intense obsession with data that can be analyzed and critiqued, even massaged if necessary. Or the reliability of 400 meters of artificial surface that starts and ends precisely every time, a constant, always there for him to run around and around as many times as needed.

Terri hands him a glass of water. Condensation drips onto his shirt when he takes a sip.

"We don't need to continue with the interview," she says, running a hand through his hair.

He dries each eye and shakes his head. "Your project is due soon."

"It's not your fault," she says, leaning into him, giving him one of those hugs that has healing powers, transferring therapeutic energy while absorbing toxic energy in return. "It's not you . . . it's life."

He sits there, wrapped in Terri's hug, the closest thing to his past he's felt since high school. "Thank you."

Wednesday
Working the Land

Jake wields the spade along the edge of a twenty-foot trench, carving out the final shape of the soon-to-be dry riverbed. With one bare hand he pierces the earth, loosening it, and with the other shifts the dirt around, creating an uneven yet natural contour, blending it in with the rest of the surrounding landscape.

The midday sun drenches him with thermal energy, the resultant sheen of sweat acting like flypaper on his skin to dirt debris, forming a gritty exterior. Jake's perpetual smile appears out of place in this state, or so a homeowner or two told him after observing him working. "This is my bliss," he responds, though it doesn't seem quite satisfactory to the observers.

Jake tosses the spade aside, rights himself from the kneeling position, and stretches his arms high into the sky, as much a salutation to the sun as realigning his posture. Forging on, he lays weed fabric down the middle of the trough, cutting large sections out to accommodate the large previously positioned boulders. Once the area is covered, he begins pulling up the larger of the river rocks piled along the embankment and placing them on the floor of the trench. One by one he places them, and maneuvers them, slowly blanketing the lining. As the rocky bed forms, Jake pulls from another of the three piles of rock, this one medium-sized, creatively placing them among the larger ones, and on which smaller rounded rocks will be placed, creating a textured and layered effect.

Had it not been for the shifting and lengthening shadow of Jake's body, a human sundial denoting the passage of time, he wouldn't have known that early morning had turned midmorning had turned afternoon had turned late afternoon when the last of the metamorphic piles, polished by rivers running wild for centuries, rests serenely in the trench. The dry river creek etches diagonally across the front yard, snaking between trees left intact from the original landscape, and through a small field of lavender, swaying gently in the breeze that cools Jake's sweat-soaked and stained cotton shirt from a race long forgotten.

Now leaned up against his truck, Jake quenches his thirst with water and surveys the natural beauty one last time with an enraptured grin before climbing behind the wheel and heading toward Sugar Loaf State Park out off highway 12 east of town. Parked and properly shoed, he works his way up through and above the tree line, arriving to one of the two Bald Mountain summits from which a 360-degree view affords him a perspective on an immensely gratifying day, new words flowing for his journal:

In solitude he veers right and upward where the trail splits. The redwoods fade, their towering perspective minimized, replaced by gnarled oak trees offering poison oak to anyone seeking a moment of respite against their trunks. "Annadel Summit—4.3 miles," carved into the faded signpost, had he cared to read it, favors well-trained and adventurous souls. It tests one's mettle as much as their conditioning. The trail transforms into long, narrow stretches of horseshoe-shaped potholes that have dried and cracked over the hot summer. An assortment of flat and round boulders dot the path; smaller, jagged rocks exposed by years of erosion jut upward in unfortunate spots.

Thursday Midmorning
Business, Pleasure, and Trouble

"Miles?" Dillon waits for a response but hears none after entering the BR&B kitchen, post-run. "Terri?" More silence greets him. He puts the two dirty breakfast plates sitting on the island counter, along with their utensils, into the sink, then adds in the empty pancake-batter bowl and turns on the water to partially submerge everything. He finds the pancake spatula sitting off to the side and tosses it in with the other items to soak. Wiping down the counter, he retrieves a clean plate and prepares himself a meal to replenish the calories burned throughout the previous sixty minutes. Just then an object crashes to the floor upstairs. He pauses, holding his breath. There are two rooms occupied: A lively couple from New Orleans, and Chase. When muted male and female laughter follows the commotion, Dillon resumes breathing and adding items to his plate.

Enjoying the solitude, Dillon takes a seat and flips through the local newspaper, skimming through each section until he spots a color photo of Zac crossing the finish at Wednesday's regional high school cross-country championships, arms raised high, finish-line tape stretched across his chest, mouth agape. Dillon reads through the article of the senior's commanding win and course record, and odds-on favorite to win CIF sectionals and finals over the following two weekends. The team also won and will join Zac in Fresno. *I'll bet Spencer is happy.* Dillon recalls the excruciating excitement during *his* ramp-up to CIF, the internal and external expectations as he won week after week that simultaneously drove him *and* demoralized him by season's end.

News and breakfast consumed, Dillon tosses his empty plate into the sink with the other items, again taking note of the odd peacefulness to the place. It has an eerie element to it, though. "Miles? Terri?"

He scratches his chest in silence, glances at his watch, and decides it's time to check in on Chase to see if he'll want breakfast, though Dillon laughs to himself that Chase has probably packed his own "chemical" breakfast. Dillon climbs the stairs, finding a cloth napkin on the steps. He stoops to pick it up. At the top of the staircase, he spots Miles sitting with attentive eyes and ears in front of the Munich Room.

"What are you doing, girl?" He walks up to Miles, who rises, peering up at Dillon. He taps on the door with his knuckles. "Chase?" The door pushes open; moans and the squeak of the bed startle him. Dillon cringes and backs away. Pulling the door shut, he spots black running tights on the floor in the doorjamb, blocking complete closure, a familiar logo on them, one he'd seen

Terri wearing that morning before he took off on his run. He stares at Miles, whose intense blue eyes stare back. Dillon's heart races, a panic flashback singeing his senses. His hand stays put on the doorknob, undecided whether to flee the scene as he sometimes wishes he'd done after last year's fateful Thanksgiving Day run. The mental table tennis match in his mind escalates, reaching that frenzied state of irrationality, forcing his hand.

He nudges the door open and peers inside. The lamp from the dresser lies on the floor split into two pieces. He wills himself into the room one small step at a time, catching the view of the foot of the bed giving way to vigorous activity. He closes his eyes, steps forward, and opens them. Shock courses up his spine, locking him in an all-too-familiar moment.

"*Wooooowoooowooo Woooooowoooo!*"

"Oh shit!" Chase says, lying on his back, eyes meeting Dillon's.

Terri, riding Chase, turns her head and freezes.

"What the hell, Terri!" Dillon erupts.

"*Wooooowoooowooo Woooooowoooo!*"

"Dillon—" Terri says, rolling off Chase, attempting to cover up.

"No, NO, *NO!*" Dillon shouts. "What are you doing?"

"Dude, it's my fault—"

"This is unacceptable, Terri!"

"*Wooooowoooowooo Woooooowoooo!*"

"I asked you to *serve* the guests, not *service* them!"

"Dillon, I know, I'm sor—"

"*Wooooowoooowooo Woooooowoooo!*"

"Dillon, really, it's—" Chase says.

"Get out now!" Dillon points toward the door with a finger jutting out from a balled-up fist, his stare aimed at Terri.

"*Wooooowoooowooo—*"

"Miles!"

Miles backs out of the room and sits down in the hallway.

"Get out!" Dillon's body trembles.

Terri jumps up from the bed, scanning the room for her clothes until she spots her top on the floor near Dillon's feet. She grabs a nearby shirt from

Chase's suitcase and slips it on, covering most of her body. She scurries past Dillon, eyes cast downward, nabbing her running tights from the floor as she exits the room.

"*Wooooowooowooo—*"

"Miles!"

Miles flees down the hallway, padding down the stairs after Terri. The front door opens, then shudders.

Suspended in time, Dillon glares at the split lamp until he senses Chase's stare, from under trampled sheets.

"I'm sorry, man."

Dillon picks up the broken pieces of the lamp and yanks the cord out from the wall outlet. Trembling under control, he wants to say something to defuse the awkwardness, but nothing comes to mind for several moments.

"You gonna want—?" Dillon stops short, recalling the empty breakfast dishes from earlier.

"No . . . no, I'm good," Chase replies. "I think I'll clean up and head out."

Dillon massages the back of his head. "There's no rush." He turns, head hung down, cheeks flushed, and strides from the room, pulling on the door until the latch clicks, compartmentalizing his past.

In the hallway the New Orleans guests from the Helsinki Room are peeking out from their room. "Is everything okay?" the man asks.

Dillon intends to nod his head, but shakes it instead. "Come on down when you're ready for breakfast. I also have the trail map ready for you."

Both guests nod and close their door. Dillon shuts his eyes a moment, lets out a low groan and heads downstairs. He tosses the napkin still clenched in his hand into the laundry room, where it misses the basket, slides across the floor, and comes to rest under his bed. Dillon backtracks through the living area and out the front door, where Miles is sitting next to Terri on the porch steps.

Terri looks back, tears in her eyes. "Dillon, I'm so sorry."

"Just grab your stuff and go," he says, exasperated.

She wipes tears from her eyes, rises, and disappears into the BR&B. Dillon takes her seat next to Miles, stroking the husky while she licks fresh scratches on his shin from some barbed wire he tangled with earlier on his run. Minutes later, Terri emerges, this time in running gear.

"Dillon—"

"Please go," Dillon says softly, as much from shame and embarrassment for losing control as for wanting to avoid further confrontation and drama.

Terri remains motionless, sniffling. Miles licks her kneecap and stares up at her until she negotiates the steps and jogs off toward the main road. Miles follows her onto the driveway, pauses, and peers back at Dillon.

"Yes, girl, new day, same problem."

Miles sits, staring off in Terri's direction until she vanishes.

Dillon leans back with his arms behind him for support and closes his eyes, letting the midmorning sun beat down on him. His run euphoria, mixed with visually painful memories, leaves him spent, but not in the way he usually enjoys. He focuses his attention on the sounds around him, whitewashing the morning away: the rumble of a truck along the county road, a crow's harsh squawk, a small plane's growly propeller chop as it crescendos and decrescendos overhead, leaving a vacuum of silence in its wake. Soon after, Chase comes out onto the porch with suitcase in hand and sits alongside Dillon.

"You okay, buddy?" Chase says.

"Yeah," Dillon says, leaning forward and opening his eyes. "My beef's not with you. Or even her . . ."

"I figured as much," he says, petting Miles when she walks up to him. "Even metaphorical death can be a bitch to deal with."

Dillon smirks.

"Sorry about the lamp."

"Nothing that can't be fixed."

Chase rises. "Racing Presidio this weekend?"

"Yep."

"Good," he says, patting Dillon on the back, heading to the BMW. "I expect you to kick my ass."

Friday Evening
Couples Therapy

"That's a write-off as well," Jim says to Maggie after she mentions the writer's conference she recently attended. "Keep your receipts for travel, food, hotel, conference fees, et cetera."

"Dessert is ready!" Doris says, entering the living room at Maggie and Spencer's home, carrying a serving tray. She hands both Spencer and Maggie a dessert plate with a three-layered crumbly square under a dollop of vanilla ice cream. She hands Jim a plate, setting her own plate and the tray down on the coffee table.

"This is soooooo good," Maggie says, her mouth half-full.

Spencer nods his satisfaction as well.

"Mixed-berry crumb cake bars . . . blackberries, blueberries, loganberries," Doris says.

Jim gives Doris a kiss, eats a bite, and continues on. "Any books that are writing-related can be written off too."

Mouth full again, Maggie raises her fork.

"And the IRS won't care she doesn't have a publisher?" Spencer says.

"They treat self-publishing like a sole proprietorship on your tax form. It's best to legitimize it by opening up a separate bank account for income and expenses, and setting up a 'doing business as' entity in the county. They'll allow it for a certain period of time."

"How long?"

"Depends. It's somewhat of a gray area, but the more you write and publish the more the IRS will consider it *actual* self-employment and not a tax write-off disguised as a hobby."

Spencer's head bobs, turning to Maggie. "You do have a number of story ideas ready to go. This would get the ball rolling."

"It is frustrating trying to secure an agent *and* write new material. My time is torn," Maggie says. "But I'm not sure about the up-front costs even if it is all deductible."

"We can swing it."

"What if it doesn't sell? I don't want to throw money down the drain."

"I have faith in you." Spencer divides the remaining portion of his slice into three, separates them, and consumes one. Forks and spoons clink on plates only removed from the china cabinet on rare occasions. He takes another bite, this time chewing more thoroughly, bridging the void.

"Go ahead, you can talk about it," Maggie says, setting her empty plate down on the coffee table.

Spencer swallows and smiles. "Did you see the updated team results?" he asks Jim.

"We're closing in."

"If we win tomorrow—" Spencer pauses a moment when he overhears Maggie ask Doris about the honeymoon at Dillon's place, returning his attention back to Jim. "If we win tomorrow it'll all come down to the championships."

"Assuming the Agras don't bring in some insurance."

"That always bothers me in relay track events like at the Olympics, where anybody can run the prelims and a different set of sprinters race the finals. And they *all* receive medals if they reach the podium."

"Swimming too."

"Not much team unity . . . if you ask me," Spencer says, though his attention is divided after overhearing Doris say "oral anthem." "What's that?"

Both women laugh, giving each other conspiratorial glances.

"Nothing, dear," Maggie says, rubbing Spencer's arm nearest her.

Spence-speak.

Jim gives a sheepish grin as Doris gobbles up the last of her dessert, then blurts out, "Did you hear about Dillon catching Chase and Terri in bed at the inn?"

Spencer sits stunned. Maggie shakes her head with curiosity.

"Chase mentioned it when he stopped by this morning with Jim's marketing plan."

"He told me that in confidence."

"Chase doesn't have the quietest voice."

"Don't go spreading that around, okay?" Jim says.

"Of course not," Maggie says in the tone of a novelist, one who enjoys taking inspiration from real life.

Spencer's first thoughts revolve around what this will do to the team dynamics at tomorrow's race. *Will there be tension between the top two guys? Motivating or destructive?*

"He's thinking about how it will affect the team tomorrow," Maggie says, jarring Spencer from his concerns.

Spencer glances her way, and around the room, all eyes fixate on him. "We'll be fine . . . we're all adults," he says. "I'm sure it's no big deal."

"You can also write off car mileage for supplies!" Doris says.

"That's right," Jim says.

"Great!" Maggie says.

After further talk about what Maggie can write off, and Chase's campaign idea for Jim—"Let Jim Worry About Your Taxes"—Jim suggests that he and Doris best be going. Doris teases him about needing to go through his pre-race packing ritual. Jim doesn't object, but becomes defensive when Spencer adds in a comment about the earlier than normal race start time and hour-long drive, to which Jim responds that he'd only been late that one time.

Saturday Morning
Presidio XC Challenge, San Francisco

Under a heavy foot, Chase's BMW's rear wheels chirp upon exiting Montgomery High School's parking lot, everybody in the car—Dillon up front, Jake, Jim, and Spencer leaned against one another in back—holding on to anything handy to anchor themselves. The digital clock on the dashboard reads 7:39 a.m., the race site approximately sixty minutes away under normal driving conditions, and the race start time in fifty-one minutes. Chase rolls his way through a red stoplight and stomps on the gas pedal, three hundred horses under his command, shooting them westbound onto Highway 12.

"Chase?" Spencer says.

"Yes, Grandma," Chase replies.

"Is this really necessary?"

"You're the numbers guy, Jimbo . . . what do you think?"

"It's going to be tight," Jim says, checking that his seat belt is properly fastened.

"You're an accountant . . . how is it you're always late?" Spencer says. "Deadlines are ominous in your line of work."

"That's why Form 4868 was created: extensions."

"A lot of good that's going to do for us."

"We'll make it, guys. Hold on." Chase brakes heavily and slips into the tight 270-degree apron, transferring them from Highway 12 to the 101, heading south . . . rapidly.

"Whoa!" Dillon groans. "I'm having childhood flashbacks of the teacup ride at Disneyland. If this is your way of getting back at me for barging in on you and—"

"Nonsense," Chase says, flitting out to the HOV lane, accelerating to eighty-five miles per hour, adjusting the frequency knob of his new Whistler cr90 laser radar detector mounted on the dash. "We're good. Besides, this isn't my first rodeo. This one time—"

"Who barged in on who and why?" Jake asks.

"Nothing!" Chase, Dillon, *and* Jim and Spencer say in unison.

Stupefied, Chase and Dillon glance back at Jim and Spencer. An odd silence of confusion swirls around the interior.

"If we'd picked up another race earlier in the season," Spencer says, "we wouldn't *need* this one as our fifth."

"We all have busy schedules, Spence. Don't worry about it," Jake says. "We do what we can. It's not life or death."

Chase's eyes flash frequently and in sequence between all the mirrors available to him, checking for law enforcement either sitting atop overpasses or entering the freeway as he guides the BMW through Rohnert Park, Cotati, down the Petaluma grade and through Petaluma. The sparse Saturday-morning traffic benefits them greatly. Except for Spencer, the rest of the passengers relax to some degree now that they're no longer negotiating tight turns, but rather streaking through the corridor across the Sonoma/Marin County line into Novato.

"You're not asleep, Jim," Chase says, smiling in the rearview mirror.

"Are there air bags back here?" Jim says.

"This car should come with air *sickness* bags," Spencer says.

Dillon reaches into his gym bag and produces a doggie poop bag, handing it to Spencer. "Miles won't miss it."

When everybody catches sight of what Spencer holds, chuckles break out.

"Maybe I'll save it for the neighbor's dog that keeps doing his business in our front yard," Spencer says. "The guy lets the dog out the front door every morning and it runs across the driveway to our lawn and drops one."

"Have you talked to him?" Jake says.

"He laughs and says, 'Dogs will be dogs.'"

"Call the city," Jim says

"I should."

"Put a sign in your front yard that reads 'No Treas-pooping,'" Chase says.

Again chuckles circulate the interior, easing the nerves that are doubly present: racing to a race, and mentally preparing for that race, their usual pre-race rituals out the window. Triage is now the order of the morning. The basics will be, in order of importance and necessity, collect their race bibs—as with all their races, they are pre-registered—and put their race shoes and club singlets on. Depending on their arrival time anything else will be icing on the cake: a few minutes of running, bathroom break, tossing in strides to undo the car ride and loosen the body up. Stretching and pre-race drills are unlikely at this point.

Cruising over a recently repaved section of the 101 through Marin the conversation tapers off, each man going inside to mentally prepare for their race, except for Chase, who maintains his roadside vigilance, occasionally glancing at the radar detector, its relevant needles and light meters passive in their display.

"Loving the new equipment?" Dillon says.

"Oh yeah. The new Nav is voice-activated, which is *sweet*!"

"It's ironic that the crooks used low tech to steal high tech," Jim says.

Chase glances at his rearview mirror.

"Too soon?"

"Pfft."

Once they have worked their way through the commerce and affluence of Marin, the scenery regresses to a lush uninhabited mountainous state, the freeway an upward twisty grade, the passengers stabilizing themselves the best way they can against the centrifugal force of each sweeping turn, the tall median a blur of concrete mere inches away, though Chase doesn't stick just to one lane if others are open. Taking tangents as efficiently as if he's running, he shuttles them over the summit and down into the recently dedicated Robin Williams Tunnel, which jettisons them out to a magnificent view of the Golden Gate Bridge. And for a brief moment the thoughts in their heads set aside their pre-race demands and they enjoy the beauty of the city on the other side of the waterway, a whitewash collage, quiet and peaceful from afar.

Centrifugal force from another sweeping curve brings the bunch back to the moment, approaching and slipping onto the bridge, the sidewalks on each side showing brisk activity at 8:14 a.m. Chase lowers his speed on the bridge, though it's still fast enough to be a jail-able offense. One tower looms over them, and soon they reach the span's apex, the pull of the city grabbing them, bringing them over the final mile and under the second tower. Chase fishes around for and finds the Fast Trac from the console tray below and plops it on the dash. He grins, catching sight of the others' expressions, everybody no doubt wondering if he'll slow down when they pass through the toll station underneath the relic steel banner with the embedded historic clock. He does ease off the accelerator, but not so much that a police officer will reward him for it.

Beep.

Chase slides over to the right lane, taking the Nineteenth Street exit. The upgraded off-ramp offers a friendlier banked turn than the previous edition, allowing Chase to zip through and into the long MacArthur Tunnel, pushing them square into the Presidio on the other side. They approach the first city intersection, a traffic light where left-hand turns are not permitted. Of course they need to make that left, and as is often the case, making a left in San Francisco entails three right turns. Chase scans all his mirrors, the three passengers steadying themselves in back for what they assume he'll likely do.

With a green light in his favor, Chase hangs the illegal left.

"Whoa!" Dillon says, pressed against the passenger door.

Chase smiles, negotiating a residential two-lane street, slowing but never coming to a complete stop unless he has to at each stop sign picketing every block. No one says a thing.

After goosing the pedal to make a "pink" light and catching sight of concerned faces in the rearview, Chase says, "It would've been a waste of a good green light."

At the last stop sign before entering the park, where the race is less than eight minutes from starting, Chase *has* to make a complete stop while an elderly man and woman make their way into the crosswalk. The car idles. Jim's leg twitches. The second hand on Chase's Garmin advances one digital second at a time, the nervous quietness inside the car palpable. He figures the tides of the San Francisco Bay move faster.

"Anytime now, Grandma and Grandpa Moses," Chase says under his breath.

Dillon nods as the couple seems to run out of steam in front of the car, now trudging, though still marching on against the sands of time.

Later than sooner the sea parts and Chase blips the gas pedal. The tires chirp, leading them into the park, approaching the on-street parking area, though Chase can't recall if it's a left or right at the upcoming fork in the road. "Which way?"

"Right," Spencer says.

"Hold on."

"Dude!" Dillon shouts, jerking to his left. "You signaled left."

"I had a 50-50 chance."

A minute later Chase angles his car in between two compacts, glancing at his watch while killing the engine. "Six minutes until race time . . . who's your Chaseter!" Chase takes the nods by the exiting group as acknowledgment of thanks. "Spence . . . TP?" Chase catches the roll Spence tosses over the car's hood.

"Best to change into our race gear here and leave the bags in the car until afterward," Spencer says. "Jim, grab our bib numbers and meet us at the start line. We can warm up with whatever time we have left on the grass field. See everybody on the start line."

More nods follow as everybody hastily sheds unnecessary clothing, dons race singlets, laces up race shoes, and tosses the leftovers back into the car. Everyone but Chase takes off running toward the race hub while he ducks and squats in front of his car, TP in hand, and takes care of business as quickly, calmly, and discreetly as possible, kicking dirt over the disposal.

He tosses the roll back into the car, locks up, checks his watch—four minutes to go—trots down a cement path through a playground, passing by a set of bathrooms that has a line outside. He works himself through the staging area, where clubs have set up base camp, scanning the area for the guys, but seeing no sign of them. Running down and onto the soccer and softball fields shrouded in fog where other racers dart in and out of the mist, throwing in last-minute strides, Chase launches into one of his own, holding the effort for fifteen seconds. He circles the field and performs two more before the starter announces one minute to go. More misty than sweaty, Chase hurries over to Spencer, who's waving Chase's bib number.

"You have time," Spencer says, handing Chase the bib. "I punched the safety pins through."

"Thanks, man." He positions the bib on his chest, getting it mostly aligned, and affixes it. Chase catches sight of the Rob Shore, his pistol raised high, and glances at his watch. "Crap," he mutters under his breath, the watch not ready to record the race properly. He readies a finger to press the Start button anyway, crouches into position, fixates on the—

Crack!

Relax, buddy. Do what you can.

With a lagged reaction, Chase lurches off the line with jittery qualms. His mind knows the team situation—win or go home—but his head, arms, stomach, and legs belie that mandate: dazed, shaky, nauseated, and heavy to be exact. "Discombobulated" better captures his state. On top of that, his watch will not provide accurate data, at least not at first; the lack of a proper warm-up and second trip to the toilet foils his mental game and peace of mind. But most important, this course, his least favorite on the series, does not favor milers—at all! Replete with hills, some long and sustained, a few squat and steep, others mixed variations thereof, it will methodically drain Chase's patented finishing kick one uphill meter at a time. Even the bone-jarring downhills have hampered his finishing form in the past, losing a toenail one year.

The late arrival had landed the guys a poor starting-line position, on the end, and as such Chase feels the pinch as the pack funnels through the narrow opening in the fence line. He slows as the field bunches up while the front-runners, including Dillon and Jim, escape unencumbered, and like an accordion, stride out, leaving Chase on the other side.

Jostling through the narrow gap, Chase lets his arms drift wide, using his hands to manage the bodies swarming him, a gentle push here, a nudge there, steadying himself. When a spike catches his heel and nearly pries his racing flats off, Chase's adrenal glands flood his system with a fresh batch of adrenaline, doubling down on the lingering rush from the drive down. He shortens his stride, taking baby steps until the threat of tripping fades.

The trail, now narrow and canted, forces Chase, running on the downside, to run lopsided, unnaturally applying greater force to the left leg than the right. The tight pack around him, toned legs of various shades of skin color scissoring, their foot strikes in close proximity to his front, rear, and right, shield his sightline. His own footsteps blindly and tentatively grope the unseen trail, steps rigid and jarring like a shaky homemade video, hampering efficiency.

A quarter mile in, Chase groans at the sight of Jake several yards *up front* where the canted terrain levels out. A quick glance to his right—*clear*—Chase slides to the center of the trail, determined to ride Jake's heels, but immediately regrets the move: his feet sink in, wobble, and ensnare his momentum; the sand trap. *Dammit!* Race conditions are unfolding faster than Chase can react to them. He labors through it as best as he can, chastising himself for not avoiding it as those to his left and right have, wisely skirting around the edges. The main pack plows right through, including Jake, whose beach-running strength leaves him ideally suited for it, going by a half a dozen runners over the hundred-yard stretch, and another handful upon exiting, his uninterrupted momentum carrying him up the first appreciable hill of the morning.

Chase rallies beyond the beach, though at three-quarter throttle where the lumpy nature of the rutted and sporadically rooted trail hampers his rhythm. A step here, right on, but the next meets with a loose rock, throwing his cadence off, his torso countering for the lack of stability. Good step, good step, bad step . . . and so he slogs along.

They rise to street level, where the guys parked, a long gradual uphill over an unmaintained dirt sidewalk Chase's extended view. He glances to the left at his BMW; thoughts of refuge come to mind. Instead, he surveys the situation, the string of runners stretched out ahead, and catches sight of Jake again, who is one position up on an Agras runner, their *fifth* man. *Crap, crap, crap.* Chase wants to latch on. A short burst is all it'll take. He routinely recruits fast-twitch muscles in his sleep. Sleep. Sleeping in. A warm cup of coffee on a foggy San Francisco morning.

Early risers from nearby neighborhoods stroll by on the left, walking dogs who stop, sniff, and require encouragement with a tug of the leash to continue on. To his right children clamber over playground equipment with squeals and smiles while watchful parents stand sedately by, observing. Moments later a tennis ball thwacks the chain-link fence off to the side, the player walking over to retrieve it yelling, "Line!"

Is this a cross-country race or a stroll through the park?

By the time he reaches the summit to veer right, Chase is no closer to Jake or the Agras's fifth man, and now the first significant downhill looms. Chase attempts to open his stride, to build some speed before the race tumbles into oblivion, but the effort is futile at best, lacking punch or effect. And before he can muster another attempt he's leaning back on his heels, braking hard, the course dropping out from underneath him. Chase loses a handful of spots until the hill bottoms out, where he releases and feels a modicum of energy, but the next hill sends him reeling again. Bogged down and no will to bear down, he churns out the twisty climb, staring at the ground passing by in vivid detail until the summit: hard-packed dirt and gravel periodically sliced diagonally with shallow trenches to allow for rainfall runoff that are incongruous to his stride, requiring adjustments on every other step to avoid stepping in them.

Around the next turn, Chase's breath shoots pains through his chest as if each lung is in a vise, squeezing every molecule of oxygen from him. Faintly dizzy, he shakes out his arms, relaxes his shoulders, modifies his breaths, each deeper and deeper from the diaphragm.

Snap out of it, asshole! We need this win!

With the Agras's fifth man lingering nearby and Jake farther on up, Chase glances at his watch for the first time, attempting to ground himself, perhaps reset and shake off the dreadful zombielike experience, but finds the current time of day on display rather than race details. Now utterly frustrated and plummeting down another rapid descent to the halfway point, Chase mutters choice cuss words, which leads to him to laugh out loud and shout, "Screw it!" Runners near him, including the Agras'a fifth man, glance over but say nothing.

With an awkward U-turn around a large, thick tree trunk approaching, Dillon comes by in the opposite direction in third place, ahead of all Agras except one, the leader.

"What are you doing?" Dillon asks.

Good question. What am I doing?

Next, Jim rushes by in eighth place, saying nothing, but his expression *challenges* Chase, reminding him of the toast he'd given Jim after finishing behind him: "Don't get used to it," or something to that effect.

Next comes Jake, who says, "Remember the dunes."

Chase remembers. The fish-out-of-water experience. The soreness, forty-eight hours' worth. His socks from that day still have sand in them.

Spence-speak.

There it is, what Chase needs, bringing it home moments before playing ring-around-the-rosy at the turnaround.

The return trip commences, a long, arduous climb, the last one of the day. A second wind fuels Chase's legs, unlike those up ahead, whose legs, he imagines, have turned to Jell-O after pounding downhill. Reconnecting with that smooth, steady groove from the sand dunes and his intervals on the track,

Chase envisions the summit three-quarters of a mile away, and the hard left that will bless him with a mile-plus-long downhill into the finish, an opportunity to turn this poor excuse of a performance around, salvaging pride at the very least, granting his club a competitive chance at the most.

Chase goes by Spencer, sensing the coach's concern and own personal sacrifice, having committed to cross-country training, to which Chase responds unceremoniously, gapping the coach, an informal apology.

After a series of hostile takeovers, Chase catches Jake, whose long legs are holding their own against shorter ones.

"Trammels, baby," Jakes says with a sly grin that contrasts with Chase's determined focus.

Chase nods and pushes on, running tangents with precision as if behind the wheel of his BMW, going by the cavalcade—Agras, Chico, Dipsean, unattached, East Bay Runners, Agras, Chico—taking no prisoners, mercilessly leaving a wake of CO_2 and sinewy debris, finally reaching the summit and banking left, at last grasping what Jake means by "trammels."

Leave nothing on the table!

Chase ignores his lungs' desire for respite and instead doubles down on the effort. Lifting his gaze on the string of runners in the foreground, he spots Jim many places and a hundred yards ahead. *Challenge accepted, buddy.* Chase picks a line along the rutted double-wide trail sidewalk, one that's served him well in the past. His foot strikes meet the ground with force, confident, in rapid succession, landing barely long enough to leave an imprint, catapulting him by several runners, those he normally doesn't contend with. Today they're fodder.

Now we're rolling, baby!

Saturday-morning recreational energy melds and rushes by Chase: a tennis ball zings back and forth between sweet spots, a grunt with each; children beg restless parents for one more trip down the slide; dogs yap, pant, and give chase, straining against leashes, ready to break free.

Sweeping by his BMW, siting proud, no longer offering refuge, Chase streaks by Jim and two others, restoring partial order to the day. Seconds later the sand pit looms again but never bears Chase's weight as he artfully skirts around it. His legs, like high-performance shocks, coil tightly under their load and explosively release, rocketing him forward, his pace increasing exponentially.

The cheers through the registration area sound faint, buffered by air whistling past his ears. Despite a gaze fifteen yards out, the world rushes toward him in surreal fashion. So surreal in fact that he no longer feels like he's in control, but rather on autopilot. His trained body requires no mental input, simply shut up and stay out of the way, just like in his most epic track race ever back in college.

You're the only *sub-4 miler in this race. . . .*

Through the accordion gate and back out on the grass field where the race started a lifetime ago brilliant sunlight slashes through the fog. Chase slants left and starts the final quarter mile around the tilled perimeter. Up on his toes he goes, barrel chest expanding, mouth wide open. With each stride his split shorts stretch at the seams, flashing striated quads. A fissure forms in his universe. Dark silence engulfs him. Again. The mind/body paradox, the impulse to stop/the compulsion to plunge into the fissure full-force, to *make* it hurt. One guy, then another, then another, he floats over clods and divots that others labor through; a ribbon of jersey colors flutter by.

Into the final right-hander, full-bore, he leans, feet blindly finding firm banked footholds, headlong with abandon by one last runner, an Agras, and over the finish line, unconcerned over *not* capturing a finishing time.

Despite no longer willfully driving his body, his momentum carries him the length of the chute, where at the end he rips the bottom tag of his bib off and holds it out to the bib taker. Chase's speed makes it impossible to snatch cleanly and the volunteer grabs at the tag several times while it flutters before retrieving it. Energy expended Chase drifts to a stop, bends over, exhausted and angry and relieved and emotionally wrung out, ready to heave but lacking the stomach to do so.

It's over. It's over . . . It's over. You did it. It's over.

Chase straightens and places his hands on the back of his head like a bird spreading its wings. Oxygen fills the deficit with every breath while the world swirls around him in stilted fashion. At times he's not sure if he's leaning and about to fall, or standing upright and rigid like a flagpole.

It's over. You did it. It's over.

"What was your . . . last mile?" asks the guy Chase passed at the finish line. "I had two-hundred yards . . . on you at the turnaround."

Chase glances at his watch, blurry eyes rapidly blinking, and shrugs.

The guy checks his watch. "Had to have been under 4:10."

Chase nods, unable to form words, shaking the guy's hand instead. He walks over to Dillon, who's down on one knee struggling to untie his shoe that he'd triple knotted in haste. Chase circles Dillon for fear of tipping over him by coming to a complete stop, all the while watching Jim cross the line complete with a satisfied grimace. Soon Spencer comes shuffle-striding around the last turn, going by Jake right before the finish line.

"Great finish, Chase," Jake says, giving Chase a pat to the back once he filtered through the chute. "Fifth, Sixth?"

Chase held up five fingers.

"Where'd you end up, Dillon?"

Dillon gives up on his shoe-removal effort. "Third."

"The second guy was unattached"—Spencer lets out a forceful cough—"you'll get second-place points for team scoring,"

"You okay, Chase?" Jim says.

"This course sucks," he says, bent over, contemplating the notion of kneeling on the wet grass to steady himself. In the end he straightens up. "You're either climbing a mountain or screaming down it. It's more like trail racing."

"No kidding," Dillon says. "Without a preview, I almost blew right past the turnaround. It came up *quick!*"

"And it's different from last year," Jim says. "I thought we were doing two loops, not an out and back."

The guys saunter back through the registration area and up to their ride, discussing their frantic drive down with other runners from various clubs along the way.

"Hey, Dillon," Chase says, approaching the BMW. "Do you have another poop bag?"

"Did you treas-poop?"

"I certainly wasn't going to wait in line."

Dillon tosses Chase another poop bag as they prepare for a warm-down, discussing their races, how it felt like a punch in the gut after arriving so late and jumping straight into it. Jim apologizes twice, but the guys wave it off, collectively adding it to one of their many road-trip adventures. Already alongside the course, they jog toward the halfway-point turnaround and back for their warm-down. Passing through the registration area, they find the results posted and stop. Spencer estimates their team score.

"I think we actually pulled it off," he says, staring intently at the score sheet taped to the bathroom's brick exterior wall.

"Really?" Chase says. "The way I ran the first half?"

"Looks that way," Spencer says. "You beat the Agras's second man again."

"Excellent!"

"And me and Jake both moved up this week."

"Nice," Dillon says. "PA Championships, here we come."

"We should arrive late more often," Jim says wryly.

Spence-speak.

"I'm hungry," Chase says. "Let's stop at La Vera's on the way home to celebrate."

Heading back to the car, Chase formulates how his Facebook post will read, the epic finish he summoned after a crappy start. It surely will garner a huge response, despite the lack of actual data to back it up. And as he concludes the thought he overhears the Chico squad, running in the opposite direction, discussing Chase's unreal last mile, the way he blazed by two of them.

I did it, Mom and Dad. Again.

Sunday Morning
Air BR&B

It takes three Spence-speaks under a placid mid-November morning sky in which a hot-air balloon drifts lazily overhead, the periodic hiss of the propane burner punctuating the stillness, before Chase relents.

"Sorry," Chase says, drawing back to the group yet again, working their way through Beardsworth's vineyards, heading back toward the BR&B fence line. "I don't feel like I ran a complete race yesterday. The legs feel deprived."

"You made up for it on the drive down," Dillon says.

"I drive with purpose."

"*Up in the Air*," Jim, Jake and Dillon say.

"Really?" Chase says. "Unintended."

"Now we're only one point behind the Agras," Spencer says.

"So by winning the PA Championships we'll earn another ten points to their nine for an overall tie?" Dillon says. "How are ties broken? And why is *this* race on Sunday?"

"A number of PA members are high school coaches, and CIF sectionals are on Saturday, so they—"

"That's right," Dillon says, watching the checkered hot-air balloon steadily descend from the sky up ahead. "You're going to have a busy weekend."

"They always are. So double points are awarded at the championships, twenty points to their eighteen."

"Got it. Win by a shoelace."

"As a club does everyone follow the same training regimen?" asks Anders, the Danish gentleman running alongside Dillon, a guest staying in the Helsinki Room.

Laughs and chuckles from the guys answer his question.

"We're like the solar system," Jake says. "Each of us in a different orbit around the sun."

"The chances of us peaking at the same time for a race is on par with a solar eclipse," Jim says.

"Sometimes a couple of us will train for the same event, like a destination marathon, but even then our training programs will differ," Spencer says.

"About the only thing we do as a group is the Sunday long run," Jim says.

"But the good news is that we're all usually in good shape when certain races come up," Spencer says.

"Does your club have organized workouts back in Copenhagen?" Dillon says.

Anders nods. "I suppose there are, but I don't compete."

Dillon glances at the Dane, who appears *very* fit and running as comfortably with them as any highly trained runner would. His physique, over six feet tall with broad shoulders, suggests he could bench press the entire open team.

"Really?" Chase says.

"Really."

"Seriously?" Chase says, his tone laced with shock and dismay.

"Staying fit is the primary objective. Anything else is not important."

"Interesting," Jim says.

"So . . . you just train . . . that's it?" Chase says.

"I have a routine, yes, but it's not born from necessity to prepare for an event. If you must label it, call it 'fitness.'"

"Really?!" Chase's disbelief slices through the crisp air. Squawks overhead from southbound geese in formation echo Chase's sentiment.

"Yes, really," Anders says patiently.

"Then what's the point?"

"Physical well being is the point. The degree is not, solely the satisfaction. I look forward to my sixty minutes each day. Americans might refer to it as a 'hobby.'"

"Is that balloon going to land out here?" Dillon says when it has all but succumbed to gravity, inching closer and closer to the ground a hundred yards ahead.

"Yeah, they do that from time to time," Jake says, his expression showing concern.

"Where's their support crew?" Chase says, scanning the area for the truck that chases a balloon from launch to landing.

"Good question." Jake quickens his pace, getting out in front of the guys. Chase immediately follows, Dillon and Jim soon thereafter.

Spence-speak.

"You don't approve of their acceleration?" Anders says.

Instead of answering, Spencer watches as Jake and Chase reach the balloon and grab hold of the rope dragging out from the basket. Both men steady the basket's drift and guide it to a safer landing spot—amidst thanks from the four balloonists—along the dirt perimeter road rather than the riskier vineyard rows fitted with stakes and wires.

"Greetings, Jake," the graying balloon operator says, the basket touching down.

The occupants cheer the safe landing.

"Hey, Francis," Jake says, letting the rope go. "Ground wind catch you off guard?"

"That'd be correct," Francis says, opening the basket door for his guests to exit. He gazes beyond the guys. "Looks like my crew is a day late and dollar short this morning."

The guys all turn to the approaching sound of a truck and balloon trailer rumbling its way down the dirt path.

After the excitement of the landing subsides and Jake introduces Francis to the other guys, Jake and Francis begin talking between themselves, preparing the traditional post-landing Champagne toast while the balloon chase crew deflates the balloon and readies it for storage.

"Dillon," Chase says, "add hot-air ballooning to your list of inn perks." Chase gestures to Francis, who has spread a red-and-white checkered blanket on the ground and is preparing to pop the Champagne cork.

Dillon scans the scene, envisioning the idea.

With the insistence of the balloonists, the guys are invited to toast the safe flight and landing. They each receive a flute of Champagne and listen to "The Balloonist's Prayer," as Francis refers to it, though Jake joins in the recitation:

The winds have welcomed you with softness
The sun has blessed you with its warm hands
You have flown so high and so well
That God has joined you in your laughter
and set you gently back into the loving arms of Mother Earth.

Jubilant flutes rise, clink, and christen lips.

Empty flute in hand, Dillon mentions his need to tend to the BR&B, and after asking for and receiving Francis's business card—as well as inviting the balloonist and crew alike to join him for breakfast—he and the guys return to running, though slower and with less concern for pace.

"Do you run *only* to race?" Jake asks Chase.

"What?" Chase says, slow to register the earlier conversation. "Oh, yeah. It's what motivated me to start running, so I suppose yes."

"Would you continue running if you stopped racing?" Dillon says. "I know I would. Running helps me work out my frustrations."

"Runners never retire; they simply do not register for the next race," Jake says with a smile.

"Or get lost in lottery limbo," Chase says. "I guess I do enjoy *running*, so, yeah, I'd continue training without racing goals. Hard to say for sure, though. Seems like everything I do has a goal attached to it."

"Create new running goals," Jim says, "like stepping up to longer distances, or wearing a shirt more often."

"Pfft."

"Running can simply be a lifestyle, an end in itself," Anders says. "A ritual to stimulate the body in conjunction with the rest of the day's needs, work for the mind, socialization for the soul. I find the pleasurable facets of a run are lost when focus centers on times or schedules, and excessive competition dulls the senses as to why you run in the first place. *Training* makes running complicated, removes the freedom of the actual movement. I prefer to run free of such impediments, not become a slave to a regimen that prescribes certain workouts that I may or may not like doing on a particular day."

"For a man of few words, Anders, that was an eloquent deluge," Chase says. "I get what you're saying. I'd miss the competition, though."

"That's what Strava's for," Spencer says. "Compete virtually."

Chase laughs. "Enticing, but not the same. I can't see the look of disappointment in the vanquished."

"Interesting . . ." Jake says.

"No hobbies?" Jim says.

"I collect technology." A cheesy grin follows.

"Bo Jackson called playing professional football and baseball hobbies," Dillon says.

"There you go," Jim says.

"Talk about marketing brilliance," Chase says. "Bo Knows!"

The group has ducked under the fence line and is now climbing the stairs to the porch of the BR&B. Inside, Maggie, Linda, and Doris have arrived early and are preparing breakfast, much to Dillon's dismay, though he does thank them before shooing them aside.

"Where's Terri?" Linda says after relinquishing the conspicuously absent employee's preparation duties.

The question leaves an awkward silence among the group gathered around the kitchen island. Glances are exchanged among the guys, directed especially toward Chase, who averts his eyes and reaches for a cardboard box he brought in earlier, which leaves Linda confused and looking to Jake for help.

Jake shrugs.

"*WooooowooowoooWooooowoooo.*"

"She's working on her thesis today," Dillon says, preparing a dozen muffin cups with sausage, egg, and savory seasonings to bake in the oven.

Miles lies down, paws her snout, and groans.

Dillon's answer doesn't completely satisfy the silent curiosity, but at least no one asks further questions.

"Check these out," Chase says, opening the box. He pulls out a light-blue tech shirt and holds it up to his chest.

"Chase bought a shirt!" Doris says.

"Excellent." Jake reaches into the box and fetches one.

"RERC Cross-Country Takes Sole," Spencer reads aloud the slogan across the front. "Nicely done."

"I printed up bumper stickers too." Chase rummages through the box, producing them.

"Do you happen to have an extra—?" Anders says.

"Of course," Chase says, tossing him a shirt. "Competition not required."

Soon the balloonists descend upon the BR&B with stories from their morning journey high above Sonoma County's countryside, commenting on the fertile tapestry of vineyards that sprawl across flat expanses, up and down hillsides, and along the picturesque Russian River, snaking its way west to the

Pacific Ocean. Dillon serves up breakfast to the hungry collective seated and standing around the kitchen island, whose varied backgrounds and paths in life merge into a serendipitous morning of strangers becoming friends.

PA/USATF TOP 5 TEAM STANDINGS AS OF 11/22/2015 (y: Five best scores tallied)		
	Club	Total
1	Agras (10-9-10-10-9-9(y))	48
2	RERC (9-x-9-9-10-10)	47
3	Chico Running Club (8-10-8-8-x-8)	42
4	Strawberry Hill Harriers (7-7-7-5(y)-7-7)	35
5	South Bay Striders (6-8-4-x-8-6)	32

Week 46 Training Summary			
Runner	Long Run	Mileage Total	Comments
Dillon	10	61	Looking forward to the PA Champs. Goal: WIN!
Chase	9.12	54	Raced like crap! Solid finish.
Spencer	9.50	59	Body is handling the intensity much better
Jim	9	44	The Agras look worried.
Jake	9	56	Chase ran the gutsiest race I've ever seen him run.

Week 12
November 16

Ding, ding, ding. "On your left," says a male voice from behind Spencer, whose workout places him on the creekside paths west of Fulton Road. Spencer angles to the right side of the asphalt's edge.

"Thanks," says the woman on the back of the tandem bike a moment later, the couple breezing by.

"Be careful of the high school runners up front," Spencer hollers.

"Okay," says the woman's fading voice along with a courtesy hand wave.

"Ding, ding, ding," comes a male voice a moment later, again from behind Spencer. "On your left."

Baffled, Spencer stays put, skirting along the edge. He's not accustomed to being passed during a run. He glances over his shoulder and smiles. "Where'd you come from?"

Jake sidles up alongside Spencer. "I was on the other side of the creek. I crossed over at Fulton, and I've been playing catch-up between your surges. Where'd you start from?"

"Where the creek path picks up at Greenvale and Fulton."

Jake chuckles. "Eugene back there"—Jake motions behind him—"said you started from—"

Beep. "Hold that thought," Spencer says, accelerating. Besides watching over his cross-country team's thirty minute tempo run, Spencer is performing his own workout, forty-five-second pickups broken up into three equal parts, where by the time he hits the final fifteen-second segment, he'll be running flat-out.

Beep. The first segment down, Spencer concentrates on his form, ensuring proper mechanics at faster speeds, accelerating and passing a couple boys from the high school group. "Head up, Rodger; shoulders back, Dan."

Beep. The bike path blurs by underneath, a smooth ribbon of black asphalt, cracks, noticeable at pedestrian speeds, fuse together, cast aside for a few fleeting seconds.

Beep. Spencer disengages the mental accelerator, his body leaning back to aid in decelerating. Rodger and Dan come by him moments later, head up and shoulders back, respectively.

"Nice one, Coach," Rodger says.

Pace steady, Jake catches up to Spencer, playing the turtle to Spencer's hare.

"What'd Eugene say?" Spencer asks.

"That you started at the 'sacred Samoan burial grounds.'"

"The what?" Breathing returning to order, mind processing Eugene's comment, Spencer pieces together the reference and utters a Spence-speak. "We parked across from their church," he says. "Their parking lot has a locked gate."

"Speaking of which, how'd your dinner go with the newlyweds last week?"

"Maggie and I realized that we'd never had a couple's dinner with them. It's always been at group functions."

"I'm sure it gave Maggie a chance to hear all about the wedding, and view the pictures—"

Beep. Spencer launches into another forty-five-second effort, overcoming easy-running inertia to top speed, then its inverse until Jake comes up alongside.

"Saved by the *beep.*"

Spencer glances over to Jake.

"Wedding pictures, discussion . . . *beep.*"

"It's the training schedule. I don't control it."

"If you say so. But you do have a knack for avoiding the topic."

"After Jim and Doris left, Maggie said that it felt like she and I were 'playing house.'"

"Are you?"

Spencer shrugs. "I told her girls play house and invite boys in; boys build forts to keep girls out."

"I'll bet that went over—"

Beep. "Not so much," Spencer says, rushing away again. "I honestly don't know the answer." Spencer lags in reaching peak speed, holding on to it for the final seven seconds. As he slows he spots Zac, approaching, strong and focused. "Nice and smooth, Zac. Nice and smooth." Zac breezes by as smooth and effortless as the tandem bike had earlier. The next kid in sight is more than two hundred yards back.

"Keep it going, Zac," Jake says. "Won't be too long before beating him at local races will be a thing of the past."

"He's certainly firing on all cylinders."

"You do know that Maggie *not* attending the wedding is her passive-aggressive way of saying she wants to walk down the aisle, don't you?"

"That's a rough transition."

"Like a quick jab before the next beep."

"She'd planned on attending the conference before the invites went out."

Off-beat and out of sync like a garage band, their foot strikes slap the asphalt.

Spencer glances at Jake, who has a smirk on his face. "Really?"

"But did she have everything booked?"

Spencer considers the idea but can't piece it all together.

"You know how it's hard to watch a race you'd planned on running in but can't because of injury?"

Spencer nods, pondering the analogy. *Beep.* Spencer responds quicker than the previous interval, hitting full speed perfectly.

"They want *Titanic* love," Jake says once he catches up and Spencer has dished out words of encouragement to his young charges streaming by in the opposite direction.

"What?"

"Most women, they want a guy who loves unconditionally. By giving everything *but* marriage places a limit on your love for her."

"So you're equating death with marriage. Not much of selling point."

"I'm sure she *loves* your deflection."

Spence-speak.

"I'm just saying that you can love her nine ways to Sunday, but if the one thing that she wants is left *wanting*, she's going to feel incomplete no matter how much reason you lay out there.

"Good job, Gavin. Focus on Don up front. Don't let him gap you."

Beep. Spencer revs up again as Sid and Oz approach, Oz laughing at a comment Sid has made. "Oz, focus. This is the time to dig in. Now, drop Sid and get a move on. Sid, don't let Oz drop you."

"Got it, Coach," Sid says, summoning the appropriate pace and demeanor.

By the time Jake bridges the gap to Spencer they've neared the end of the creekside path at Willowside.

"I'm parked here," Jake says, extending a hand to shake Spencer's. "Say hi to Maggie for me."

Spencer manages an acrobatic handshake, slowing, grasping, releasing, pivoting, as his watch summons him. "I will." Spencer reverses his direction and speeds off. Pushing forward, leaning back, weaving through his squad, he doles out instruction and encouragement and considers Jake's marital commentary. Often such advice comes disguised as lessons learned from those with shaky relationship track records, but Jake's self-actualized presence lends a weighty hand to the discussion, an attribute Spencer admires. *What am I scared of?* If he can answer *that* question, he can conceivably ascend Maslow's hierarchy of needs as well. Why is he stuck? Can all the personal and professional responsibilities he accumulates in his life crowd out others, commitment after commitment except the one commitment?

As the sun slowly concedes its presence in the sky, Spencer keeps wondering: *What am I scared of?*

Thursday Late Morning
Gone Fishing

Under Billy Mill's black-and-white frozen moment of triumph, Jim rummages through a dozen boxes in the garage until he finds the one that stores his three-piece fishing pole. It hasn't been used since the backpacking trip he, Jake, Chase, and Spencer took in the Trinity Shasta region several years earlier. He snaps it together, inspects it thoroughly, and disassembles it. He rummages around for some other equipment, loading it all into a small day pack, the three pieces of the pole poking out the top.

"Find it?" Doris asks when he walks back into the house.

"Yep," he replies, gathering food items for his run and fishing adventure out at Armstrong Woods. "I should be home—"

"Just have fun and stop worrying." She wraps her arms around him. "Jake can't make it?"

"He's at a tech expo."

Doris cackles.

Jim grins. "I know."

"My mountain man," she says, giving him an embarrassingly long kiss afterward.

"You goof," he says once the mock mauling concludes.

Jim steers his Subaru alongside the meandering westbound, tree- and vineyard-lined Russian River, hangs a right in Guerneville thirty minutes later, and heads up to the state park's visitors' parking lot, fee-free and nearly empty. Ready with the light pack on his back, he jogs toward the trailhead, ascending immediately into solitude among the majestic, towering redwoods.

With the PA Championships three days away, he scales his efforts accordingly on the steep and rooted terrain; no need to burden the body excessively. He recalls the first time he ran/walked this route up to Bullfrog Pond to go fishing with Jake back in junior high, the day he became a runner, the day he realized running could be more than punishment doled out by his Little League coach for striking out—ten laps around the baseball field for each one after the game, if memory served. It was a Saturday morning when

Jake's mom—who kept a scornful eye on Jim during the drive there and back post–Condom Condemnation Act of '89—dropped them off for the day, complete with fishing poles, beef jerky, and cans of Sunkist orange soda. They didn't have day packs back then, just cloth grocery bags that they stuffed the food items in, carrying their poles in a free hand while they ran up the trail in long shorts, though Jim's hill fitness at the time paled in comparison to Jake's, who was gracious enough to slow down and walk on the steeper inclines with Jim.

By the time Jim negotiates the initial switchbacks and the trail's intensity diminishes, the carefree kid of yesteryear emerges, ambling along with no deadlines or timelines to guide him, sneaking peeks here and there of the sheer drop-off just a foot to his left, sensing the thrill of tumbling into a different kind of worry with one bad step.

Running with young Jake set the stage for the freedom Jim experiences in running today. While it doesn't always shoo away the doubts he harbors, it at least allows him to put them into perspective, place them outside himself to evaluate objectively. And though he rarely solves a dilemma the respite from juggling matters internally feels like a vacation nonetheless.

Jim reaches the steepest incline of the day, slows to a fast hike, bends forward, and places a hand on each quad, aiding in the uphill assault, a trick he learned from one of the better ultrarunners in the club who said that some hills are better tackled in this manner rather than running them, ultimately conserving energy. It seems to work, though it looks and feels silly, hunched over like a knuckle-dragging caveman.

Upright and running, additional hills press Jim's cardiovascular system, lifting him higher and higher toward the campgrounds and the pond where he and Jake had acted out scenes from Mark Twain's classics: Jim playing Huckleberry Finn to Jake's Tom Sawyer. There had been an old log that had lost its battle to sudden oak death disease many years before, stretched out into the pond from the shore, and on it they'd take their shoes and socks off, cop a squat, and cast their lines, snacking on the bounty they'd brought with them.

The campground surroundings appear smaller to Jim in many regards upon approach, like a grade school shrinks in the mind of the adult who revisits it with their own child. The fallen log is no longer there, either removed or dissolved back to nature. The current drought has taken its toll as well, the pond a former shadow of itself. But none of this sullies the nostalgia Jim senses, unpacking and piecing the fishing pole together, and then walking around to an area with good exposure to the pond, where he can cast in toward a patch of tall reeds. And once line has been cast and lure submerged where desired, Jim reels it in until it jumps up out of the water and dangles near the pole tip. And like the angler from yesteryear he repeats the process, a steady rhythmic cadence of patience that Jake instilled in him.

It's unlikely he'll catch anything more than pond scum and debris, but that's not the point. Eventually he casts away and lets the lure dangle underneath a bobber he's added, sits down, and chews on beef jerky while sipping Sunkist orange soda, watching the shadows from the afternoon sun shift around him, the tall trees nearby playing their part as sundial.

The afternoon ambience lulls Jim to sleep, and upon waking he gazes upward, large clouds drifting in like the first carnies to arrive for a circus, announcing the arrival of the big storm forecasted for the upcoming weekend. "Storm of the century," the news called it, but it *is* California, as Chase would say, so who knows. Jim chuckles under his breath.

Jim closes his eyes and imagines the race in progress, the wet slop they'll have to run through. A long dry summer followed by a dry autumn often leaves him and the others mentally and physically spoiled, unprepared for the wet conditions of *true* cross-country. Here he harks back to past races where course conditions have been a factor. His mind's eye conjures up the tactics and strategies that come with it, the adaptation necessary to compete and not just survive. Immersed in the imagery, key leg muscles twitch as he visualizes himself hurdling the old log on the backside of the course while others may step on top of it to go over, confidently plowing through every mud puddle, bouncing back up without hesitation should a misstep along the slick grass send him to the ground. Three laps, two miles each, the largest field of competitors they've seen all season, everyone's quest the same: club bragging rights fought with nothing more than swift legs and courage.

By the time Jim completes his PA Championship visualization the sun has disappeared behind the thick grove of trees that blankets the land between the pond and the coast. It will be another two hours until sunset, but the day always seems to end earlier out here. And with that, Huck Finn packs up his gear and goodies, and runs back to his car, a mostly downhill affair, recalling Tom Sawyer's wisdom from years ago: "Downhill running is tax-free running; take advantage of it."

Thursday Afternoon
First Annual North Bay Landscaping & Technology Expo

City legs are unsuited for this type of terrain and best left for those with sole in their soul. He hops and stutter-steps from one foot to the other, lunging over, stepping on top of, and swerving around a minefield of—

"What do you think?" says the man standing beside Jake amongst a small group in front of a software vendor's booth.

Jake reengages with the demonstration in progress, a young man extolling the latest mobile integrated version of AutoCAD 360 and its applicability for landscapers. "Seems like a lot of work to map out where a tree goes."

"But it has the new Smart Pen feature, and it's integrated with Dropbox so you can share files with your team and clients. The 2-D and 3-D capabilities alone are worth the steep learning curve."

Jake stands patiently, uninterested in furthering the conversation. "True." He half wishes he'd skipped the expo, confined to the large, breezy Veterans Memorial Hall, and joined Jim on his run at Armstrong Woods. "I'd rather spend my time out in the field getting a feel for the property than artificially tinkering with it on a computer. It gives me a better perspective."

The man dressed in slacks and a button-down shirt strokes his goatee with an index finger and thumb, nods, and directs his attention back to the demo. Jake listens to the software rep hype the ability to view landscaping designs on an iPad, which he's now interacting with, for another minute before returning to the ultimate paragraph of his "prose poem," recalling his run up at Annadel earlier that morning where he ran for a short while with a trio of local junior college students.

. . . potential ankle twists—

"Hey, Jake," says another man who wanders up, much older than Jake, with white hair, a tucked-in plaid shirt, and a leather belt holding up faded jeans.

"Hey, Franklin," Jake says, offering a handshake. "I didn't expect to see you here."

Franklin grunts. "The kid's out in Alexander valley finishing up a job." He chuckles. "Like I understand any of this tech crap."

Jake smiles. "It has some benefits, but as Ellen Glasgow is reputed to have said, 'Not all change is growth, as not all movement is forward.'"

Franklin cocks his head to one side.

"In other words, change for change sake doesn't always improve on the tried and true."

"As long as I have the kid he can deal with it. It's his business when I retire." Franklin starts to laugh but instead produces a phlegmy cough. "Although I do like these laser rangefinders." He retrieves the device clipped to his back pocket. "I can stand in one spot and practically measure the entire area, then hand it off to the kid and he does his magic on the computer."

Jake regards the device. He knows about it, but skipped the earlier demo on it. If he isn't interested in software to design and plot out a yard, gathering measurements with the device is moot. Besides, Jake enjoys walking around a client's yard, gathering the measurements he needs. On occasion he'll take a picture of an area if an unusual aspect presents itself. Deep observation and scant notes are all he needs.

"See?" Franklin has measured the distance from where they stand to the back wall.

"Walk with me," Jake says before he reads the value. They head toward the smart irrigation system display, Jake taking the same type of steps he does while out on a client's property, mentally tallying each one. Arriving at the row of tables he stops, guesstimates the distance to the wall and adds it to the total in his head: *126 feet.* He reads the measurement off Franklin's one concession to technology and smiles.

"Seriously?" Franklin says.

"Close enough."

Franklin coughs. "You should audition for one of those whisperer TV—"

"Jake!" says a middle-aged man who pats Jake on the back. "Great job on the waterfall out at Bodega Bay. I swear it looks like a scene straight out of Yosemite. Submit some pictures to *Landscape Architectural Digest*. You might pick up a nomination."

"Hey, Norman," Jake says. "It's been a while. Still with Elysium Gardens?"

"Earthy hands, happy soul."

"Norman, this is Franklin. Franklin, Norman."

The men shake hands.

"I need your opinion, Jake," Norman says, "on these new auto-sprinkler models."

As Jake recites the latest info on one brand, Franklin excuses himself with, "Way over my head, gentlemen."

"Many of the smart irrigation controllers," Jake says, "tout how you can remotely control their systems, but the reality of the matter is that once it's configured you rarely need to adjust the settings. Definitely go with the models that have moisture-control sensors, though. They sense if it has rained and shut the system down until the next cycle. Some have weather forecast data fed to the system wirelessly to perform the same action, but again, overkill and a marketing point."

Norman divides his attention between listening to Jake and peeking at the different models on display, most of which are either integrated with a laptop or smartphone.

"They also have a hefty price tag," Jake says, watching Norman ponder the shiny new objects. While Jake steers *his* clients away from extravagant purchases that have little use over the long haul, he does acquiesce to the more affluent set, such as the former San Diego couple living up on Skyfarm who have money to spend and want the latest and greatest technology. In such instances, Jake seeks Zac's expertise in setting up the remote-control aspect, computers, smart phones, tablets, and whatever other device is available for the client to track the rate of plant growth while on vacation.

"You going to check out the new mobile communication packages?" Norman asks Jake. "I hear you can Skype with clients *and* show onscreen design schematics simultaneously."

Jake smiles. "I think I can manage a conversation without a package."

Norman laughs, turning to leave. "Fair enough."

Jake steps to the side and out of the way as a small group approaches the vendor's table. He rereads what he's written earlier and continues on:

> *Fitter, younger explorers may extend him on less challenging terrain, but on this trail, they struggle to stay on his heels. Gracing them with Irish step-dancer form, he easily disappears up the tortuous, 1,600-foot climb to the summit, humbling even the most prideful soul.*
>
> *Jake D.*

Friday Afternoon
RERC Room Housekeeping

Dillon is in the middle of making the bed in the renovated RERC Room steeped in deep purple and green tones. Above the headboard, wallpaper depicts a cluster of hot-air balloons dotting a blue sky at sunrise. On the wall across from the foot of the bed hangs a five-piece oil painting of the entire Peanuts Gang on loan from a club member, who knew Charles M. Schulz and regularly skated at the Snoopy Ice Arena throughout his youth. Charlie Brown and Snoopy are hoisted by Lucy, Schroeder, and Peppermint Patty, with Franklin and Sally on the flanks in a joyous celebration of friendship and community. A plaque near the doorway lists the RERC's hall of fame inductees from 2008 onward: Darryl Beardall, Mort Gray, Carl Jackson, Brendan Hutchinson, Dan Preston, Pamela Horton, Al Tagliaferri, Bob Holland, Jim Ray, Kathy Van Riper, Mike McGuire, Ralph Harms, Shirley Fee, Jerry Lyman, Jon Hermstad, Brad Zanetti.

"*Wooooowooooowooo Wooooowooooo.*" After sitting quietly in the room, overseeing Dillon's handiwork, Miles trots over to the doorway.

"Room looks nice," Terri says when Dillon catches sight of her leaned up against the doorjamb. She kneels down to pet Miles.

"Thanks for stopping by," he says, unfurling the flat sheet, attempting to figure out which side faces up. He and his ex used to argue over such trivial things toward the end. "It's supposed to go wrong side up," she'd say. That never made sense to him. He assumed she was messing with him, pushing buttons. To this day he doesn't know which is which.

"It goes the other way," Terri says, stepping up to the bed on the opposite side.

Dillon nods, flips it over, wrong side up, and unfurls it so that it billows and floats outward toward her.

"I want to apologize for last week . . . the way I . . . handled the situation." Dillon adjusts his side of the bed while Terri does the same on her side.

"It's okay."

"I reacted poorly. It wasn't like you were, well, doing just anyone. I—"

"I know." She smooths out the sheet, yanking it taunt from the corners. "I'm sure it was a painful experience for you." Together they take hold of the comforter and bring it up from the foot of the queen-sized bed and slide it up over the length of it.

Dillon nods again, though somewhat uneasy with her assessment, owing to the fact that he's never told her, or anybody, about what happened between him and his ex. He places the decorative pillows, grapevines knitted on them, across the bed and smooths out the comforter until taut like a stretched muscle ready for action. Miles walks up to the bed, nuzzles it, and backs away, pleased with their teamwork.

"I am sorry, and if you're up for it, I'd like your help again . . . I mean if I haven't screwed things up between us."

Terri meets Dillon at the foot of the bed and leans in for an embrace that catches him off guard. He relaxes enough to appreciate her acceptance of his apology. Dillon stands awkwardly after the embrace, gives the room a once-over, and moves to adjust the drapes as the afternoon sun pours in, making an appearance after the last big storm has passed and before the next *bigger* one is forecasted to hit the area.

"Okay, well—" Dillon says.

"Does the Munich Room need tending to?"

"This is the last one."

"I'll check the schedule for the rest of the week." Terri strides toward the door, giving Miles a pat on the head. "I can work Sunday morning while you and the guys are kicking Agras's butt." She pauses at the door and turns her head back toward him, her hair twirling. "Righty-o?"

"How's your thesis coming along?"

"It looks promising," she says, flashing her wicked smile and exiting the room with Miles in tow.

One conflict addressed, one more to deal with later, Dillon stares back out the window, dark clouds crowding the horizon, ready to storm the sky. His thoughts turn to Sunday, *the* big race, kicking Agras's butt, the prospect tingling up his spine and tickling every hair atop his head. *Game on . . .*

Saturday Morning
Dream Big, Dream Often

This is quite a story, what we're seeing here tonight. Chase Brandon, from Green Bay, Wisconsin, now living and training in Santa Rosa, California, a relative unknown a few months ago until he shocked the running world with his five-thousand-meter track-and-field finish at the Olympic trials in Eugene, nabbing both the A standard qualifying time and *the third spot on the Olympic team.*

And here he is now, the solo American in the finals, holding his own and running with the lead group: two Kenyans, an Ethiopian, a German, and a Czech, who is currently leading the group. It was the Czech who staged a surge at the three-thousand-meter mark that separated the men from the boys, and this lead group now has thirty yards on the fading boys.

Chase looks comfortable sitting on the shoulder of the young Kenyan phenom, who is heavily favored to win this event, as well he should. Until the Czech's surge the pace had been pedestrian, and that certainly favors Chase with his kick. I think he stands a good chance of medaling here tonight under the lights of Rio's Olympic

Stadium. And how would that look, another gold medal to go with the one he already won in the fifteen hundred meters two nights ago, a rare double that has only been accomplished by "King of the Mile" Hicham El Guerrouj at the 2004 Olympics, and the "Flying Finn" Paavo Nurmi at the 1924 Olympics? I'm sure he can picture it now, perhaps even taste it, a pair of gold medals hanging around his neck. What do you think, Phil?

I agree, Paul. He certainly has nothing to lose by staying with these gents. His kick is top-notch, and if he can handle the Kenyans' upcoming surges, then he has an excellent chance. I'll tell you, I was duly impressed the day I witnessed him race in Olso a couple months back at the Bislett Games. He wasn't even a blip on the radar going into the last lap, and out of nowhere, Chase roars down the backstretch like he'd stolen something, and by gosh, by the time he crossed the finish line in first, he had! I turned to my good Norwegian friend and said, "who in blazes was that?!"

Three laps to go as they pass by the finish line. That last lap was a spirited sixty-three seconds. The Kenyans are trying to pare down this group before they hit the final lap—

Wait! Chase has moved swiftly to the front. Quite a cheeky move this far out.

I think he's attempting to rattle the Kenyans, who have been switching off pacing duties, trying to control the race. Chase's move here is a good one.

Well, time will tell. It certainly has dropped the German runner, who can't hold on to the back of the Czech's heels, who himself appears to be struggling to stay with the Ethiopian just ahead of him.

The two Kenyans are looking at each other and undoubtedly discussing strategy. I think they were caught off guard with Chase's move. The Kenyans are well known to exhibit team tactics on running's biggest stage.

And Chase is well known for saying that anybody on any given day can be beaten, and the Kenyans are no exception in his mind.

Two laps to go and Chase has slowed some after a fifty-eight-second lap.

That may have done him in, I'm afraid. It was a nice attempt, but against this world-class field it may have been a skosh impetuous—

Whoa! The Czech has taken up the charge now! As Chase eased back the Czech moved out from behind the Kenyans and overtook them all. Unbelievable! I *thought I had noticed subtle hand signals three laps back between Chase and the Czech. At the time it didn't seem like much, but I now believe they've formed their own international alliance, attempting to set something up for the bell lap and break the Kenyan dominance.*

Whatever they're doing it's taking its toll. Unable to cover the surge the lead Kenyan has motioned his younger countryman forward.

The younger Kenyan has moved out and around, the Ethiopian right on his heels, and Chase has latched to the back of the train.

Now they've spit the elder Kenyan out the back!

Six hundred meters to go and the Czech has slowed the pace, taking a quick peek over his shoulder. That may have been another signal, because Chase immediately moved forward as if to resume the lead, but instead stalled alongside the Kenyan, who now looks concerned as the pack glides down the homestretch and into the bell lap.

The young Kenyan is boxed in all right, but he has time to break free . . . if he's patient.

That may be a problem. He's trying to fight his way out as they hit the far straightway, and now the Ethiopian has also moved up right behind Chase, further sealing the youngster in.

Oh my! Chase just gave the youngster a lesson in track etiquette with a short jab from his elbow as the Kenyan tried to push his way out of the box. Chase waggled his index finger afterward. Not today, upstart!

It may be too late, but the inexperienced phenom needs to slow down and slip out the back door, and go around the bottleneck, but instead he's panicking.

It's too late. Chase has left his post and is making a mad dash to the finish line. The Ethiopian has spread out and is running up on Chase. The Czech is starting to tie up, but still holds the lead.

Thirty meters . . . twenty meters, Chase has pulled even with the Czech, the Ethiopian is on Chase's shoulder. Hold on to your bowler hats, we're in for a snug finish!

Under a downpour, Chase raises his arms high above his head, slowing after an easy six-miler just beyond the parking lot entrance to his condo. He mocks crowd noises during his saunter over to the soggy grass that stretches the length of the Windsor Town Green, removes his shoes and socks, and starts running hundred-yard striders, continuing with his internal post-race monologue throughout the recovery sections.

I think I need CPR. That was the most dramatic five thousand finish since Prefontaine's '72 Olympic debut against the venerable Lasse Viren, who won on that day in Munich.

And the results are up: Yes! Chase, the Ethiopian, and the Czech, gold, silver, bronze.

What a race. The Kenyan youngster was certainly schooled. It's a hard lesson but there will be other days.

Chase is wrapped in an American flag now, smiling and waving at the crowd who are on their feet, celebrating the yank's remarkable double-gold-medal performance.

"Meow," Dogma says after Chase has completed eight striders, walked barefoot and soaked up the stairs to his condo, and entered.

"Yes, Dogma, it's treat time," Chase says, locking the door behind him. "I won double gold."

Dogma turns, arches his hindquarters, and offers it for petting. "Meow."

"High-five right back at you."

Sunday Morning
PA XC Championships: Runners on the Storm

The rain does more than fall from the sky; it bolts from the heavens, a launch strike of biblical proportions. The guys—minus Spencer—stand huddled under a tented tarp in the heart of Golden Gate Park's Lindley Meadow, staring out at the torrential downpour that slants at an unnatural angle, their view grainy, bordering on abstract. The women's race just wrapped up and judging by the thigh-high mud marks on all of the female racers milling about, it had been ugly out on the course. Race officials are frantically re-marking part of the oval course deemed unsafe, where a mudslide has formed at miles two and four, when some of the women racing through it found themselves sliding on their keisters after a faulty step or two. Dillon can't recall if a cross-country meet has ever been canceled due to weather. Cross-country is on par with football in that regard, sans protective gear. No rain delays, or make-up races. You take what mother nature throws at you and play on.

Nestled on the northern border of Golden Gate Park and flanked between John F. Kennedy Drive and a long quarter-mile row of eucalyptus trees flapping in the wind sits the long narrow, grassy expanse of Lindley Meadow. On calmer weekends the meadow hosts family picnics, BBQs, and live entertainment. But on one Sunday a year, late in November, the meadow swells with adult harriers of all ages, looking to cap off the three-month regional grand prix series and crown individual and club champions.

"Hey," Dillon says as Kate walks up, still in her racing gear, soaking wet with mud streaks up and down her body.

"That was fun!" she says, shaking her head like a dog, water spraying out in all directions.

"Nice job. You looked strong at the finish. What place did you end up?"

"Not sure," she says, wiping water from her face that has trickled down from her hair. "I was top ten on the last lap until I went down. Not sure how many passed me before I got going again. I passed a few back." She turns to her side, craning her neck around to gain a better view of the red cherry that has formed on her left butt cheek.

"Ouch!" Dillon says, grimacing.

"Could be worse. Good luck out there, and be careful." She approaches him as if for a hug. He receives it without hesitation, muddy as it is.

"Thanks. You heading out?"

"Maybe. With this rain . . ."

"Wouldn't blame you."

"I'll stop by if we do leave early," she says, turning to walk away.

Dillon watches her head toward another covered tarp and disappear under it.

"Bib numbers," Spencer says, rushing in under the tent cover. He lifts the rain hat from his head and pulls the stack out from the race packet. "Dillon . . . Chase, me, Jim . . . Jake."

Dillon takes his—409—and gives it a couple squeezes, balling it up until suitable for the trash bin.

"What are you doing?" Spencer asks. "You're not supposed to alter bib numbers in any manner."

Dillon smiles. "I don't want any sharp edges."

Jim seems to accept the idea, knelling down to pin one to his race jersey. Jake chuckles. Chase appears disturbed by the messiness of the act, taking great care in centering his on his jersey and preserving the crisp corners. Spencer stands in disbelief.

"It's an old tradition from high school. One of the guys needed some toilet paper, so he waded up an extra bib to make do."

Chase nods in appreciation of the idea, though Spencer isn't any more at ease.

"Don't let the officials see it. They'll disqualify you."

"I fell, someone accidentally grabbed it . . . don't worry."

"Yeah, don't worry," Jim says with a wry grin. "Let's warm up."

The guys don what they each think will be suitable warm-up gear and start off. Dillon inquires about the course, which Spencer explains consists of the same two-mile loop repeated three times. The start is down in the meadow they've been standing near, running west through it before jutting up and onto the gravel and dirt path that hugs John F. Kennedy Drive, which slopes modestly downward and always guarantees a fast start in the opening three-quarters of a mile.

After skirting around numerous puddles and dodging other clubs running in the opposite direction they reach the westernmost point of the course, where two quick, ninety-degree turns require delicate negotiation. Even without the current downpour these two turns are tricky. Today they'll be brutal. Between a narrow muddy path bordered by slick grass, and dozens of runners jostling for position before heading into a winding and, in some spots, sandy section that can easily separate front-runners from back runners, it's deceptively nasty for those unaware. Dillon doesn't say it, but he's made the same assessment. After a full racing season of warming up with Spencer, Dillon concludes that Spencer's course-preview talk is not only the high school coach inside him but also his way of mentally preparing for the race, talking out loud. No one ever seems to mind, and perhaps benefits from it in one way or another.

A mile into the warm-up and running through another, though smaller, meadow—Chain of Lakes Meadow—two distinct paths have been laid out by the women's race: grass trampled into submission, and a well-worn muddy track that has so many foot impressions on it that appears pulverized. And with another race soon to start—the master's race—these tracks will be further defined and more difficult to negotiate. The previous discussion on the car ride down on whether to go with spikes or not now leans unanimously toward wearing them despite the couple of spots where they'll cross over asphalt. Too much power applied at the wrong time in the wrong spot can send a runner lurching forward, slipping and scrambling for balance and ultimately out of contention.

After negotiating a three-foot-high log beyond Chain of Lakes Meadow, they slop their way up a slight incline that's single-file only and contains several elongated murky puddles where any step can end in an ankle twist if an unfortunate root or rock or depression lurks.

Beyond "Puddles Alley," as Jim coins it, the course takes on another long stretch as part of its general oval-shaped configuration. Initially it's wide enough for two runners to run side by side, assuming each runner *shares* the trail, which rarely occurs during the heat of the battle. Again, another opportune section to work the field, getting a jump on someone before Puddles Alley and forcing them to follow and play catch-up, a subtle tactic that may pay dividends at the end of six miles in these conditions.

Chase makes a pit stop at the decrepit bathrooms near the tunnel that leads out onto the famed Polo Grounds. As Chase curses the stench, the guys take cover in the tunnel, performing stretches that don't require sitting down on the wet, and in some places flooded, pavement.

"See that guy there," Spencer whispers to Dillon, using his head to gesture to a guy with black matted-down hair who's in the middle of the Agras club, running by.

"Yeah."

"That's the ringer."

"Really? You weren't kidding." Dillon sizes up the ringer's form: compact motion, quick turnover and a propensity to run up on his toes. Dillon recalls Jake saying once that Spencer's "ringer" lament isn't entirely accurate, suggesting instead that guys like him *only* run the bigger meets, the ones with higher stakes such as qualifying spots to even bigger races, forgoing the smaller ones in lieu of training.

"He's a sub-thirty-minute 10K-er on the roads," Spencer says.

"Yeah?"

Jake and Jim nod.

It's been a while, but my PR is 28.49.

"Don't worry too much about him early on. He'll wear himself out churning through this slop," Spencer says.

"Was that Bernard?" Chase says, rejoining the guys, who resume their warm-up back out in the rain, which is dumping harder now.

"Yep," Spencer says.

"You can take him, Dillon," Chase says. "He'll go out hard and get eaten alive by the terrain. He's a tough road man, but this is a whole different ball game!" He spreads his arms wide, raising his face into the rain.

"Keep that in mind for some of the other top guys too," Jake says. "Some may run conservative on different sections."

"No guts, no glory," Jim says.

The guys hit the longest hill on the course, though it has nothing on anything they have trained or raced on this season. It resembles a gentle rise with a couple twists and turns to it, and today, owing to the rain, some unfortunately placed and quite large mini-lakes that ruin the best tangent between bends in the trail. Based on the traffic pattern from the women's race, most have skirted around it, with few exit tracks coming out from the heart of them.

The gradual climb will feel much different by the time they tackle it a third time, however, when precious finishing spots lay on the line. By not surrendering to mental or physical fatigue, or the conditions, instead bearing down here can create a vital gap up to the crest of the hill, taking advantage of the welcome but tricky downhill back into Lindsey Meadow where a dicey right-hander on slick grass will test their agility and propel them along 150 yards into the finishing chute.

Warm-up complete, the guys take shelter back at the RERC tent, shaking off water that has accumulated on them. The master's race is in full swing, and the front-runners are coming through the meadow on their second lap. The PA announcer rattles off their names. Jake and Jim shout out encouragement for fellow club runners passing by while Dillon looks on in silent appreciation, watching the battle within the war unfold, projecting himself into the mix.

Dillon switches out his drenched shirts and socks and begins his seated stretches, half listening to the women discuss their races, and Spencer speak of Zac's commanding CIF sectional win the day before, which triggers Dillon's competitive juices to flow stronger, further bolstering his confidence.

Soon his mind drifts from the surrounding din and concentrates on the race twenty-five minutes away, going over the season to date, the guys he's beaten and who've bested him. He sizes up the ringer standing nearby under another tarp, searching for anything about him that will show his hand: is he intimidated by the weather? Was he recruited because he can go toe to toe with Dillon? Or Chase? As far as Dillon can tell the ringer is unfazed by the moment, shows no sign of fear at a championship event. Cool, calm, collected, leisurely stretching, much like Dillon is. Despite Jake's take on Bernard's ringer status, Dillon chooses to retain the label "ringer"; it has a motivating *ring* to it.

Dillon doesn't avert his gaze toward the ringer when he and a couple teammates glance in Dillon's direction. He tips his head up, acknowledging their nod at his presence. He breathes in deeply, exhales, switches to a different position, and closes his eyes, visualizing the course, running brave, undeterred by the chaotic weather that lashes out. He pictures his stride, lifting knees high and sailing over the log on the back side of the course while others step on it. He envisions himself gliding along the straightaways, taking the shortest route between any two points, splashing through puddles and, with a little luck, annoying the runner next to him with said splash. It'll be the little things throughout the race that'll add up and take its toll on the fittest contenders.

Moving into his last seated stretch, Dillon pictures the last half mile, charging up the final hill and dropping anybody with him, negotiating the turn at full speed by going wide as Spencer suggested, plummeting like a rock onto the meadow and applying the right amount of torque, trusting his spikes for proper footing, echoing Dillon's high school coach's famous last sprint phrase: "Turn and burn, Dill Weed, turn and *burn!*"

Dillon opens his eyes to the squawk of the public address announcement. "Ten minutes . . . the start . . . men's open . . . Ten min . . ." The words warble in the gusty wind, but Dillon's toe-tapping nerves fill in the blanks.

Dillon slips on his spikes, laces them up extra tight, makes his way out onto the wide dirt pathway along JFK Drive, and launches into a stride straight into pelting rain. Were it not for his jacket, his singlet and dry multiple layers underneath would've been soaked by the time he reached the end of stride one. He slows to a trot, shaking out his legs and arms. He spins around, revving up again and again, and four times more before gliding back underneath the RERC tarp. As the guys strip down to the essentials, Dillon can't help but grin, musing over what a causal bystander may think of them all shedding clothes to *go out* into the storm; disbelief or the word "crazy" comes to mind. Certainly the usual Sunday morning, Golden Gate Park crowd has been held at bay, instead sheltered in warm confines, or perhaps at best indoors on machines that simulate exercise.

Such thoughts further fuel his resolve.

Dillon trots across the meadow, scanning the wooded area where a trickle of other competitors are exiting, finds a hidden unoccupied tree to water, and heads to the start line, past a bundled-up Rob Shore, wishing luck to those competitors he's come to know in the past three months. He reaches the spot where the RERC guys have staked out a claim on the start line, pats Chase on the shoulder, and bolts out for one short strider to get a feel for the mush they'll be running through in the mad dash off the line; each foot strike splashes a sheet of water left and right from the point of contact. *Excellent.* Dillon smiles, takes a knee, then the other, retying his shoes, giving each soaked shoelace an extra cinch that wrings muddy water and adding a triple knot for good measure. He trots back to the start line as an official walks along it, ensuring a fair start.

"Come on! You call this a storm?" Chase blusters into the sky. "Blow, you son of a bitch! Blow! It's time for a showdown!"

"*Forrest Gump,*" Jake, Jim, Spencer, and Dillon say in unison.

Nearby runners turn in their direction, some confused, some amused, some clap their hands, one yells, "Yeah, baby!"

Overhead, thunder reverberates, shooting an ominous chill over the meadow.

"I think you upset the gods," Dillon says.

"I did not see that coming."

The guys shake hands with one another and give silent nods of *Let's crush this.*

Dillon and Chase line up in front; Spencer, Jim, and Jake directly behind. They hunch over at Rob Shore's command, "Runners to your mark!"

Rain thunders down; wind thrashes through the eucalyptus; the sanctity of the moment disrupted.

Crack!

Off the line they stampede, *chop, chop, chop, splash, splash, splash, muck, muck, muck, squish, squish, squish.*

Protective elbows flung wide, Dillon charges forth, intensely focused on an imaginary line toward the short hill to the muddy sidewalk. Out of his peripheral vision he surveys each flank, lean and fast, and once content a shifting field on either side will not swallow him up he relaxes and coasts, biding his time until *bursting* up the hill onto the path. Perfectly placed to churn out the next five-plus miles, letting the ten runners in front duke it out for the top stops early on, Dillon settles in, his eye on the one anomaly, sitting alongside two other Agras runners. Briefly appraised, Dillon dismisses the ringer and instead focuses on energy-efficient strides, conserving valuable resources for the trickier spots later on.

As if in a dream state, giddy and at times chomping at the bit, Dillon floats with minimal effort throughout the first loop, where little change takes place among the leaders' positions. Back through the meadow, where the PA announcer is identifying the front-runners, Dillon listens intently after his name has blared across the field, to gauge how the club is doing. Chase's name is announced three spots back, and as the voice warbles and fades, Dillon catches Jim's and Spencer's names six and eight spots later.

Awesome!

Lap two, back on the downhill path along JFK Drive, Dillon shifts gears when the guys up front start pulling on him, a mid-race surge to weed out the pretenders. He splits a pair of runners from two different clubs, both who veer to opposite sides of an elongated puddle. Dillon tested the waters on the first lap and, with nothing lurking underneath, stays true: *Splash, splash, splash, splash, splash.* Five strides and a grunt to his left later, Dillon exits the puddle half smiling in front of the duo.

On the backside of the course, gliding over the log for the second time, Dillon sits in eighth place, thirty yards behind the two leaders. One he doesn't recognize, probably running unattached, disappears up Puddles Alley. The other is an Agras runner Dillon has been moving up on all season long but has yet to beat. Ten yards back from them is another Agras runner leading a small group of the usual suspects that Dillon has at one time or another dispatched of. And directly in front of him roams the less-than-comfortable-looking ringer. His awkward stutter-step over the log earlier told Dillon all he needs to know: the ringer is out of his element. Sure, on a dry course, stable footing, his road racing fitness may script another scenario. But not today.

By the time they exit Puddles Alley, Dillon is glued to the ringer's heels, pressing him, and once clear of the tight quarters, Dillon surges to go around while there is still time before the trail narrows again. The ringer is no slouch, however, and fends Dillon off, forcing a disgruntled Dillon to fall in line. The low-hanging, waterlogged evergreen branches on each side make it hazardous to use the edge of the trail, and the cagey ringer runs right down the middle.

Dillon peers over the ringer's shoulder; being outmanned by the conditions notwithstanding, the ringer continues to contribute, allowing his teammates to add precious yards and gap a rival. Dillon's mind reels. Losing ground at this stage threatens his ability to make it up as the race progresses in this slop: the elements will work against him, the crappy footing, gale-force winds thwarting urgent progress, stranded in no-man's-land, goals slipping away . . .

Dillon reins in his spiraling thoughts. *Work the problem.* Ten yards ahead, the trail balloons wider. He syncs his steps with the ringer's, attaching as close as possible without clipping the guy's heels. Reaching the wider spot, the ringer veers to the right where previous runners have created a visible path. Dillon accelerates at the same moment, but to the left, and despite catching an elbow from the ringer when they merge together beyond the puddle—as well as getting a tree-branch slap across his shoulder—Dillon stays the course and beats back the ringer, whose footsteps recede over the next fifty yards.

Dillon has room to roam and rides the momentum, regaining lost ground where the race filters through an opening among the trees before *the* hill.

"Go, Dillon! You got this!" comes a voice, and though Dillon doesn't see who shouts it, it's no doubt Kate. She stayed to watch, out in a torrential downpour; that says something, says everything. Her presence inspires him; he passes two runners on the hill, taking the best tangents as if no puddles exist, much to the chagrin of two unsuspecting spectators who scatter from the wall of water sent their way.

Lap three, through Lindley Meadow again as if on a merry-go-round, more hearty cheers from the club trumpet out from under the tarp. Dillon begins the final lap in fifth place. The rut through the meadow appears haggard, no longer able to defend itself after thousands of foot strikes against it, most in long spikes. The wind distorts the PA announcer's words. Treetops whip and thrash around. A club tent loses its moorings and sails downwind.

Dillon's quads bark for the first time as he ascends the short hill to JFK Drive. The pace hasn't caused it. The sloppy course may have, but more likely the culprit is the cold rain that sheets down on them. Working hard, producing copious amounts of energy to maintain a competitive pace, yet taxed to stay warm at the same time, vying for precious resources exacts its toll. For several yards, Dillon runs without the proper use of one arm, then the other, using one for balance and the other to give each quad a quick warm massage, rubbing the hand up and down. He returns back to normal form right before the dicey double left-handers, gearing up like a wind-up toy, intent on catching and passing the Agras number-two man—*whooooooa! Whoa, whoa, whoa.* Dillon has never skated a day in his life, until now: despite spikes, his right foot glides out from underneath him. Off balancing, left arm windmilling, he teeters perilously along the trail's edge. All in and no desire to regain control by slowing he combines quick baby steps, momentum, and agility to steady himself. Risky, but it works. Somehow. Eagerness building, passing the Agras number-two man through the sand pit, Dillon quells the surging adrenaline and excitement, the desire to make things happen *now*, sooner rather than later, instead of parsing it out for a strong finish.

Passing a Chico jersey through the smaller meadow moves him up to third place, his eye now on second, approaching the log for the final time when the unattached runner catches the log wrong and somersaults right over it, disappearing on the other side. Dillon has already committed to hurdling the log and prays that the guy will not spring up. He doesn't, but as Dillon soars over the log the guy lies crumpled up where Dillon is projected to land with flesh-piercing, tetanus-inducing spikes.

Messy landing imminent, Dillon stutter-steps midair, plants a foot on the log, and launches himself as far as he can beyond the fallen runner. The last-second decision is not as powerful as he hoped for. Dillon descends from the log, the other guy's body stretched out and now squirming, Dillon's lead foot ready to land on an outstretched defenseless arm. Dillon can't help but wince at the thought, landing hard and waiting for the scream that'll jeopardize Dillon's chances of winning and effectively end the other guy's day. The landing: soft, squishy . . . but no scream. The guy's arm moves just enough to avoid puncture wounds that would've made for an interesting story in the ER.

Counting his lucky stars, Dillon pushes aside the nastiness of the fall and soldiers on. He loses sight of the leader of the race, the Agras runner, up Puddles Alley, but once through it cleanly he catches sight of him among the trees: twenty yards tops, not unmanageable, but the Agras runner moves with the body language and poise of the undefeated over the relatively solid footing that remains until Lindsey Meadow. If Dillon wants to catch him, he'll have to start now and close the gap before they reach the summit of the final hill, because after that there'll be little chance or time to pass him; and as Dillon knows all too well he's been *owned* by the Agras guy all season, and when one competitor owns another competitor, history tends to repeat itself. Ask Ewing about Jordan, Mickelson about Woods, Lochte about Phelps.

Dillon narrows his sights onto the back of the Agras jersey, creating a tunnel-like vision between him and the leader. Everything outside the imaginary tunnel walls blur. Sounds morph to white noise. The hill, five and a half miles in him, under him, on him. No turning back now, no giving into the past, letting it define him. Dillon bears down, squeezing the seemingly empty tube of toothpaste for all its worth, trying to turn it inside out if possible, not sure if anything will come of it. Pain signals raise their ugly heads, SOS flares sent up from the legs. *Yes, I see you there, I feel your pain, but it's not over yet. We're seeing this through.*

Skillfully guided like a marionette his arms and legs rise and fall, determination shifting down the kinetic chain, through years and tens of thousands of miles and into the ground, the gap closing, excruciatingly slow but closing. Around the bend the summit emerges. Dillon's focus, unwavering to this point, has memorized every stitch of the Agras jersey, the pattern of his foot strike—slight supination on his right foot, neutral on the left—but with daylight in sight, the old familiar unselfishness creeps back into his mind: second is good too; no shame in that. Running doesn't score the same way other sports do, winners and losers, a binary version of success. He's beaten back the ringer, done his part. Now's the time to preserve his current position, take second place, and hope the rest of the team comes through.

Same old Dillon. Settle for mediocrity when the big carrot lies within reach. Attainable or not left wanting, a haunting question for weeks, sometimes months, afterward. You're not selfish enough to win the big ones. You have to *want* to own them. Make it yours and no one else's. The state championships that eluded him in high school, the collegiate conference championships junior and senior year: all runner-up. JW always said every runner has at least one more ounce to give than they think they have. They just have to be willing to extract it no matter the mental, physical, or emotional toll. Do you want it or not? It's really that simple.

Over the summit, Dillon snaps out of his defeatist past to a very vocal Kate, jumping up and down, yelling from the turn toward Lindley Meadow, "Get him! Get him! You got this!"

Two things happen in that moment. Three if you count the crack of thunder overheard that reverberates across the sky and down his spine. One, Dillon reengages, peeks at the spectator to his left and watches her eyes drift from him to the next runner; without urgent foot strikes pressing upon him and the spectator's extended gaze he guesses thirty yards or more, plenty of space to take risks. And two, the Agras runner up front, rounding the corner, glances back.

You're mine! Turn and burn, Dill Weed, turn and burn!

"Go, go, go!" Kate shouts as he passes by, waving an arm like a third-base coach sending the runner home for the winning run. "Nobody's behind you!"

The Agras runner reaches the meadow's base as Dillon starts his descent toward it, following the line he'd taken the previous two trips through. Unbridled, Dillon glides down, closing the gap to within five yards after the Agras runner struggles to regain his previous speed after an iffy, perhaps pressured, descent, the hunted showing signs of fear.

Each foot strike, each plant, six spikes aerating the meadow, anchoring Dillon's body and pushing him forward into a slanting rain that batters his jersey, RERC hermetically sealed to his chest.

Two yards back, less than fifty to go.

Plant, dig, willpower, push, *go!*

Half a stride back, twenty yards to go.

I want this!!

Frantic PA announcements mix with vocal cheers mix with the howl of rain that races from sky to ground and thuds against the muddy surface upon arrival, its force bouncing each droplet back up and melting into a white noise of excitement, an electricity that surges through Dillon's entire being.

Side by side, ten yards from the line, Dillon catches a sharp elbow on the arm, yet the pain doesn't register.

Five yards, three yards, one yard.

Dillon *thrusts* his chest across the imaginary finishing tape, across so many self-imposed limitations in his life. Stillness pervades, every last ounce of effort expelled, an eerie displacement from Earth, weightlessness. The muddy slip-'n'-slide chute rises to greet him with a *smack!* back to reality, shunting him forward uncontrollably before coming to a rest. He lies there, breathless, a sea of clad legs, muddy shoes, and the occasional galoshes on both sides of the chute dancing around, fixing his gaze on the mud-caked right shoe supinating ahead, and then the shoe's owner passing off their tag to the volunteer, who affixes it on the leader board.

Dillon rolls over and is immediately belted by raindrops that sting his face. He squints up through the cold, harsh sky at a number of jacketed arms reaching for him like an octopus, pulling to right him before the stampede begins. Reluctantly he rises, dead weight until his feet are under him and he can continue through the chute under his own power. He rips the bottom half of the mud-streaked, rumpled bib number off, handing it to the taker. The tag passes from the volunteer to another volunteer tasked with placing it on the leader board that's shielded by an oversized plastic trash bag held by yet another volunteer who is soaked despite being dressed down in water-resistant clothing.

Dillon staggers out from the chute, his eyes never straying from the tag's journey, a lion tracking a gazelle. About to post the tag below the one on the board, the volunteer pauses a moment, glances up, and yells toward the finish-line judge. The volunteer nods at the answer lost in the finish-line din, struggles to straighten out the tag twisting and flapping in the wind, but finally coordinates both hands to accomplish the task before placing it *above* the Agras runner's.

Dillon throws his head back, the rain washing over him, mud rivulets streaking downward and dripping off his face, back to their source. Exhaustion mixes with euphoria in those oxygen-deprived moments, an aura of lucid mental clarity, an unfiltered glimpse between the blurry line of his conscious mind and subconscious one, critical judgment suspended, where the past doesn't burden him and the future is not yet envisioned.

Lowering his head, he wipes his face with his jersey and spots the runner-up Agras nearby, talking with a woman.

"Nice finish, Chip," Dillon says, offering a handshake.

"Right back at ya. You timed that perfect."

"Not sure about perfect. More or less worked out. I'll take it."

"Sorry 'bout the elbow."

"No worries. Tight quarters, a lot on the line."

"Gotta love cross-country."

"Nationals?"

"We'll be there."

"Until then."

"On my God, oh my God!" Kate says, rushing up to Dillon. She embraces him like he's been the sole survivor of a train wreck. "That. Was. Awesome!"

When she breaks the embrace, Dillon yanks her back and lands a deep, soulful kiss that lingers and lingers and *lingers* as the rain anoints them. "Sorry," he says, reluctantly concluding the kiss. "Had to share this feeling with someone."

"Wow! That was some first kiss."

"Get a room," Chase says, coming out from the chute, giving Dillon a hearty slap on the back, water spraying in all directions. "What a mess out there."

"You beat Bernard?" Dillon whispers, catching sight of the ringer coming out from the chute.

"Not so tough—"

Bernard passes by, pats Dillon and Chase on the back, gives them a nod, and joins his teammate. Dillon and Chase acknowledge the ringer's effort.

"Where'd you end up?" Chase asks. "I lost track of you guys after the last turn."

Dillon grins, a delirious one.

"Holy shit! You won?"

"Got him on the line."

"Oh man, you know what that means?"

"I'm making breakfast?"

"Winner sex!"

Dillon's quizzical expression leaves him speechless.

"What's winner sex?" Kate says.

"It's better than makeup sex," Chase says. "Be sure to hydrate." He winks, turning to see how the race is unfolding behind him.

Dillon stands tongue-tied, but Kate nudges him. "After that kiss . . ."

Delirium still intact, Dillon grins.

"Nice job, Spencer! Where's Jimbo?" Chase says, standing alongside the chute, giving Spencer a high five that misses terribly when Spencer tries to return the high-flying greeting *and* motion up front.

Chase, Dillon, and Kate glance around, but as far as they can tell, Jim hasn't come in yet.

"There he is," Dillon says, pointing three spots back *behind* Spencer. "Spence beat Jim."

"You go down, buddy?" Chase says.

Jim is covered from head to toe in mud. "Someone wanted to know my shoe size and clipped me from behind." Jim twists his body to get a better view at the damage: if there had been blood from the spike's punctures it's no longer apparent. "But I made up for it and then some. Spence was on fire today. He looked possessed when he blew by me."

"When did I pass you?" The guys are corralled off to the side, peeking back toward the finish for Jake's arrival, which has been announced over the PA system.

"Through the meadow on the back side . . . mile five."

Spencer coughs. "I didn't see you."

"I said, 'Good job.'"

Spencer shrugs as Jake exits the chute with a big smile on his face.

"Gentlemen," Jake says, "if I never race again, it was truly an honor to end it on a high note in the mud. *This* is what cross-country is all about!"

"You think we won?" Jim says.

"It looks promising . . . I beat their *fourth* trammel," Jake says. "He ran without conviction."

Dillon, Chase, Jim, and Spencer exchange excited glances at the possibility. Spencer rushes over to the board to tally an estimated score, but the first board has been replaced by another, so the guys stroll back to the

RERC tent to change clothes. Dillon bids Kate goodbye, thanking her for sticking around, and asks her out on a date in the near future. She accepts amidst cheers and clapping by the rest of the guys standing nearby, Chase adding, "Finally!"

Sheltered from the elements each regales those club members remaining with animated stories. Chase tells of his epic battle with five guys, including one Agras runner, over the last three miles, each throwing surges at one another in an attempt to drop the pack. None gave an inch, and it was Chase's patented miler kick at the end that left them chasing him. He lifts his muddy, sopping-wet spikes and kisses them, garnering laughter from all.

Spencer talks of a new level of focus never before experienced, as if the inclement elements narrowed down his field of vision, leaving his mission clear and unfettered. That he passed Jimbo surprised him. He'd seen him up front at some point early on but after that nothing.

Jim gives his normal subdued recap, more or less ruminating on his tumble, though he does admit the adrenaline rush from it gave him new life.

Dillon speaks of the final half mile where he acknowledges Kate's spirited cheering as the catalyst that compelled him to *finally* "go for it."

Jake simply smiles, telling the guys that there are two kinds of runners: those who run and those who run like there's no tomorrow.

Forgoing a warm-down, despite the lessening rain, they swap anecdotes for the next twenty minutes until the results of the open race are posted. Spencer grabs his cell phone, and he and Dillon rush over to the results board. Dillon reads off the club names in finishing order as Spencer taps them into his XC scoring app.

"That should be enough," Spencer says. He taps icons, studies the board, reviews the app's results. Taps more, studies hard, reviews harder.

"No?" Dillon says.

Spencer gives a subtle head shake and cups his hand to cover his mouth.

"Really?" Dillon takes a deep breath, holds it, and reviews the board, scanning the top twenty-five, hoping against hope that their season *has* ended on a high note. He and the team have come too far to settle for runner-up. The captive breathe escapes. "Wait!"

"What?"

Dillon points to an unattached runner in the top ten. "I counted him."

Spencer enters the change into the app. A smile forms, growing immensely.

Dillon stares at Spencer, waiting for the shoe to drop. It doesn't. "Yes! Yes, yes, a thousand times yes!"

They race back to the tent, announcing the news to an ecstatic group, whose celebratory roar sweeps across Lindley Meadow, over the Golden Gate Bridge, echoing all the way up to Sonoma County, the drought over, both literally and figuratively.

FINAL 2015 PA/USATF TEAM STANDINGS		
	Club	Total
1	RERC	67
2	Agras	66
3	Chico Running Club	60
4	Strawberry Hill Harriers	53
5	South Bay Striders	51

Week 47 Training Summary			
	Long Run	Mileage Total	Comments
Dillon	0	48	YES! Finally won the big one.
Chase	0	42	Look out, nationals, here we come!
Spencer	0	51	This season was something special.
Jim	0	43	Best PA finish for me.
Jake	0	57	What a great way to celebrate the ups and downs of life.

Week 13
November 23

Wednesday Late Afternoon
Portland, OR

"Where're you going?" Maggie says when Spencer steers their rental car *northbound* to I-5 off I-84. "Did you forget where my parents live?"

"We have time for a quick run in Forest Park," Spencer says, scanning the signage overhead, searching for the Fremont Bridge exit.

Maggie flashes a smirk. "Trying to minimize your time with my dad?"

Spence-speak.

"Don't worry, I didn't tell him about the department chair position, so he doesn't know you turned it down."

"Thanks, but we didn't get a chance to run this morning. I haven't run there in a while. Have you?"

"Not since I moved down south with you. Where do you want to run?"

"I was thinking Wildwood from Germantown."

Maggie smiles. "I love that trail."

"Me too."

Along St. Helens Road they drive, hugging the Willamette River, its south-to-north flow against the grain for the Pacific Northwest. The route floods him with memories: the many cold, wet, sweaty, tired miles he ran along it; veering up Saltzman Road and into Forest Park; the stillness of those morning runs, quiet and remote; the slap of shoes on wet trails; running across the St. John's Bridge more times than he drove over it in his car; living a Spartan existence a block off the University of Portland campus, visible on the bluff across the river.

Parked at the trailhead, Spencer and Maggie exchange their travel wear for running gear in the front seat, looking out for peeping toms, peeking at each other, and laughing like teenagers at summer camp. They hike up the short, steep incline that marks the entrance to the Wildwood Trail and begin running, Maggie leading the way, discussing where they will turn around, the memories the trail brings back, and how beautiful it is running amongst the densely forested "urban wilderness," as travel brochures refer to it.

They meander under a thick canopy of Douglas fir, western hemlock, and western red cedar, rays of sunlight filtering through and reflecting off wet ferns that brush by them. Two miles into their trip down memory trail, Spencer slows to a stop. Maggie glances back, stops, and returns to him.

"What?" she says. Her breath floats like mist amongst the mossy surroundings.

"Something's amiss," he says, scanning the area, both up and down the trail, and off to the sides.

Maggie swivels her head around as well, but doesn't understand what he's talking about or looking for.

By the time her attention shifts back to him, Spencer has dropped to one knee in the moist ground, his gaze and smile directed at her, an open ring box in hand. "I may not remember the first time we met, but I imagine it somewhere along this stretch."

Maggie places a cupped hand to her mouth, covering the gaping surprise that forms, though her eyes, equally wide and filled with shock, betray her disguise. She nods.

"Will you marry me, Maggie Deckingham?"

His proposal lingers several moments in the stillness of the forest, raindrops thumping oversized maple leaves. "Are . . . you sure?"

"I'm *literally* groveling in the mud."

Maggie's laugh echoes around them. "Yes, you are." She kneels and extends her hand, on which Spencer slips the ring. Betrothed, she reaches for him and plants an extended kiss that only breaks when voices rise in pitch, announcing the arrival of three runners who flash by, extending apologies and athletic maneuvers to skirt around the couple who chose to share a moment in the middle of forget-me-not trail.

"It's lovely, Spence," Maggie says as they stand and she gazes at the ring. "How—?"

"Dillon and Linda offered a few suggestions."

"Well, you did good." She leans in again to kiss him. "We'd better head back. I can't wait to tell Mum and Dad. They are going to *love* the news."

Spencer leads the way.

"You better not trip and forget that you proposed," Maggie says. "I have a ring for proof this time."

Spence-speak.

Thursday
Thanksgiving Night

Robyn is curled up in Jake's lap, head resting on his chest, fast asleep as he lies stretched out on the couch, Bukowski's book in hand, reading the penultimate poem. Linda rests two cushions over, playing host to Jake's feet across her lap as she reads through Maggie's latest manuscript pages. The grandfather clock ticks along, nearing 8:00 p.m.

Robyn's early slumber is the result of an active Thanksgiving Day, acting as host and entertainer and informant and networker for an extended Catholic family of Jake's and Linda's parents and grandparents, brothers and sisters, nieces and nephews. Also in attendance, and enormously overwhelmed, the lesser procreators from Jake's running circle: Dillon, Chase, and newlyweds Jim and Doris, who brought along enough homemade pumpkin pie to feed the entire Dearborn homestead, and had split their time between two locations: dinner at Jim's parents' place, and dessert with Jake and company. Dale arrived as dinner was being served, carrying a bottle of wine from local hundred-year-old vines, which brought on enough jokes to last the evening. Miles was also in attendance, though she spent more time dodging rambunctious children and their short arms jutting her way than anything else.

Chase had agreed with Dillon's comment that sitting at the completely occupied twenty-two person table, sandwiched somewhere in the middle, platters of food brimming from end to end, resembled a scene from a war movie, soldiers sitting around the mess tent. Laughter filled the boisterous room, with several comments on how respective parents *did* act like drill sergeants at times, which brought on follow-up comments from the "drill sergeants" about unruly and ungrateful behaviors from said soldiers. Chase also quipped on how long it took for a platter to make a full lap around the table, and how he could run a mile faster.

Football games were watched, though Chase was unable to view all the commercials due to the "mayhem," as he referred to it, in the house. At times, Chase and Dillon acted like stray puppies.

Robyn spent the majority of her time showing off for "Dilly" and "Chasey," performing cartwheels, parading around in her grandmother's old hats, and talking in a silly voice, mimicking Miles. When the family clan dispersed after a second helping of dessert, she took to drawing, showing the guys her rendition of them running in the park. Of course Jake was the tallest of the group and shepherding the rest with a pitchfork, though Robyn said it wasn't a pitchfork but instead a rake. In it she managed to capture her father's scruffiness, Dillon running alongside Miles, and Chase chasing Terri, who held a large timepiece, presumably Chase's. Jim had a dour look on his face as if he'd eaten an entire bag of Sour Patch Kids, and Spencer ran with a clipboard and had a balloon bubble stemming from his mouth with the word "Hey" written several times in it.

Several toasts were celebrated: Dillon's new life in Sonoma County; Doris and Jim's marriage; and the guys' "epic," as Chase called it, PA Championship win during the storm of the century, as well as winning the overall open division grand prix—a first for the RERC club. This spawned talk of how well they might fare at nationals against the country's best clubs: best-case scenario top three. They also toasted Spencer's and Maggie's engagement announcement that came by way of a text message with an attached picture of Spencer holding Maggie's ring hand up as "proof." Spencer had taken the opportunity in the text message to remind the guys of where and when to meet for Sunday's run, which gave them all a good laugh, as well as to ask Jake to ask Linda about using the minivan for their road trip to Bend, and that he'd already made the hotel reservations for their trip; the guys acknowledged and thanked Spencer for his organizational efforts.

"Time for bed, sweetie," Jake whispers in Robyn's ear. She stirs but doesn't open her eyes. He kisses her cheek, rubbing his chin against it. She giggles. "You still want to go for a hike in the morning after Daddy's run?" She nods. "Then you need to go to bed, okay?" She yawns but her eyes remain closed.

"I'll put her to bed," Linda says, gathering up the loose pages from the manuscript and stacking them on the coffee table. "Come on, sweetie." She rises and extracts Robyn from Jake's lap. Linda nuzzles and kisses Jake's cheek and hoists Robyn over her shoulder. "Come to bed soon."

Jake watches Linda carry Robyn off, her head resting on Linda's shoulder until both reach the archway, where Robyn opens her eyes and waves good night. Jake waves back until they've turned the corner. Jake resumes reading until the pages thin and their words run dry, reflecting on the existential gamut of the author's life for several minutes afterward. He closes the book, places it on the coffee table next to Maggie's work, and extinguishes the table lamp, retiring to bed.

Friday Morning
Moving On

One year, one day. The magical passing of his and her birthdays, four seasons, twelve months, and umpteen Hallmark holidays. No more "this time last year" thoughts. A Gregorian reprieve. Time to move on.

Dillon coasts down Richardson's Trail at three-quarter throttle, leaving behind more than the ten miles run. The crisp morning air greets him warmly, nips at his face in the way a grandmother pinches a grandson's cheeks during a holiday visit.

Farther down his descent, rounding the hairpin turn, he slows and drifts toward the outer edge as a group of cantering horses approach, slowing to a walk when their reins are pulled on by their riders. Cherry hellos are exchanged all around by humans while equines snort and jerk their heads at the subdued pace, or gaze at the two legged Dillon with big brown eyes, or lean their heads just off the trail for a sample of wild grass before rider corrects the horse's behavior.

Through the turn, returning to his previous pace amongst sturdy oaks that harbor no judgment, Dillon lets his mind wander again, acknowledging the relief that fell over him last night after getting home from the Thanksgiving Day festivities at the Dearborn homestead: at last he said her name.

Rebecca.

At first a simple mental thought, followed by a whisper to himself, then out loud when he *finally* returned her call, causing Miles to awaken, stand up, and *talk*.

The phone conversation wasn't particularly long, just long enough to say hey, ask how she was doing, and apologize for blaming her for *everything*, that for his part he came to recognize that viewing himself as an athlete 24/7 and living his life occupationally and socially as such precluded him from being the supportive husband and grown-up *she* wanted or understood. His forgiveness was met with sorrowful tears and a heartfelt "thank-you," to which he replied, "take care," hoping to move on but not before she told him to not let her bad decision ruin what might be a good thing with Kate; she'd heard through the grapevine. He promised he wouldn't and hung up. That was enough. Enough to touch base, acknowledge her existence, express his shortcomings, and let bygones be bygones, a gesture and admission he hopes will aid him in other areas of life as well.

Through the pedestrian gate and onto Channel Drive, Cobblestone beckons, enticing him toward her at more than a leisurely pace. Dillon gives into the temptation, leveraging the pavement's hard surface, gravity's tug, and his free mind.

Sound bites of "Hey, Dillon" and "Did you hear . . ." from a small group of runners coming toward him wash over him as he breezes by, responding with a cursory nod. Moments later a slower pack approaches, giving him room to pass by, none whom he recognizes. Their solemn faces and voices, not in keeping within a morning group run, send chills down his spine. Like the imp to the perverse his pace involuntarily quickens, at speeds that would invariably, though futilely, incite a Spence-speak, past the park ranger station that exhibits frenzied activity.

Spread across the asphalt a pack of road cyclists approach, bunching up to their right at the sight of Dillon barreling toward them. Dillon holds his breath momentarily, diverting his attention to his ears, hoping to pick up useful clues as to what he's rushing toward a dusty parking lot for. His pace, their pace, a combined thirty miles an hour, leaves little to discern other than he *thinks* he hears Jake's name.

Dillon's lungs demand oxygen. He gulps in what he can, short of hyperventilating, but he remains behind in the count. His legs slog down the final quarter mile as if churning through thigh-high surf. His arms and hands pummel an imaginary punching bag. The Sherwood Forest–like canopy, dark and foreboding, the first stretch he ran with the guys so many Sundays ago, roils like the aurora borealis.

Around the bend Dillon bursts into bright sunlight and commotion, halting him in his tracks: first the sight of an ambulance, whose back doors are closing; several other emergency vehicles sit scattered in various spots— local police, the sheriff's department, park rangers, and a fire truck is now screaming down the road toward the scene; and in the middle of all the chaos, facing Dillon, angled toward the side of the road, rests a black Tesla with a sizable body-shaped dent on the hood, and a cracked windshield, whose vanity plate reads MOVE AWN.

Fear grips Dillon as the ambulance pulls away, at first with lights strobing and sirens wailing, but moments later silent as it disappears down Channel Drive toward town.

"Dilly, Dilly, Dilly," comes a frightened voice, rushing toward him, followed by another female voice hollering, "Robyn, come back!"

Before Dillon can comprehend what's going on, Robyn wraps herself around his legs, crying and talking and crying some more and talking even more, though none of what she says makes sense.

"What happened?" Dillon hollers right as the fire truck kills its siren. His words echo in the void.

"Robyn, don't run away like that."

Dillon rubs Robyn's head, her words still gibberish.

"What happened?" Dillon repeats, scanning the area for Jake.

Linda shakes her head and whispers, "There was an accident. Robyn, sweetie, we need to go."

"Don't tell me . . . ?"

Linda's pained expression halts Dillon's question. He can see the stoic nurse in Linda's eyes, the clinician, then the protective mother not yet ready to explain to her daughter why Daddy took a ride in the ambulance. Dillon fights the tears welling up behind his unbelieving eyes. He focuses instead on anger, the sight of the driver of the Tesla sitting in the back of a patrol car, shoulders slumped, head down, face ashen. Eyes set hard, Dillon fixates on the driver, mentally crucifying him until he feels Linda's hug.

"We don't know what happened yet," she whispers. "We arrived after . . ."

Dillon unclenches his jaw and fists, all aching.

"Robyn, sweetie, we need to—"

"I want to stay with Dilly," Robyn says, squeezing Dillon harder. "Can I see Terri and Miley?"

"Sweetie, we have to—"

"Let me watch her while you . . ." Dillon fights back tears that need to flow. "We'll be at the inn."

Linda stands there, now looking like the despondent wife. She brushes a tear from her eye. "Okay, sweetie, you can go over to Dillon's for a while. I'll come pick you up later."

"With Daddy?"

Dillon bites his lip hard, trying to hold it together. Blood trickles out.

Linda covers her eyes with the sunglasses from the top of her head. "I'm going to see how Daddy's"—her voice cracks—"doing." She bends down and gives Robyn a kiss on the top of her head, squeezes Dillon's shoulder, and mouths the words, "*thank you*," then rushes off toward the chaos.

Dillon tastes metallic on his lip. He scoops Robyn up from the ground, places her in his arms, and starts walking. He speaks to Robyn, though he has no idea what he says, distracting them both from the scene until he reaches his pickup. He settles her into the passenger seat and buckles the seat belt around her, fumbling with the straps to accommodate her size, his mind drifting, wondering if he had started his run earlier, placing him at Cobblestone sooner, that perhaps—

"That's too tight," Robyn says, squirming under the pressure.

"Sorry. Is that better?"

She nods. "Can we see Miley and Terri? And Jimmy and Chasey and Spencey too?"

"Yes we can," he says as he buckles himself in and steers them toward town. He dials Terri's number. He hopes she can at least stop by for a short while on her day off. It's still early, but he calls Chase, Spencer, and Jim, leaving brief voicemails for them to call him back as soon as possible.

"I didn't get to see the birds and bees with Mommy and Daddy today on our hike," Robyn says, staring out the window toward the park, clutching a stuffed bear Dillon didn't notice earlier. "Tweet, tweet, tweet, and buzz, buzz, buzz . . ."

Dillon caves. Tears rolls down his cheeks, mixing with the salt from his run, cascades over his swollen and bloody lip, and drips into his lap.

Friday Night
Midnight Run

There's light, moonlight, two days removed from a November full moon. Jim's eyes have long adjusted to its paleness on the unpaved side of the creekside path somewhere between Willowside and Fulton. Heading east, moon overhead, his shadow runs alongside him, keeping pace, though he hardly cares. It isn't Jake, his best friend, his college roommate, his best man, his movie buddy, and the constant reminder irritates him, urging him to run faster, but still it shadows him.

Going to the movies seemed like a good idea when he set out and bought a ticket, but halfway through the quirky independent film, he bailed, no longer interested in the premise that held no promise of shared quips and quotes with his childhood buddy.

Still dressed in jeans, T-shirt, and sweatshirt, he took to running from the downtown theater, attempting to fill the sudden void in his life, a life that had been replete with friendship since he was eight years old, when they met, Jake reasoning with a much bigger kid on the school playground who was giving Jim grief for being "a skinny runt," that to harass another was akin to chastising one's own shortcomings in front of a mirror, and wasn't that self-defeating? The bigger kid sized up the just-as-skinny-but-taller Jake and decided to move on to less philosophical skinny runts.

Though he can't feel them, Jim knows his arms are pumping in rhythm with his denim-clad legs based on the jingle of car keys dangling from a hand. He isn't cold, though the crisp midnight air rushing in and out of his lungs reminds him that winter is fast approaching.

When his breathing hits unsustainable levels, he backs off until his mind re-engages, prompting him to push the limits again, holding the agonizing thoughts at bay. At some point the cotton T-shirt under the fleece sweatshirt he wears clings to his skin, soaked in sweat. On the fly he removes the bulky top and wraps it around his waist. The air instantly chills the wet shirt against his skin; another welcome distraction.

He rushes up the ramp to Fulton and dashes across the road. Headlights from an oncoming car light him up, erasing the shadow to his left and creating a longer shadow to his right. At the sound of a horn honk, an act deemed unnecessary given the adequate buffer, Jim flips the driver off, crosses the median, and dashes across the other lane, dropping down the ramp, back onto the dirt path. Again at full steam until his lungs ache, and again easing off, Jim carries out his emotional fartlek until he returns once more to the downtown theater, the pace slackening as he approaches his car. His heart thumps under the wet cotton, pulsing and echoing in his ears in the still of the night that has turned morning. His breaths create foggy billows, and inadequate running attire chafes his inner thighs. Soon his body will cool and the chill will engulf him. Even fatigue from roughly twelve miles run in an estimated sixty-five minutes is a welcome respite. The cacophony of sensations suffuses from head to toe, but most important, the head, where nothing matters, a state he hopes to nurture into a deep sleep, counting off the first of many, many days in mourning.

Saturday Daybreak
The Dam Bursts

From his condo, Chase jogs toward Foothill Park, a detached effort at best. He needed to get out of the condo despite the early hour that followed a night of tossing and turning. Dogma had stared him down on the couch long enough, and Chase harbored thoughts on testing the nine-lives-of-cats theory. Scrolling through Facebook left him further deflated from all the outpouring of sympathy for Jake. Gaze narrow in focus, body numb, he floats along to the white noise of minivans and SUVs shuttling kids off to soccer practice.

He enters the parking lot and stops off at the bathrooms before heading up into the trails, but after one short climb that leaves him breathless, he slows to a stop on the dam and bends over, placing hands on knees as if he's run the race of his life. Still hunched over, he lifts his head, staring off into the lake held in place courtesy of the Army Corps of Engineers. His narrow field of vision blocks out the sides of the lake as it stretches east, disappearing into the bank of trees a quarter mile away. He rocks his head, no longer able to contain the bile that has for the past twenty-four hours churned inside, set in motion years ago, his body trembling. He straightens up, clenches his fists, closes his eyes, and opens his mouth, the dam bursting with venom, "*Fuuuuuuuuuuuuuuuuuuuuuuuuuuuuuuuuuuuuuuuuuuuuuuuuuuuuuuuuuuuuuuuuuck!*"

Saturday Late Night
Spencer's Weekly Email Addendum

Spencer sits comatose on the bed at home, staring at the blank email on his laptop until Maggie enters the bedroom and snuggles up to him.

"I don't know what to write," he says.

Maggie rubs his shoulders, his mind as empty as the email page. Exhaustion also factors into his mental state. After flying back from Portland Friday morning and learning of the fateful news from Dillon, Spencer had to drive the boys team down to Fresno for the CIF finals at Woodward Park. And after marshaling all his energies toward Zac and the team's efforts on Saturday morning, Spencer drove them back home, half celebrating their successes en route and half processing Jake's death.

"It's like a deep, dark void I can't comprehend," he says.

"I'm truly sorry, honey. How's Jim handling it?"

"Doris said he goes out for a run every few hours." Spencer turns to Maggie. "I love you."

Maggie nods.

"I mean it."

"I know."

He leans in, kisses her, and buries his head in her bosom while she massages his back, the band of her engagement ring grounding him.

"I'm sure none of you have slept much," Maggie says. "Tell them there's no group run. It's going to hurt too much *not* having Jake there to banter with."

Spencer lets out a muffled sniffle, gives a faint nod, and lifts his head, drying his eyes. He types out the subject, pauses a moment, and deletes the group recipient distribution list, replacing it with the guys' individual email addresses. "Jake used Linda's email address," he says, now imagining what Linda is going through, and little Robyn with a *y* . . .

From: Spencer Lingard <MarathonMan@gomail.com>
To: Chase Brandon <ChaseMeIfYouCan@gomail.com>,
Jim Greyson <JimG@gomail.com>,
Dillon Percy <BRB@gomail.com>
Subject: Sunday's Run . . .

Gentlemen,

I'm not up for running tomorrow morning, as I'm sure you're not either. Let's touch base after the weekend on whether or not we still want to travel to Bend next weekend.

Signing off,

Spencer

P.S. Zac won CIF today down in Fresno, and he says thanks for running with him on Percy's Loop. The team also placed 2nd; our highest finish in school history.

Sunday Morning
Breakfast, No Run

"Dilly!" Robyn shouts, upon opening the door at the Dearborn homestead.

"*Wooooowooowooo Wooooowoooo.*"

"Miley!"

"She wanted to come see you," Dillon says, standing there holding two bags with breakfast items, one warm, one cool.

"Hi, Dillon," Linda says, appearing at the door. "Come in. Robyn, sweetie, you can play with Miles later. Go wash up. Dillon brought us breakfast."

"Mom, it's *Dilly* and *Miley*. Come on, Miley."

"*Wooooowooowooo Wooooowoooo,*" Miles says, trotting off behind Robyn across the living room.

"How's she doing?" Dillon asks, following Linda into the kitchen.

"She has good and bad moments." Linda gathers dishes and utensils. "One moment she understands that he's not coming home, then the next she spots his truck out front and rushes to it. I finally parked it at the neighbors'."

Dillon unloads containers from the bags and opens them up, placing serving spoons into each. "How are you doing?"

"Without sleep it's hard to tell."

Dillon watches Linda prepare Robyn's plate, dark rings under her eyes, a stoic yet fragile demeanor.

"How are you doing?" Linda says. "No run today with the guys?"

Caught off guard about the run, Dillon hesitates, reading the room, unsure what to say. He clears his throat. "No."

"I figured as much when I didn't see Spencer's email."

"There was one, but—"

"He probably didn't want to upset me. I see them before . . ."

Dillon walks over and takes hold of Linda, whose brave exterior has caved, and hugs her. He can hear light weeping in his shirt.

"Mommy's sad because Daddy stopped breathing and can't have breakfast with us," Robyn says, entering the kitchen.

Linda pulls back and wipes her eyes dry. "Yes, sweetie, that's right."

Dillon turns his back to Robyn and Linda to hold things together when Robyn says, "I told him he was too scruffy. Is that why he won't breathe anymore?"

"No, sweetie. I liked his scruff," Linda says, giving Robyn a hug, a kiss on the head, and handing her food plate. "Thank Dillon for breakfast."

"Mom, it's *Dilly*. Thank you, Dilly. Come on, Miley. We have things to discuss."

Dillon sucks in his swollen lower lip and sniffles. "I can't even imagine." He prepares plates for Linda and himself.

They take a seat at the table in the kitchen, eating until the grandfather clock from the living room chimes nine times.

"When I was moving Jake's truck, the glove compartment popped open and this journal fell out," Linda says, pulling it from the side table and handing it to Dillon. "I always wondered where Robyn got the idea to carry a notebook around with her."

As Dillon chews on a biscuit, he accepts the earth-stained journal and opens it.

"I read through it last night when I couldn't sleep. I think there are some things in there that you and guys might enjoy."

Dillon thumbs through many pages of running entries, coming to a page with the phrase "Footfalls in Annadel" written across the top. "I'll share it with them."

"Jake's grandmother stopped by earlier this morning," Linda says, sipping her coffee. "She told me a cute story about Jake I'd never heard. The whole family was spending a week up at their cabin in Tahoe one summer, the summer he started running every day back in junior high. Well, his grandmother didn't think it was good for him."

"Like mother like daughter," Dillon says. "At Thanksgiving, I heard the jokes about his overly cautious mother."

Linda smiles. "Both were very happy he married a nurse."

Dillon chuckles.

"Jake shared a small room with his grandfather and would set out his running gear on the porch before going to bed so as not to wake anybody up in the morning. But when he woke up the next morning his shoes were missing. His grandmother had hidden them. Jake complained to his mother about it, but the next day his shoes were hidden again. So on the third day, still no shoes, he puts on three pairs of socks and goes off on his run, and when he gets back the socks have holes in them. Ruined. The next day his running shoes were on the porch."

Dillon smiles. "I guess shoes were a *safer* option than socks."

"That and she's frugal."

Linda's story lingers until they finish breakfast, fragments of Robyn's conversation with Miles from the other room drifting into the kitchen.

"Are you guys going to Bend next weekend?" Linda says, clearing the empty plates from the table.

Dillon shrugs, rising to his feet. "We haven't talked about it. Not sure our hearts are in it."

"You should. You know he'll be watching over you."

Dillon nods. The idea of running seems distant; the thought of racing seems pointless.

"Let Spencer know that he can leave Jake on the emails."

"Sure thing," Dillon says, walking out the front door, Miles in tow and Robyn waving goodbye, brave-girl tears streaming down her cheeks.

Week 48 Training Summary			
	Long Run	Mileage Total	Comments
Dillon	5	46	There are no words.
Chase	6	38	Life isn't fair!!!
Spencer	0	39	His was a life well lived.
Jim	26	79	Godspeed, Jakey . . .
Jake			

Week 14
November 30

Wednesday Evening
Go/No Go

> From: Spencer Lingard <MarathonMan@gomail.com>
> To: Team Thirsty Boys <SundayRunDL>
> Subject: Nationals . . .
>
> Dear Sirs,
> I wanted to send out a quick email to check on everybody's
> thoughts regarding running nationals this weekend. Linda
> called last night and suggested that we run in Jake's memory. I
> like the idea. Anybody else in?
> Signing off,
> Spencer

. . . I will reply to your email after I've had sufficient time to reflect on its content.

From: Chase Brandon <ChaseMeIfYouCan@gomail.com>
To: Team Thirsty Boys <SundayRunDL>
Subject: RE: Nationals . . .

I'm in. We can take the Bimmer.
Chasester

From: Dillon Percy <BRB@gomail.com>
To: Team Thirsty Boys <SundayRunDL>
Subject: RE: Nationals . . .

In.
Cheers,
Dillon

From: Jim Greyson <JimG@gomail.com>
To: Team Thirsty Boys <SundayRunDL>
Subject: RE: Nationals . . .

Gentlemen,
I'm in, but my legs are trashed so don't expect much from me.
Jim

From: Spencer Lingard <MarathonMan@gomail.com>
To: Team Thirsty Boys <SundayRunDL>
Subject: RE: Nationals . . .

Dear Sirs,
Jim, don't worry about it. We're all reeling from the loss. We'll
do what we can and leave it at that. Linda gave me the number
of Jake's friend Salvador. I'll call him to see if he'd like to run in
Jake's honor, otherwise we'll race as an incomplete team. Our
hotel reservations are already in place as well as our race entry

applications.

Signing off,

Spencer

Friday Late Morning
The Long and Winding Road Trip

Miles nudges open the BR&B front door and pads out onto the porch at the sound of a vehicle approaching.

"*Wooooowooowooo Wooooowoooo.*"

"Thanks for covering tomorrow," Dillon says to Terri, picking up his overnight bag from the floor, his racing shoes laced together through the bag's handles. "Linda, Maggie, and Doris said they'd help out if needed. We'll be back late tomorrow night, so there's no need to come in on Sunday."

"Race strong tomorrow." She walks over to him, gives him a long hug, kisses him on the cheek, and gazes deep into his eyes. "Jake will be there in spirit."

Dillon nods, letting the hug go on longer than he normally cares for, though deep inside he appreciates it, the soulful quality it embodies.

"Hey," Chase says upon entering.

"Thanks for picking me up."

"Not a problem."

"And again . . . sorry." Dillon pats Chase on the shoulder, glances back at Terri, and heads out to the BMW.

Walking hand in hand, Terri and Chase follow Dillon outside, pausing on the porch to share a goodbye kiss.

"Good luck, guys!" she says, waving as the car exits the property.

"*Wooooowooowooo Wooooowoooo.*"

"How'd I end up shotgun?" Dillon asks.

"Jim needs sleeping room, and Spencer prefers the additional safety buffer." A reserved smile crosses Chase's face.

Nobody comments further on the seating arrangements and, predictably,

Jim dozes off as soon as they hit River Road, making their way east toward Calistoga.

"Congrats on the engagement," Dillon says.

"Man, sorry, Spencer," Chase says, shaking his head. "Congrats as well."

"Don't be," Spencer says.

"How'd Maggie's parents react?" Chase says.

"They practically fainted during the Thanksgiving dinner toast."

"I'll bet."

"Is Salvador joining us?" Dillon says.

"Yeah. He has family in Portland so he's up there now. He'll meet up with us at the race tomorrow. He ran the Seattle marathon this past weekend, so he's not fresh."

"Nice he's willing to fill in," Dillon says. "How long to Bend?"

"Seven to eight hours, depending on traffic. And Chase."

"We'll stop in Weed, gas up, and eat if we're hungry," Chase says. "We have snacks on board."

"I brought food too." Dillon rummages through his bag for the extra banana bread loaf he baked that morning.

"Between that, what I brought, and what Doris sent along, I'd say we're set for a few days of driving."

It doesn't take long for drowsiness to creep up on Dillon as Chase negotiates the switchbacks up and over the grade that separates Napa and Lake Counties. Through fading eyelids, Dillon spots the Robert Louis Stevenson Trailhead as they crest the summit where a group of hikers are on their way up to Mount Saint Helena. Once off the mountain the pastoral landscape flows by without distinction, completely lulling him to sleep.

It isn't until the sound of voices invades Dillon's subconscious that he stirs from his slumber. Unsure how long he's been out, he glances at the dashboard clock: nearly two hours, the landscape now desolate, agricultural, and flat, extending north, east, west, and south into a brownish haze that blurs the horizon. He flexes his leg muscles and yawns, tuning into the words from the ongoing conversation.

"Band on the Run," Spencer says.

"Paul McCartney and Wings?" Jim says.

Spencer and Chase nod.

"Your turn, Jim," Spencer says.

"What are you playing?" Dillon says.

"'Run' song game," Spencer says.

"Duck and Run," Jim says. "Three Doors Down."

"Don't Stop Runnin,'" Chase says. "Y&T."

Dillon watches Spencer enter Jim's and Chase's answers into his cell phone. "You want to join?"

"Sure. What are the rules?"

"You have two minutes to come up with a song or forfeit your turn. 'Run' or a derivative of it can be in the song title or band's name."

"Okay. I assume 'Born to Run' has been taken?"

Nods follow.

"We reserved that one in Jake's honor," Jim says.

"Fitting," Dillon says, peering out the windshield, deep in thought. Cruising well above the posted speed limit, they pass a long caravan of semis filled with consumer goods, produce, cars, household items. "'Running on Empty.' Jackson Browne."

Everybody glances at Dillon.

"Taken?"

"No," Spencer says, adding it to the list. "My turn. 'Keep on Runnin.' Journey."

"Shoot," Jim says, shaking his head.

Chase chuckles. "Your two minutes start now, buddy."

Dillon smiles, working on his next song: "Run, Runaway" by Slade.

They reach the end of the barren northbound I-5 experience at Weed, where Chase pulls off the freeway and spends several minutes driving around searching for a gas station, though he's already passed two.

"I need to pee like a racehorse, Chase," Jim says, shifting around in his seat. "Gas is gas."

"But I get reward points with Chevron."

A collective groan springs from the backseat.

"And gas isn't gas."

"Not this again," Spencer says.

"Chevron uses Techron, which is—"

"Well, piss is piss," Jim says, irritation and urgency colliding.

"Here we go," Chase says, pulling into a Chevron station.

Jim opens the back door before the car comes to a stop, jumps out when it finishes rolling, and sprints toward the minimart's main entrance.

Dillon steps out from the car and stretches his arms high into the sky, watching two rental vans drive by with painted windows that read BEND OR BUST! Painted images of a running shoe's sole are stamped around the dire and misquoted sentiment. "Win or go home" better captures the mission, but Dillon doesn't care that much. The caravan does remind him of his first road trip, high school freshman year, though: a group of fourteen high school boys comprising the frosh/soph and varsity divisions for the Mammoth Cross-Country Invitational. Two of the team members' parents had offered to drive the team up in their respective Winnebagos. They played card games, including poker, using large elbow macaroni for chips. Dillon recalled the camaraderie that spawned from that trip, hanging out with friends who joked, laughed, and competed like there was no tomorrow.

Of course he can't forget the sleeping arrangements and racing conditions on that inaugural road trip: on the hardwood floor of the Mammoth High School gymnasium the night before the race, alongside other teams from around the state; the 9,000-foot-elevation assault on his lungs a minute into the race, wrecking havoc on his sea-level training until he hit the three-quarter-mile mark, where his second wind kicked in and sent him into the finishing chute first with a course record, beating out the state's previous year's best freshmen and sophomores, his performance a testament to his potential at a young age, that effort taking its toll on him in the chute as he struggled to breathe in the oxygen-deprived environment, gasping for minutes. Afterward he slipped on his sweats, where a bee had worked its way into a pant leg and proceeded to sting him, his hopping around trying to remove the sweats and gulping thin air giving rise to both laughter and concern to those watching. *Good times.*

Jim has a relieved expression upon returning to the car, and once the gas tank is topped off, they take a quick vote about stopping to eat. A unanimous nay sends them on their way along a two-lane highway with periodic passing lanes, though they're never in opportune spots, as Chase laments whenever they get stuck behind a semi truck or an out-of-state motorhome.

"Run-DMC," Spencer says.

"Spence, mixing it up," Chase says. "How 'bout, and nobody laugh . . . 'I Ran' by—"

"A Flock of Seagulls fan!" Spencer says, chuckling.

"Pfft."

"Okay, my turn. How about this one," Dillon says, "'Run Like Hell.' Pink Floyd."

"Man!" Jim says. "You guys are killing me."

"I was so tired at the end of my first 10K road race that I started chanting the opening lyrics to that song: '*Run, run, run,*'" Chase says. "The closer I got to the finish line, the louder I chanted, and the other runners ahead of me pulled off to the side. Everybody was cheering me on that last hundred yards . . . it was pretty awesome."

"Okay, here's another old-school one for you," Spencer says. "'Fox on the Run'—"

"You already claimed that one," Chase says.

"That was by Manfred Mann. Sweet later used the same title for a different song," Spencer says.

"Well, look at you . . ." Chase says. "Jim?"

"I need a minute."

"So who's winning?" Dillon says.

"We're not keeping score," Spencer says.

"We could—" Chase says.

"Nooooo . . . why must *everything* be a competition with you?" Jim says with more irritation than when he had to pee like a racehorse. "We get it, you have the most toys. Give it a rest, already."

"Sorry, man, I—"

"Let's just have fun," Jim says. "'Runnin' Down a Dream.' Tom Petty."

Jim's dream echoes in the quiet interior several minutes before he apologizes for his agitated response, allowing the game to continue on, whiling away the last of the California miles, distracting the guys from the heavy weight on their emotions, but upon approaching and crossing over into Oregon, Spencer's temperate mood changes.

"'Runnin' with the Devil,'" he says with a hint of dormant frustration. "Van Halen."

"Problem?" Jim says.

"Oregon does that to me," Spencer says. "Four years of college here and I never heard the end of my California roots." He gazes at the perpetually green landscape streaking by.

"I thought their beef was with L.A.?" Dillon says. "You know, the '*Beat L.A. Beat L.A.*' chant during sporting events. Man, that gets annoying."

"Happens at the Giants game when the Dodgers are in town too," Chase says.

"Californication," Spencer says.

"FYI," Dillon says, "Southern California doesn't give anything north of Valencia a second thought."

"That's the problem," Jim says.

"And they should," Spencer says. "Sacramento is the state capital. And we have the water."

"I didn't notice it much during my time at the Dub," Dillon says. "I suppose with the rise of Microsoft, Starbucks, grunge rock, and the *Frasier* show, they became their own California."

"'Run Through the Jungle.' CCR," Jim says. "Oregon has Nike."

"Nike is a marketing genius!" Chase says. "They have perfected the ability to sell an idea rather than a product: 'Just Do It.'"

"And that's good *why*?" Dillon says.

"It makes more sense to grow a business vertically than horizontally. It costs too much money to manufacture, so offloading it overseas allows businesses to grow and manufacture brands instead, without limits."

"So *more* commercials," Dillon says, shaking his head. "Every day, it's like I wake up and the world is trying to sell me something, lurking around every corner I turn, stalking me online, then every web page tracking what I may have said in an email, and every other page I view after that has an ad for it. It's a never-ending assault on my senses, and for what, to liberate a few dollars from my wallet? It's hard to live in peace when anything I look at, read, review, or watch is constantly telling me what to buy to make me feel a certain way. Enough already!" He snatches a chunk of banana bread and stuffs it into his mouth, teeth grinding away.

With the BMW stuck behind a motorhome and no passing lane in sight, a quiet timeout ensues as the tires' methodical hum over the black asphalt fills the void.

"'Take the Money and Run,'" Dillon says. "Steve Miller Band."

"Hey, it's my turn," Chase says.

"You snooze, you lose."

"'Run to You,'" Spence says. "Bryan Adams."

"You can have my turn, Chase," Jim says.

"'Runnin' Wild,'" Chase says. "Airbourne."

Dillon sighs. "'Runaway Train . . . ' Soul Asylum."

"I get it," Chase says. "It can be overwhelming, but for a company to promote their product out there they must rise above the constant buzz and multitude of viewing options the consumer has today. A simple TV commercial no longer cuts it. Sports is about the last bastion of live TV left. Everything else is recorded and watched later, skipping the—"

"Aaron Rodgers's fumble, brought to you by Butterfinger candy bar," Jim says.

"'Run with the Pack' by Bad Company," Spencer says. "Doesn't it bother you that everybody hates commercials?"

"Some are entertaining," Jim says.

"It is crappy that I have to endure a thirty-second spot in order to watch a sixty-second YouTube video," Spencer says. "And often with poor production value. I actually had to sit through a commercial the other day online in order to watch a *product* promo."

"Especially the old Gatorade commercials," Jim says. "The Chris Legh one narrated by Keith Jackson was inspiring."

Chase shrugs. "How else are companies supposed to advertise their products?"

"I don't know . . . email? Twitter?" Dillon blurts out. "Anything that allows you to opt out if you're not interested. I know you're always saying it's all about branding but I'm so tired of being branded, branded like . . . cattle." He turns his attention to the passing scenery, Upper Klamath Lake to the left and an informational road sign to the right informing travelers that the Oregon Institute of Technology campus exit is one mile ahead. "And don't get me started on Gatorade and their Gatorade Sports *Science* Institute."

"Good thing you don't own a business," Chase says.

Rubbing his forehead, Dillon massages his thoughts. "Yeah."

A heavy collective sigh launches a long stretch of silence, everybody gazing out a window, thoughts miles away until Chase increases the volume of the satellite radio receiver—which, ironically enough, is commercial-free as Dillon is quick to point out—so that music soothes their emotions: Mike and the Mechanics. Everybody chuckles at the song playing.

"'Silent Running,'" Jim says. All eyes peer in his direction. "What? It's my turn."

Spencer grins and adds the song to their growing list.

"Feel better?" Chase says, glancing at Dillon.

"Metaphorically speaking."

Night has consumed day by the time they reach Bend, driving along the freeway that has a speed limit of forty-five. Chase accommodates the odd limit for a freeway after Spencer cautions him about Oregon's "energy conservation speed limit" fines. Chase isn't sure what that means, but heeds it nonetheless, if for nothing else than fatigue from eight hours behind the wheel.

They find their way to the downtown hotel suite on the main drag, the venue that serves as official headquarters for the National Cross-Country Club Championships. The other guys stretch outside in the nippy air of the high desert sequestered along the eastern edge of the Cascade Range, where the Deschutes River runs wild, while Spencer goes inside. Spencer states his last name when the stout night clerk asks for the name under which the reservations have been made. She types it in, makes additional entries, and requests his credit card. "That's one suite for two nights, correct?"

"It should be two suites for one night."

The stout woman types more commands into the computer, but repeats her original statement.

"See here," he says, producing the printed confirmation email for her, "two rooms, one night."

The stout one grabs the confirmation and stares at it for several moments. "Darla?" she hollers. "Could you come here?"

A skinny woman wearing a heavy jacket comes out from the small office behind the reservation counter, where a printer is shooting sheets of paper out onto a tray. "Whatcha got?"

The stout one hands her the confirmation.

The skinny woman scans it and says, "Two rooms, one night."

The stout one points to the computer screen.

"Oh," the skinny one says, looking at the confirmation email again. "You booked it through a third-party website instead of with us. It's looks like they muffed it."

Spencer stares disapprovingly at the blame game playing out before him. Both women stay silent with unblinking eyes as Spencer forms words. "Look, I booked it through the site that had the special rates for the event . . . how could it have *muffed it?*"

The women glance at each other before the skinny one speaks. "Sir, I don't know, and we're sorry, but—"

Spencer lets out a deep sigh. "Just change it. We've been on the road all day, and we're tired and hungry."

The stout one types on the keyboard. "We're all booked tonight because of the—" she stops short, catching Spencer's stone-faced stare. "I'm sorry, sir, but we only have the one room that you reserved. We can get some rollaways for you."

"Dammit!" Spencer follows his vocal displeasure with a noisy sigh, looks down at his shoes a moment, and out through the front door window at the guys standing by the car, who are talking with fellow runners he recognizes from the PA. "Fine," he says, pulling out his rewards card for the hotel chain. He places it on the counter while the skinny one reaches for the phone and orders up two rollaways.

"I'm sorry, we don't accept rewards cards," the stout one says, glancing at it.

"What the hell? This is West Coast Suites, isn't it?"

"Yes . . . but we're an independent. Those are accepted in California and Washington, for the most part."

"Typical," he says, staring at the stout one.

"And in Portland," the skinny one says.

Spencer rolls his eyes as if that's any comfort. "Look, the website didn't specify that when I booked—"

"What's up?" Chase asks, coming up from behind Spencer. A tired yet concerned Dillon and Jim flank Chase.

Spencer turns around. "Where to begin," he says as if ready to explain a long, complicated lecture to his students who failed to read the assigned chapters. "First, only one room tonight. Second, because we're not in *Portland* we can't use my rewards card for a free night. Third—"

"It's okay, buddy," Chase says as Spencer's voice rises and passersby take long looks in the guys' direction. "We'll sort things out." He pulls Spencer back and faces him away from the counter, turning to say, "We'll only need—" He stops short while Dillon converses with the women behind the counter. Chase guides Spencer outside. "Let it go. We're all tired right now."

Spencer nods, separates himself from Chase, and stares off into the distance toward snowcapped Mount Bachelor, ignoring the joyous chorus from a group of runners heading into the hotel's banquet room, where the race director has organized a spaghetti feed for all the clubs. Several minutes elapse, allowing Spencer to let the reservation SNAFU go when he hears his name called.

"Here's a keycard. We're all set," Dillon says, handing one over to Spencer. "If we want to stay tomorrow night they'll comp it, no problem. They also comped dinner tonight and breakfast tomorrow." Dillon stares at Spencer. "They are sorry . . ."

Spencer takes the keycard, wondering what it cost Dillon in trades to smooth things over. "Hey, guys, can we skip the race dinner?"

"Agreed."

"Yes."

"Definitely."

The lack of objections comes as no surprise, given the circumstances. Jake's death made national news owing to the high-profile nature of the vehicle involved. The last thing Spencer wants is a constant stream of condolences.

The guys settle into their two-room suite, Chase calling dibs on one bedroom while Spencer calls dibs on the other. Neither Jim nor Dillon protests, and when someone from the front desk drops off their meal vouchers, and only one roll-away—a second one is not available due to the full house—Dillon offers it to Jim, opting himself to take the couch, which looks comfy enough for one night, where sleep will unlikely come anyway.

Beds claimed, and amenities explored, critiqued, and (by Spencer), criticized, they head down to the hotel restaurant, bypassing the banquet room, where a booming voice is making announcements about the next day's race. Nothing much is said after sitting down until some time into their meals.

"Spence, what time is the race tomorrow?" Chase asks, eating a heart-healthy plate of pasta and mixed vegetables. Between bites he scrutinizes Spence's four-course meal. "We're not running a marathon tomorrow."

"Open race is at twelve forty-five," he says, shoveling another portion from plate number two into his mouth.

Dillon wonders if the late race start time will aid in sleeping, but he doubts it. He dislikes races that don't start in the morning. It makes him feel lazy, like he has to rest and do nothing until race time.

"Oaf," Jim says. "Late races are the worst. Hard to plan what to eat."

"I don't mind them," Chase says. "I'm used to running at lunch anyway with a full breakfast under my belt."

"A real breakfast or a chemical one?" Jim says with a smirk.

"Real . . . and a protein shake midmorning."

Dillon chews on bread soaked in spaghetti sauce—the first such dinner that doesn't come from the breakfast side of a menu in a long time—the traditional meal his high school coach had instilled in him the night before cross-country and track meets, though once he had it for lunch before a night track meet and burped the tomato-based sauce throughout the race. *Not* good times.

"Seriously, Spence, what's with all the food?" Chase says.

"Getting my free meal's worth."

Dillon smiles. Chase laughs. Jim snorts.

Spence returns a halfhearted grin.

"Shit!" Chase says ten minutes after the lights have gone out in the suite.

"What?" Dillon says reflexively, then realizes he's not at the BR&B tending to a guest. He recalls the lady who had come downstairs sleepwalking, searching for her cat, wondering why Miles didn't respond promptly to her call of Lulu. When Miles did speak, the woman went about trying to prepare a cup of tea until her husband came looking for her and guided her back to their room.

"He can't hear you," Jim says from the nearby rollaway.

"Why not?"

"Earplugs," Spencer says from the other bedroom. "Chase!" The name ricochets off the walls several times until it loses strength.

"What?"

"What, what?" Jim says

"The sheets are scratchy." He emphasizes the point by scissoring his legs around; *swish—swish—swish—swish—swish.*

"They feel fine," Spencer says.

"I'm used to a higher thread count."

Spencer snorts. "You know what Jake would say."

The room waits in silence for the answer.

"Lord love a duck?" Chase says.

"Pampered tastes leave you hapless in the everyday world."

Chase's legs swish several times. Jim chuckles. Dillon ponders the wisdom that Jake bestowed upon the guys.

"Jake ever tell you about his first cross-country meet?" Jim says.

"Not sure," Chase says.

"Don't think so," Spencer says.

Dillon shakes his head, realizes the room is dark, and says, "No."

"You met his mother at Thanksgiving, Dillon, so you heard how super cautious she is about everything. We used to call her the 'bubble-wrap mom.' So when Jake told her he was going to run a race at school, she told him he had to wear a cup like the other sports required."

Dillon smiles, and a pair of chuckles come from the bedrooms.

"Now, Jake had never played a team sport, so he didn't know anything about jock straps or cups, so he's in the bathroom at Spring Lake five minutes before the start of the race trying to figure out how to put it on."

More chuckles fill the darkness.

"Old Coach Munson is yelling his name, so Jake ditches the jock strap, figuring the cup is the important component to the whole contraption."

Jim chuckles a couple moments.

"So he stuffs the cup into his running shorts, trots over to the start line, and starts running as soon as the gun goes off. He's gets a hundred yards into it and the cup slips out and onto the ground."

Collective laughter grows.

"He stops, turns back, grabs it, and continues on running with it for the entire race."

The image of a junior high boy running a race carrying a protective cup sends Dillon into fits of laughter along with the rest.

"He's finishes second behind me, and at the end of the chute, Munson is there and says, 'Son, what are you carrying?' And Jakey shows him and goes 'My cup, sir.'"

Suppressed laughter is now the order of the moment so as not to miss the rest of the story.

"Munson can't decide whether to yell or laugh out loud, and just stares at Jakey. Jakey goes, 'My mom made me wear it so no one kicks me in the nuts, sir.' Munson goes, 'Lord love a duck! Now I've heard it all.'"

The suppressed laughter no longer holds, and Dillon suspects that he isn't the only one stricken with a watery form of laughter, especially when it dawns on him where the "The Great 'Cup' Escape" idiom comes from.

"My favorite Jake story is how he meet Linda," Spencer says a minute later after their laughter fades. "Jim knows this story. Do you, Chase?"

"Probably not."

"I convinced Jake to come run with me at a road race up in Mendo County. A 10K. I didn't want to go by myself so I told him it was a *country* road race, and he reluctantly agreed. We show up and there are a few other PA runners, but nobody serious, so it's going to be an easy race to win. They always had great awards, like vacation trips and such. Anyway, we take off and Jake and I are two hundred yards in front of the field a half mile in, so we set it on cruise control and run side by side. Somewhere around mile two we come to a fork in the road. There's an old pickup truck on the side of the road with a grizzled guy in dirty overalls leaned up against the hood. He has what looks like a CB radio mike in his hand. I ask, 'Which way?' and the guy motions us to the left. So we veer left. A couple minutes later something doesn't feel right. It's like we crossed into another world. I glanced around and it looked like we were heading into the hills, where no one ever comes back with a good story to tell, if they come back at all. Next thing I know a motorcycle is roaring up behind us. It's a cop and he's flagging us down because we'd been steered the wrong way. So the cop does a U-ie and takes off back down toward the course. We turn around and I'm steamed because we were leading the dang race, now we're running around like lost sheep out in the country. And let me tell you, Dillon, if you haven't been up there, it can be a little unsettling."

"Welfare nation," Chase says.

"Got it," Dillon says.

"So I take off fast, adrenaline fast. Jake is jogging in place where we'd turned around, hollering to me, 'Spence, I think we can cut through this field and get back on the course. It'll be quicker.' I glanced to the left. There's an old dilapidated barn, rusty trucks up on blocks, overgrown bramble as far as the eye can see, barbed-wire fencing all around. I said no thanks and kept running. So I reconnect with the course but not before giving a piece of my mind to the volunteer at the fork in the road, who shrugged. That boiled my blood, so I go blazing down the road, passing tons of people who all think I started late. I kept half expecting Jake to pop out along the side of the road but he never did. I ended up winning the race by some miracle, but no one at the finish had any idea what had happened until the cop told them.

"Impressive you won after all that," Dillon says. "Must've been a great first-place award."

"Two nights at a B&B there in town."

Dillon chuckles.

"So I'm waiting around for Jake to come in but after twenty minutes he hadn't shown up, and I'm getting worried . . . like *Deliverance* worried. I asked around about him but nobody knew anything. I ask the cop and he said he'd go back out and look for him. And just as he says this, I see a car pull up next to the finish line and out pops Jake, big smile and all. Linda was heading to work, driving along the racecourse when she sees this guy running through the pasture and ducking under some barbed wire, snagging his shorts in the process. She stops, rolls her window down, and asks him if he's all right. Jake said he looked up, saw her smiling at him, and said, 'I am now.' He called that their first date, her cleaning up his scratch marks from all the thickets he'd scrambled through."

"He called it the best wrong decision he'd ever made," Jim says.

Whoops of excessive energy and excitement in the hallway crescendos and fades.

"My favorite Jake story," Chase says, "was the day he called me and said he wanted to do a track workout with me. I was like 'Hell yeah!' He tells me to meet him at the little elementary school on the corner of Willowside and Hall Road, out by your place, Dillon."

"Yep," Dillon says, chuckling at the direction the story is heading.

"So you know. Well, I didn't."

"What?" Jim says.

"I get there and, yes, there's a track, but it's an old *dirt* track, with weeds for an inside curb, ruts on the turns, and a few potholes on the straightaways for good measure."

Spencer laughs. "That's right. I forgot they had one there."

"Yeah, so I'm shaking my head and Jake's got this smirk on his face. Of course I have a few choice words for him. As we start warming up he tells me he wants to see what it's like to wear my watch for a few minutes. I say sure and hand it over. I give him the lowdown on how it works and what it tracks. Then we discuss the workout—five one-mile repeats with a three-minute recovery, if I recall, and each mile ten seconds faster than the previous one—and after we've changed our shoes, I ask for my watch back. He says no. I'm like, what? I need my watch and he says he'll give it back on the first mile repeat I can *guess* the split, within a second or two. I thought he was joking until he trots over to the start line and shouts, 'Release the hounds!'"

The rumble of belly laughter gathers momentum in the room.

"I was pissed, so I take off and catch him, add a few more choice words, pass him, and settle into a pace that I think is good. I really have no idea, flying blind like that. We finish the first lap and I holler back for at least a split and all he says is 'Feel it, baby.' I grumble some more and continue on. When I hit the finish and start jogging, Jake catches up and goes, 'Well?' I go 'five . . . .thirty-two.' I look over and Jake shakes his head. Faster or slower? I ask, and he says, 'Just feel it.' I tell him I can't feel it. I need some feedback at least. He says 'close.' That's it, 'close.' We finish the recovery lap and start into the next mile repeat. I get up to speed and try to make a subtle adjustment so it's faster than the first, but of course I have no idea if I was high or low, and Jake wasn't helping out with the pacing. It was the most frustrating workout I think I'd ever done."

The guys are chuckling pretty good now, Chase running without technology guiding him.

"Anyway, when he said I was close after the third one, I felt dialed in and went with the flow on the last two, though I never did guess right, and I had a sneaking suspicion he wouldn't have told me if I had. Before we started warming down, I was dying to know my splits and I practically ripped the watch off his wrist. He wanted me to guess what they were first, but I flipped through the splits without saying anything. Surprisingly enough there was only a two-to-five-second variation from my goal times. It was a little more erratic than I preferred, but I had to admit that it was fun running those last two without knowing. It reminded me of the first time I ever ran a mile race."

"Jake always did like challenging us by adding variety to our runs," Spencer says.

"It is easy to stick with convenience at times, basic routines," Jim says.

Dillon processes the stories told, wishing he had known Jake longer.

"I don't have any running stories about Jake," Dillon says. "I didn't know him as long as you guys, but the thing I'll always remember about him is the time he came over to my place, and he and I transformed the front of the BR&B. His whole approach was very Zen-like."

"He called it 'yard walking,'" Jim says.

"I generally don't like asking for help and am even less likely to accept it when it's offered, but there was something about the shared labor he offered. He was easy to talk to for some reason. No judgment one way or another about anything I said or did. Anyway, I'd never bonded with someone as quickly as I did with him."

The silence that follows has a shared quality of reverence to it.

"Colorado." Dillon laughs. "He was always chiding me about referring to San Francisco as 'Frisco.' I had no idea what he meant at first."

Chuckles follow.

"He's also the one who came up with the name Percy's Loop."

After several minutes of latent chuckles that taper off, the room draws quiet only to be disrupted by the light next to Spencer's bed, eliciting a groan from Chase and shielding of eyes by Jim.

"What are you doing?" Dillon says, watching Spencer turn a clock radio around on the kitchenette counter and toss a wash towel over the coffee maker display panel.

"Covering up the lights," he says, placing one of his T-shirts over the red light on the TV console.

"Ohhhhhh boy," Chase says.

"Says the man who can't sleep without earplugs," Spencer says.

"Or on *normal* sheets," Jim says.

Spencer turns his light out, stays still, then flicks it back on, grabs another shirt from his bag and walks over to the digital panel on the heater that glows green. Once covered, and after adjusting the triple layer of curtains for a second time, Spencer appears satisfied that he's extinguished all the light pollution in the room. He turns off his light and settles back into bed.

Sleep eludes Dillon, owing in part to the rare nap he'd taken in the car. Chase is still tossing and turning, and will undoubtedly continue to do so for the foreseeable future. The heater unit kicks on and off, keeping the sub-twenty-degree December temps from imposing their will on the room. Occasional muffled voices grow and fade outside their door. A weighty door slams shut down the hallway, leaving behind a vacuum of silence. Dillon stares at the dark ceiling, settling into a long night of restless sleep, stuck on a semi-uncomfortable couch.

At some point Chase stops moving, Jim starts snoring, and Spencer is crawling back into bed after visiting the bathroom, but not before returning to the bathroom to shut the door because of the streetlight shining in through the small window. Dillon's eyes have just closed, the world retreating from his mind—

Anngt! Anngt! Anngt! Anngt! Anngt!

At first Dillon lies there with eyes wide open, unable to process the blaring sound. It sounds familiar, as if from a distant memory, perhaps grade school, the buddy system coming into focus. Spencer's light comes on. Jim ceases to snore. Voices can be heard in the hallway outside their room.

Anngt! Anngt! Anngt! Anngt! Anngt!

"Chase!" Spencer yells.

Jim rolls off the rollaway and onto the floor. Dillon grabs his phone and presses a button; 3:14 a.m.

A determined fist pounds on their door, prompting Spencer to race to and open it.

"You need to evacuate," the deep voice wearing a fireman's helmet says. "Now. Please follow the escape route."

"Shit!" Chase says, grabbing his stuff and tossing it into his bag.

"Leave everything," the deep voice says. "You need to go now."

A cacophony of voices sweeps into the room from the hallway, growing louder and more strained, drowning out the guys' voices.

They all reach for their phones, toss on nearby clothes and shoes, and pad out the door, falling in step with the other disheveled runners, all who look like they are being directed to a 4 a.m. shuttle bus for the start of an ungodly race start time. They descend two flights of stairs, pass through the emergency exit to the back parking lot, and are smacked with the chill of a clear night in central Oregon, stars crisp and bright. They wrap their arms around themselves, shuffling from one foot to the other to keep warm, jostling among the other hundred or so guests doing the same dance. An outside observer may have thought a pre-dawn ultra trail race is about to begin; all that's missing are headlamps.

Despite several questions asked by Spencer and Chase, as well as others in the crowd, no useful information is passed along until forty-five minutes later, when it's announced that they can all go back to their rooms. It was a false alarm: concern over smoke spotted in the woods alongside the hotel. The news is met with groans and sighs, both of relief and disbelief.

Most of the crowd heads back to the crowded emergency exit they'd come out from, but the smarter crowd, including the guys, goes around to the front of the hotel and enter. Spencer gives a suspicious glare toward the two night clerks he dealt with earlier, accusing them of the dubious smoke sighting. Chase and Dillon give Spencer a firm shove from both sides to speed things along.

By the time the hallway outside simmers down and the guys return to their beds it's 4:09 a.m., and no one seems quite ready to go back to sleep.

"Shit!" Chase says, his light now back on.

"What?" Dillon says.

"I lost my earplugs in all the commotion."

"You really need them?" Spencer says.

"I can hear flies mating in the next county without them." He's now rummaging through his bag.

"Will gum work?" Jim says.

"It might. You have some?"

"Yeah." Jim turns a light on and grabs his toiletry bag. "Doris sent some along in case I needed to pop my ears over Shasta."

"Is that a good idea," Dillon asks.

"It'll be fine." Chase splits the stick in half, chews and softens each of them, and molds each for an ear canal, making squishy adjustments. "That'll work." His voice rises several decibels. Soon his area darkens, and after ten minutes of shifting around under the sheets, he settles down.

Dillon stares at the dark ceiling as Jim snores and Spencer makes another bathroom run, the world fading from Dillon's conscious mind.

Saturday Morning
Wake-up Call

The faint sound of a cell-phone alarm lugs Dillon from a deep sleep. He opens his eyes once the owner of the cell phone squelches the droning tone. *That was a short night.* He lies there, orienting himself to the strange surroundings until another sound prevails, and it isn't a pleasant one or a quiet one.

"Shit!"

No one responds, because either the others are still asleep or Chase's pampered tastes are no longer news. Chase strides through the open area and into the bathroom, fiddles with his ears, and rocks his head side to side like a swimmer trying to unclog an ear of trapped water, but to no avail.

"What's wrong?" Dillon asks, watching Chase turn his head sideways to the mirror and strain to look inside the canal. Dillon yawns and blinks his eyes several times before he remembers the chewing gum. "Chase, are your ears plugged?"

Chase wiggles his head, lowering it below his waist at one point.

"Chase?"

"What's *wrong*?" Jim says.

"I think the gum you gave Chase last night is stuck in his ears."

A sleepy chuckle comes from underneath Jim's pillow.

Chase now stands over Dillon, shirtless. "Dillon!" he shouts, which causes Dillon to snap his head back. "Dillon, the gum in my ears . . . I can't get it out." His voice grows louder with each word.

"What's with all the shouting?" Spencer says, tossing a pillow over his head.

Jim's amusement swells.

Chase emphatically points to his ears.

Dillon mouths the words, "*What's wrong, buddy, having a Hubba Bubba moment?*"

"What?!"

Jim is now in full-blown laughter.

Spencer rises up in his bed, a smile forming.

"I can't hear you!" Chase says, loud enough that the first floor can hear *him*.

Spencer breaks out laughing. Dillon can no longer contain his humor. Chase straightens up and peers around at the silent movie of panoramic laughter igniting throughout the suite. "You guys suck!" He storms off to his bed, pulling out his cellphone.

"What do you think, Dillon?" Spence says. "The best way to remove dry gum from the ear canal?"

"I'm thinking a trip to the ER is the safest way."

"Yeah, dry gum is tough to scrape off a school desk."

Dillon pulls out his cell phone and searches for the nearest urgent care center in Bend. He finds one, calls the number, asks for a quick consult, confirms the need to go in, and announces his findings. "We should have plenty of time before the race, assuming the rest of the hotel didn't do something equally ridiculous."

"Great," Spencer says, and lies back down on the bed.

"Guys!" Chase returns to the main area. "I think I need to go to the hospital to remove this shit!"

Jim pulls out a stick of gum, starts chewing it, and blows a bubble

Spencer chucks a balled-up sock at Chase, pelting him on the back. "Put a shirt on, Nipple Man!"

Chase swivels toward Spencer, to the gum-chewing Jim, and to Dillon, catching the urgent care number on his phone held up for viewing.

"You guys *really* suck!"

The guys rally over the course of the next hour, Chase using a moistened cotton swab in a few failed attempts to soften the dried, neatly molded noise-canceling gum. He refuses to talk to the others after they give him various ill-formed sign-language gestures.

It's 9:45 a.m. by the time they pile into Chase's BMW and are bound for urgent care. After much debate about who will drive the BMW, Chase decides Dillon is the man, though Dillon's trouble with starting the car gives Chase pause on this decision. Content with a scientifically formulated breakfast in hand, Chase waves off the guys to go eat; he'll text them when gum-free.

Complimentary breakfast consumed, Dillon, Jim, and Spencer head back to the hotel suite to gather their gear for the race while Chase bides his time at urgent care. They grab Chase's stuff as well, or at least they hope they have, owing to the long text message he sent about what to bring along. Some details may have been overlooked. "He'll survive," Jake would've said, Jim notes to the guys, and they laugh a subdued laugh. With an extra night comped, the guys don't have to pack up all their belongings. Spencer concedes it's as a nice thing to have as an option, coming back to the room after the race to clean up before heading home.

At 11:06, Dillon receives a text message from Chase that Operation Gum Removal was successful, along with additional reminders of what to bring. Dillon worries more about starting the BMW and keeping it in mint condition. Once they scoop up Chase, who gives his baby the twice-over before taking control, they jet over to the race venue. Being entered in the last race of the day makes it difficult to find a parking spot, and Chase isn't willing to *squeeze* his baby into certain spots that are best left for compacts.

Once parked and standing outside the vehicle, Spencer checks his watch and says, "Okay, it's eleven thirty-five. Keep in mind that for this race we need to report to the check-in tent thirty minutes before the race, so plan your warm-up accordingly. Make sure you have on the correct shorts and jersey. They'll be checking for any deviations."

The others nod, deferring to Spencer's leadership skills.

"Probably best *not* to ball up your bib number at this race," Spencer says in Dillon's direction.

Dillon nods.

"Bathrooms are over there," Spencer says, pointing to a row of Honey Buckets and glancing at Chase. Fiddling with his Garmin, Chase nods and Spencer swings his arm around. "Check-in tent is there, and you'll have to enter from the far side."

"Can we warm up on the course?" Dillon asks.

"Yes, but be mindful of the race in progress. The master's race should wrap up soon and the open women's race goes off in ten minutes."

"You okay, Jim?" Chase asks.

Jim turns his head away from where he's looking.

Dillon spots where Jim has been staring and shakes his head. The other guys follow the same sightline. There stands a billboard across the highway that reads: DEARBORN TRACTOR REPAIR, BEND, OR.

"Let's go, guys . . . we can do this," Dillon says, patting Jim on the shoulder as they begin walking off toward the course. "Is that Salvador over there in the green sweats?"

As the guys wander away from the car, Chase continues fiddling with his Garmin, attempting to clean off the sticky substance that engulfs it. One of his energy gels has split open and coated the face cover. While the Garmin fires up fine, the gel has penetrated every nook and cranny of the face piece and hard rubber band. He puts it on, makes adjustments to it, first loosening, then tightening it, but nothing feels comfortable.

Chase glances up at the sound of his name, and sees Spencer waving. Chase gives it one more attempt, this time with spit. He rubs it vigorously, dries it, and fastens it to his wrist. No better.

He lets out a deep resigned sigh, flips the Garmin into the center console, and locks up the car, trotting off to catch up with his team.

Saturday Afternoon
Atop High Places

The vista from above consumes Jake, splendid in all its pageantry. He always did like the view from the top, a higher perspective on life. He peers down at his boys toeing the line, their hearts heavy. It isn't supposed to be like this, but then again life rarely follows any earthbound plan; Jake always accepted this notion, undeterred by its fragility.

Corralled in the starting area they perform strides: one, then a second and third and so on, each man adjusting their mind-sets for the big race. Jim's right elbow has a sharper edge to it, jutting out in a more pronounced way. Jake feels pity for the poor soul lined up on that side of Jim, for they will bear the brunt of his angst-laden motion. Dillon has a solemn look about him, standing there shaking his legs and arms out, his focus shifting up and down the long start line, sizing up the competition. Rubbing an ear, Chase trots up next to Dillon, says something, and launches into another stride. Dillon cracks a smile. Chase always knew how to loosen the cork on the group's bottled-up emotions. Spencer converses with Salvador, finishing up the last of their strides, no doubt discussing course conditions and race strategy. That Spencer invited Salvador, dressed down in RERC colors, was a big step for Spencer to concede, adapting to circumstances beyond his control.

Before long the stragglers cease jutting out from the start line as an official walks down it. The Earth dangles in suspension, serenity from afar, anticipation up close, and like a cracked piñata a flood of colors rushes out and onto the pristine golf course.

Jake's boys appear swallowed up in the middle of this mass explosion of colorful confetti, but it isn't cause for concern; they have 10,000 meters to sort things out, split into four loops, over mild rises in terrain, along dirt paths that skirt around duck ponds, across large grassy expanses including fairways, and a three-foot-high hay bale added for good measure to break up a runner's routine lest they get complacent.

After a few minutes of stampeding, the sinewy mass jockeys for position, approaching the first turn that leads to the outer circuit. Jake's boys have started smart, drifting away from the vortex, freeing themselves from getting sucked in along the barricades. Dillon and Chase lead the RERC contingent as usual; grouped together, Spencer, Jim, and Salvador follow fifty yards back; all five in the upper quarter of the field as it elongates and takes shape.

It's more than pride that swells Jake's heart, watching over them. He knows the pain they endured in getting here. "Dying is harder on the living," as is often said. That's not to say he won't miss things himself. To watch an activity you love from a distance has its charms but it's not the same. The fleshy part of life—the often messy, frustrating, confusing, and incomprehensible part—make living *living*.

Dillon forges ahead of Chase, though more aggressively than is prudent on this day and against a national-caliber field, but that's Dillon: *leap* before looking. Chase shadows Dillon for as long as possible until Chase's tempered tactics unhitch him. Running side by side, Spencer and Salvador move steadily ahead of Jim, whose form evokes a battle-weary soldier, there in body but not spirit. Perhaps he's overwhelmed by the enormity of the field, a size much larger than has been seen throughout the fall, though Jake knows better: Jim's heart flutters like a hummingbird, burning up desire that sends him reeling into the throng.

What might've been? The PA Championship victory and season grand prix win were special accomplishments, born out of five guys with a single desire, despite careers, families, and personal issues, to excel beyond the other clubs, the ones with more talent, more resources. True, all the other clubs have careers, families, and personal issues as well, but few commune in the way he and the guys have, in ways only a close-knit community can: long Sunday runs, Sunday brunches, BBQs, club meetings, holidays, weddings . . .

Throughout the first loop, Dillon takes risks on slippery slopes, throws surge after surge through the one wooded section and across vast flat expanses dotted with snow patches, passing competitors at will. Chase settles into a large group strung out two and three wide, exercising caution where deemed necessary, but it does leave him conceding a spot here and there. Spencer and Salvador remain in close proximity to each other, occasionally trading places at certain junctures. And Jim struggles and struggles with not only form but tangents and large packs that bunch up on the slick sections and cut in front of him.

Around and around they trek, lap after national club championship lap, running the same groove they have before, the field for the most part one long single-file string of runners from all over the country, each attached to the other by sinewy bonds of camaraderie, bonds forged over the length of the season, literally over hill and dale as well as mud, wind, sun, rain, and, in RERC's case, grief.

Having reached the top five, Dillon's aggressive start eventually exacts its toll: shoulders sag and stride length shortens, bearing the fate of anaerobic demise, swallowing pride as competitor after competitor overtakes him, though not without spurts of energy to hold off or stay with them, until that too fades.

Chase's "tour" of the course presumably leaves him a solid gear to work over the final mile as he gains on Dillon, but he too lets others drift by uncontested until someone from the Agras squad comes by, pats him on the shoulder, nods, and presses on. Chase latches onto the guy's heels, but a hundred yards later his body returns to its default mode for the day.

On the wooded uphill slope, Spencer moves ahead of Salvador, whose marathon legs remind him that 26.2 miles of hard racing on city streets requires more than seven days of rest to race properly; he relents, encourages Spencer, and watches him shuffle away into a sea of club uniforms.

Jim sweeps through the S-curves of the last lap, the dicey section that induces runners to take shorter, quicker steps, but Jim's lapse in attention halfway through sends him down in one sudden motion, sliding along on the muddy and beaten-down golf course. Coming to a stop, he curses something wicked, attempting to rise, but the next group of runners coming through hasn't received the memo of a man down, and two more runners slip, land in the mud, and slam into him, bowling him over. More wicked cursing spews out from Jim's mouth. Righted and running, mad, muddy, inspired, he sprints along the course like a man on a mission with nothing to lose.

Back to regular form, Jim catches and flashes by the group he'd initially been with before the misstep, churning through the slop left behind by thousands of previous footsteps. One by one, and at times two and three at a time, Jim leaves no doubt that he has a fire in his belly, his Saturday throw-down revived.

Singular focus and the sense of having thrown caution to the wind spread across Jim's face as he blows by Salvador, swinging his arms with anger, his speed increasing with every foot strike, his pace making the others look slow and tired, as if they don't realize the finish looms in the foreground. It doesn't, of course, and after a mile and a quarter of thrashing like a prizefighter backed into a corner, Jim hits his limit, form rigid but still throwing punches.

Jim catches Spencer, who's exiting the outer loop and heading for the finish. Spencer glances over to Jim, whose face shows the strain of his adrenaline burst. Jim backs off and falls into step with Spencer, who motions to where Chase is, thirty yards up front, coasting and about to draw abreast of a fading Dillon.

Jake watches them come together two hundred yards out, among the constant stream of rabid racers giving everything they have left. His boys have already spent their emotional cache. Now they run four abreast, unrushed, forcing the other clubs to veer left and right to move around the running processional.

Fifty yards out, no one from the group making any moves, Jim offers a hand to Spencer, who's on the left, and a hand to his right toward Chase. Both accept. Chase offers his free hand to Dillon, who grasps it, raising it high above their heads. Jim follows suit with his, Spencer's, and Chase's arms.

Joined as one they trot the final yards, to additional cheers and heartfelt comments by the race announcer, cross the finish line, and unlock their hands, wrapping arms around one another's sagging shoulders, walking through the wide chute, and melding into the sea of racing stories.

Jake smiles, a broad one. Sharing race stories and going long on Sundays with the boys . . . he'll miss these the most.

"We'll probably get disqualified," Spencer says as he and the guys thread their way through the throng of finishers, some one hundred of them communing in an ever-growing orgy of fatigue.

"Screw it if we do," Chase says. "Runners make this race, not bureaucrats."

"You okay?" Dillon asks Jim, who looks like he's had a mud wrap some time in the last half hour.

Jim chuckles, nods, and shakes his head. "Perfect!"

"We showed them," Dillon says.

"Jake would've hated this course anyway," Jim says. "Running laps around a golf course . . . too pristine for his tastes."

"He'd have laughed at the hay bales out there," Dillon says, which makes the others chuckle.

As the guys stroll around, orienting themselves to where they've left their belongings, a couple of PA club members stop and speak with the guys, trammels offering condolences and racing memories they have about Jake.

The guys find their stuff and dress for a warm-down, but decide they'd rather clean up and hit the road for home. Walking back to the car, Jim pulls out a Ziploc bag, produces some beef jerky, and chews off a hearty chunk. Chase looks over and puts his hand out. Jim places one in it, as well as in the other outstretched hands that follow.

"He would have loved this part," Jim says, biting off another chunk. "Fuel is fuel."

Sunday Late Afternoon
Lake Illsanjo

The sun hasn't yet set but its last rays strain to filter through the trees as the guys solemnly run up Spring Creek toward Lake Illsanjo. Other than "hey" to one another, a habit-induced "morning" to a passerby, and Jim thanking the guys for joining him, nothing more is said. The silence commemorates their first Sunday run without Jake as Jim leads the group, each carrying a chunk of dried mud cake from Spill Gate.

They returned home very late the night before, and agreed to do their Sunday run later in the day instead of the morning. The starting spot had been altered as well, to Spring Lake instead of the post-race BR&B tradition. Dillon said he found it fitting, since he'd first met Jake there. Spencer never once objected to either decision.

Reaching the dam that holds Lake Illsanjo in captivity, they slow, walking out to the middle of it and standing quietly in the setting sun's colorful hues, not a soul in sight. Breathing in check from the hill climb, Jim nods to the guys and they spread out along the paved path, behind the low wooden railing, facing the lake, still and peaceful. Jim gazes at the clump in his hand as if it had been only yesterday that he and Jake canvassed the meager lake for the mud cakes, coming up with the idea to make it part of a new shoe-initiation rite of passage.

As much as he tries to hold it back, a tear breaks his composure, dampening the clump in is hand. With a finger, he massages the escaped emotion into the cake, steps back, and slings it in a high arc toward the heavens, watching it sail over the glassy lake. "Lord love . . . a duck," he chokes out when the cake breaks the surface of the water with a *plunk*.

Dillon tosses his next, the mud cake sailing high into the sky until gravity pulls it back down, splashing into the lake. "Lord love a duck."

"Lord love a duck," Chase says, heaving his farther than the others. It splashes and disappears underneath the surface, the ripples beginning their outward journey.

Spencer steps back, launching the last of their offerings. "Lord love a duck."

They stand in reverent silence, watching the four concentric ripples move outward from their respective epicenters, interweaving with the others at some point until they lose strength.

Jim breathes deep through his nostrils, exhales, and faces the guys. "Thanks again," he says, wiping away another tear.

"Don't mention it," Dillon says, patting him on the shoulder. "This was a fitting way to say goodbye."

Except for Jim, they all move to continue the run. "I'll catch up in a minute," Jim says, turning back toward the lake, straining to pick up the remnants of the ripples.

The mud cakes have long settled on Lake Illsanjo's bottom and will dissolve with its brethren in due course, but the ripples on the surface continue to travel, however faintly, outward 360 degrees times four, north, east, west, and south toward their respective shorelines, eventually and quite gently lapping up on the shore, forever scribing in time Jake's presence.

"Is this heaven?" Jim says under his breath, once last movie quote for his friend. "No, it's Annadel." As he turns to catch up with the guys he pauses a moment, catching sight among the abundance of cattails at the water's edge a white swan standing stoically. Jim grins. *Right.*

"Do you think Jake will say 'Lord love a duck,' you know, *up there?*" Chase asks when Jim rejoins them.

"Only if the Big Guy says something funny," Jim says.

"Metaphorically speaking, of course," Dillon says.

"What do you think Jake's first order of business will be?" Spencer says.

"Ask the Big Guy to go for a run," Jim says. "Up a very long hill."

"Mount Sinai," Chase says.

"That sounds about right," Dillon says.

As a flock of southbound geese squawk overhead, the guys clear the dam and return to Annadel's succulent womb, continuing their Sunday eulogy, running headlong toward winter.

Week 49 Training Summary			
	Long Run	Mileage Total	Comments
Dillon	8	33	
Chase	8	28	
Spencer	8	46	
Jim	8	76	"Lord love a duck."

Footfalls in Annadel

The dry twig snaps, breaking the predawn slumber, awakening ancient Pomo footfalls that came before him. Old-growth redwoods stretch high, basking in autumn's first sun rays, outlining the meandering trail below. The ground shifts subtly under the weight of his shoes, set to a rhythmic cadence, dispersing pillowy clouds out from underneath, forever scribing the journey both in soil and socks.

The season's warm days and quick-cooling evenings infuse the air with the aroma of anise that permeates his nostrils, harking back to adolescence and his first days of trail running. Ahead, wild turkeys rustle in dry leaves a safe distance off the trail. He never pays them much attention, though once a rafter of turkeys hindering his progress scattered as he approached, except for one loner, who frantically trotted ahead some fifty yards before stepping to the side, lost its footing, and tumbled several feet down the embankment.

His sleepy body slowly shakes off the remnants of a long night's sleep, recalling Sunday's morning ritual with the same autonomic response as breathing. His effort varies throughout the early miles in tandem with the terrain, the heart shunting blood to legs where the trail soars above his sightline; then, reaching a plateau, diverting it back to other extremities, warming hands against autumn's nip.

Unlike city sidewalks that lack variation from one concrete slab to the next, the park unfolds like an obstacle course of dry riverbed crossings, elongated etchings across trails left behind by snakes seeking warmth, narrow wooden bridges, steep climbs and precipitous descents. Meanwhile fawn nibble on wild grass, clover, and twigs unaware of mankind's fabricated existence. It doesn't take long for his body to wake up out here.

In solitude he veers right and upward where the trail splits. The redwoods fade, their towering perspective minimized, replaced by gnarled oak trees offering poison oak to anyone seeking a moment of respite against their trunks. "Annadel Summit—4.3 miles," carved into the faded signpost, had he cared to read it, favors well-trained and adventurous souls. It tests one's mettle as much as their conditioning. The trail transforms into long, narrow stretches of horseshoe-shaped potholes that have dried and cracked over the hot summer. An assortment of flat and round boulders dot the path; smaller, jagged rocks exposed by years of erosion jut upward in unfortunate spots.

City legs are unsuited for this type of terrain and best left for those with sole in their soul. He hops and stutter-steps from one foot to the other, lunging over, stepping on top of, and swerving around a minefield of potential ankle twists. Fitter, younger explorers may extend him on less challenging terrain, but on this trail, they struggle to stay on his heels. Gracing them with Irish step-dancer form, he easily disappears up the tortuous, 1,600-foot climb to the summit, humbling even the most prideful soul.

Jake D.

Acknowledgments

I want to thank the following friends who took the time to read the early drafts of this novel, and provided me with invaluable feedback: Liz Bernstein, Lorinda Miller, Alec Isabeau, Suzanne Bair, and Larry Meredith. Special thanks goes to Eric Bohn, Kenny Brown, and Eric Walker who not only assisted in providing feedback, but inspired the story with the many, many Sunday long runs in Annadel. The conversations and camaraderie that sprung from them were both priceless and timeless. Also, to Mark Spencer, who provided the vital content edit and helped shape a stronger and more meaningful story, and Rachelle Mandik, who handled the tedious copyediting aspect.

Made in the USA
Las Vegas, NV
15 December 2023

82963053R00288